KURGAN

Copyright © 2015 by Blue Dome Press

Originally published in Turkish as *Kurgan: Sarayın Yıkılışı*,
Sütun Yayınları, 2011

18 17 16 15   1 2 3 4

Published by Blue Dome Press
244 5th Avenue, Suite D-149
New York, NY 10001, USA
www.bluedomepress.com

Library of Congress Cataloging-in-Publication Data
Boztaş, H. Şaban, 1980-
[Sarayın Yıkılışı. English]
Kurgan : fall of the palace / H. Şaban Boztaş.
pages cm
ISBN 978-1-935295-57-0 (alk. paper)
I. Title.
PL249.B69S2713 2015
894'.3534--dc23
2015000171

ISBN: 978-1-935295-57-0

Printed by
İmak Ofset, Istanbul - Turkey

KURGAN

FALL OF THE PALACE

H. Şaban Boztaş

NEW JERSEY • LONDON • FRANKFURT • CAIRO • JAKARTA

New York

The Ufis

The wind blew mightily. During the day, the sky was clear blue, and when seen from above, the deep valley resembled an eddy. High cliffs in the valley walls seemed like they were trying to protect the valley from the fierce wind, which scattered red dust everywhere.

Looking down from these cliffs, one could see a small forest. A thin stream of dust clouds rose from this copse, the leaves and branches of the trees shaking violently. A few people were watching the storm. One of them seemed to be deeper in thought than the others. His clothing also made him stand out; while the others were in soldier's uniforms, he wore a black robe, embroidered in red. Beside this small battalion was a motley group of hunters, their clothes in tatters.

"Sir, we're just hunters and we're here to serve our king. We have no other goal," said one of the hunters.

"I know that," said the man in the robes. His name was Atarcat. "If you just shut up and let me think more clearly, then you can go," he added, moving away from them.

The hunter, whose name was Kette, shut his mouth and glanced at the two hunters around him. They were anxious to return to their homes, to see their wives and children.

"Kette, are you aware of the trouble you've gotten us into? Because of your greed, we're going to die here," said Kette's friend, who stood next to him.

Kette feared that his friend was right, though he would never admit it.

"You say that, Tui, but it was because of me that we won Gelpagoren's title as the best group of hunters! Don't ever forget that."

"Since it was the most desirable thing for us…" said the third hunter, joking.

Kette didn't mind this teasing and said, "Lets not talk about this, now. I wonder what Atarcat is thinking."

"He charged the wisest person in the country with investigating your mistake. I guess our end will be a disaster."

Kette sniffed his nose and said, "I never knew you would all be such cowards. If I knew this before, I would've gone hunting with my sons. Even if they're little boys, they are brave as their father."

"I'm sure they are," Tui replied. "But I hope that they're not as talented as their father at getting themselves into trouble."

Kette stared at Tui with anger. "Be quiet," he said. "Atarcat is coming."

"Tell me exactly what happened," Atarcat said.

All of the sudden, the three hunters looked at each other with fear. The soldiers next to Atarcat were the special guards of King Kalsor; everyone in the land knew how brutal they were.

The hunters, therefore, decided to be more honest. Kette started talking: "Sir! Me and my friends went hunting, like always. These are the places we know very well. We know which animal is hidden in which place. Other hunters are not brave enough to hunt in this valley. This is our major place to hunt."

Tui and Huyaf were scared because their friend was taking too much time with his explanation. They knew that Atarcat could grow angry in only a minute. On the other hand, Atarcat was listening to Kette very quietly.

"Carry on," he said.

"Sir, when we came here recently, we saw a blue sapling. We didn't understand what it was. We spoke with villagers, but they only told us to stay away from it. According to the elders of the village, this tree could belong to the Fire Creatures. However, we didn't listen to them and came here anyway. This time, we were here seeking this tree instead of hunting. As we came here, we saw that this tree was growing faster than the other trees. In a few days, it reached its full height. As we approached it, we saw that there were black spots on its leaves. These spots seemed to be alive.

"Another time we came, we saw that these spots were knitting cocoons that were like silkwarm cocoons. We decided to stay the night. When we woke up in the morning, we saw that the cocoons were torn. And those blue birds were flying around the tree. We decided to give some of these beautiful birds to our king, as a gift. So, we caught a few of them and brought them to the palace. This is all we've done and all we know, my sir.

"I would like to add one more thing. My friends are only here because of my curiosity. Otherwise, they would never have come here. Their only fault is staying with me. That's why, if anyone should be punished, it should be me, and only me."

The soldiers were disturbed becuse of Kette's willingness to give advice. However, they wouldn't dare to speak near Atarcat.

"Did anything else happen?" Atarcat asked. "You aren't forgetting to tell me anything, right?"

"No, sir."

"Have you seen anybody else walking around here?"

"No, sir. We saw nobody. Right, my friends?"

Both of them stepped forward, saying, "Yes," simultaneously.

Atarcat put his hand on his chin. His eyes deepened. "Okay, you may go," he said.

The hunters' faces brightened. They bowed so far they touched ground, and then greeted Atarcat and the soldiers. To avoid the soldier's angry stares, they ran away quickly.

After the hunters went away, Atarcat and his guards watched the helix appear by chaos until night fell. He tried to figure out what this enigma – which mixed blue and green – could possibly be.

When the sun was about to set, the soldiers' commander approached Atarcat and said: "Sir, the sun is setting. For your security, we must return to the village. According to our king's order, your safety is our priority."

Atarcat was still watching the chaos. Thinking he hadn't been heard, the commander moved closer. Atarcat suddenly turned toward the soldier.

"Yes, we must return to village," he said. "One of you must go to King Kalsor."

"May I learn the reason, sir?"

"I want the king to send those birds here."

The commander obeyed the order without understanding the reason.

"Yes sir!"

***

After sending a soldier to get the birds from the king, the group spent the night in a nearby village.

The village was located on a plain between mountains covered with forest. Most of its residents were farmers. Though many of the villagers were called hunters, all they did was keep wild animals from their crops. Nobody in this village, or in Gelpagoren's country, ate meat.

The arrival of Atarcat and his guards scared the villagers. In this village, not even the elders could remember the last time strangers had arrived. The strangers' silence and seriousness only increased the anxiety. They only addressed the villagers if absolutely necessary, using short, commanding sentences. The oldest one among them didn't even speak at all, though it was not out of arrogance – he was lost deep in thought. Atarcat and the soldiers retired to their rooms to rest. The commander stationed one of them as a guard, and gave the others orders about turn of duty.

It was obvious that it would be a sleepless night for Atarcat. He was standing in front of the window. In the darkness of the night, he tried to watch chaos's lights in the distance. Earlier, when he'd given orders about the birds, he'd felt afraid. But now that fear had dissipated. This was the first time he had witnessed such an event, and if his predictions were correct, then this could be the most important discovery in the history of the country.

But for the time, all they could do was wait until morning. With sunrise, the secret between the birds and the tree would come to light. As Atarcat's predictions grew more vivid, he felt his body growing weak. He lay down, and sleep took him.

In the morning, the commander knocked on Atarcat's door. Atarcat leapt up like an arrow. "Yes," he said.

The commander entered and greeted him. "Sir, your man brought the birds. They're in a cage," he said.

Atarcat took a deep breath and said, "Okay, lets go back to the valley soon."

***

Holding the cage in his hands, Atarcat descended from the lookout atop the valley. Despite the commander's insistence, Atarcat went alone. To avoid any trouble, the soldiers waited atop the cliff, praying. They watched Atarcat nervously. He walked with calm, careful steps.

When he reached the plain the soldiers sighed with relief. However, he was walking directly into the chaos. Once more, the soldiers watched him with fear.

A strong wind was blowing. It was difficult for Atarcat to walk through this violent windstorm, but he persevered. Objects carried on the wind were hurled towards him; he raised his hands to cover his eyes. While moving through the middle of the chaos, the wind began to die down. He would prove that his predictions were wrong.

When the wind began to slow, the smoke screen of scarlet, black, blue, and green began to fall apart. Seeing the huge blue tree appearing in front of him, he was astonished.

He watched the tree for a while. He'd never seen this kind of tree. Birds like those in the cage were flying over its branches and all around the tree.

He slowly left the cage on the ground. Once more, he looked through the tree, which was the source of the chaos. "It looks as if it's made of light," he said in wonder.

The birds were squirming in the cage. Despite their fluttering, not one feather had broken on their wings. Smiling, Atarcat opened the small door of the cage. The birds all flew towards the tree. Three of them landed on different branches. A few minutes later, they all began to fly around the tree.

"You, blue tree! These birds are your children. You grow angry when they are away from you. This is the secret of your chaos! I will use your power to help my country prosper. For now, I've known enough of you. But I'll be back very soon. I shall take the first steps in a partnership that will last forever – with you, and perhaps with your ancestors."

Then, Atarcat headed back to the rim of the valley. Before he could make the ascent, the soldiers descended to him very quickly. They were convinced that everything was fine. They welcomed Atarcat at the base of the cliff.

"Are you okay, sir?" the commander asked.

"I could not be better. Because of what you have witnessed today, you have acquired a dignity that shall be told for generations. Now, it's time to return to the palace."

Fall of the Palace

"Come on Mabel! Won't you tell us where you're taking us? We're in the middle of the ocean!"

"You should learn to be more patient. Otherwise, you'll get no taste from any surprise!"

Due to the noise of the propellers, they had difficulty hearing each other. Mabel looked at the girls who filled the helicopter. He felt like a stack of shriveled flesh.

They were four young women. Three of them were sitting in front of him. This was the only helicopter of its kind in the world. The girl sitting next to Mabel wasn't talking to the other girls facing him because she was feeling privileged. She was also trying to not laugh at others' jokes.

Then, all of the sudden Mabel cried with joy and the girls enthusiastically joined him.

"Sir, in three minutes we'll arrive," the pilot called from the cockpit. Mabel composed himself; he didn't want to be out of sorts.

"There you go ladies. In just a minute, you'll have an opportunity that very few get."

The same girl insisted on learning what the surprise was. "Please tell us, Mabel! I'm about to have a stroke from curiosity," she said.

Once more, Mabel felt abominable hearing such words. He leaned his head against the windowpane and watched the ocean. After five or ten minutes, he said to the women: "We're here."

The women clapped with excitement. The helicopter was fixed on a point in the ocean. The pilot and Mabel were watching outside. One of the girls yelled cheerfully: "Did we come here to fish?"

Mabel ignored the question. He locked eyes with the pilot. Both of them saw the air bubbles forming on the ocean. A dark sphere, as big as half a football field, rose from the dark waters.

"Oen, you're wonderful man, my friend. No one like you shall come to this world again," he muttered to himself. Then he turned to the pilot and said, "Set us down."

The upper part of the glass sphere opened like a watermelon. The girls were watching through the windowpane. Though they were not aware of how exciting the situation was, they were still astonished, as they'd never seen anything like this before. The helicopter landed on the runway atop the sphere. Mabel and the girls walked away from the helicopter by bowing their heads.

**

"I hate this," Oen said, throwing his racket to the ground. "I'm done."

Saru laughed and said, "This is the second time you've quit, Oen. Trust me, leaving every bad match unfinished won't make you feel good."

While the roof opened above, downstairs in the huge sphere, Oen and Saru were playing tennis. When the helicopter landed, they shielded their eyes with their hands.

"Looks like Mabel is in the mood to entertain again..." Oen said.

Mabel's frivolousness spoiled Saru's pleasure. "I'm afraid this means we'll have to postpone some of the work," he said. Saru paused for a while, and then said what came to mind: "There's no better time to speak to him seriously. Things are getting out of our control, don't you think?"

"Come on, Saru. Let's not give him a hard time. You know he likes to have fun. This isn't new," Oen said. The helicopter moved away. As silence returned, Oen and Saru could hear the visitors.

Mabel hugged his friends warmly. For a moment, Saru almost felt regret for what he'd said. Almost. Instead, he moved decisively toward a decision. He would speak to Mabel.

***

Oen, Saru, and Mabel were children of some of the world's wealthiest families. Their families had long been close, so the three of them became friends.

Mabel's family owned the world's biggest banks. Saru's family ran an energy conglomerate. Oen's family was the leading power in maritime and airline transport. From Oen's family's factories, ships, airplanes and helicopters were designed, built, and exported.

The three friends were all over the age of thirty. Having grown up with extraordinary wealth and privilege, many people considered them quite snobby. They were aware of this because they didn't have many friends outside their circle. Even though they attracted enormous attention anywhere they went, it was very difficult for them to make close connections with new people. They were very isolated.

Compared to the other two, Mabel was a bit thinner; some even considered him unattractive. With sparse hair and body like a dry branch, he resembled someone who needed to be protected from the wind, lest he be blown over. Perhaps because of this, he was always the most frivolous and sybaritic; he was constantly seeking material pleasure. Mabel was always meticulous planning the friends' newest adventures. These revelries, which angered his family, were so lavish they scared and sickened people. As such, his family trusted his younger brother more. Mabel was terribly ambitious, but also terribly impatient. He was constantly on the move, pursuing some new fancy. His lack of patience, however, doomed all these pursuit. He wanted to finish so quickly that he would abandon any cause at the first sign of struggle.

On the other hand, Saru was a source of pride and confidence for both his family and his friends. He was decisive and meticulous, and as such, his life was not terribly exciting. He had jet black hair and deep black eyes. But he didn't trust himself, and was always petrified of making mistakes. Saru adored Oen. And though he didn't approve of his behavior, he considered Mabel a close, if out of character, friend.

In fact, both men adored Oen, who everyone viewed as being the best of the bunch. He was constantly away on family business, attending to voyages at sea and in the air. He loved the freedom and struggle of his family's work. He was a principled man, who struggled without harming others, and who never let his greed do damage.

The ship the three of them were travelling in was built by Oen's family. It was very comfortable, and was a cutting edge design. Deriving its energy from water, inside the ship was a home, study quarters, crew quarters, and a below desk observation area where Oen could marvel at the sub-aquatic life. Oen had spent years dreaming about this very project. Four years before, he'd finally convinced his family he was old enough to oversee construction on his own. He had personally witnessed every moment of this ship's design and construction.

**

"What's going on with you?" Mabel asked. "You two look like dead men."

They didn't want to respond, but Oen felt responsible for giving an answer.

"You know exactly why we're like this. We've got to finish Saru's Project. We're presenting it in a few days."

"Yes, but you said it was already finished."

"It never hurt to double check, did it?"

They were in Oen's living room. Mabel was trying to convince the other two to join him on yet another adventure.

"Oh come on," Mabel insisted. "Don't give me excuses. The trip will only take a day. Maybe it will inspire you guys to create excitign new designs."

They were silent for a long time. Saru was trying to hide his nervousness while Mabel was impatiently waiting for his friends to say yes. Oen was trying to behave naturally.

At last, he stood up and went to the big window overlooking the sea.

"We've worked too hard on this project, Saru. It's nearly done. It'd be good to rest for a day. We'll come back to the project with fresh eyes, and will be able to see the problems better."

"OK, fine," Saru said. "If everyone agrees, I won't be selfish."

Mabel was so happy he ran to Saru. Then he said, "It's not selfishness, my friend. We understand your concerns. This voyage will make you feel better, don't worry. Don't think too much! You'll give those Egyptians something more valuable than the pyramids. Don't worry at all."

With a modest expression, Saru said, "No one can build better than the Pyramids, Mabel. Please don't exaggerate."

Saru's Project was a grand new hotel being built by the Pyramid of Cheops, in Egypt. The hotel was designed as two pyramids diametrically attached to each other. It looked like a giant oasis in the middle of the desert. Due to the economic growth and importance of Egypt, the project was incredibly prestigious.

"OK then," Mabel said. "We better get going before night. We don't have much time. Only bring things that are absolutely necessary. We've got two countries to pass down to the ocean cost."

***

In the evening they got to the faraway place Mabel mentioned. First, they had a helicopter journey from the ship to the airport, then from airport to this distant land they had a small jet plane travel. After they left all their stuff in a hotel located on the ocean coast, Mabel had the group get into a luxurious car.

Due to a change in weather, and the long travel, they were exhausted. Despite this, no one objected when Mabel offered to drive around some. He drove happily, singing songs. Their car traced a river they planned to camp along.

Mabel parked the car. Oen and Saru went down to the river, to watch the water flowing under a bridge. This left Mabel alone with the women he'd brought along. Without his friends, Mabel felt empty. He wanted the girls to cure this emptiness. He demanded they get on top of the car and dance, to entertain him.

As they came back from the water, Oen and Saru saw the women dancing on the roof of the car. Saru was disturbed, but didn't want to say anything. Oen helped him out.

"This is too crazy, Mabel. I can't say I find this enjoyable." Mabel smirked, "You haven't seen my surprise yet."

"Surprises, surprises!" Oen said. "Is there no end to your surprises, my friend?"

"No, even my death shall be a great surprise!" Streching out his head towards Saru, he added, snarling, "Believe me, Saru. Even my death shall be a great surprise!"

"Stop it! This is bullshit, Mabel! You're starting to annoy me."

"Let's have some fun then," Mabel said. Then he held out the bottle of alcohol in his hands and laughed again: "Unfortunatelly, my friends began to show loyalty to their loved ones. A very big loneliness is waiting for me impatiently."

"If you pull yourself together a little bit, then you shall see that there are people ardently waiting for you."

While talking, Mabel's words started to slur. In order to clear his mind, he took off his shoes and soaked his feet in the river. His friends were waiting for a great speech.

"Who, or what, is waiting for me so ardently?" Mabel asked.

"How many women truly loved you for who you are, not for what you have in this world? You know the ones who truly care for you. Other than them, I know it will always be a disappointment for you," Saru said gently.

He then put his hand on Mabel's shoulder. "Is there anyone here who wants the best for you more than we do?" Saru asked.

"Of course not. We joined your fun, but after this, we have to be more responsible. People expect a lot from us. *Everyone* – but especially those we love.

"When we're old, and we hear the footsteps of death, we need to look back and feel we've lived lives which will allow us to easily accept the Angel of Death's invitation. This isn't so hard. The kind of life you're living isn't the only way to be happy. You should understand this and be with us. We all want you to be with us," he further said.

"What the hell are you saying, Saru? Are you encouraging me to kill myself?"

Saru didn't respond. He knew Mabel wasn't speaking to him, but was talking with his iner voice. Oen again interrupted: "You're talking bullshit, Mabel. Wash your face if you need to. Let's not talk about this now. We have plenty of time in the future."

Mabel desperately washed his face. While cold water dripped from the tip of his hair, he called out, "Do you think there's any water in this world that can extinguish the fire inside of us?"

His friends preferred to respond with silence. Mabel reluctantly joined them. Just as they were beginning to feel at peace, gunshots rang out in the hills. They turned toward the sound, and the girls, screaming, huddled close to them. Saru and Oen were confused and didn't know what to do. They looked for shelter behind a rock or the base of a tree. Distantly, they watched the lifeless lights of bullets falling from the sky; they feared more.

Finally, Oen composed himself and dragged the group behind a rock. Only Mabel refused to join them in hiding.

Saru called angrily out to Mabel: "Hurry up, come over here, Mabel. What the hell is going on? Where did you take us? God damn, get over here."

The bullets echoed through the silent night. Mabel, perversely, seemed to be enjoying himself.

"You cowards!" he said and then laughed. "I thought a little excitement wouldn't be too bad. But you ruined my surprise. Come on, there's nothing to fear. Get over here."

Mabel's recklessness only made them more terrified.

"Come on men, be excited! The guns are from a battle between two hostile tribes. I gave them some money to start a battle tonight and to perform a symphony for us!"

Hearing this, Saru went crazy. He ran to Mabel and grabbed the collar of his shirt, saying: "What the hell are you talking about? Tell me what all this means, immediately. This time, you've gone too far!"

"Don't be mad, my friend," Mabel slurred. "All this happened just as I told you. I arranged tonight for us."

"You mean this night, where we don't know where we are, and where a war is happening next to us? You paid for this to happen?"

Oen came out to them while the girls still cowered behind the tree.

"Mabel," Oen called, and then he punched his friend in the face. Mabel stumbled and fell into the water. Saru pulled him to his feet. Oen moved to punch Mabel again, but Saru stopped him. Oen still had his fists clenched.

"Over there, people are killing each other and you're having fun. Right? And you've brought us here as your partners? I won't repeat what I'm about to tell you again: stop this battle right now, just like you started it. Otherwise, one of the people who dies will be you."

Mabel wiped his bleeding nose. A deep sense of guilt started to overwhelm him. He expected this kind of reaction from Saru, but not from Oen.

"They're already at war," he protested. "I only gave the money to one side to make adjustments for tonight. If I hadn't done this, the battle would've happened anyway – it just might have been yesterday, or might be tomorrow."

"Don't try to just yourself. Do just what I told you and let's get the hell out of here," Oen said.

"OK," Mabel said. "At your own sweet will. There is a satellite phone in the car. I'll do what you said, Oen Atara, you genius." He went to the car, mumbling the whole way: "What if I told you that your family's ships carry the weapons here! You think you know everything…"

After ten minutes, the guns stopped. This made everyone feel a bit better. But the tension hadn't fully lifted. One of the girls screamed: "A car is coming."

The lights of a car meandering through the forest, appearing and disappearing among the trees. From afar, it almost looked appealing.

"What's next Mabel? Will someone kidnap us and demand a ransom from our families? Is this your new surprise?"

But Mabel was surprised, too.

"Believe me: I have no idea what it's about."

"Some other cars are coming, too. We better hide somewhere. Tonight, we're having a run of bad luck," Saru said.

Mabel looked at Saru. "If some people really have plans for us, it'll take only a few hours for them to make it happen. This their country, my friend. And these men are well aware of their land. That's why I'm not moving anywhere. You may hide whereever you want. But you better hurry up because they're about to come."

Oen and Saru glared at their friend. They anxiously waited for whomever was about to arrive.

The moon emerged in the sky. The fog which started to descend on the surrounding mountains was given a blue tint by the moon. It was a very soft light.

The first car pulled up. As it turned around, its headlights drew a half circle in the hills. Two more cars arrived. Soldiers got out of these cars and formed a perimeter around the friends. Then a fourth car pulled up. A few civil man got out of it, following by an older man. Only one car kept its headlights on.

The old man said, "Good night, ladies and gentlemen. You've chosen a very good place to have fun, Mabel. However, I wish you'd told your father beforehand."

"Why do you think I'd want to inform my father, dear ambassador?"

Saru suddenly interrupted: "Sir, we only..."

The Ambassador quickly interrupted Saru, saying: "I didn't come here to listen to you guys. At this moment, your families are very concerned about you and they're impatiently waiting for you to return. I shall help you to leave the country in an hour. Any questions?"

Because his behavior was so cold, nobody said anything. In fact, they found his cold demeanor comforting; it made them feel safe. The Ambassador turned to his assistant.

"Let's get out of here," he said, grimacing.

His assistant called to the friends: "Please get into your car. One of our men will accompany you." One of the civil men got into the friends' car.

"What?" Mabel asked. "Is this idiot going to drive?"

"Shut the hell up, Mabel. Just shut up," said Saru, clenching his teeth. Then Mabel, lifted up his hands, meaning that he gave up.

The Ambassador and his assistant spoke to each other while getting into their car.

The assistant said, "They're a few rich snobs. Their kind get you into trouble whereever they go."

Proud of his job, the Ambassador said, "You should not talk about your future bosses that way. Well, I shouldn't have to tell you this; one day you'll learn how much respect you must show and to whom. Or else there'll be someone to teach you. Let's get rid of these "rich snobs," by taking them to the airport as soon as possible. I don't want any trouble."

Then they got into the car. At the airport, the pilot received his instructions from the Ambassador, not Mabel. The girls were strapped into their seats. They'd stopped crying, and were staring silently into the night's darkness. One of them whispered something to other. The one who listened stopped for a while and then burst into laughter. The others tried to understand what was going on but after awhile they began to laugh.

They were having an attack of nerves, and the laughter reverberated off the walls of the aircraft. However, Oen and Saru were not affected by the laughter. They looked at the girls with pity. Mabel, on the other hand, was collapsed in his seat, the bottle at his feet. With an open mouth, he was about to zonk out. Everyone looked at him. However, he saw noone, and he began to snore. When he grew short of breath, he changed his position by reflex. Once his breathing returned to normal, he kept talking nonsense in his dream.

***

Oen was a little annoyed when Miryom told him that there was guest waiting for him in the dining room. He greeted the guest with an insincere manner. "Good evening," he said. Then he pulled a chair out and sat down. "I didn't know you would come."

"I wanted it to be a surprise," she said, a green-eyed, white-skinned woman named Arin. "I canceled the trip and came to you."

"I'm overjoyed," he said, though deep down, he was waiting for Miryom to finish his service. Because he was eating very lightly in the evening, it wasn't hard for Miryom to prepare his dinner. For Miryom, preparing dinner was like easy peasy lemon squeezy—it usually consisted of boiled vegetables; the only nod to gastrointestinal diversity was an array of exotic spices. Unfortunately, when Oen's friends came, then she was obliged to cook a different dinner for everyone.

"I want to speak to you," Arin said. She didn't like to belabouring her point or broaching a subject indirectly. She usually cut right to the heart of a matter, motivated by the stress of wanting to say many things. Oen was trying to guess what she was about to say.

"Sure, I'll listen to you," he said with a fork in his hand; Miryom had quietly, and quickly, brought out his dinner. He stared at Arin's freckles (which he believed was the source of her power over him) and her hair (which was red, the color of maple leaves in autumn). Because he still couldn't figure out what color her freckles were, he couldn't do anything about giving a specific name. However, on a green-eyed, fair-skinned, red-haired woman, these freckles were quite precious. She wouldn't be the same without them.

"Lately, I can't help thinking about the point we arrived at," she said. "Or, rather the point *you* arrived at."

"What's the point?" he asked. He frowned, his face taught. The two of them sat very still, staring at each other.

"You're knocked out. What's wrong with you?" she asked.

"I'm so tired. You know this project took all my energy."

"I don't think you have a problem with your work. I thought such a project would inspire you."

"Arin, I'm sure you've unnecessary misgivings."

Arin couldn't restrain herself anymore, and unburdened all her concerns: "Do you remember that old man the other day? The one who wanted your help for his sick child?"

He wanted to stand up but could not; he refrained from making any movement because he didn't want to manifest his current physiological condition. He stared with meaningless eyes.

"Yes, I remember. So what?"

"You thought he was a liar, but I found out that his child really was ill."

"So? It's none of my business. I'm not able to take care of everyone' s problems. There are lots of organizations that help such people in this country."

"He has no social security. You're not the first person from whom he asked help, but no one has helped him. His poor child is dying. His immune system is destroyed due to poor nutrition."

"Arin, as I told you before I can't take care of everybody's problems. Besides, how did you learn all this?"

"After leaving you, I followed him and I spoke with his wife and neighbors."

"Arin, why did you do this?"

"I don't know, Oen. I guess I wanted to know how a person who cares about others, who loves and wants to see like through the eyes of others, could be so insensitive. Although he's in a position to help others, why is he a mere spectator?" Arin said, looking right into Oen's eyes. He couldn't hold her gaze, but she continued.

"I guess, if you start rethinking your friendships, it would be good for you and for us. What do you have with Mabel except a menial understanding of each other's lives? His selfishness consumes all your beauty. Why are you in such conflict with yourself? Instead of staying firm with your principles, you chase after silly adventures with your friends. Don't you see how tired it makes you? Those who love you—including me—are growing exhausted with you. All the good you want to do is being wiped out."

Arin stood up. Her vocal cords were fresh, and she could scream and yell as much as she wanted. Oen, however, watched quietly.

"Oen! You were the most perfect man I knew. I want to think you still are. Please, listen to your heart and use your own head. You'd be happy doing good things for people instead of chasing coarse pleasures."

Oen took a deep breath. He furiously threw out all the air from his lungs. He just wanted her to leave.

"Can we just drop the subject?" he finally said.

While Arin finished her last words, Oen's head reached over the table, wide-eyed and disbelieving. He took a bite of boiled vegetables. With the hands of his soul, he was pushing Arin towards the door in order to start the process of forgetting the subject.

"You're exaggerating. There is always someone else to help them," he said with a frozen expression.

"Sure. *I'll* help them. We even took the child to the hospital yesterday."

She put her hands on the table. She wanted to announce these sentences to whatever man had inhabited Oen, a man she could no longer recognize. She couldn't stand this man standing in front of her. He looked like a monk in a vow of silence. She then left the room, the house, and went out to the garden.

Oen watched her leaving the house from the window. Watching her go was always attractive to him. When Arin disappeared, Oen barely controlled himself. Miryom came in.

"Do you need anything, sir?" she asked.

"No," he said, turning away from her. "Thanks. Comfort yourself."

Miryom began to clear the table. Oen wanted to gather his thoughts, which were like vultures or lizards, into the nearest corral in his mind. He looked through the contents of his thoughts. They seemed too many... He began give them names, one by one, and gave them forms that he could tolerate. He turned vultures into hawks. He likened lizards to the ones he watched on documentary films. Then, he gathered these new creatures somewhere deep in his brain, and knotten them up, one by one.

Miryom was gone. He was all alone in a big house. The weight of darkness, which he hadn't felt since adolescence, appeared and began to shake his soul. The house fell into pieces. The ceiling went vanished, but there was no light or air.

When he realized that he was looking out the window, he called after Arin.

"For months, everything I've done has turned me a piece of rotten cloth. I know all my mistakes. Every single day I get angry with myself. And I don't want people to talk about my mistakes anymore. Even if everything seems to go haywire, I want to restore order, but I can't. In order to ease the pangs of my conscience, I try to cover old mistakes by making new mistakes. I'm like an ostrich... I'm burying my head in the sand. Every time, I go deeper, but each time, I take less air. Maybe I'm on the brink of going insane."

It was nearly evening when he left the house, which had begun to feel as if it was a grave. The sun's last light was like a red whip in the hands of celestial cavalryman who rode the purple clouds, the whip making deep wounds on the earth. He heard the voices of small insects who looked like spirits as they wandered around. The sea was on the horizon with its opened mouth getting ready to swallow the sun. Birds like black spots moved forward to the mouth of the sea: returning birds, lost birds, appearing birds... Creatures everywhere were seen by a burning eye, their slippery forms were hung in the air.

Oen didn't know how he came to this shore. It was the hour when everybody was running to their homes, to their families and their hot meals. Instead, he was constantly moving because he imagined that sharp knives, axes, and swords were falling all around him from above. He couldn't dare to look at the small houses on the slopes near the sea. By the time he turned his head, he feared losing his balance and falling down. A wet breath came off the ocean and caressed him. Oen was trying to walk and to ignore this moisture which hit his nose, ears, and fingertips.

On his left side there were those houses appearing from the forest, and on the right side there was a dragon, there were knives, axes, and swords flowing behind the fire. In front of him was that fire's blur. He tried to walk without moving his head. The only thing he could hear was the water whispering... It was the kind of closed-off state where one's mind could journey...

He tried to shut down his thoughts. He didn't want any two words or symbols coming together to form any meaning.

Yet no matter how hard he tried, a sense of anguish was pursuing him. For a moment, everything he could perceive around him was wiped away. He stared into space—into the veins of the past...

He remembered the days just after university, when he got his first job as an architect and put all his effort into his work. In those days Oen was bounching off the walls; he wanted to make the best of it, and wanted to be proud of himself. Therefore, for many days he examined the field where they would construct a building and memorized all the things around the site. When he finished collecting data, he put himself into the shoes of every person who visited the field and imagined an artifact by looking through their eyes. Some days, he thought of a tree near that field; he tried to figure out what kind of building this tree would like to see nearby. Some days, he flew low by helicopter, and he thought of birds regarding what kind of building they would like fly over.

After examining the surrounding area, he paid attention to the requests of the employer and he designed an environmentally-friendly building. At his first job, he achieved a great deal of success, which led him to rapidly rise at the peak of his profession. He has been a source of great pride not just for himself, but also for his family and friends. Sometimes, he even visited those friends—those trees, birds and hills—from whom he got his opinions.

Things should have gone this way: he was the only child of a perfect family. His school life was full of success, and all of his friends considered him an "Angel." However, lately he felt like he lacked a heart and mind. He didn't know how to clean this darkness which had leaked to all the vistas of his spirit. He remembered the day when he rejected a poor man who wanted his help.

He was murmuring, in conflict with himself. "The weak ones cannot live," said a voice inside of him.

Then another voice responded: "If it is so, then death is coming for you."

"I'm not a weak one!"

"Sure that man received a negative answer from you. But somewhere, he's fluttering with a small glimmer of hope. To stay alive, one needs hope. And yet you've completely lost your hope. So tell me: who is the weak one?"

"I listen to you for weeks but I don't remember a day in which you were ever this cruel."

"You're the cruel one, Oen Atara. All you had to do was sign a check. A life depended on it. This simple move could have saved a child's life. Actually, this was an excellent opportunity for you to be human. You could do that favor;

by acting modestly, you could ignore gratitude. But you could not! At that moment, because of your arrogance, you thought that you were one of the owners of life. You decided that those who are weak should not live. You fancied yourself a small God."

"That's enough. Enough!"

"You are not the one who decides whether it's enough or not. You see that you're here because of your decisions. You don't keep your mind and your heart with you. Well, let's go back to our subject. You lost the chance to save a life because of your arrogance. Because you have such a dark soul. You missed an opportunity when evil inside you was in the darkest position. If that child has days to live, then he shall live... You didn't bring either that child or yourself into existence. But you thought so! Do you think I'm lying?"

"I do bad as much as everyone, and I do good as much as everyone. Do we all keep the goodness and the badness inside us? Does everybody's soul go through inner turmoil from time to time? Don't people we consider to be the best do things considered persecution by to others?"

"I don't have the answers to these questions. I only told you what you needed to hear. And I spoke honestly."

Oen suddenly began to see ahead of him. His mind returned from the place it had gone. Even though he was near his house which was far from city, when he saw the lights of a small town he hadn't visited before, he felt relaxed, his loneliness and discomfort lifted.

In one large street, there were the lights of a half dozen houses. People were with their families, preparing to enjoy their meals. Some of them were living happiness in that very moment. Oen roamed through the streets without thinking of the reason he was there. There was nobody around. He was jealous of people who were at their homes, with their families.

He saw a place where there was much light. He came to a taphouse, which was the place for old fishermen, who were constantly stopping by. Without listening to his mind, which was telling him to stop, he went inside. Not knowing anybody inside or with whom he would talk made him feel comfortable. He thought he could spend a few hours there. He could even find a place to stay for the night if he felt too tired to go home. He climbed up a few stairs. Then he pulled a door from where there was a little light filtering outside.

A few fishermen were seated at a table near the door. The scent and sound of the place was very familiar to Oen. He shivered. The walls were covered by trees, which were shaped like lids. The tables and chairs were handmade. The owner of this place was sitting in front of him. The calm steps of waiters mixed with the sound of the music inside. He sat at a table next to the door. From there, he could see the whole place. Everyone behaved as if it was the first day of their life.

One of the waiters came over and received Oen Atara's order. In a few minutes, his table was garnished with various food and drink. He ate a few bites of fish and bread, and then began to drink. The night was getting along. The best thing for him would be to zonk out. However, he couldn't go home—there were strange noises coming from his stomach. He ran to the toilet and got sick.

***

All things coming out of the human body arouse disgust. Though people gain beautiful things when mixing various elements found in nature, they throw everything up when it comes to an upset stomach, bloated with a mixture of various dishes. Are the fossil remnants of life always so disgusting?

He entered the toilet. The nausea in his stomach was stopping. He still prefered not to trust his stomach. He was having difficulty standing. He tried to regain his consciousness. He sat next to bowl and closed his eyes. He felt the smell of urine mixed with the scent of soap. He waited there for a while. Strange things were coming into his mind and then disappearing. They were thoughts he'd never had before... When did they come and why did they wait for his weakest moment to show up? Even to search for an answer seemed a burden for him. Looking around, he thought about what differentiated this place from a place where picnics were held. Lines and scents... Lines showing God's hand; true scents... Here was the scent of the toilets.

He felt wetness on him. Water was dripping onto him, very slowly. He shivered a little but he didn't move. He thought of the reasons to not be here right now. There were dozens, even hundreds of reasons, but he didn't want to count them right now. He wanted a long corridor to be laid in front of him. Maybe he could get rid of these strange thoughts by walking down this corridor.

"Just look at tiles, they're white and clean..."

"Is it white or a taint?"

"It's clean."

"Surely some murderer must have white hands?"

He closed his eyes and lifted up his head. He began to follow the light of the lamp behind his eyelids. Red, blue, pink... Then, he lowered his head and opened his eyes. He thought he could spend some time in transient blindness, but he saw darkness and spots floating within that darkness. Everything seemed so drab and colorless. He panicked, hoping to see their true colors. Maybe he wouldn't see things as he'd seen them before. He was sweating, but his mouth was dry.

He felt that he should stand up and go back inside. He felt dizzy. Everything was spinning. He felt like he could hear the electrons spinning around him. Was he also spinning this fast? Or was it the feeling one gets when they're close to death? His wheat-skin seemed to be darkened, like flour-sprinkled bread. He looked at the mirror. The thing he feared was happening. He felt as if all of his cells were moving around. His face was like a ball of dough changing shape...

"The bread is here?" a man who appeared in the mirror said.

He looked at his face very carefully. He didn't know the man in the mirror. He looked more closely. He began to know him a little. Then, he began to relax.

But all of his features—his eyes, mouth, nose and ears— kept shifting shapes again. They moved faster and faster. He was watching this change with fear. Colors were disappearing and the light was weakening. Feeling the pressure coming from his stomach, he perceived that his throat was burning. He bent his head and a bitter taste spread in his mouth. His eyes were aflame. He vomitted, then opened his eyes. He saw some puke in the washbasin. Then he turned on the faucet to clean out the basin.

He felt he was seeing things a bit more clearly, but then he felt the pressure in his stomach. This time, though without the bitter taste, he vomitted once again. He looked in the mirror once more. The colors were much more vivid. He turned on the faucet and washed his mouth and cleaned the basin. He let the water run for a long while, listening to its voice. He saw his long curly hair and handsome face. After checking his teeth and strecthing his lips, he saluted himself and he left the toilet. There was only one thing in his mind: without the possibility of vomitting, would the colors be so clear?

He left the taphouse where no one knew him. He wasn't thinking of going home. There was nowhere he wanted to go. He headed towards his car. The breeze coming from the sea was cooler. He threw himself heavily into the car seat. He felt lighter when he started driving. He headed towards the city, to see places he hadn't seen before.

After parking his car, he began to walk through the city's streets. There were parked cars, open shops, a few people walking... He was feeling better. He walked as if he was light as air. He felt the atmosphere of the new place, the different scents, colors, and tastes... Then he felt exhausted. He felt his cells burning. He began to hear the sounds of his body's mechanics. He heard the rustle of his blood vessels, the vibrations emitted by the heart to the body, the opening and closing of his lungs as he took a breath. A chill again...

"No, this can't be," he said to himself. Then, his heart rate accelerated. He was trying to take deeper breaths. He wasn't aware that his knees were growing wobbly. He looked like a phantom wobbling around. He wasn't sure how long he walked for. He arrived at a dark place. He arrived at a crossroads. Without thinking, he went left.

"Why did I choose this side?"

"Maybe it's because there's some dim light here."

***

He came inside the darkest room of the hotel, sat on a chair in front of the window, and lit a cigarette. He was very tired. After finishing smoking, he laid down on the bed without opening the sheets. He curled into the fetal position. Suddenly, he started to perspire and he waited for the warmth to spread through his body. He lingered with this feeling for a long time. When there was nothing to think about, he wished his girlfriend were with him. He wanted her to look at him with real eyes. He imagined her coming next to him. He closed and then opened his eyes and felt a fragile wind, a nice scent. Without opening his eyes, he caressed her hair in his imagination. Inside, he was saying "my love," but in fact, he never believed that he had a lover...

When saying "my love", he was first remembering the smell of her hands, which moved him deeply. Is there a way, other than scent, to leave such an indelible impression on someone? She was filling Oen's soul just through her scent. Her hands were the most delicate branch of his mind and heart and were extending him into life.

During the moments when he was seeking trust, behaving childishly or trying to protect her, he would hold her hands—sometimes softly, sometimes very tightly. The existence of these hands were vital to his heart's functioning. Seeing how happy she was when he kissed her little finger made Oen feel extraordinary powerful. Every time he tried to walk towards those hands, fluttered to reach them, he felt like he was flying. He never believed that he could find a woman who would give him peace as much as she gave him.

Trees, earth which drank rain water, freshly cut grass, tea, meals, mother, child, sweating, gasoline...

How much space all of these things occupied in his mind! This was the necessary consequence of being a human being in this day and age. All of these things were stuck involuntarily to his soul. He realized that when he met the smell of her hands.

When he was with her, he felt like a leaf which had landed on windmill propeller. In order to move, he needed the wind. But the wind could take away that leaf at any time, and this was extraordinary interesting. Overcoming a harsh winter and reaching spring, getting life's energy to become a bright green leaf, waiting for some more water from ground to be able to keep smiling to life, experiencing drought days, hitting the bricks and at last running towards that windmill... He was a leading actor in this adventure that seemed very ordinary. To be able to breath without thinking much about the past or the future was, however, possible for him only when he was with her. Since the first time he smelled her, these kind of thoughts were passing through the desolate corner of his mind.

To be yourself, just like a desert...

"For a man who has found what he was looking for but could not complete what he found, how long would he be able to have her?"

"Never," he said. He was not even bored of speaking by himself for that long.

***

Inside of human beings, there is a secret place. No matter how much beauty you put into that space, it's still inclined to evil feelings. That place is the land where emotion roots. When one is surrounded by beauty or evil, failing to do what must be done is the collapse of the soul. We never realize whether we have made the right decision or not.

These thoughts raced through Oen's mind, but he didn't expect them to orient his actions. Yet these thoughts obsessed him.

Midnight had already passed. Smelling bad scents, he left the hotel. There was a different darkness in the area. He plunged aimlessly into the streets. He was curious what thoughts they would arouse within him.

He thought of women who fell in love with him. He decided to call the first one who came to mind. Ebri was his first real love. Memories flooded back... A small smile spread briefly across his face. After his memories of Ebri, Adila came to mind. He thought of her for a while. Then, came the last love. Still, she was unreachable: Arin.

He thought the care he'd put into each relationship. Beginning and endings... How interesting that to reach this state of reflection, he had to give up the palace where he lived—or even tear that palace down. Why did people only learn during times of trial and error? The small differences which determine a person's character were very important to people, all of whom breath the same air, have the same needs, and share the same problems.

He was thinking of these differences and the women. He wanted to speak with all of them and hear Oen Atara in their words. Maybe those who were closest to him would see his mistakes more clearly. Didn't Arin awaken this idea within him through her speech?

Now, where were they and what were they doing? If he told them that he wanted to speak with them, would they come? Arin for sure would come, but he wasn't sure of the others...He decided to call three of them. He was excited. He thought that he had found a way to save him from this depression.

He called three of them and gave them an appointment in an all night cafe. After he finished the calls, an icy trembling overtook his entire body.

***

His wandering led him to a slightly dangerous part of town, where a criminal air hung menacingly over the streets. In a minute, three women he loved would be meeting one another. He didn't think he had the courage to put what he was thinking into words; he wouldn't go to meet the women.

Ignoring the cars splashing water on him, he walked into the street, where there were many shady-looking people. He looked down the dimly lit street.

Upon seeing a well dressed man, many of the women— prostitutes, he assumed—waited for Oen to approach, hoping to get lucky. He wasn't sure what to do. He listened to his body, clenching his teeth, feeling his eyes burning.

Light and shadow flowed on both sides of the road. The women started to catcall him with offers. Their faces were hidden behind makeup. The smoke of their cigarettes was mingling with their fake hair and showy outlooks. They were trying to hide their work into night's darkness sometimes with their silence as hell and sometimes with their sorrowful life stories that they never tired of telling. When a shadow appeared in the street, they emerged in the lights of the street lamps on their dim corners.

He looked at the people and thought of their work. The quickest way to earn easy money... His eyes began to burn and his nose began to ache.

"Why do we die tearfully? What's happening to me?" Oen asked. "Why isn't sleeping with someone solely for material purposes considered a crime in the eye of law?"

Thinking about this upset him. He was trying to run away from the glances of the women of the street, trying to understand their speech and to reach the end of the street. He didn't know why he didn't want to go back and why he needed to reach the end of the street. Their voices were like the bullets of hunters chasing their prey in the dark.

As he was walking in this mood, he heard a moaning and timid voice. He turned back and looked at the owner of the voice. A middle aged woman, her good looks wasted on her work, came into the street from where she was hiding. Oen felt a desire only to speak with her. But she acted quickly and fell into his arms. This close proximity upset Oen. He tried to resist her as she attemped to take him back to the hotel room.

Her entreaties won out, and they entered a hotel room. The woman came close to Oen.

"Stop it!" he demanded.

She was surprised. She tried to understand what he really wanted. Oen sat on a chair.

"Are you a police officer?"

Oen shook his head in "no."

"Are you a crazy man then?" she asked.

Oen lit a cigarette.

"If you're thinking of scaring me to squeeze money out of me, you'll be left empty handed," she said desperately.

Oen ignored her. He motioned that she should sit down. She was no longer scared and did what he asked. She wouldn't take her eyes off him.

Oen smoked his cigarette. Her bag was right under his feet and was half-opened. When he looked into it, he saw the barrel of a gun shining. He imagined her holding this gun in her hands... Pulling the trigger and bullet jumping toward its target from the barrel.

When he finished his cigarette, he turned to face her. She was silent. He handed her an enormous sum of money.

"Rejecting this would be stupid, but this is too much. All of this for sitting in silence?"

"No," said Oen. "Some of it is for the gun in your bag."

***

"Mabel! When will you be on your best behavior? Could you please tell me what kind of nonsensical things you've done?"

"Whose side are you on, Saru? Didn't you see? He insulted me officially. It was good to have that happen. Ah, nevermind. I'll talk about it way too much tonight."

"I didn't hear anything wrong in his words. The only thing he's done was to count some of the things you screwed-up. Didn't you want all of these things known by everyone?"

Mabel didn't say a word. He looked angry and straightened the collar of his shirt. Then, he left, sayinghe would wash his face. While he was gone, Arin arrived in front of the theater, right where guests were entering. Seeing her, Saru immediately ran over.

"Arin, welcome. The only good thing about this mess is you. Did you know that?"

Arin smiled. She seemed curious. "People are talking about something outside," she said. "Is there a problem?"

Saru answered her unwillingly. "The problem is, of course, Mabel. He pushed one of the journalists around."

"I wouldn't worry about it. I'm sure they're both content with their situations. I'm sure once they leave, they'll be hanging out together!"

Arin was looking around while speaking to him. Her eyes were searching for Oen. She hadn't seen him in a few days. After meeting with his ex-girl friends, she had a strange feeling of conserving him. She wanted to see him as soon as possible. Instead of having a chip on her shoulder, she couldn't help but feel so worried about him.

She was trying to play it cool towards Saru: "I called Oen from the road but couldn't reach him. Do you know when he'll be here?"

Saru laughed. "I just spoke to him. He'll be here in ten minutes." He then looked at her with wide eyes. "Are you OK?" he asked.

"I'm OK," she said.

"Well, I better welcome the guests. Before having more trouble, I want to get this night over with."

"Everything will be wonderful. Don't worry, I'm here."

"I know that," he said, turning for the door.

Arin sat in her seat, turning frequently to look for Oen. Looking to the front of the theater, she saw Mabel instead, and recoiled.

"Don't be scared little girl. It's me, Dracula!" Mabel said.

"Mabel!" she screamed, "you scared me." She punched his shoulder lightly.

"How was it, Miss Muhammed Ali?"

"Dracula's about ready to get his butt kicked."

Mabel laughed. "Oen's a lucky jerk," he said.

"Hey, he's your friend! Please say nice things about him."

"By the way, where is he? Is Mr. Perfect going to miss his best friend's project presentation?"

This made Arin angry. She understood that Mabel hadn't seen Oen lately.

"If you ever looked outside yourself," she said, "maybe someday you'll see what's going on around you."

"Boy, you, too, Arin? I don't know how I got surrounded by such angels. Let me be a tough devil."

***

Arin ignored chose to ignore Mabel after that. Her eyes were focused on the door. Then, she found what she was looking for: Oen was speaking with Saru. He was well-dressed, but his demeanor was very strange. Arin remembered their last conversation; her heart filled with deep pain. She immediately wanted to apologize to him.

Oen seemed very calm and a little bit lackluster. Arin watched him moving his body very slowly. She thought that the joy in Saru's face was shadowed by Oen's unease. This meant that Oen was shaken up even more than she thought...

Oen left Saru to look after the newly arrived guests. He headed towards Arin and sat next to her. Their greeting was lackluster. Both of them tried to speak without looking at each other's faces, but they failed.

"What were you speaking with Saru about?" she asked. She was trying to make a cute expression on her face.

"Nothing. Greetings, the usual... He also wanted me to make a speech. That's why I got a bit excited." He was about to smile, but then his tension overwhelmed him.

"I think a speech at the opening ceremony is a good idea. That was smart of Saru. After all, you've supported him the most."

"I've always been excited to work with Mediterranean people. However, this project is his endeavour, not mine. I only gave him a little advice about the method."

"Even if that's true, you're one of the best known architects in the world. It was helpful, not just for your business, but your friendship."

"Yes" Oen, said. "He's a a sharp old bird."

His face paled. Even though he tried to pull himself together, he couldn't get rid of his inner turmoil. Arin realized this when he sat next to her. With a deep sense of compassion, her heart sank and she couldn't look into his face.

Everyone took their seats in the hall. The plan was for a small presentation and then cocktails downstairs. Everyone present was used to the successes of Oen and Saru. The crowd murmured quietly amongst themselves.

The lights shut off. The noise finished. Scenes of the presidential palace built in Italy and right after that, the Cheops Hotel, reflected on the stage. Saru wanted to begin with the work of his friend. As soon as the presentation, which included a light music, finished, Saru came to the podium, serenaded by applause. He greeted the invitees:

"I thank you for being here with us. I would like to invite the man I called 'the best architect in the world,' and my best friend, Oen Atara up here. I don't think anybody can introduce this project better than he can. Yes, it's true that I made the drawings, but the soul of this work is in his mind. Let's give him a warm welcome!"

The guests acclaimed him very much. Arin applauded with a nice smile and watched him moving from his seat. Oen looked around and then leaned into Arin's ear: "Would you wish me good luck?" Then he looked into her eyes.

When she saw the depths of despair in his eyes, it curdled her blood. She was filled with something terrible and didn't know what to say. What she felt was a precursor to remorse, but she was so afraid of saying the wrong things that she stayed silent.

As soon as Oen squeezed her hand, he faced the podium. While the crowd waited for him to begin his speech, he stared at them blankly, silently. Saru, Mabel and Arin were waiting for him. He cleared his throat. His friends and Arin thought that everything was fine and relaxed. Oen took his hand into his jacket's pocket. A cold metal touched his hand. He slowly pulled the object out of his pocket. His hands were under the podium and noboby could see them. Then, he slowly lifted his arms up. People who were watching him very carefully saw the gun in his hands. Oen lifted up the gun a little more to make everyone see it clearly. The bright part of the pistol flashed for a moment and then suddenly disappeared.

After a few seconds, when he was sure everyone was watching him, he put the last part of his plan to action.

A gunshot rang out in the hall. Women screamed, men opened their mouths in shock.

Oen fell to the ground. Arin fainted and Mabel was petrified with fright. Saru felt giddy. No one in that place could do anything initially. When the scene began to clarify, the private security guards ran to Oen.

Someone screamed, "Call an ambulance immediately!"

Sleep of Emptiness

*F*irst there was burning, then a coolness, a bit of moisture and some air. He realized his existence. However, he was unconsciously thinking; why he wasn't seeing or hearing anything? He was hanging fire in a deep darkness. The only thing he could perceive was a bit of air and the coolness. Air was circulating around him very slowly. At the beginning, Oen thought himself a piece of flesh in front of this air circulation, because he couldn't see or hear anything. There was no sound, no light and no conscious to understand the situation...

The air was wriggling like a snake. Each time he touched himself, he felt the coolness. Then the air wriggled again. This time, Oen felt agile and inhaled the air. As the air got into his nostril, he sneezed immediately. Then this sneeze became a spark and finally ordered the blood in his vessels and veins to move. The red liquid began to move slowly. Even the blood didn't know how long time waited.

The blood rubbed against the wall of his vessels. Oen heard the voice of this rubbing, which he considered very strange. It was like time had only just begun. He didn't know how long he'd been here...

After getting over its initial dizziness, the blood began to circulate in the vessels. As it was speeding up, its color was becoming clear. As it was becoming visible, the sounds and the crowd inside Oen were increasing... It was like a light music pushing the blood forward with its soft hands. The clearness of the vessels made the blood happy.

Then, the blood reached a piece of muscle. It knew this piece of flesh. This was that motor that sent it on its journey. As far as it remembered, its name was "heart." Both blood and heart were in love with each other. Blood filled the heart. The heart was inactive. As far as blood remembered, the heart was pumping blood into the vessels; in other words, it was pumping life into vessels... Blood filled the heart, waiting for it to respond. It was exhausted from moving through the vessels without the heart's strength; it didn't know how to make the heart resume its old movement. Then, all of a sudden, the blood heard a voice:

"You can't give me life by wandering inside of my empty rooms. Deliver a part of yourself into my own vessels. You need to sacrifice a part of yourself for this to happen. Could you do this?"

"Yes," said the blood. "Show me the way."

"Send a little of yourself to the right vessel. I can send over the rest."

The voice of heart was trailing away. That's why the blood hurried up and did what the heart said. And then, it waited... The blood didn't know how long it waited, but noticed that one of the surrounding rooms was illuminated. The heart had begun to work. Then, new blood came to the first blood and dispersed through the body.

He began to lighten. Oen was perceived all his senses. He had eyes, hands, ears, and nose but there was no stimuli addressing them. There was no time, no place or direction.

When the blood began to wander his vessels in a normal rhythm, Oen occupied himself with the voice of his body machine for a while. He could almost hear the voice of every organ. It took maybe a million years or only a fleeting moment...

When he fully regained his consciousness, he had to endure his mind's pressures; it shrieked because there were very few things that would give him the opportunity for his senses to work. He wanted to speak and scream. However, he could not control his voice or ears. He was exhausted, but he didn't know if anyone else would hear him; he wasn't sure anything existed beyond himself. This situation, too, may have lasted for a million years or only a fleeting moment...

He was in emptiness. Because of the silence around him, his body's voice was cut-off. Was he alive? Or was he dead? He wasn't in a mood to understand the question. All he wanted was to hear some voice. A deep feeling of loneliness came over him. There was no direction for him to go. He wanted to take a step, run and see the places he wanted to go because the colors in his mind began to return. However, there was no place, no direction to go. This situation took a million years or only a fleeting moment...

His mind had opened itself. Then, a tree grew in his mind. A giant tree with its lush leaves and branches stretched up. However, he couldn't imagine either a wind or a bird settling on a branch. Then, the tree disappeared... For a moment, when the tree appeared, his loneliness vanished. But now that it was gone, he was consumed by nihilism.

He wanted, profoundly, to cry. The burning in his eyes and the pain in his nose were forcing him to tears. However, he failed because there was no memory of a cry...

Oen was all alone in the middle of the emptiness. All he could do was wait.The most painful thing was that he couldn't realize how long he waited. Then all of the sudden, he heard a click. There was something approaching him. A small thing, but it was existing...

He waited for a while, then the sound was cut off. At that moment, he realized that he was able to turn his head right and left. He stared around but couldn't see anything. Then he heard the click again.He tried to understand which side it was coming from. He looked around, but he was overwhelmed.

He woke up again in the emptiness.The last thing he remembered was the click. Somewhere near him, there was someone else. They were alive and moving. Whatever it was, he wanted to see and touch it. While turning his head to right and left, his hands moved slightly. To feel the presence of his arms and hands right next to his head made Oen delighted beyond belief. After awhile, he realized that they were his own arms and hands. For the first time a word came into his mind:

"Sound! Where are you?"

Oen was speaking to himself, deep inside, a place that no one could hear him. For the first time, Oen felt sorry, but he couldn't cry. Sleep began to walk around his head. Oen gave up...

When he woke up, hc was delighted to be remembering many more things. The concept called "time" began to form. The more he moved, the more he remembered things. He tried to move his hands; he only made a small movement. Stirring his little finger seemed a great success for him. While he was delighting over this moment, he heard that familiar click again. He felt good. The sound was gradually approaching. This made him excited. He was all ears. For the first time, he felt very close to the sound. The click resumed. Whatever was coming, it grew closer to Oen. He was happy in that moment. The owner of the sound stopped. All sound went away. Oen broke down. Then, a pain shot through his head. He was tired, so tired.

When he woke up, he turned his head right and left. Even though he couldn't see anything, it gave him pleasure. He moved his little finger. Next, he moved all his fingers, his hands and arms.

He felt a shock in his head. For the first time, he felt his feet and tried to move them. By means of the experience he gained from moving his hands, he moved his feet for a very brief time. He felt pain in his left toes. He didn't know why he had the pain, but he enjoyed it... He was loving any kind of information. He loved regaining the feeling that he was alive, loved the colors of life, the smells, the other stimuli. He was gratefully accepting these gifts, gifts that he didn't have to work to receive. A small burning sensation was sending Oen to the moon and back.

Once more, he fell asleep. Then, he woke up. This awakening was very different from the others because he was feeling the breath of a living being over his aching fingers.

Whatever it was, it was touching his fingers with its tongue. Like a flame, the breath burned his fingers. He was trying to figure out what it was, but he was also afraid of this living thing that was pulling him back to life.

Trying not to move as little as possible, he tried to bend his head to look at his feet, but he failed. He felt that small creature's hard, sharp teeth. The small creature got its teeth into Oen's fingers. He felt pain and wanted to scream, but couldn't make a sound. After breathing five or ten times, he began to get used to this new pain. Everytime the pain pulsed through his head, he felt grateful to be alive. If it were possible, Oen would kiss this creature biting the bottom of his feet. Because he couldn't move much, he gave himself to this creature's motion.

After awhile, the creature pulled his teeth from Oen's toes. Then, a sharp coolness like a knife spread through his entire body. When the coolness dissipated, the creature blew its breath again, and Oen felt a flame on his fingertips. A pinch of breath...this burning thrilled him. Despite his deep loneliness, this burning reminded him that he was alive. It made him want to be *more* alive. And as his ambition for life increased, so did his life.

He discovered time. From his heartbeat or his breathing, he could estimate when he was going to sleep. As the duration of time between each breath increased, he was falling into sleep. For now, the only values he could measure were paucity or abundance. For instance, the time the creature spent at his feet was much less than the time Oen spent in the emptiness. He was aware of this distinction.

He wanted to fall into sleep again because something new was happening every time he woke up. However, according to his primitive calculations, there was more time before he would fall asleep. He desperately thought of the creature. The knowledge of something else existing filled him with joy. When he was thinking, he fell into sleep.

He woke up with the breath of the creature. He tried to move but couldn't... The creature was doing the same things as before. When the creature left, Oen worried more than before. Of course, he was deeply wounded by the creature's teeth. Despite the pain, he was much more concerned when the creature left.

He closed his eyes and thought about what the creature could be... There were only a few colors and a tree in his mind. Because of this, he tried to build an image of his only friend. He wasted his time by thinking of how much time had passed between his first visit and his second. Then he fell into sleep again. When he woke up, the same things happened. This time it was much more insufferable than before. When the pain finally began to lessen, Oen relaxed and once more fell asleep.

He woke up. This time there was nothing around him but silence... He tried to calculate the time to learn when his friend was going to come. He waited for a very long time, but there wasn't a click or pain. A sadness covered him. As his sadness became stronger, it gave way to anger... He tried to force himself to move, but each time he moved, he felt a deep pain in his muscles. As the pain spread to his whole body, he grew angrier. He was behaving like a tiger who wants to get rid of his chains.

No matter how hard he tried, he couldn't get any results and he had to calm down. When his cramping finished, he tried to hear even a small click; he listened to hear whether his friend had come. He forced himself to move again, but he failed. His rage grew even more.

With full steam ahead, he overloaded his vocal cords. A cry echoed in the emptiness. Oen's throat and lungs burned, as if they'd been scalded by nitric acid. When he heard his voice, he was astonished and afraid. This was the first time he had heard his voice. After waiting awhile, a few syllables came out in a whisper. He liked his undertone. From now on, he began to make strange noises by himself. By hearing these meaningless noises, he was losing his consciousness. He forgot about his friend.

When he got tired of making noises, the first thing that came to his mind was an image of a tree. For a long time, he thought of a tree—its branches, leaves, and birds flying around it. The object was much more clearer than ever before. He remembered that this object was called a "tree"... He said "Ttttt" by himself and then he said the other syllable inadequately: "Ree."

Oen liked it very much. He repeated it many times. Sometimes in a low voice and sometimes by screaming...

He got tired and slept and woke up. His voice and the name "tree" were in his mind. Without thinking of his friend, he repeated the things he had done before sleeping. While he was repeating the word "tree," he remembered the word "leaf." And then, the word "bird." He repeated the new words before he slept.

He was remembering everything he said every time he woke up. He was constantly remembering new words. He struggled with words until he had enough of them to be self-sufficient for a man.

He woke up. This time, he didn't want to speak. He tried to strech his body, which he could move more freely than ever. He wanted to get rid of the fatigue that had settled between his muscles. He realized that if he stretched as soon as he woke up, his muscles relaxed. He felt his weight. It was as if something was pulling him to one side. He felt it at the bottom of his feet. He tried to understand what it was. Whatever it was, it was enhancing its power.

Oen had to give up. He felt something soft on his feet. It was easily penetrating into his feet. The substance wrapped around his femur and wrist. He was get rid of the emptiness...

It was water! He was in the water up to his knees. He stayed there for a while, filled with excitement and fear. Suddenly, there was a hardness beneath his feet. He touched it with his his fingertips. It was really rough. In fact, it was much rougher than the thing he felt on his knees. Moving his fingertips encouraged Oen. He tried to move his legs. When he was convinced that he could make it, he tried to lift his right leg but his hands were motionless. He fell into the water as he lifted his leg. He took a deep breath because of the fear and panic. A small amount of water entered his mouth and his trachea. By coughing, he spit it out. However, Oen wasn't reacting against the surprises as quickly and accurately as his lungs. He was astonished. Because he wasn't seeing anything, he had difficulty balancing. The bulges and holes at the bottom of the water were obstructing him. At last he found a level place to stand and then he stood up.

He was out of breath. Then he took another breath, one that would satisfy his lungs.

After some time, he overcame his fears. He wasn't going to wait motionless in the water. He slowly moved one of his feet forward. The base beneath him was still stable and Oen didn't fall. This situation encouraged him and he took one more step. With the confidence of this motion, he took many steps. As he was moving forward, he realized that the water was getting shallower. Then the water vanished. Now his feet were stepping on dry soil and a little grass. He felt the heat and confidence of soil and could smell grass. The scents and the sounds gradually increased. His eyes began to burn because a light appeared around him. He waited for his eyes to get used to this new environment. When he was sure that his eyes were relaxed, he slowly opened his eyelids. His eyes were seeing for the first time. Hundreds of lush trees were swaying in front of him, just like the one he was trying to revive in his mind this whole time.

He was straining to keep his eyes clear under these new circumstances. Because his eyes hadn't met any stimuli before, they didn't know the correct responses to give. In order to understand what the objects were, he examined everything around him. He couldn't move from where he was. As he was looking at the objects, he remembered their names, their smells, how soft they were... At last, his mind grew tired of this work. His eyes began to black-out and he left himself on the soft grass and went to his real sleep.

***

It was a very soft awakening. Feeling his face on hard ground filled his heart with a confidence. He waited to enjoy it for a while. His body was rested and breathed a sigh of relief.

He suddenly stood up and looked around in order to try to understand where he was. The place was a little bit different from the other place – or it seemed different to Oen. Instead of feeling fear or suspicion, he seemed self-satisfied. He was happy with the things he was seeing, the scents he was smelling; a warm wind was blowing...

He tried to enjoy the feast that was given to his senses. The name of the wind or the name of the flower he smelled didn't matter to him. He only cared about converting the existing world into a form that his mind could understand... This was all Oen was doing. From now on, there were many names and pictures in his mind. However, he didn't have any memories of these things. That's why he would make his decisions unconsciously.

He took a few steps and enjoyed walking. After taking more steps, he stopped next to a tree. He knelt down and touched the tree trunk. He felt its hard shell with his fingertips. He pulled off two pieces of the dead barks. It was very strange for him to pull off a piece of trunk without having any reason. He tried to understand why he had done that. Afterwards, he looked at his body; he was nude. His behaviour was just like a timid animal. He pulled a few hairs from his arm. He got hurt and then thought: "Did the tree get hurt, too?" He couldn't know.

He stood up. His curiosity to explore was throughly awakened. The last thing he remembered was water. He looked towards the side where he remember it, but there was no water. He was on a plain that looked like it was pressed between two hills. There was no sun in the sky. He couldn't figure out where the lightness came from.

He heard the sound of bird and immediately turned that way. From one of the trees a bird flew into the air. Oen watched it. During that time, he saw many – in the air, in trees, on the ground. He didn't approach some of them. He watched some of them very closely. Just as he saw more animals than he could count, he saw a multitude of flowers.

He got tired of exploring. He threw his body down to the meadow and began to watch the blue sky. He compared himself with the living creatures he saw. Though he studied the other animals, none of them studied him. Without curiosity, they were doing what they needed to do and they were going where they needed to go. He couldn't make any sense of his thoughts. On the horizon, where the hills met the sky, he noticed a black curtain. It was the first time he'd seen this curtain. Though he shivered, he was drawn to this curtain. He was glad its darkness was far away. He fell into sleep.

The next time he woke up, he found some rags next to him. He asked loudly: "What is it? It looks like a different thing. Is it a leaf? An animal skin?"

He couldn't understand what it was. He began to carefully examine the rag . He saw that it wasn't a single piece; it was many fine yarns brought together. For a long time, he examined the cloth. At last, the cooling weather forced him to hug the cloth.

As the weather got warmer, he left the cloth where he first found it. He left the place. He wanted to see new places but when he thought of the cloth, he turned back. He possessed this object, and it was useful to him. He wanted to leave it in a safe place. He was very anxious about the wind carrying it away from him. He squeezed it into a tree hole that seemed safe. But he didn't feel at ease. He thought of the tree hole and then removed the cloth. After a very long struggle, he decided to wear the cloth. At the beginning, it disturbed his naked body, but he got used to it after a little while. He felt himself much safer.

He went to the corner of the bright field. He hadn't been there before, and he saw new flowers and animals. He even tried to greet some of them, but hearing Oen's voice, the animals ran away. Oen went back to the where he'd first woken up. Once again, he lay down. He watched the bright sunless sky and the darkness that fell on the horizon... The black curtain drew his attention, but for the time being, he slept.

When he woke up, he felt his blood circulating through his body; he had a bellyache. His mouth was dry. His body was decaying because of these troubles, but he forced himself off the ground. The pains grew stronger. He walked through the places he visited before, but he couldn't find anyting that would save him from these pains. He find the thing that would help him.

Then, he began to run. The animals he passed were scared and ran away from him. His eyes weren't seeing where he was running. When he ran out of breath, he stopped. The pains had decreased a bit. He looked around. From the opposite hill, some kind of animal was descending. When he looked carefully, he saw that these animals were monkeys. They were coming down the hill in single file. When he looked more carefully, he saw that the monkeys were coming from the black curtain. When they came to a tree, some of them began to scream and the others accompanied them. The baby monkeys that were hiding in this tree came down qucikly, crying with joy, and the adults gave them fruit. The babies choked down the fruits. Ocn was very surprised. He examined the movements of the babies' hands and mouths. These movements were very familiar to Oen, but he couldn't figure out why.

He succumbed to his curiosity and walked towards the monkeys. Seeing him approaching, the bigger monkeys began to scream and throw stones. He had to retreat and find a safe place for himself, waiting for his fear to pass. His eyes were still watching the monkeys when his bellyache started again. While he was massaging his stomach, he realized that the things that monkeys threw weren't just stones... In a panic, one of the baby monkeys had thrown fruit to Oen. As they were already sated, the monkeys were no longer interested in the fruit. While the baby monkeys celebrated being reunited with their parents, Oen used the opportunity to slowly move toward the fruit. As he was paying all of his attention to the fruit, one of the monkeys cried. Oen was petrified with astonishment and fear...

When he realized that this call wasn't meant for him, he began to crawl towards the fruit. There were only a few steps between him and it. As he got closer to the fruit, its size grew bigger. The red color of its skin made him feel overambitious. Oen was crawling calmly and silently. He ignored the smell of fresh grass and the mud dirtying his hands. He stretched out his hands and took the fruit and, without moving, he examined the shape of it.

He focused on its scent, which he liked very much. He remembered the baby monkeys biting into the fruit. Then,

Oen realized that he had teeth, too. He put the fruit, which was called "apple," into his mouth. Apple juice exploded into his mouth. He enjoyed the taste. He began to turn it in both sides of his mouth. This didn't satisfy him. He began to crush it with his teeth. His hands began to tremble. A few more monkeys cried, but this time Oen didn't hear anything. The apple melted thoroughly in his mouth. His mouth was so full he needed to swallow. His entire body was pressuring Oen's mouth to swallow immediately. Oen swallowed. Filled with pleasure, he almost attacked the rest of the apple. Regardless of anything going on around him, he quickly devoured up the apple.

He was relatively relaxed but wasn't full up yet. The bites he ate had given the feeling of hunger to Oen's wild ambition. He suddenly stood up and ran towards the monkeys. Seeing the hunger in his eyes, the monkeys scattered in different directions. They'd already had their fill. They weren't going to struggle with this hungry creature.

With wide eyes, Oen searched for an apple under the tree. He found a few, and ate them immediately. When he was full, he felt sluggish, and soon fell into a deep sleep.

***

He returned to the tree where the monkeys had been, but he couldn't find any monkeys. Oen was starving. When he abandoned hope at the tree, he began to look around, hoping to find some apples, but he had no luck. He was tired from searching and growing hungrier.

He began to think about what to do. He spoke to himself: "The monkeys came down from the hill. They went out of the darkness. There must be some of these red ones over there. Who could bring me a red one?"

He sat down and thought some more. He stood up and thought, he walked and thought. He couldn't find a way out... There was a fountain near the place where he was. He saw animals drinking water. He went there and, just like animals, drank from the water of the fountain. The taste of the water seemed much better than the taste of apple. In order to suppress his hunger and thirst, he filled his stomach with water. However, the feeling of hunger didn't leave. When the water spread through his body, his stomach was empty again...

Oen made his decision and made his way towards the hill. While climbing, he watched the valley below and enjoyed the ascent. He had difficulty climbing the hill; it was rocky and wooded in some places. He kept his fear on one side and his exhaustion on the other. Even so, he was a prisoner of his hunger, and he had no idea about that black curtain waiting for him. That's why, sometimes he hesitated to continue... But each time, the hunger and the curiosity forced him forward.

As he arrived at the middle of the hill, he got some rest and studied the valley. He tried to imagine the location of the path where the monkeys came when they were coming down. He believed he was on the same path.

When he was able to breathe normally again, he carried on his way. As he neared the top, his fear added to his exhaustion.

He finally reached the peak. There was a vast plain. At the edge of this plain, the black curtain, its consistency like mud, fell from the sky. It seemed to be waiting for Oen.

With trembling hands, Oen began to look around. He wanted to see something breathing and his wish came true. A ladybird ran towards the curtain and passed to its other side. This gave Oen courage. From the moment he began the climb, this was what he'd waited for.

He slowly approached the curtain and watched the consistency of the mud; it seemed to be flowing. His nose was about to touch the tree. The silence forced him to go forward. He first stretched out his hands. This movement was very strange to him. He wondered why a human being risks his most critical limb for a situation like this. However, he didn't think much about this matter. When his left hand got behind the curtain, he felt a little coolness. It was pleasureable. He put both of his hands, up to the elbow, through the curtain. His hands were in a place and he didn't know what that place was. How strange: to know something exists but not to see it. To Oen, this was very strange and exciting.

He tried to estimate how thick the curtain was. Considering that the animals were getting in and out of it, he figured it should not be so thick. He withdrew his hands. For a moment he looked at his hands and feet very carefully. He admired the the work they do. As these thoughts were passing through his mind, he pulled himself together. There was a darkness to be discovered in front of him. His stomach's insistence was increasing.

He debated whether he should pass slowly or quickly to the other side of the curtain. At last, he made his decision. He would pass just like the animals. He dove into the curtain...

After taking a few steps in that cool weather, his feet stumbled on a rock and he fell down. At the moment he fell down, the the world around him came alight. Seeing the light made him relax.

"It was easy," he said from inside.

This side wasn't terribly different from the other, except that it had better weather and the colors were much clearer. He felt much more mentally alert. There were lush, flowering bushes. When he took approximately a hundred steps, he arrived at a meadow of tall, yellow grass. To its left was a small pond, which served as a sort of boundary between the meadow and the grove of bushes. Oen began to walk that way. A flock of birds flew very low over the meadow. Oen felt the need to bend down because one of the birds almost passed his ear.

For a long time, he watched the water. He saw a group of trees on the opposite side. He began to run towards the trees with joy: they were full of red fruit. When he got close to the trees, he thought of being careful, just in case the monkeys were around. Maybe there could even be creatures other than monkeys...

When he was sure that he was safe, he approached the tree, plucked an apple, and ate. He ate more and more, until his stomach was full. When he had finished, he saw a winder-like plant behind the trees. Then he noticed small pink and red fruits between the leaves. He quickly ran that way, plucked one of the fruits and smelled it. Its scent was different from an apple. He liked it. He ate a few of this fruit, which was called strawberry. After, he drank some water from the pond and laid down right next to the water. Then, he sunk into a deep sleep.

He woke up. He was asleep on his back and when he opened his eyes, he saw the sun, but he wasn't surprised. He remembered more and more each time he awoke. He spoke to the owner of the dazzling sky: "One day, I shall wake up before you, The Sun!" he said. He sat up and looked over his surroundings.

It was very quiet. The sounds of birds, the whisper of the wind, the singing of insects... He knew all of these things. For a long time, he talked to himself. He was enraptured when he turned back and saw that the apple trees and strawberries were still there.

"I have everything I need here," he said to himself.

However, after awhile, he began to think about why he remembered these words. Where did he learn all these? He ran towards the apples and strawberries because he was hungry. He ate his fill and examined his surroundings. He tried to reconcile the things he remembered with other things. Even though he wasn't good at this, by seeing the landscape, some of his pain went away.

He saw a bird's nest somewhere nearby. Seeing a human being approaching it, a mother sparrow left the nest. Oen climbed over the tree in order to see the bird's nest. Three baby sparrows, with their red skins, were opening and closing their mouths. Their innocent behaviour led Oen into deep thoughts, but he couldn't stay long – the screams of the nearby mother made Oen climb down from the tree. When he moved away, the sparrow's mother returned to her babies.

Oen spent all his time thinking about baby sparrows, monkeys, and other living creatures. He tried to find out where he came from and why he was alone. He was feeling much more powerful and clever than the other animals he had seen. All these things he had seen looked so facile, and he could not keep asking himself why he didn't have all these before and where they were in the first place... Hopelessness, fear and meaninglessness mauled Oen. He laid down and slept.

Here, Oen learned the difference between day and night, and the existence of days, and sometimes he woke up at night. He searched for the answers to his questions. At the end of this long period of thought, he maintained control of his mind, except for his memories. He could supply all his needs here. However, Oen couldn't resist wanting more. He wanted to see the sunset and was also hoping to find the answers to his questions behind the black curtain. He was getting tired of only eating apples and strawberries. Because of these things, he decided to pass back to the other side of the curtain.

Compared to most people who embark on a journey, he had a great deal of freedom. He had nothing to carry with him, he'd left no one behind. He chose to leave when the sun was at its highest point. In order to reach the black curtain, he had to descend. He moved slowly and carefully. While he was looking around, he kept saying the words, "Let's see what's there."

Sometimes his feet ran into soil, and he was feeling the lukewarmness of the soil. And sometimes, sharp stones and gravel stung his feet and wounded him. He was saying, "I wish I had something to protect my feet." He had no time to cope with that.

He was where he wanted to be... He wanted to look at the curtain more closely, but this time he was in a hurry. He threw himself into the darkness of the curtain. After taking a few steps, he barely stopped himself by hitting his head against a tree. After a lighting flash appeared in front of his eyes, he regained consciousness. He looked around.

"It seems that there's nothing much here," he said. Then he lifted up his head: "If we don't count the trees, of course."

While he was thinking about where to go, all of the sudden a child appeared from the back of a big tree. Oen was overcome with joy. When he began walking towards the child, his eyes almost popped out of his head. The child ignored Oen and began to walk in the opposite direction.

***

The child was ahead of him on a road. He was trying to keep up with the child, and was curious where the road was headed. It was a humid day, and the earth was covered with grass. The few stones embedded in grass were smooth, as if they'd been rubbed by water for hundreds of years. As they neared the curtain, the child slowed to wait for him. The scene started to change. The colors of various trees, the sounds around, were suddenly all different. This change surprised him.

At the black curtain, the child suddenly stopped. Oen's heart began to beat quickly. Then, the child started to walk again.Just as the child was about to disappear behind the curtain, the scene changed again – a vast darkness was pursuing them. It was only a few steps behind Oen, who started to run in fear.

"Wait!" he screamed. When the child saw that he was running after him, he began to run, too. But Oen was faster. When he reached the child standing next to black curtain, he stopped and looked back. The two of them were bathed in different amounts of light. The child had more.

Because he was afraid, Oen couldn't understand why he was here. The child looked at him. His cute face made Oen relax, temporarily. Confidence replaced his fear, and he looked at the black curtain in front of him. Why wasn't the child walking? He was thinking of lots of questions about this place and the child. Here they were, by the curtain, so why didn't they walk? Was there something to fear behind this curtain? He watched the darkness that was like a thin black paper flowing down. He wanted to see what was behind it now. He reached out his hand. However, an electric shock stopped him. The back side of the curtain wasn't to be seen. With curiosity and fear, he returned to child.

"Do you know what's behind the curtain?"

He waited for the answer.

"Why don't you walk? Aren't you afraid?" he asked again.

He asked all these questions breathlessly. On the other hand, the child smiled him and then began to run. All of a sudden the curtain opened...Seeing a new scene, Oen began to run, too. They were in a forest with different colors, sounds, and climates. All these things were happening beyond his control. He had less fear and wonder than he should have felt. He stopped and looked around. The child was very far away, but with his white cloth he was to pick out, just like an egg white in a salad.

"Wait for me! Let's walk together. I don't know where we are. I need a guide. Do you live here?"

The child ignored him, carried on running and when he came to the curtain, he stopped. Oen caught him by running.

"Why don't you answer me? Do you understand me? Are you deaf?" he said.

The child smiled again.

"Tell me, why don't you speak?"

The child suddenly began to collect a bushy plant's yellow fruits. When his palm was full, he sat down and began to eat them.

"You mean that you're hungry? I guess I am, too. What are those you're eating?"

The child didn't answer again.

"I guess you don't want to speak," he said and began to collect the yellow fruits. When his palm was full, he sat near the child. He took a fruit from his plam and brought it to his mouth. As he took the first bite, he spit it back as if he had swallowed a piece of fire. He never expected that such a pretty fruit could have such a sour taste. He still continued to eat it, but it was really hard to swallow. However, as he continued to eat, he felt that his sense of taste adapted to this fruit and his stomach approved.

"Its taste isn't too bad," he said. "What is its name? I guess this is something not a lot of people eat, because I've never had it before."

These sentences sounded strange to him. He ate the last fruit and he swallowed more easily.

"I've eaten lots of fruit, but this one, for the first time. Really. In fact, I may eat much more. Would you want some?"

The child grabbed Oen's hand that was about to reach for one.

"What? What happened? It's only that I want some more fruit. Would you let go of me?" He stopped. "Or does eating more kill people? Oh well, however you like it. See, I'm done. That's enough for me."

"What's your name?" Oen asked. The child smiled again, but didn't answer.

"OK, it's understood. You don't know how to speak. Well, then we communicate with sign language." When he said that, the child began to chuckle.

"What do you mean? Do you understand what I'm saying? You little devil!" he said and then caught the child and began to tickle him. After squirming to the left and right, the child got free. Then he burst into laughter. When he was about to choke, Oen left him. The child stood up and as he was carrying on chuckling, he was ready to run again.

"Funny, right? Since this morning, I've been the only one talking. Right now, you know me much better than I know you. That's why I won't talk to you anymore, until you talk to me. Did you get that? No more speaking! No more speaking until you tug at my sleeve and want me to look at your face," he said and then sat next to the child.

He was still thinking of the curtain. "The way to understand everything is to follow the child. Yes, yes this is the best way. I shouldn't lose him." When he finished thinking, he turned to the child and took a deep breath.

"Haven't you finished yet?" he asked. The child shrugged his shoulders.

"Where do we go? Would you tell me?"

All of the sudden, the cheerful expression disappeared from the child's face. A deep grief came over him. Oen was on edge. After finishing his meal, the child turned his back to Oen, as if he wanted to be alone. He looked at the black curtain and began to run, quickly. The curtain opened again and again the scene changed. There was no forest. From a distance, the blue of the sea and the remains of a settlement were seen and the child was running in this place. Oen, on the other hand, was following him. Oen was dazzled with the colors, which had so much tint.

In this ruined place, which was stone covered by lichens, the child stopped and then Oen stopped. The child was waiting next to a couple of columns. Oen came up beside him.

In the place where the child was looking, a beautiful girl with black curly hair was sitting. Oen was astonished by her beauty. Instead of feeling a spasm caused by the pleasures of the body, a fatherly coolness spread inside of him. This was someone who needed protection.

When he swallowed it was like a dry wind rushing through his throat. As he looked at this girl, vessels of courage and fear invaded his ports. He tried to recover from this storm by forcing himself to swallow again. Then, he greeted the girl. The girl answered back.

"In a world that I don't understand, to meet such a beautiful girl like you has made me very happy." This was all he could say... He was proud of himself for his courage.

"Maybe, you would like to answer my questions?" he asked.

"It depends on the questions you ask," the girl said.

"Actually, I don't remember anything. I don't know where I am. This is the easiest way to explain my situation."

"To remember is the result of things that have existed and been lived. Maybe, it's only that you cannot unleash the words from your mind."

"The words remain imprisoned in your brain," she continued. "They stay there until the spirit experiences their real meanings. According to me, if you don't remember, then you don't live."

"Yes, I've heard these words before," he said. He paused in surprise. He felt like a lightning fired in his brain. He thought as if he found all the answers to his questions.

"All right, I'm dreaming. People can realize in their dreams that they're dreaming. Yes, this is only a dream."

He sat on a rectangle-shaped stone; he seemed relaxed.

"Such strange things only happen in dreams ..."

He started laughing, about to become hysterical. The young girl and child didn't seem to care about his mood. Oen calmed down.

"Yes, this is a dream. In a little while, I'll wake up and everything will become normal."

Then, he took a handful of soil from the ground. He pulled some of the grass from between the stones and then he tossed them into the air.

"Dream, dream, dream. I know this sentence and I remember what a dream is. However, I don't remember that I ever dreamed," he said inside himself.

"It's like I've been here before. Nearby a very beautiful sea... a place just like this.... I mean, this is a film of moments I've lived, shots that were taken by my brain."

The girl who was sitting on a cylinder-shaped stone said: "Do you want this to be a dream too badly? I hope it's as you want."

Then, she stood up. Her white dress was flapping in the wind, her hair was streaming. She approached Oen; her scent was painting the wind orange and light green.

She streched her hands, saying: "Do you think this is a dream?"

He felt as if she was touching him with her hands, that they were getting into his blood vessels. He quaked deep inside his body. His sweating became a small river and flowed down his spine. As he looked at her eyes that were like an empty piece of paper waiting to be written upon, he couldn't decide what to pray for: to pray that this was a dream or that it was real?

"Dreams belong to your life. But you've never seen me. How could I be a dream?"

Oen was astonished and looked at young girl. At that moment, they heard a strange sound. They stared at the child, who was sitting on the ground picking his left wrist with his lips. They went over to the child.

"Are you OK? What's the problem?" they both asked. The child was slightly cross eyed, and he ignored their questions.

"He looks scared," the girl said.

"Why is he scared? As far as I know, there's nothing around that makes him scared."

"When kids are scared, they do strange things like this."

"Do you know him?" Oen asked.

"Sure. He comes and goes all the time."

"You mean that you've seen him before?"

"No, but I feel like I have."

"I don't understand. What's going on with me? When will this meaninglessness end?"

He stood up and looked around. With two hands, he picked some of the hairs under his chin.

"My God, please help me! Where am I and who are they?"

"If everthing seems meaningless to you, then why do you ask questions? I may tell you something about this place. Here, whatever way you choose for your life, you willl reach the same ending. When you were a little child, if you were playing with a knife and your mother was busy, say you accidentally stabbed out your eyes? You would be blind now. If you try to rebuild your life, moment to moment, so many small, minor probabilities have determined you now are. If any one of those went a little differently, you'd be a different person right now. Your fate has chosen your life to have this shape."

"You mean, a kind of captivity."

"I don't know if it works that way."

Up to that moment, the child seemed relaxed. But all of the sudden, he started sucking his wrist again. Then his body began to shrink.

The child began to sleep, curled like a fetus. Oen turned to face the far away sea.

"Enough of this!" he shouted.

"You'll wake the child," the girl whispered. This shut Oen up. The girl was showing the child a great deal of affection. She wanted to show some of it to Oen, too: "I would like to help you find answers, but I have many things to do. It seems to me that this is not the place for you."

Oen didn't say anything. While he was watching the woman who was looking at the child, he heard some voices behind them. He looked. An old woman and a little girl were looking at him. The old woman said:

"The dress looked very nice."

"Not that nice!" the little girl protested, angrily. "You've made the shirt very long. If someone sees it from a distance, they'll think there is a woman inside. I don't understand where you found this dirty yellow color. It's disgusting."

"No, damsel! It's really nice and that's flat. Why are you so good at finding flaws in things, regardless of your age? I don't understand it."

"I do nothing! You just think everything you make is perfect, which is crazy."

The old woman's face flushed with anger. She glared at the girl.

"Never mind! They do whatever the hell they want. Let's go pick some flowers, my little dear. What do you say?"

"That's a good idea. As you say, lets leave them do whatever they want."

The little girl was picking at Oen's cloth.

"Ha, you've made a pocket as well. Very smart," she said and then laughed.

The old woman turned to the young girl, saying: "You need to give us permission. We also don't like this situation, but rules are like this, which you know."

The young girl yelled with anger: "Get the hell out of here! You've been buggering around since yesterday."

As the young girl was shouting, one more old woman and another little girl came from the ruins. The new ones looked like the old ones. Oen looked at these new faces very carefully.

"They look exactly the same," he murmured. "What the hell is going on here?"

The young girl said: "This is not about you. They're the pains in *my* neck."

She turned to the others and carried on shouting: "And these things just keep coming!"

As she finished her sentence, another old woman and little girl emerged. They looked like the others. Oen looked at the young girl.

"Don't waste your time with them. You carry on your way with the child. The child will take you to your answer. You can be sure of that! However, the first thing you should do is get away from here without asking anymore question. Do you understand me?"

Oen only could say, "yes."

***

For a while, he looked at the ground absently. He felt the child moving on his knees. After rubbing his eyes, the child stood up quickly, as if he was late for an appointment, and then began to run towards the curtain. Oen thought that the same things would happen again. He was about to stand up, but he was indecisive whether to go with the child or stay. The child wasn't speaking, however the girl was speaking to him. He thought that maybe he could find the answers to his questions from the girl.

What answers am I looking for? My questions: Where am I, who are they, where do I go and how did I get here?

It would be better for him to not to ask these questions. The child was still waiting in front of the curtain, looking at the darkness.

After thinking for a while, Oen acknowledged that the little girl was right. To go with the child seemed much more safer to him. He looked at the child, who was waiting along the path, which resembled a road cut from snow. The child was waiting for Oen. And Oen waited for girl to say something more, but she had fallen silent. When he looked into her eyes, there was an expression that said that she wanted go away. He wanted to know about her; he imagined the possibility of falling in love with her, making her happy. However, he wasn't excited.

"You should go with him," said the girl, snapping Oen from his reverie.

"It seems I have no other choice." *Never mind*, he said to himself. The he walked down the path. He wondered whether the darkness was following him or not. He looked behind and saw that the darkness *was* following him. He looked at the girl and the darkness that was following her. He started to walk away, but then stopped and turned back once more. The darkness was about to swallow her. Only the wind could hear what she was trying to tell Oen.

"When you leave your body into the arms of sleep, clean all the thorns that stumbles on your feet. For each leaf that falls from the spirit tree and for each bird that sings songs on the spirit tree's branches, please elegize! Put your palm under the branches of the tree, so that leaves and the bodies of the dead birds slip away from your hand and then cover the ground. And after seeing each of them off, sprinkle water in the heart of the tree, so that the new ones replace the ones who has gone... Let your heart be awake to the greed which is settled inside of us like a snake and waiting to flow from our teeth into our brother's skins...

"Wish that you will have a new door at the end of each of your trips and that you'll write your epic with your own fingers. When the wind that has touched the first wise man who found God in his heart touches your heart, you shall seek shelter in a hair-raising darkness. Your homeland shall be the holes in trees and caves. Your companions will be the worms. Because you won't fit in the darkness and will feel safe only in the ground. And no emptiness will be able to cover your forest's fires. You shall turn your left cheek to the one who has hit your right cheek, so that he may hit it, too. Either the devil shall die between you or else war shall be your heritage. Maybe someday you shall meet someone who loves the same cave and worms and shall want you to walk into the light. The devil shall put his toys between you and your new friend."

***

He and the child were all alone in this forest when he started hearing unfamiliar crying sounds. All of a sudden, the curtains disappeared. He began to walk next to this child; he believed the child knew where they were going. They were moving forward in the forest where daylight was seeping through the trees. The ground was sometimes dry and sometimes it turned to marsh. They walked about three hours. When he looked around to find some place to rest, he saw the child was standing in front of a rock cavity that looked like the entrance of a cave. They were so tired and sat down where they were.

"Where are we?" Oen asked. Again, the child didn't answer him. His black hair was stuck on his sweaty forehead. Drops of sweat hung indecisively on the ends of his hair. His face had an exhausted, dull expression. He looked around. Evening was about to descend and the two of them were hungry. They had to find something to eat. The child stood up and faced towards the direction where the sun rose. He looked at the bushes with hungry eyes and ran that way. Oen wanted to go with him, but something stopped him, and he sat down beneath a tree. He stared at a series of tall, thick-trunked trees. This place was foreign to him. He leaned against the tree's thick trunk. The bark of the tree stung his back but he paid the pain no mind. He was tired, hungry, and was about faint from tiredness.

Soon, the child came back with a snake and a lizard in his hands. Thank God, Oen thought. He was so hungry his vision was blurry. The child left the animals and began to gather some brushwood. Oen desperately stood up to help the child. When they finished picking up brushwood for a fire, the child brought a few branches of a tree that was five or six meters away and began to rub them together. Oen watched the miserable movements of this child's thin arms and he told him to leave the job.

"Let me do it. Here, see? You tire yourself recklessly."

The child only smiled. They cooked their hunt over the fire. After they choked down the meal, they drank water from a fountain. The child lay down on the grass and Oen leaned against the same tree as earlier.

"Thanks for the meal," he said. Then, they lay in silence.

"Of course, I can do that, too," he said. "It's not that hard. First you find a snake and then catch it from the head and hit with a stick. The lizard is an easy hunt. I can do that, too. I'll find our next meal and I also want to tell you that my hunts will be bigger; maybe it'll be a rabbit or a big deer."

He then stood up and put his hands to his temples, imitating a horned deer. He moved towards the child. The child was watching him, laughing. For a while, this game carried on. *I'm going off the deep end*, he thought. He also imitated a monkey and a lion. He was jumping, screaming, waving his hands and stomping his feet. When Oen stepped on one of the cinders spread around, he suddenly screamed. However, this didn't stop him, and the fun continued.

There came a deep darkness. Oen was watching the fire.

"It's needed to keep the flame alive," he said. Then he stood up and picked some brushwood and threw them over the fire. By blowing on them, he set them aflame. When he finished, he lay down on the grass and watched the sky.

"Where am I? What kind of exam is this, God?" he wondered quietly. Then his eyes slowly closed...

"What kind of exam is this, God? What kind of exam?"

He suddenly woke up and cried, "Fire."

The fire was about to die. He picked up a few branches and kept the fire alive. Then he sat down and relaxed. At that moment, the child woke up and saw everything. When he looked at the child where he was sitting, they locked eyes by the light of the fire. Once again, the child burst into loud laughter.

"What is it? Why are you laughing?" he asked as if embrassed about what he had done. The child turned his back. He watched the child, who laughed until he fell asleep.

"I should sleep," Oen thought aloud. "Maybe tomorrow, when the sun rises, I can find the answers to my questions."

He was lost in the forest. He felt resigned. He had seen strange scenes and curtains. However, in this forest, everything was normal. Maybe he'd lost his memory? Or maybe he'd become an addict and overdosed? It was also possible he was in a dream. *Maybe I'm a part of an experiment or a voluntary guinea pig*, he thought.

While he was thinking of all these, he found himself in the corridors of sleep.

A shiver interrupted Oen's sleep. He woke up and looked around but he couldn't see anything. By straining his eyes, he found a few braches and kept the fire alive again. He looked around and said, "what is waking me up from my winter rest?" He didn't know how this kind of parlance came into his mouth; it was not how he usually spoke. He thought that maybe it was because he was sleepy. He lay down on the grass and watched the sky again.

All of the sudden, he saw silhouettes circling around him. He was scared to death. He couldn't breath. His chest was swollen and his heart was beating so fast one could see his chest vibrating. After waiting for a while, he saw the silhouettes approaching the child. He tried to figure out what they were doing. If they were going to harm them, he thought they would've harmed him first – not the child. His whole body was rigid. Could this be a dream?

The silhouettes began to swirl around the child. They were muttering among themselves. They were swirling, stopping, talking, and then swirling again. The sounds of feet and clothes were heard. Were they cannibals or strange creatures? What would they do to the child? Were these silhouettes murderers or members of a tribe?

All these questions made his head hurt. He began to shout towards the silhouettes, but then he realized no voice was coming out. He tried to throw a stone at them, but he couldn't move.

When he finally gave up, he was drenched in perspiration. The silhouettes were in the same position. *What did they want?* he thought again. The silhouettes knelt down. The sounds seemed like the sounds of hyenas which had been hungry for months. He felt nauseous. He was about to faint from the pain. He wanted to cry, kill, and destroy. When he felt better, he ran towards the silhouettes. His body ached, as if he'd been burned by the fire. With the movements of his hands and feet, he scattered the silhouettes.

Then, he saw the child's lifeless body. He had been torn apart by wild teeth. Blood pooled around his body, congealing on the ground. Oen jumped from the cliffs of his terror, soaring like an eagle: he had to do something to help. He knelt down. He tried to stop the bleeding with his hands. When he looked up, he saw that one of the silhouettes was his best friend.

"Please, help me!"

His friend handed him cloth to stanch the flow of blood. Another friend handed him some water to clean the wound. Another friend handed him some medicine.

"That's OK," said the chorus of silhouettes. "We think he'll be fine."

Oen raised his head and looked at the silhouettes around him. He was petrified, his face was burned. All the faces he saw were the faces of children. He was nauseated, dizzy, and then everything went dark.

Gepose's Wound

When he woke up, the daylight seeping through the leaves warmed his face. His muscles were cramped and he tried to move a bit. He tried to understand where he was. He was trying to use all his senses like a wild animal. Dewdrops were playing on the leaves. He got up and started walking into the wind. He came to a high hill. The things he saw at the bottom of the Gepose Hill dazzled him. A small but perfect city spread across a flat plain. He watched the city with a mixture of fear, joy, and curiosity. A river flowed through the middle of the city. He could easily see small boats on the river's surface. Looking closely, he could even spot people down there. A shephed grazed his herd in the cool of the morning. They seemed to be a happy flock. Their sounds mixed with the wind.

"Who the hell are you?" a voice said, surprising him. Turn around slowly, so we can see your face. Are you a thief, huh?"

Oen overcame his fear and turned around.

"I'm one of the people who has lost his way. I have no bad intentions because of my wretchedness. My body is very tired..."

He looked at the man, who had a long, grizzled face and broad shoulders. He was pointing a gun at Oen. Another man moved behind Oen, bringing a knife to his throat.

"You look like you have an honest face," the man with the gun said after a moment, slightly lowering the gun. "But I'm not convinced."

"Instead of showing mercy to a man very much in need, you're threatening me. Please, have mercy on me, so that my anxiety might pass," Oen pleaded.

The one with the knife kept its cold blade pressed to Oen's throat.

"You have unneccessary doubts," Oen said. "I find myself in an unknown place. The one who is playing this game on me has made me forget everything."

"You're the one I'm not sure about," the man with the gun said. "I think you'll be my prisoner. How about that, huh? Your fate will be decided later on."

The man with the knife hit Oen on the back of the head, knocking him to the ground. They tied his hands, and then they nudged him with the knife's blade, urging him to his feet. They led him away from the city, into the depths of the scary forest.

The man opened the door of his lonely house in this dark forest. It resembled a small stony castle. He pushed Oen inside.

Oen found himself in a damp and dimly lit room. He glanced around the house quickly: there was a table, a few chairs, and some tools. It didn't resemble a place where he'd be getting any answers...

The Price of Centuries

The smell of the jujube trees was spreading through the streets of the city. Oen found himself walking down an empty street. The darkness between the white houses made them all look alike. He could hear faint voices, the soft sounds of the herd in the mountains, the gentle whisper of the river.

He thought he saw somebody and he suddenly crouched next to the bottom of a wall. However, as he saw that nobody was coming, he continued. He'd come to the city looking for help, but he wondered why the people who are most likely to help him always run away in his dreams. He laughed at his desperate situation, and this helped him muster up his courage. He began to walk more confidently on the street's stones and stared at the houses and the streets. He perceived that peace was the city's defining characteristic. However, in the back of his mind, he knew he could still face unexpected events here.

It was late at night. His mind vacillated between the fireflies, the possible surprises lurking behind every corner, and his own courage. At the beginning of a corner, not finding an opportunity to think about which direction to go, his steps led him to the city center. The feeling of being followed by someone was blowing at his back, just like a cold wind. As he took a few steps, he heard a voice.

He leaped out to where the sound was coming from. When he turned the corner, he saw a person trying to lift another person, who was lying on the ground. The person on the ground was an old woman and the person trying to help was a young girl. Even though he wanted to help them, he still waited. But the girl saw Oen. When she didn't respond, Oen braced himself and spoke to her.

"Poor old woman, what's wrong with her? Please, let me help you," he said. Then, he immediately tried to lift the woman onto his shoulders. However, her body felt stiff. He quickly checked the woman's breath and heart. The woman was dead. The young girl looked like she knew it and was looking very calm. There were no tears in her eyes. Instead, she looked very serious. When she heard Oen saying, "poor old woman, she's dead", she winced. She moved back.

"Don't be afraid! I won't harm you. I'm needy and helpless and can do no harm."

"You're walking through the night just like a thief. Who are you, stranger?"

"I'm a loser in the game of fate."

In Oen's head, a voice whispered: "It is the Creator who has thrown me into this abyss, full of people I've never met. He sends me to the places I do not know. Well, never mind. Let's hold a funeral for this old woman. Of course, you are not thinking of leaving her here."

"Now, get out of here! I shall do my duty by myself," the girl said.

"No!" said Oen. "You can't carry her by yourself. Please, let me help you."

She thought very quickly and desperately accepted the offer. The two of them carried the dead body, first into the garden and then into the house. In the single-floor house, all the rooms opened to a large hall. They lay the body in this hall, and Oen said, "What will happen now?"

"You ask too much. A person should not poke his nose into everything in an unknown place."

"You're right. I'm in a city I do not know and I'm in a stranger's house. This poor old woman is dead in front of me. I'm talking too much because of my confidence."

"You're talking like a nut."

"If I'm a stranger, you are, too. This is where my confidence comes from."

"But here is my house and you're the one who is much stranger in it."

She went to a room. It looked like a kitchen. Then she came back to the hall.

"Shut the door," she said. "Don't let the insects in."

Again she went to the kitchen. She came back with a pot full of water. Various flowers, and dirt, were in the water. She knelt down in front of the dead woman. She dipped her fingers into the water and then touched her fingers to the dead body. Oen looked at the elegance of her fingers and the sparkle of the whiteness where her little finger and her wrist met. She didn't notice his gaze.

After she finished cleaning the body, she turned to Oen. "Come on, help me. I have to take her down."

The two of them took the dead body and walked into a narrow hall. There, they left the body on the ground. The girl opened the two wings of a door and Oen heard the sound of flowing water.

"Come on, hurry up," she urged him on. "Or else it would be disrespectful."

"Why did we bring the body here?" Oen asked.

"Don't stick your nose into everything."

The girl lifted the body into the water.

"Wait, what are you doing? Did *you* kill her?" Oen said, fear in his eyes.

"Even if you're a stranger, you want me to trust you. Okay, but you should trust me, too. My mother died a natural death. This is nothing other than finishing my last duty for her."

Oen sat down and said: "I find this very strange to understand. I mean, this is a really strange thing."

"Why? How would you do this?"

"I don't know. If it was my mom who died and I was all alone, I guess I wouldn't even be able to move."

Oen began to wonder whether he had a mom or not. He was lost in thought, and when he came to, the girl was gone. He found her in a large hall at the house's entrance.

"Stranger who helped me," she said, "there are not many strangers who come to this city. But I see no badness in you. I know a place where you can stay, where you'll be treated well. I'll take you there."

They passed through many streets and arrived in front of a big building. Oen couldn't notice the details of the building because of the darkness. She knocked on the door and told Oen to stay a bit behind. When the door opened, she talked with someone, though Oen couldn't see them. When they finished speaking, the one who opened the door said: "Welcome stranger. We'd be pleased to host you. Come in, come in." When Oen entered, the girl left. Oen tried to study the house. He couldn't place why, but he felt very safe.

"There is a room on this side where you can rest. Let's go this way." The host showed the way. They climbed a few stairs and then came to a room. The host turned on a lamp and showed Oen the room.

"The pleasure is mine," Oen said. "I thank you so much for hosting a man who lost whatever he's known. A man like me, who has lost his way."

"Please, don't make yourself tired. We'll have lots of time to talk tomorrow. Good night."

There were only white painted walls, a bed at the foot of the wall, and a lamp in the corner of the room. The cool of the stone floor was giving him refresing breeziness. He threw himself on the bed, beginning to relax. Lying on his back, looking at the ceiling, he tried not to think about all the bad things he had experienced and fell into sleep.

***

"Uselya! Let your eyes lighten the sun!" said the old man.

"Let the light of helplessness lighten our day," Uselya replied.

"Your mom finished her journey of suffering and went to the real country. Is that true?"

"Yes, last night I sent her body to a place where her spirit will be the companion."

"She was good and benevolent, for sure. There is no creature that complains about her in the sky. She had fully opened her heart to love and to life. One day, we will also go to the real country. I hope that she will be one of the people who meets us there."

"We should make the same wish for all of us."

"Well, Nagun told me something about last night. You didn't send her off by yourself." There was a softness in his eyes and mercy spreading from his luminous face out to the girl's eyes.

"Yes, this stranger helped me."

They were at the edge of a large clearing. It was being prepared for a large meal, and it was big enough to hold hundreds.

"His manners and demeanor didn't trouble me and then I took him to Nagun," she said.

"I know that, my child. Well, I want to speak to this stranger. If you see Nagun, please tell him to come to me with the stranger."

Uselya motioned to the temple side: "Look, he's coming. May I go back to my work? This place should be ready for tomorrow's lunch. I have lots of work to do."

"Where are your assistants this morning?"

"I woke up early at the crack of dawn and wanted to work until they arrive. Excuse me," Uselya said.

It was a flat space in the open air surrounded by trees. Ten long rows of tables were set up for the diners.

"Good morning Master Ridar," Nagun said.

"Good morning, Nagun. Come here. Would you like to take a morning walk with this old man?"

"I'd be honored, Master."

"I want to talk a bit about the stranger."

"He's still sleeping. He must have come from a long way away."

"I have an inkling that Uselya has some doubts about him," Ridar said. They were walking by the river towards the temple side.

"May I ask something from you Nagun, my son?"

"I'd be honored to be at your service."

"You shouldn't speak this way. The beauty of the words is deceptive. I am afraid of my ego being deceived. The only difference between us is my age. I'm older than you."

Master Ridar stopped and looked out across the river.

"When the stranger is awake, dress him with clean clothes. Feed him and take him to the temple. Okay?"

"I'll go immediately, Master Ridar."

The young man didn't say another word. He walked towards the library. Ridar went towards the temple. It was a big temple with a colossal dome surrounded by eight little domes. It was near the river and had a big garden with colorful flower beds.

Ridar entered the garden of the temple. He saw Viroy, who was working in the garden, watering sirfon flowers.

"Have a good day Viroy. I see that you're enjoying the sirfon flowers."

"Have a good day, too, Ridar," Viroy said, continuing to water the flowers.

Viroy finished his work and turned Ridar. He was an old man, too, and they resembled one another. They looked at each other's eyes.

"I see shadows on your face. Are you ill?" Viroy asked.

"No, I'm fine. I'd like to speak with everyone soon. Could you please inform the other workers?"

***

Nagun opened the door and came inside the room. Oen was awake and watching the city from the window. He turned back and said "Good morning" to Nagun.

"God bless your day," Nagun said. "I hope you had a comfortable night. I brought you some things to eat. Here are some clean clothes, too."

"I'd like to thank you for your favors, but I'm not sure how I should do it."

"I'll be outside. When you finish, please come to see me. First, we'll have our meal and then I would like to introduce you to our city."

"I'd like that," Oen said, and Nagun left him alone.

When Oen finished his work, the two of them went to the temple. They greeted the Workers and the people who were inside. After, Nagun and Oen sat down, Ridar met them.

"Welcome to our blessed city, stranger. I apologize if that seems rude. I called you 'stranger' because I don't know your name."

"I don't remember my name... I don't even know whether I had a name or not," Oen said.

All the Workers were surprised. Ridar continued with his questions.

"What kind of trouble could make you forget everything about yourself?"

Oen stared at the white-haired, white-bearded people who were looking at him very carefully and decided to explain what he'd been through.

"In fact, it's not that I don't remember anything. I don't remember how long it was before, but I woke up from sleep. I felt as if my body had been replaced with my spirit. I'd been hanging in emptiness for a while. I couldn't see or hear anything, but I felt the wet touch and striking of a creature. Then my feet touched the water and I walked. As I walked, a light appeared around me and it got stronger..." Oen told them about his journeys across the plains, to the city and deep into the forest, the people and animals he met on the way, the black curtain and the change of scenes—all he could remember.

Nobody could look at each other's eyes. They were too shocked to talk. Ridar stood up and then other old men did.

"I would like to welcome you again as the oldest man here," he said. "It seems clear you've been dealt a bad hand by fortune. Until you find your way, you'll be our guest and Nagun will look after you. You can go with him now."

***

The next day when they were having their meal, Oen said: "You're embrassing me with your favors. I don't know how to thank you."

"We eat what our Creator has given us. All people have their share and rights upon these favors. The flavor not shared is only for the stomach."

They continued to eat. Nagun looked up and smiled.

"You missed the times when the meat was fresh. Meals were much more delicious."

"Why do you say that? I like this meal," Oen said.

"We only eat fresh meat a few days a year. All other times we eat dried meat."

"I'm surprised."

"Because we butcher the animals only two days a year. The two days when the day and night are equal with each other."

"I still didn't understand anything."

"When the day and the night are equal with each other, the lightness cover the darkness those days. The regret destroys the pain. The knives do not hurt. The tears extinguish the fire. On those days, the animals don't suffer. That's why we butcher the animals only on those days."

Oen lost his appetite when he thought about ending the existence of a creature for one's own survival.

"You don't need to feel guilty. Eat your meal comfortably. Make sure that all the animals died without pain. We do this to stay alive. We try to achieve this in the most noble way," Nagun said.

"Ridar allowed you to go into the library. If you wish, we can go there," he continued.

"I'd be really pleased," Oen replied.

Then two of them left the house and walked through the library. They came into a space bigger than Nagun's house. It was well-lit inside and all the walls were white. Oen looked around in wonder.

"Would you like to help me clean? We'll still have time to visit the city and talk," Nagun said.

Oen looked at Nagun, who was blonde and had blue eyes. He was short, and looked very young.

"Of course I'll help you."

"Then, take the broom and come with me. Let's start over here."

After they cleaned for a while, Nagun asked Oen a question. "Does not being able to remember make you sad?"

Oen paused and thought for a while. "Of course. This emptiness always draws me back like a cannonball. If only I could remember the names of those I loved, at least..."

"Your trip seems very strange to people. Well, if you came here with no name, then we'll give you a name so that everyone can recognize you."

Oen carried on sweeping. He ignored the suggestion.

"Then, we'll call you Oen. It means 'conscience, inner man'. It is one of the words of our language, but many people are not knowledgeable about it.

Oen felt something familiar as he mouthed the name to himself. It was very strange.

"Why not!" Oen finally exclaimed. "You showed me your hospitality and friendship. You can call me by any name you want. Oen. Yes, it's a very nice name. Have you ever given someone a name before, Nagun?"

"No. I haven't."

"I guess the elders usually do this?"

"There is no such a ritual here. The names of the newborns are known already."

"How is it that? Could you explain more?"

"In this city, the names of the newborn babies are given according to names on the purple rock."

Oen was surprised again.

"The purple rock is located a bit outside the city. Hardly anyone go there, except the Workers, and they go there only when they have certain duties to fulfil.

There was a mesmeric fascination in his tone of voice as Nagun said, "Thousands of names are written there. These words are the ones our ancestors learned from the Creator. For each newborn child, the name is given from there. There is a certain sequence for giving a child a particular name."

"I wonder if the name Oen is written there?"

"No, it is not. I learned it from our language's wordbook. If you were born here, you would then be given a name from the purple rock."

"I see. What's the meaning of your name?"

The two of them stopped working and looked at each other.

"The meaning of the names written on the purple rock are only known by the Workers."

"Workers... Are they the elders we saw in the temple?"

"Yes. The Workers are the ones you spoke to this morning. They are the guides and long-term sufferers of our community. They're called the 'Workers' because they perform the most demanding job; in other words, they're doing the leadership and management jobs. They're responsible for every breath in this city. To be responsible for this community requires a great deal of effort. They mostly get hungry and thirsty when they perform their duties. A small pain of someone from the community means major suffering for them. We show a great deal of respect and loyalty to them."

Oen was listening to him as a child would. When they finished speaking, they carried on sweeping. When they finished that, Nagun went outside. Oen looked through the bookshelves. He was about to reach the thickest book when he heard the sounds of Nagun's feet. He pulled away.

"Now, let's put the books on this rug and dust them."

Oen handed Nagun the books, one by one. When they finished aligning all the books on the floor, they finished cleaning the shelves. Then, they put the books on the shelves again.

"Here," said Nagun, handing Oen a book. "This is my favorite book. All the words in our language are written in this book."

"It's purple," Oen said. "Just like the rock." Then he looked at his friend, who was thumbing through the book with a smile.

"Here, look!" Nagun said. "Your name is written here."

He handed the book to Oen.

"Since we speak the same language and understand each other, I'll assume I can read."

"So, the place where you came from used the same alphabet. As far as I've known, this alphabet is only read by our people." His eyes gleamed innocently.

Oen took small steps while reading. It was as if he'd forgotten his blonde friend. Meanwhile, Nagun continued to organize the books.

"There are too many words about love," Oen said.

Nagun didn't disturb his friend. He silently carried on working. His mind was full of words. He mused upon the stars being an inspiration to the poets. Then he got into an inspirational mood as if speaking with the stars in the sky. He had questions like, "Which star is the house of a poet?"

on his mind. He believed that poets were the ones holding onto the stars – they were the birds nesting there.

When Nagun finished alinging the books, Oen said, "It has lots of words about love and blessings. As far as I've read, I didn't see a bad word in it."

"Love and blessings are the basis of our society."

"I would like to know more about this."

Nagun sat beside Oen, who closed the book.

"Then I'll tell you all I know," he said.

"When babies are born, the Workers perform a ceremony here, in order to get rid of bad seeds in the babies' hearts. They chant the prayer of the beautiful words, so that their hearts and minds meet goodness and beauty in this world. In order to live with goodness and beauty, we treat each other well, we speak kindly. If a flower of goodness has not blossomed in a heart, then that heart is covered with a poisonous grass of evil. Welcoming everyone, showing them affection and expecting love – this is what our soul needs."

"So it means that you're planting your seeds into another's garden? Afterwards, you reap the fruits."

"No, we plant the seeds into the other's garden. And then, the growing trees and flowers reach into our gardens. They connect us."

"Your words are very charming. I'm glad to have a friend like you. I wish I had similar words to tell you. Friendship isn't supposed to be one-sided."

They looked at each other with affection. Then Nagun said, "We're finished. If you want, you can help me water flowers in the backyard."

Oen looked at him with smile.

"Let's go, then," he said.

Nagun began watering the sirfon flowers. Oen liked these flowers very much. They had all shades of blue, and even a few shades of purple.

"I'm curious about many things, Nagun. Why did Uselya place her mother's body into a channel under the house? This seemed very strange to me."

Nagun smiled: "This is not a strange thing, my friend. We're sending off our dead to the real world."

"Why don't you prepare a nice funeral? Don't you think this would be much more beautiful?"

"We're born here; we live and die here. The place we go is our real country. To go there gives us happiness. If we prepare nice funerals for our dead, the hearts of the ones who stay in this world fill with pain. The memories hurt them. The quiter the journey, the less sorrow there is. The Creator lessens the sorrow."

"You mean that every house has a gateway that opens to the channel?"

"Yes, every house has that gateway."

"This must be very hard for those who lose their relatives. To have to endure the pain of death all alone..."

"Death in this world means a birth in a real country. Why should we feel pain for people who are born in a place much more beautiful than here? We all wait for our turn to go there."

Oen began to believe that his friend was right. He thought, "Maybe here is my real country." Then, he sat beside Nagun and held out his hand to help clean the grass.

"No, there's no need," Nagun said. "If you want, you can water the flowers."

"It was a very hard night for Uselya. She won't see her mother again," Oen said as he started working.

Nagun smiled: "As I told you, she went to a place where all of us go. Don't worry, Uselya is fine. She may come to visit you at night."

"Why do you think this?"

"Because you helped send off her mother. She would want to thank you."

Nagun smiled again.

"Why don't we talk about you for a bit," Oen said, tired of piecing together the mystery of himself.

Nagun was relaxed, as if he'd been expecting the question.

"I try to protect the books in which our sacred teachings are written. I protect them in order that they'll reach future generations. I love to be with books, smell and read them. As you may guess, there isn't much else to me."

"Isn't your family here?"

"Of course they're here. Some days I stay with them. Other times, I come here, to this library."

"Don't they miss you?"

"Of course they do, but because I'm working a very important job, they say nothing about being far away. Their only concern about me is that I do my job well."

"Well it doesn't seem like your job is too difficult. Why are they so anxious?"

"Even if it seems very easy, here, a job only reaches it's goal if it's done with love. You have to love books. Think about it: if you water flowers without love, they die the next day."

"Are flowers and books really that sensitive?"

"Sure. They're as sensitive as all living things. Mountains, rocks, animals and every kind of plant... Don't ever forget that in universe, the biggest scale is in the human heart."

"In that case, what's on the other side of love on the scale? Is it evildoing? Is it the very spirit of everything that's evil?"

"The human mind thinks in words and perceives with names. You know the names, but you should not bother yourself reflecting too much upon all those things on the opposite side of love. Don't let them become established in your mind, lest they may direct you towards evil."

"I'm trying to understand."

Being engulfed in thought, he said, "It doesn't sound so plausible to me, but it's OK. My mind often plays tricks on me."

***

There were a few flowers left to be watered. Oen looked at the ground.

"Please bring this water to the flowers that need to be watered with love. Don't waste this water."

Then he faced the sun.

"Please don't make this water evaporate!" he pleaded.

"I know what I've been taught better than you do," the sun replied. "What the ground deserves stays in the ground. What the cloud deserves goes to the cloud."

"I know what I'm taught, too. What flowers deserve go to flowers; what little creatures wandering inside me deserve, go to them," the ground said.

Oen shuddered and stood motionless where he was. Then he heard the flower's voice: "Don't bother this man who has lost his way. There is no badness in his heart. It's only because he thought that he gave me water."

Then the flower turned to Oen: "Don't worry about me. People put me in a wonderful place. Indeed, it's the most beautiful place I could live. They watered me with love, and I am coming up roses now."

Then three voices went silent.

"That was very strange," Oen said.

"Were you speaking with the flower?" Nagun asked.

"Yes, with the flower, ground and sun."

"I speak with the stars most," Nagun said. "It's strange. Until meeting you, I'd never felt the same feeling of friendship that I felt with them. I guess I was waiting for you to awaken the meaning of the words I've learned all these years."

"If that's true, then I want to tell you something. The one who has been on an island alone for years is only understood by the one who has no one but God around him."

Nagun was deeply affected by Oen's words.

"We're done here," he said. "If you'd like, we can go into the hills. From there, we can watch the city, and we can talk more."

Then, they began to walk towards the hills.

****

"Look Oen, Uselya is here to thank you. And she also brought you the most beautiful, sacred gifts."

"Welcome, Uselya. Your visit makes me happy."

"I came here to thank you."

"Come on," Nagun said. "Let's have our dinner together and thank our Creator."

Oen and Uselya didn't talk too much. Oen was watching Uselya's hands. As he watched, he shuddered, just like those who had seen Moses' white hands. He kept dreaming about Uselya as he watched her eating... Oen hardly heard the question his friend asked him. Nagun was wondering whether he liked the dinner or not.

"It's wonderful," he said automatically.

"We had a nice day with Oen. Did you know that, Uselya?"

Nagun finished his meal and was leaning back. He seemed happy.

"He helped me in the library. We cleaned the place. He watered the flowers and he even spoke with them," Nagun said laughingly.

"He's curious and is a quick learner," he added.

"I guess this is normal for people who don't remember the past. There must be a big emptiness inside them," Uselya said.

Oen sensed some implication in her words.

"Yes, but I'm sure he'll remember everything very soon," Nagun said.

Uselya left the table in order to bring some figs for dessert.

"They're from our garden. Good food for our guest."

Oen ate some, but couldn't taste very well.

"Everyone has been so kind to me here. I really, deeply appreciate it. I feel at home here."

"We treat every stranger the same way. This is a city of goodness."

"Even if your words make me feel good, the expression in your eyes is off-putting," Oen said.

Uselya didn't say anything. Nagun didn't understand why Oen was being unkind towards her. In order to make his two close friends reconcile, he suggested they leave the table to watch the night sky.

Even if this would be inconvenient for Oen, he wanted to stay with his new friends, especially with Uselya. He was totally besotted with her. So the three of them went to the roof of the house. Nagun looked at the sky and opened his hands from side to side:

"Hello, my celestial friends. I would like to introduce you to my earthly friends. They're Oen and Uselya. Their hearts are full of goodness. Tonight, they would like to speak to you."

The two of them looked at Nagun, whose words brought a sudden smile to their faces. As soon as they flashed a smile at each other, Oen shivered with excitement, but Uselya tried to be serious, wiping the smile off her face. She glanced away when she caught his eye again. Then she told Nagun: "Stars like the crazy ones. Did you realize that they livened up when they saw you?"

"Please, sit down," Nagun said.

Then three of them sat on the cushions and watched the sky for a while.

"Can you speak with the sky just like you spoke with the flowers, Oen?"

Oen smiled.

"Maybe, you should choose one of them as a friend tonight," Nagun said. Then he added, "Come on, choose a friend. Tell me which one is your friend."

Uselya waited for a while. Then, she indicated a rickety star with her index finger.

"That's my star. That's my friend in the sky. I chose it."

"It's near the horizon and watches all the other stars from the bottom. It looks a bit sad and forgotten," Nagun commented.

"Oen, you choose one, too," he added.

"I think it's not true to find a friend in the sky before finding one on earth," Oen said. A deep silence descended upon the scene as they all knew that his last sentence was meant for Uselya.

Symphony of Existence

"We must hurry up, Oen. Otherwise, we shall be late!"

Nagun was ready, wearing clean, white clothes, and was trying to help his friend get ready. Oen was going to see Uselya. His emotions were conflicted. His heart was shaking; he felt pain, fear, and happiness at the same time.

He called out to his heart: "Do these feelings crush you? I feel like I'm losing light..."

The two of them embarked for the place. The sun was setting. The whole community was walking towards the sacred place, wearing their white clothes. They were gathering for the vow ceremony. According to their beliefs, everything that is thrown into the waterfall would reach the place it should have reached according to the intentions in a person's heart... This was also the best time to send presents along with the best wishes for the people of the Blue World. The Workers oversaw this ceremony.

When Nagun and Oen came to the largest area, they saw many people. Large torches were burning. Atal, with his long white beard, greeted Oen. He was an old man of profound wisdom conveying their teachings to the youth.

"Oen," Atal said. "Is this the first time you've seen such a ceremony?"

Oen smiled and said, "I don't know what I've seen or not. However, I don't remember something like this."

Atal looked at Nagun with regret.

"He's learning very qucikly," Nagun said with childlike enthusiasm.

The chief cook Masu came over. They greeted each other.

"You worked too much tonight to prepare this great feast. How can we thank you?" Atal said.

"Everyone here does his job. And everyone deserves to be thanked. The Creator forgives our failures, we hope. We also hope that the Creator increases our well-being."

Masu turned to Oen. "We are all happy to see you here," he said.

Oen expressed his satisfaction by bowing his head. After awhile, Masu and Atal left them. Oen's eyes were looking for Uselya. Then Tabe came over. He was the one who collects firewood from the forest for the temple and for the needy. They greeted each other. While Nagun was teasing a small child, Oen began to speak with Tabe.

"You spend most of your time in the forest, right?" Oen asked.

"I do."

"Do you go deep inside the forest?"

"Sometimes."

"Well, did you ever meet with Zelor?"

Tabe's face changed and he touched his beard.

"You know him?" Tabe asked.

"Yes, Nagun told me some things about him."

"I sometimes meet him in the forest."

"And then?"

"Then, I give him some goods. The ones he needs. For example, oil for his candle. Because he reads at night. In fact, maybe I shouldn't have told you all this. When I found him crying his eyes out, I never showed myself; I was hiding from him."

Tabe went quiet and looked at the sky.

"Yes, he's the bleeding wound of this city."

Oen felt deeply sad.

"The first time I saw him, he asked me why I was looking after wood instead of gold."

"And what did you say?"

"Gold is one of the things that fire melts. Wood is useful for people in every way. He smiled when I said that."

Tabe understood that Oen was sad about what he was telling him, so he stopped talking when they approached the crowd. He then said, "Whether it is wet or dry, crooked or straight, wood is of a great benefit for everyone. But gold ore needs to be found in rock and then extracted and processed many times. The more it is processed, the more valuable it becomes. As it is difficult to refine it into pure gold due to many physical and chemical processes, refining the ore eventually makes the person greedy for more profits. Zelor could find a place to live only in that remote woodland away from the Ador city because of this greed he put in his heart."

Then Nagun came back, telling them it was time for feasting. When Oen and Nagun took their seats at the table, they saw Uselya.

"Uselya's here," Nagun said. "Let's sit with her."

Oen's heart was in pain. He began to speak to himself: "Dear sky... You covered everything and you can easily see her. Dear flowers! She comes to smell your odor. Dear ground, dear skies! You all are lucky because you see and touch her every day. It doesn't matter how close I am to her, I can't be happy with her. It is as if she pulls me in close for more pain and suffering."

These thoughts even started to make Oen jealous of Uselya and everything that belonged to her. When they sat down, Oen heart's began to beat faster. Occasionally, he would look at Uselya and try to figure out how interested she was in him. He tried to calm himself.

"I didn't see you on the morning walk, Oen," she said. "Didn't you go today?"

He was shocked to hear this. If she had wanted, she could have seen him.

"I was there, just like whole community. Since I live here now, I had to fulfill my duty."

"They're starting," Nagun said, interrupting. Oen looked around in order to understand what was going on.

All of the sudden, the crowd went silent. A group of twenty or twenty-five people with flute-like instruments in their hands came to the front of the tables. The sound of their instruments rose up into the sky. The sound was both sweet and a little hair-raising. It represented the Creator's "BE" order when creating the universe.

In order to represent the departures between galaxies, all the instruments took turns playing solos. The sound of the orchestra was telling the story of the universe's creation.

The galaxies and solar systems, the mountains and seas, the ground and the seeds that were thrown into the ground—they all had a role in the story. The orchestra then told of the eggs thrown into the water.

In the next part, the world looked like a heaven. The world was greeting the sun and the other galaxies, and then began its rotation. The souls of the human beings were placed around the world. They were all turning around the Blue Planet, praying and giving thanks.

After this part, they told the story of the devil souls, and how their laughter came between the souls of those who were praying. The panicked souls of the people were running in different directions. The Messenger souls came and tried to help them. In emptiness, horrific things were happening.

After this part of the story, there was a long silence. In the penultimate section, the Messenger souls were crying for the souls that were drifting into emptiness. In the last part, the immense Mercy of our Creator was told.

Afterwards, Ridar's voice was heard: "People who stay faithful to their word of this sacred city! Don't forget to thank our Creator. Pray for your friends and brothers and sisters more than for yourselves. You'll get many things in return. Let's pray for the mistakes we unconsciously make. Whoever gives the best of his or her body and soul, you have found the most valuable treasure. Everyone should know the limits of their own essence. Respect is the consciousness that grows by knowing the essence of ourselves.

"Dear Ador people! We are gathered here to get closer to God. The Merciful God never left us in darkness. God loves all of us. To keep your bodies, hearts, and souls pure and clean is the most valuable virtue. Right?

"Dear Ador people! Let's pray for forgiveness of our mistakes. God help us!"

Everyone joined Ridar's prayer. Oen was so enthralled with the fascinating ambiance that he could collect himself only after the long prayers. When they all finished praying, they ate their meal.

"Are you enjoying the meal?" Nagun asked. "If not, maybe you should blame Uselya. She prepared it, after all," he teased.

Oen tasted the food in front of him: the bread, meat, vegetables, fruits and syrup.

"How could I be angry? This is wonderful. We should all thank her."

"If you finish all the food, that's thanks enough," she said.

Time was passing quickly. Oen was so tired, he couldn't tell if he was happy or not.

In the distance, Ridar and Yorin sat together, speaking.

"Yes but we can't do anything without being sure," Ridar said.

"You're right," Yorin said. "There is only one way to be sure. But it may cause pain..."

Brooding over it for some time, Yorin further said, "Having the same thoughts as you makes me uncomfortable."

"I pray we're both wrong. Uselya has changed very much since he came here. She was like a growing flower, but now she begins to fade. I wonder if she has the same thoughts. Maybe she is also suspicious about it," Ridar replied.

"Maybe she just misses her mother. After a while, I'll think she'll be better," Yorin said.

"I fear she won't be. Lamenting is forbidden, after all."

"I don't mean that," Yorin said harshly. "Missing someone is an innocent feeling." But he caught himself, and said he was sorry.

Ridar was beginning to worry that Oen's arrival was bringing discord to the community.

Yorin thought that it was good to talk about Zelor. It wasn't the time to think about those kind of things. There would be another ceremony soon. Ridar called one of the assistants, to check on the preparations.

"What if it happens just the way we thought? Then what shall we do?" Ridar asked.

"We should discuss it with the others and then decide."

"Of course we'll do that. But I was wondering *your* opinion."

"The best decision will be made. Don't worry about that, my old friend."

"Stop treating yourself badly," Ridar said, taking his friend's hand.

"Our Creator will show us the right way."

"You were always my closest friend. Right or wrong, you were always with me. You really are a great person. Maybe we should have sent you to the Blue World," Ridar said, smiling.

Yorin was affected.

"You're getting older. What do you think about sitting down and crying together?"

Ridar only smiled.

"We shall be together. In a much more beautiful place where there is no human weakness. I wish you would be more positive about this," Yorin said.

Ridar had always liked his friend's powerful attitudes. He was the leader of the Workers. But he needed his friend right now: how could he bear the responsibility of this city, these people, this temple, the White Waterfall, Zelor, Oen... all alone?

"I shall inform Usat to start the ceremony. Let the Workers take their places."

"Stop, Yorin. Don't hurry up. There are people who are not ready yet."

"I don't hurry. I wonder why you're so strange tonight. You aren't ill, are you?"

Yorin began to walk towards the Workers. People had finished their meals. The Workers and assistants took their places. One of the young assistants blew the trumpet strongly. Then, everyone stood up. Everyone walked in single file towards the Workers. Atal led them. Oen was trying to understand what was going on. He began to walk with the crowd, just like Nagun and Uselya.

When Atal came in front of table, a Worker put a white scarf on his right shoulder and a black scarf on his left shoulder. Atal continued walking in order to form a circle. Yorin had the same scarfs on his shoulders. The farmer, Maysen, had the same scarfs on his shoulders. So the line went on like this...

Oen was trying to figure out the meaning of this ceremony and decided to ask Nagun. Uselya was walking in front of him. He looked at her body. She took small steps. He watched her black hair covering her white dress. He wanted to touch her hair. But Uselya was completely absorbed in the ritual, just like the others.

The young disciple Anset put the scarves on Uselya's shoulders. The people were forming big circles that fill the entire place. Then Anset put the scarves on Oen's shoulders. The black scarf was heavier and it was very difficult to carry. He realized that his body was out of balance and his body was leaning to the left side. He even thought of asking Uselya for help. He was wondering whether everyone was feeling this way. He was exhausted.

"Nagun," he said slowly.

Nagun didn't say a word and carried on walking behind Oen, who thought of throwing the black scarf away. When he saw that the circle was about to be completed, he felt better. When it was complete, Ridar called out: "Never despise making favors! Do favors even if they are small!"

Ridar sat down, and Anset called: "Everyone come here again, to throw the black scarves from your brother's shoulders."

Then Ridar stood up and asked: "Who's going to throw away the load on Atal's shouder?"

Sonmer, the carpenter, stepped forward.

"Let the favors Atal has done save him from his loads. I witnessed that he helped Maysan's father, who was working at home on his own."

Then, Sonmer approached him and threw the scarf away. He put the scarf on the ground in the middle of the circle.

Then Maysan came forward. The same thing was done for Maysan. Then Parel, the farmer, and Nefon, the fisherman, came... Oen was waiting his turn to come.

Then, Uselya came. Lugas – the Worker – spoke for her: "She works too hard for her patients. She is always the first one to arrive at work."

Then Lugas took the scarf from Uselya's shoulder. Oen felt better at that moment.

Then Anset came and spoke: "Who's going to take Oen's load from his shoulder?"

Everyone waited for Uselya to go and take the scarf, but that didn't happen. Oen was scared as he was waiting. He looked at Uselya and at last she stepped forward. Uselya took his load from his shoulder and left it in the middle of the circle with the other scarves.

Then Nagun came forward. Oen took the scarf from his shoulder and explained to the crowd his favors, just like the others done.

At last, Anset came to the middle of the circle with a torch in his hand and burned all the black scarves.

"Let the fire destroy the evil."

***

When Oen and Nagun reached home, they went to bed. Oen thought of the day and wanted to speak with Nagun, but he was already asleep. He had many questions prepared for the morning.

When he woke up in the morning, he realized that Nagun wasn't home. He thought maybe he went to the library. He went to see him there, but he wasn't there. He thought maybe he was with his family. Oen walked through the streets of the city. When he turned the corner, he saw Karsiyan, the cheerful youth.

"God bless your day, Oen," he said.

Oen greeted him and asked for Nagun.

"Not long ago, I saw him going to temple."

"Is that so?"

"He left you alone? It doesn't matter. We are all your friends now. Please excuse me, I have to go be with the shepherds now."

Then he left. Oen continued walking through the streets. When he came to the blacksmith shop, he heard Bachar and his assistants calling him from inside.

"Oen! Come and join us! We hope you didn't have your meal yet."

Oen greeted them and went inside.

Bachar, the balding, slim blacksmith, welcomed him. With a friendly grin on his face, which also showed the signs of tiredness, Bachar said: "My wife's soup and bread are very delicious. Will you join us, Oen?"

"Sure, I'm very hungry."

"This morning, I saw Anset and Nagun going to temple together."

"Yes, he wasn't at home when I woke up."

"Anyway, let's have our meal."

"It's so nice that we've shed our loads. Now we can live another year."

"It was very tiring, though."

"Yes, but it was worth it. The weight of a human being's load is as much as the universe's weight. This is because the responsibility of finding God is given to human beings. The ceremony last night was to lighten the loads we carry," said the blacksmith.

"I'd like to ask you something," Oen said. "Last night, what if we hadn't taken the loads from our shoulders? Then what would happen?"

The blacksmith's face paled. He wanted some water from Mashka, his apprentice, who ran to get some water from the fountain. This city had lots of fountains on its streets.

"As far as I remember, no such thing has happened. However, if it had, everyone would retake the loads and everybody would have to carry those black scarves for one year. That would be a shame for us. At that point, mother earth wouldn't give us any food, which would be a disaster."

"I was really scared last night," Oen said. "I didn't think my load would be removed."

"You are a good person and do favors, just like us. Now that you're part of this city, everyone loves you. And you love us. I think this is enough for everything."

Then, he turned towards his apprentice.

"Where have you been, Mashka? I'm thirsty. When you finish your meals, do not forget to pray."

"If you do this ceremony every year and people get rid of their loads, then there must be some trouble," Oen said.

"You think so?"

"Yes, I believe that good people can be mixed with two-faced people."

Hearing Oen's word, the blacksmith began to laugh and said, "In this city, everyone knows that God sees what is hidden in the heart!"

When Oen finished eating, he left the blacksmith's shop–with permission, of course. He went back and checked the home and the library, but Nagun was not there.

***

When Nagun and Anset walked into the meeting room of the temple, Ridar turned to Uselya and said, "Fate is the book that God knew before and that people write with their choices. For the things that have happened, you can only feel regret or happiness. Regarding this situation, there is nothing for you to regret, my girl. It was not your fault and you had no responsibility for it."

He grew quiet as the two men entered the room.

"Our oldest one, is anything going wrong?" Nagun said. "What is the reason for this silence?"

"Come here, my son. Come and sit down here. There are things we need to talk to about."

They waited for a while.

"Anset, could you tell our Yaves brother that we wait for him?"

Nagun didn't understand anything. Why was nobody speaking? Why was Uselya crying?

He could not speak to Uselya at such a moment.

Finally, Anset found Yaves, who was taking care of his students. Anset told him Ridar's message. With his pure white beard and wrinkled face, the sagacious Yaves looked much older than the other Workers. He was a small man with a short beard, a long nose and eyes like two burnt holes in a blanket.

"Tell Ridar that I'm coming soon, my son," he said.

He asked his student, Kolin, for his rod. His students were surprised; they'd never seen him use his rod before.

"Are you OK, sir?" Kolin asked.

"I'm fine, don't worry. I'm a bit tired, that's all. I'm a little busy, don't forget what I told you," he said and he left.

Meanwhile, Oen was in the library. He looked through the shelves and books. He loved books. He wished all people would love them. He took a book randomly and looked inside it. He started to talk to the characters in the book. Then he fell into deep thoughts... He hadn't felt this alone since he had arrived.

"Some children don't cry near their mothers, but they don't go far enough from their mothers that their mothers can't hear their cries. It appears you're far from your mother," said a strange voice. "Let me wipe away your tears."

He ended his monologue when he looked up and saw an old woman watching him.

"My name is Pana. Are you OK, my son? I accidentally overheard what you said. When a man begins to speak with objects, that means the situation is extremely bad. Tell me, what happened?"

His hands were trembling. He didn't know what was going on with him. He couldn't make up his mind. The old woman slowly knelt down near Oen.

"Please, you can trust me. Tell me: what makes you so sad?"

As soon as Oen told her about himself, he unconsciously put his head over her shoulder. She began crying with him.

She touched Oen's hair. She thought, *coming here with no past makes him sad. Even though he is loved, and loves, he is still lonely.*

Then she said: "Poor little man! You've been through some bad luck."

"Uselya," Oen moaned, though his head was still on Pana's shoulders.

He repeated the word many times. Pana looked through his eyes.

"These tears are for the sorrow of love."

She prayed to be wrong.

Oen bowed his head. She waited for Oen to say something. However, he didn't say a word.

"Come on, take it easy! Let's go to the garden and water the flowers. Fresh air will make you feel good."

***

"Life is just like a river. We all jump into that river without making a choice. We all complain about being here, but somehow we are not willing to leave," Pana said.

"Yes, staying here does seem more attractive," Oen replied.

"I'm very old, Oen. If you interrupt me, I'll lose my train of thought."

"Excuse me."

"This river is beautiful. But sometimes, we have to go ashore and think about where we're going... Once, we're on the shore, we may see more beauties, too.

"You too, should go ashore and watch the speed of the water, its eddies and cliffs. Don't worry, you're not wasting your time by doing this. Because the shore is also a part of life."

She stopped and then added. "By the way, the violets look beautiful. I want some. Promise me that you'll plant these into my garden tomorrow or after tomorrow."

"Sure, I enjoy doing it."

"Come on, bring some more water here. Let's see if Nagun's come."

Oen did what she told him to. He watered the floweres. Nagun was nowhere in sight.

"I have to go now," Pana said. "But remember to try to find out when you should go ashore."

***

There were still four people inside the temple's meeting room.

Ridar said: "There's no need to worry. Yasev, you go with Nagun and bring Oen here."

Then he turned to Uselya.

"You, my dear, go home. Being here may be bad for you."

She looked at him.

"No, I want to stay here."

"Uselya, my dear."

"I can stand it. I'd like to stay."

Yasev and Nagun looked at each other.

"Come on Nagun! Let's go!" Yasev said, hoarsely.

They left. When they reached the library, Nagun said, "It seems as if the whole city is in mourning. Everyone seems to know."

"We need to stay strong."

"How can I tell him this?" Nagun said, stopping, hitting the wall with his fists.

"Let me tell him. I'll explain. First, we go to the temple, and then follow God's way later."

They found Oen.

"Oen," Yasev said. "I need to talk to you."

Nagun began to tremble. The three of them sat on a cushion together.

"Nagun, our friend is very tired. And I'm thirsty. Could you bring us something to drink?"

Nagun stood up and went to bring something to drink. He looked indecisive. Oen was very anxious.

"I see anxiety on your face."

Oen didn't answer.

"You came to this city as a man who doesn't remember anything."

"Yes, that's true, sir."

"Don't worry, this will end today. The Workers found a way to give your past to you."

Oen recoiled.

"Don't you like this news?"

"Of course."

In fact, he wasn't sure whether he wanted to remember his past or not.

"I promise, everything will be all right. To remember your past may hurt you, but I don't believe you have a bad past. Maybe this way, everything will be better for you. You should be strong!"

"I'd like to ask you a question."

"Sure."

"I came here from somewhere else, right?"

Yasev looked at him suspiciously, but then shook his head yes.

"When I remember everything, will you send me away?"

After a long silence, Yasev looked at him.

"This city accepted you and people see you as a brother. How could you think of this?"

"This city..." Oen said, trailing off, unable to speak.

At that moment Nagun came in with three drinks in his hands. They drank and then departed together.

They barely spoke on the walk. Something he couldn't put into words scared Oen. It all felt like a goodbye symphony for Oen.

Then, they arrived at the temple and walked in through the meeting room. Ridar and Uselya were there. They greeted each other and sat down. Then, Ridar told them to wait for a while. Seven more people came. They had flutes in their hands.

"Here they are. Oen, they will help you. Now, let's go downstairs."

They all went to a cabin downstairs. There was only a small window in this cabin. Ridar whispered something to Nagun, the librarian, and then Nagun run quickly away. After a while, he came back with a book and tripod.

"You must be brave, Oen. Because fear prevents you from seeing the truth. That feeling is like a snake strangling you in your weakest moment," Ridar said.

Ridar was just like a doctor. His face had an expression that suggested he could overcome any, and all, difficulties.

"Let's start, Oen. The light of God be with you."

Sakin, the oldest of the flutists, stayed, but everyone else left.

Oen was alone with the flutist , a tripod, the book, and a water bag. Then Sakin left the room and closed the door.

The room was dim and silent. After awhile, he began to hear the sound of music. He took the book and looked in the pages. The pages were empty. He didn't understand anything, so he put the book on the tripod again. He began to walk around the room. The music's peace was increasing. His breathing began to quicken. The moments began to resemble the first moments he remembered.

"Are they going to send me back? I don't want that..."

He began to walk faster.

No, he thought. *They would've told him if that were the case.*

The music grew quieter, but the voice in his head grew louder.

How long will I be here?

All of the sudden, his eyes caught the water bag on the floor. *They left a lot of water. That means I'll be here all night.*

He was relaxed then.

What is this book? What does it mean? Why are the pages empty? Is that supposed to represent my memory?

Then the music began to quicken. He began to walk faster.

He only saw the wall... The shapes of objects appeared and then disappeared. The color of the light changed, from purple to red...

The wall in front him vanished, and then it grew bigger. The music grew faster. *Am I running? Walking?* In the light, there was music, the light grew bigger and bigger, and then it was gone.

In its place there was a wall opposite him and a window in it. The window was half eaten by the wall. The wall was eating the window. Then the window was lost.

Oen was thirsty. The water bag was on the floor, but he couldn't find it. *The water bag was on the floor. Where is it? This is a big place. How can I find it? I'm sweating. I'm thirsty. Where is the window? Where are my hands? Where's the water?*

The opposite wall looked like a camel. *I'm thirsty. The camel is going... The camel is lost.*

Then a lion appeared. There were two of them, an older lion and a baby. Then the old one ate the baby. Oen ran, and ran, but then the lion was gone. *Where did the window go? The music is here. Is the window close to the music? Let me see the other wall. There's a white pigeon. There are different birds flying.* Then, they were gone.

Oen fainted.

He woke up in the middle of the next day. He was dying of thirst. He finished the water in the water bag.

Outside, the musician Zanka took over playing the flute. He could hear Oen moaning inside. Zanka did not care about it; he just kept playing the flute for twenty four hours, until Uta took over.

On the third day of darkness, Oen was absolutely unconscious. He was lying on the floor in a fetal position. The only thing he perceived was the symphony of fate playing outside.

At the end of the seventh day, Ridar, Yasev, and Nagun came into the cabin. Nagun opened the door with fear. Oen was lying on the floor. Nagun tried to pick him up. Oen was still moaning, pressing the book to his chest.

"Can you tell us who you are?" Ridar asked.

Oen tried to look into Ridar's eyes. He tried to see him up close.

"My name is Ayzer, Ayzer, Ayzer…"

Yasev, Ridar, and Lisel, the seventh flutist, looked at each other.

"Nagun! Find a few people and take Oen to the library," Ridar commanded. "But go at night, so no one sees you. Be careful. This has to be a secret."

Ridar turned to Yasev. "We must go, too. Then we'll speak with the others."

He turned to the musician, saying, "Give him some water. It will revive him."

Then he handed the musician a yellow powder wrapped in fabric.

"This will make him feel good. Let's go, Yasev."

Then two of them left. The musician made Ayzer drink the water.

***

Nagun was watching his friend, who lay under the blanket, sweating. Oen was opening his eyes from time to time. Nagun was praying for his firend's sorrows to end.

Since the night before, Ayzer had slept. His friend still called him Oen.

"Oen!" he said. "Do you hear me?"

Ayzer didn't react.

"Do you remember, Oen? The first day we met? That was the time I felt good things would happen. However, look at what's happened. You've become someone who could not be accepted by this city's soul."

He couldn't help his tears.

"Remember? You told me the story about the man lost at sea and the man alone on the island. I wish you could be that Oen again.

"That day, Ridar entrusted you to me. The first day we shared this house and library. Do you remember, Oen? Speak my friend, come on... Whatever happens, my love for you will stay the same. You'll be my best friend forever."

He carried on crying.

"Come on, my friend. You have to be strong now. Open your eyes and smile. The city will give you the things to be happy, just like it gave you your history. Now, please, open your eyes."

Ayzer needed a few more days to wake up. This was what Ridar said. The medicine had to be given regularly. Nagun left the room and returned with a cloth. Then he wiped his friend's sweat.

"Don't leave me, my friend," Nagun pleaded. "This shouldn't end like this. Don't leave me, Oen. Death is not the sorrow of reality."

He burst into tears. He thought of the days he spent with Oen and Uselya. He relived them in his mind. Ayzer was breathing very slowly. As he watched Oen, Nagun fell into a deep sleep.

Yasev came and woke Nagun up.

"Come on," he said. "Go to your bed and sleep. I'll watch him."

Yasev studied Oen's face. Was he really Ayzer? He didn't want to believe it. But there was no evidence to show otherwise.

"Poor child. What kind of destiny you met with! You've done such terrible things. Don't you have any inspiration in your heart that shows you the truth?"

Then Yasev fell silent. He began to watch Ayzer's face again. That night and the next day, Ayzer slept. Nagun and Yasev waited beside him.

Ayzer opened his eyes very early in the morning. He stayed in bed for a while with his eyes fixed to the ceiling; he felt his life flashing before his eyes. It was like he existed outside of time, like his past became his future and his future became his past. He was exhausted, feeling as if his ankles, knees, and wrists – all of his joints had been dislocated.

In his mind, he thought of how familiar everything seemed. He was walking the streets again, heading towards the house where he had been born, where he'd grown up...

***

When he came to the house, a few memories began to materialize.

"My mother and my father have gone to the real country when I was here. Now, his younger brother, Ulsem, should have been staying here. Ulsem. *My* brother.

"Yes, he's my brother."

Since the time he had arrived as Oen,   Ulsem had been treating him more like a brother than a friend. Now his brother was married. He met his wife, Seya, who was a very beautiful woman. He was very proud of his brother, who was making his wife very happy.

The sun was about to rise. He passed in front of Uselya's house, but he couldn't look at it. He turned back to the library where Yasev and Nagun were still sleeping. He went into his room and sat down on his bed. He waited just like that for a long time. He thought of Uselya and their happy moments. .

Ayzer remembered how they would frequently meet and walk late at night. He was very excited during those walks. Sometimes, he would wait a long time for Uselya to come. Sometimes, he would hold her hands and begin to run with her up to one of the hills close to the city.

He recalled how his hands once met hers while climbing up a hill in the dark to watch the stunning vistas of the city from the top. When they passed through dark streets and climbed up to the top of the hill, Oen told her to watch the stars. He went to get some papers he had hidden beneath a rock. When he turned back, Uselya was still watching the stars.

"Shall I watch more?" she asked.

"Yes, but just watch the ones I tell you to watch. First, look at the brightest one. That one. See?" he pointed.

"Yes, I see it. Very nice."

"I want you to read a letter that I sent you from this brightest star." He handed her the paper. She was confused with joy, and began to read. Then he showed her another star, and then passed her another letter he sent her from that star.

For a long time, Uselya was busy reading the letters. She wasn't strong enough to speak, and tears fell from her eyes. He touched the tears with his fingers.

"Why are crying my darling? I didn't mean to make you cry...

"I love you!" he said gently.

"You've taught me the most beautiful love. You're in everything I see. You're the fountain of love for me," Uselya said.

Her head was on his chest. Uselya was very happy.

**

Ayzer found himself once again sitting in bed without moving his face from the wall. He took a deep breath and then turned back to his memories with Uselya. The ones they passed watching the stars on the hills...

All of his memories about the city were circling in his head. Yes, he was born here. He had turned back to the place where he had come from. Instead of feeling shame, he was praying not to be born. When he thought of Uselya, he was feeling deep regret.

He stood up and came to the window in order to see her coming out of her house. However, he didn't have the courage to look at her.

Yasev came into the room. Ayzer hugged him and began to cry. Yasev waited for him to calm down. Then, Nagun came into the room. When he saw his friend, he began to cry, too. As he stepped towards Ayzer, the Worker stopped him. Nagun stepped back. The two of them waited about fifteen minutes for Ayzer to calm down. When Ayzer quieted down, Yasev told him to stand up and then turned to Nagun: "You stay with him. I shall go to the temple and turn back."

Then he left the room. Ayzer and Nagun cried together. When Ayzer calmed down, he said: "I'd like to speak to Uselya. Please, my friend, can you tell her I want to speak with her?"

"Of course. I'll go and tell her. Don't worry."

Nagun wondered how he could tell his friend that Uselya was ill. When the book of fate was read, poor Uselya fell ill.

"Please go, Nagun. Please."

"Okay, I'll go in a minute. Now, take your medicine and don't worry, you'll speak with her. Okay? I'll get you the medicine now. Wait here."

When Ayzer drank the medicine, he began to feel sleepy. He wasn't reacting to anything.

***

Nagun walked through the streets aimlessly. He didn't know where to go. He had to find a story to tell Ayzer when he returned. He thought of going to Uselya's house. Then he changed his mind. He was confused. As he turned back to the house, he saw Ayzer.

"Will she come? Will she speak to me?"

"Now, it would be really hard for her to speak with you, I'm sure. You should give her time, Oen."

Ayzer didn't react. He knew his friend was right.

Ridar arrived and spoke to Nagun.

"We should finish this very quickly and be careful that nobody learns. You know that he has to be judged and has to be punished according to the decision given."

Yasev's head began to turn. Seeing this, Ridar said, "Don't give up! Everything should be done according to our Lord's rules and the rules of our ancestors. You know this. To show him mercy is unnecessary and is our misfortune."

Yasev looked into Ridar's eyes and said: "Sir, with all due respect, nothing like this has happened in our city before. I'm not sure how you can expect the decision to be right for him."

"How could you say that?" Ridar said, growing angry. "There are rules about this and everything shall be done according to these rules."

"You're right, sir! I shall do whatever is needed to be done." Yasev relented.

"Then, Ayzer shall be judged at court tomorrow. I shall speak with the other Workers. You shall be with us. Tell Nagun to look after Ayzer and take him to court tomorrow."

***

The birds flew from the cedar trees. The wondrous sound of the waterfall could be heard. There were a few people in the courtyard of the temple. Yasev left there in silence, trying to overcome the trauma of the shock.

***

The next morning, in Ador City, things happened that had never happened before. Ayzer and Nagun came into the meeting room. Nagun was told to leave. Everyone in the room became deeply upset when they saw Ayzer's whole body trembling. The Worker Dolatin greeted him.

"Ayzer, do you know why you're here?"

Ayzer's eyes dropped in fear; he couldn't say a word.

"First, could you tell us who you are?"

Ayzer's lips parted, trembling, as he looked up to see Dolatin facing him. He looked just like the other Workers, except his dark blue eyes had visible reddish veins on the whites of his eyeballs. He had a commanding presence.

Ayzer took deep breaths to compose himself before speaking. Then he said: "I am the son of my father, Serkinte, and my mother, Kamin. I was born in Ador, and was given the name Ayzer from the purple rock. I grew up with love and was taught with mercy and affection in the hands of great teachers. I was sent to the Blue World in order to spread our teachings. I ended my thirty two years of life with my own hands. Afterwards, I was sent back to Ador. Here, I read my book of fate and now I'm in front of you."

"Could you tell us again why you were sent to the Blue World?"

"I was sent to the Blue World in order to spread the holy teachings of this city," Ayzer said.

Dolatin asked again, "Could you explain exactly this duty, Ayzer?"

"It was about preventing the world from being dominated by hunger, war, poverty, unfair death, injustice, hatred, and vengeance. And to embed love and tolerance into people's hearts."

"Well, in order to fulfill this duty, what are the things given to you here? With what kind of equipment were you sent?"

While Ayzer answered, he fixed his eyes at one spot on the wall.

"The things given to me were a clean heart, seeing eyes, hearing ears, and a more open mind than the people in the Blue World have."

"Before leaving here did you swear on anything?"

"Yes, to be faithful for the things entrusted to me."

Then came a long silence. Dolatin asked again: "You, the son of Kamin and Serkinte and brother of Ulsem, have you been faithful?"

"The answer is not in my words; it's about being in front of you, sir."

Dolatin took a deep breath.

"Your book of fate has been read by the Workers. Because of the result of your life and the things you've done, you'll be punished."

Dolatin fell silent for a while and then carried on: "Ayzer, until the doomsday, you shall live with this sorrow or you'll pay the price according to the way that the old ones have chosen. So, the price will be paid either by the old ways or it will be left to your conscience and we will do nothing about it. We leave the choice to you, for that is the tradition of Ador community. It's an opportunity for you to get rid of your sins."

"You're the wisest men of this city! You've protected our legacy very well. On the other hand, I'm a helpless prisoner. I can't know which of my sins is the biggest one. Being unworthy of my city? Or to feel ashamed towards Uselya, who has had to give up her dream of forming a family with the one she loves? Or not to look after the people who needed me in the Blue World? I wish you didn't give me the choice."

He was crying his heart out.

Ridar said, "Ayzer, my dear! There are reasons for us to leave the choice to you. However, for now, they're non-apparent to you."

They left the temple together. Ayzer was thinking of the thousands of mistakes made during his lifetime. He had a stange hope inside him.

Nagun took Ayzer home. He refused to eat though he was hungry. He sat down on his bed, and delved into deep thought, fixing his eyes to the wall. Then he stood up, regardless of the dizziness and headache he had. He began to walk through the room. There was a great silence. No one knew what would happen.

A few birds settled on the window. Though all the energy in the room was telling them to go, they stayed.

"We want to know what's going on," they said. "He always looked at us with love."

The sorrowful ambiance hovered over the entire room. "Go away," the room said. "Now is not the time to ask questions."

"We didn't come here to cause any problems or cause sorrow for anyone. However, if you say so, then we will go."

They were about to fly away, but when Ayzer approached them, the birds waited there without moving a muscle.

"You're Uselya's birds. I knew you. Please tell me: how is she? I know that she doesn't want to speak to me, but tell her that I want all her sorrows. Tell her to give her anger and disappointment to me. Tell her how much I love and miss her."

The child inside of Ayzer spoke just like this. When the birds flew away, Ayzer called Nagun. He wanted to talk to him.

"Nagun, tell me what to do? I'm in a big trouble though I have no evil in my heart."

He knew Nagun wouldn't answer. So, he kept on speaking.

"This is the point where resignation begins. Either suffering or destiny. Trying to attribute a meaning to the events that happened and trying to understand what and why they have happened . This means a resignation to suffering. To accept everything and look for the light that shall come up in the darkness. This is the real resignation. At first, you stay where you are, and then you have reasons to give in to defeat."

He looked at his friend. "This is not the time to feel sorrow; it's time to cry."

He approached him and said, "Now, go and tell that I want speak to her. I shall find a solution. Come on, my friend. Oh, please, help me!"

Nagun looked at Ayzer: "Okay. I'll go and talk to her, but you've things to think about before I do. You have to do that. I think you should choose the first punishment. Thus, you carry on living with us and with time, everything will be all right. Please, promise me you'll choose the first one. Then I'll do anything you ask."

"No, it is not going to be like this. First, I want to talk to Uselya. Afterwards, I'll make my decision. I want you to respect me."

Nagun was a bit hopeful now. "OK. I will," he said, and then left the house. He felt sure now to go and talk to Uselya.

When Nagun came back, he told Ayzer that Uselya didn't want to see him, and he felt a deep sorrow. However, Nagun handed him a letter she had written. Nagun went outside and Ayzer began to read the letter...

***

The day you were sent Blue World, the morning was very clear. Now it is different...The first night we met, it was like a dream. It felt like losing and gaining the closest person in the world, all at once.

Your coming was like an unforgivable sin. I want to be far away from you because I don't want you to know what I feel inside. Why am I the most unfortunate lover of this city?

Why did I lose my real world when I'm still here?

***

Ayzer felt his blood curdle. For a long time, he remained stoic. His mind kept on reading Uselya's letter, over and over again. He stood up.

"I have no one to trust except God."

He went outside, next to Nagun.

"Nagun! Let's go to the temple. I have made a decision about my punishment."

The Birth of the Heart Snakes

He woke up shaking. In front of his eyes were endless pebbles. He might have been on the ground for hours. He waited for all of his body's parts to wake up. Finally, he lifted his head. He didn't know where he was and for how long he'd been there.

Slowly, he stood up. He looked around. He was close to a lake. It was a place where a human could feel happy. There was no place to go; he understood that this was where he would serve his sentence.

He began to move towards the lake. Would he really serve here? If so, it wouldn't be that hard. He moved closer to the lake and sat down on a rock. He thought of the ways to escape...

Yes, I could escape. But even if I have the chance, I have no right to. There is a purpose for my being here.

Then, he began to muse... It was very silent. He wanted to know what Uselya was doing and how she was. Would they have a chance to live together?

Is this the price for a life with Uselya? No, it was the price for what he had done. All he had was the hope of forgiveness.

God, what kind of silence is this?

He was thirsty. When walking towards the lake, he realized that he was barefoot. He went into the water up to his ankles. He drank a handful of it. It had a different taste. Then he heard some voices. He looked behind him. There were different types of animals and they were approaching him.

I guess my punishment is that they'll feed on me. He was scared of his thoughts. He heard the voice of a turtle next to him. He looked at the animal with fear, but the animal passed him. It drank some water and went back to where it came from.

***

He began to watch the animals. The smell coming from them did not disturb him.

I guess my punishment isn't related to the animals. My punishment is to be alone. I have everything. I have water. I have ... And then it struck him: where would he get food from? He stood up quickly.

"What happened," asked the turtle.

Ayzer tried to understand where the voice was coming from. Ayzer looked at the animals and then the turtle.

"Did you speak to me?"

"Yes, I did."

"You can speak?"

"Yes, I learned to speak long ago. But for a while, I had no one to speak with."

Ayzer was surprised. He realized that he wasn't dreaming.

"Why don't you speak with others?"

"They can't speak."

"It is hard to understand you."

"Everyone talks to each other but I'm only one who can speak your language."

"Really? Well, how did you learn it?"

"I already knew how to speak."

"I mean, where did you learn my language?"

"How did you get here?" the turtle asked, ignoring Ayzer's question.

"I don't know."

"Me either! I can't answer your question."

"Okay, then. I guess we'll understand each other very well."

"Yes, you're right."

"It seems hard to get out of here. Life must be difficult for you."

"Not really," the turtle said. "Life isn't too bad."

"But what about drinking water? There are these steep, rocky banks."

"Yes, that's true. Drinking is difficult."

"It must be exhausting to go up and down every day. And the dangers of the rocky parts…"

"You don't know this place yet. If you did, you would know what we actually worry about."

"What does that mean?"

"You'll understand my words in time."

The turtle began to walk towards the other animals.

"Wait, come back! I didn't understand. What are you warning me about?"

The turtle didn't say a word and carried on walking. Ayzer followed the turtle.

"Where are you going? Could you please answer me?"

"It can't understand you," said a voice. "Whatever you want to ask, ask me. You're scaring the other animals."

Ayzer looked around.

"I'm behind you."

When he turned back, he saw an owl on a bush.

"Don't be surprised. Ask me whatever you want to know."

"You can speak, too?"

"What do you mean by 'too'? Here, nobody else can speak your language except for me. You must be tired and confused."

"No, I'm not confused. The turtle just spoke to me."

"Why are you insisting on not understanding? Here, it's only me who can speak your language."

"But, but... just now..."

"Excuse me, but I have no time to waste with your rubbish. You come to our land and then ask too many questions. And also, you don't believe what I tell you. According to me, you should go back to where you came from. Immediately. Or else, you'll be all alone here. I'm the only one who can speak your language and I won't talk to you anymore. Never."

The owl turned and flew away.

Ayzer waited for a while. He tried to figure out what was going on.

"It won't be like this," he said. He went among the animals.

"Didn't you guys see it? The owl just talked to me," he said.

The fox turned to the owl and said, "I think he's going crazy... He keep saying that one of us spoke to him."

"Yes, yes you're right. He's crazy."

"Poor man. To lose your mind is the worst experience a human can endure."

"One of you, speak to me. Please. What's going on? Why can't you answer my questions?"

Ayzer stayed where he was. At that moment, the owl flew away. All the animals moved as a pack towards a hill in the distance.

"Where are you going?"

He knelt down where he was.

"Whatever. Go away. I'll find what I'm looking for on my own. Or, it will find me."

He watched the animals disappearing.

"I will find it!" he called after them. "I don't need you!"

When the animals disappeared, Ayzer was all alone. It was the middle of the day. What would he do when night came? He tried to calm down. The silence started to make him feel better. Maybe it wasn't such a bad place. He thought he should begin to look around.

No, you're here for a purpose. You must be prepared for anything. This is the price of your salvation.

As Ayzer was thinking, a squirrel appeared.

"Come on," it said. "It's no good for you to just wait here."

"You can speak, too?"

"I'm sure what you're about to see will be much more surprising."

"I'm used to surprise by now. Don't worry about me, my little friend."

"We're not friends yet."

"Why is that?"

"Because you ignore my advice. Come on, stop talking and come with me."

"If you don't tell me where we're going, I'm not going with you."

"It's your choice," said the squirrel. It turned back and began to walk towards the other animals. While walking, the squirrel was grumbling to itself.

"How stupid these people are! They think they're the smartest creature in the universe. Yet they eat all the time, and never replace what they eat."

It turned and looked at Ayzer. He hadn't moved.

"You'll see in a minute, poor man."

Being alone made Ayzer anxious. The squirrel laughed at him.

"Yes, you'll see in a minute. Let's see what you'll do then. When you want help from me, I'll ignore you. You're the smartest thing in the world? Nothing happens to you? Here, the stupid man goes the wrong direction." He sighed to himself.

"I can't look anymore. Oh, God, I can't look anymore. This will be your end, poor fool. Turn around!"

Not hearing these appeals, Ayzer was walking towards the lake. He was really thirsty. He drank a handful of water. Then, a second. However, this one made him feel an ache in his stomach. He didn't care much and carried on drinking. This made him feel much worse.

"Now you'll see what happens when you don't listen," the squirrel said.

Ayzer couldn't move. Something resembling a fish began to emerge from the water. Ayzer stepped back and began to watch this creature. It had a tail like a crocodile, teeth like a shark, a horrid tongue coming out of its mouth...

He was still watching it with admiration. It was looking around, as if trying to find something. It emerged from the lake. It had four legs, and a back that was as strong a horse's. The creature walked on shore for a while.

"This is what you're scared of?" he said to the squirrel.

"It doesn't scare you?"

"No, there is nothing to be afraid of."

"Really? Maybe you can talk to it and convince it not to eat us."

"I can do this."

"Come on, then. Let's see how brave you are."

Then Ayzer turned towards the creature. He really was going to talk to it.

"Today, God's helping you. You didn't die," the squirrel said. "Yet."

Ayzer was breathing deeply. However, he saw the creature was going back to the water.

"Next time, I'll speak to it," Ayzer said.

The squirrel admired his courage but didn't want to admit this.

"I agree with you. You should try later on, so that you'll be able to stay alive longer," the squirrel said.

"I accept that. I'll go with you now. Not because I'm scared, but beause I'm tired of you insisting."

"Why didn't you follow the others?"

"If we're going to be friends, don't ask me anything about this. Okay?"

"Okay," the squirrel said. "I'll tell you everything when the time comes."

The two of them began walking to the other animals.

"I still don't get your courage," the squirrel said. "It seemed silly to me. Why not just run?"

"I'm not surprised that you wouldn't understand."

"I suppose if I ask you why you're here, you won't tell me?"

"No, you can ask."

"Then, I asked: why are you here?"

"There's a price to pay and I'm here to pay that price."

The squirrel looked as if it didn't understand anything. Ayzer didn't tell him anything more. The squirrel didn't ask anything more.

"It's not the fear I see in you. It's curiosity. Fear is the mother of the most daring moves," the squirrel said.

"It's like a man who is dying from hunger and steals wheat from the king's warehouse."

"Yes, it's just like that. However, the thing in you is an ambition to know."

"You think so?" Ayzer asked.

"Sure. People don't know their limits and that's why they are very interested in new experiences. This madness ends when your body mixes with the soil. Just like the beginning, the ending is also beyond your control. That's why, the most smart among you is the one who gets wise help from others. This is the only way to get power and knowledge to work for you."

Ayzer didn't answer back. He wanted to sleep and couldn't resist anymore. He fell into sleep...

"Come on, wake up! Wake up, you lazy human. Come on, we want to talk to you."

They went to the tree where all the animals had gathered together.

"You," said the old wolf. "Welcome to our forest. As long as you stay here, you'll be our guest."

Ayzer greeted the wolf by shaking his head.

"Yesterday, you told something to this squirrel."

"About what?"

"About Orga. You You said you are not scared of the thing in the lake and that you will speak to it."

"Yes, I will. Since I can talk to all the animals, then I can talk to what you call Orga. But not when it's hungry," he said, smiling.

"It's always hungry," the old wolf said, wryly. He started to walk. "Come with me," he motioned to Ayzer. They walked together.

"I know why you're here, Ayzer. Others don't know about it. I am old friends with Ridar. And he told me that you'd come here."

Ayzer was only listening.

"You can never leave."

"For now, I don't have a problem with that."

"Then, you can help us. You can help us to get rid of this creature. Orga. You're human and you can defeat it with your mind."

"Why do you want to get rid of it?"

"Because it will destroy the other creatures here."

"It's a living thing, too. In order to stay alive, it's very normal for such a creature to do things like that. Nobody can be blamed for filling his stomach when hungry."

The old wolf smiled. "You don't understand. It doesn't let us reproduce. It kills us when it's not hungry. Since it arrived, the lake has pulled away from us."

"Or maybe it only seems that way because you have been running away."

"Believe me, we should be done talking about this. We need to rebuild our lives here, and you will help us."

Ayzer considered this. After a while, he spoke again.

"OK, I'll help you. I don't know whether my mind and power shall be enough to overcome this creature. I can only accept the offer if we work together."

"Sure, we'll all do whatever we can. We only want some help from you, not for you to do all the work."

"I have one more condition."

"What is it?"

"I want to try talking to it first. To see if that helps."

"It doesn't help, but do as you wish."

"Will it come to shore again today?"

"It will. It has slept hungry for a week. Everytime it comes ashore, it grows angrier."

"Then, we agree."

"Monse," the wolf said.

"I didn't understand."

"Monse. It's my name. It's nice to meet you."

***

When the night had finished, Ayzer was already gone. The animals went to the lake in the early morning.

"Come on, Orga. Come out and meet me. My name is Ayzer. Come, so that we may struggle and make sense of our existence. We are not afraid of you," Ayzer said, pacing the shore.

He walked towards the water with courage. He wanted speak to Orga as soon as possible. He wanted to bring good news for Monse and the squirrel.

I'll save you, little squirrel. And I'll save me, too, he thought, waiting near the lake. *Yes, I'll get through this without getting hurt. Everyone will be grateful.*

He felt strong and happy as he waited for Orga, checking the surface of the water every so often. He thought of Uselya, and Ador. He thought of the life he had left behind. Ador – and Uselya – those were his only truths.

All of a sudden, he heard a voice. He looked around and saw a baby squirrel.

"Get back to your mother, little squirrel. It's dangerous out here."

The baby passed Ayzer, moving towards the lake. As it neared the lake, Orga popped out of the water with a fierce noise.

Before Ayzer could save the baby, it ran to its mother. Orga tried to attack Ayzer, but he caught its jaws. Orga tried to break free while Ayzer trapped its right legs.

He was sweating. As the animal's jaw moved, his back hit the ground, painfully. He grew very tired. Despite this, he thought of Uselya, and he began to squeeze Orga harder. His hands were like snakes on Orga's neck. Soon, Orga stopped. It was clear Orga was hurt worse than Ayzer. Then, Orga pulled back.

He looked and his hands really had turned to snakes. *What is this?* he thought. Maybe Ridar had given him this power. Orga pulled away in pain, slinking back to the water, and Ayzer collapsed with exhaustion on the rocky shore.

***

He woke up shaking. His eyes widened as he saw all the animals shouting and cheering. He narrowed his eyes again, with a terrible tiredness overcoming him. He hardly realized the old wolf beside him. In the wolf's eyes, he saw the anxiety resembling Ridar's eyes. When he saw that his hands were still snakes, he began to run, screaming in terror. The old wolf was following Ayzer from behind. The wolf jumped on Ayzer, overwhelming him. The wolf was very anxious...

Uselya, Orfin and Zelor

*D*ays and nights passed. Uselya returned to life again. Her sorrow passed with the love and compassion of her community. Everyone was happy to help her feel better, but Nagun thought that to show too much compassion towards her was wrong. He worried too much care and compassion would make her feel weak. He believed that things could be resolved only when Uselya was truly ready to face up to them. He thought that no-one around her seemed to have his good sense to follow a right strategy. He therefore assumed responsibility for helping her in a more intelligible and sensible way, and he had great confidence in himself.

***

"There were mornings when I had presents left from happy nights."

Uselya looked out of the window. Nagun didn't say anything, he only listened. He thought that for the time, no one could speak the same language that Uselya spoke.

"I'm very tired, Nagun. Ayzer, whom I loved, fell to pieces."

A few weeks passed. Once more, Nagun and Uselya were together.

"Do you know what kind of punishment they gave him?" she asked.

Nagun was irritated. "What difference does it make if we know?" he asked.

"Please, if you know, tell me. Don't worry about me. There's no steady place left in my heart for sorrow."

"What matters is whether he can complete his punishment or not. We should pray for this."

"Two days ago, I would've been angry at that request. But now I want him to be well."

"This is what we have to bear."

Looking into the distance, Uselya asked, "Have other people who have gone to that world made mistakes? Or is Ayzer the only one?"

"Of course there are people who make mistakes."

"But none of them had returned before. Why did you hide the truth from me?"

"I'm sure there are reasons for everything."

"Please tell me where he is, Nagun. For my own sake."

Uselya looked into Nagun's eyes. "If you don't do this, I'll do it. I swear I will," she said.

Nagun was astonished. Then he spoke to her with the indifference of someone who, underneath, was very worried.

"Ridar's waiting for me. We have to prepare for tonight's ceremony. Will you come? It'll be a nice wedding ceremony," he said, trying to stay composed.

When he was leaving her, Nagun heard Uselya speaking to herself: "I had mornings... Since Ayzer's been gone, the mornings have turned into nights... I need him to come back. I need him to return. Where is he? My anger and compassion need him. God help me!"

That night, Uselya was still standing at the window.

The only person who can take me to Ayzer is Zelor. I am sure he knows where he is.

She thought of the time she'd spent with Ayzer. Should she go now or in the morning? She would take the road at night...

***

She was very far away from the city. When she stopped walking, she saw a light coming from the hill. Her heart began to beat like it did in the old days, with Ayzer. Finally, she could see the hut.

In front of it was a short, old man with a big wrinkled mouth and protruding eyes. His big ears could be seen through his fluffy white hair. She was frightened of this strange looking dwarf.

"Please, don't be scared. I wouldn't hurt you," he said.

Uselya didn't say a word.

"Don't be scared of my appearance. I just came to visit Zelor. I came a long ways."

"Me, too," she said.

"Then we'll visit Zelor together."

When they came to Zelor's hut, they called him, but no one answered back. Then, the dwarf climbed through the window and asked Uselya to come in, too. She did.

"He's not here," said the dwarf.

He took a book from the table.

"I'm sure he didn't give up without a fight," he muttered. "He's from Ador. He's much stronger than his father."

Uselya didn't understand what he was saying.

Where is Zelor? she thought. *This man is scaring me.*

"You know him, right?" she asked.

"Sure. Did you think I'm a thief or murderer?"

"No, why would I think that?"

"I can see how scared you are from your eyes. I've known Zelor for a long time. I came here to visit him and ask his help. Do you live in Ador?" he asked, though he knew the answer.

"Yes, I do."

"Can I ask what kind of help you're seeking?" she said.

"Sure, you can ask. I've been looking for someone for a long time. I learned that Zelor knows where he is."

Uselya nearly jumped out of her skin when she heard this last sentence.

"Who are you looking for? Since you came all this way, he must be very important to you," she further inquired.

The dwarf sat down in Zelor's chair and looked at his book with anger.

"Yes, he's very important to me," he said in anger. Then he gave her a dark smile and asked, "Why are you here? You're very far away from Ador."

Uselya didn't know how to answer. The possibility of looking for the same person was preying on her mind; she thus made up a story on the spot: "Zelor was going to make me a gold necklace, and I have come here to take it. I must go back before anyone notices my absence."

"Zelor isn't here, so you must wait. Come on, sit down and have some rest. The morning is about to come. I don't think we shall wait too long."

The dwarf fell asleep, but Uselya spent the night awake in fear. In the morning, the dwarf awoke, asking if Zelor had come.

"No," Uselya said.

The dwarf's face was much scarier by daylight, so Uselya avoided looking at him when she spoke.

"We should look for him," the dwarf said. "I think I know where he is."

"OK, then. Let's go," Uselya said.

The dwarf opened a door that led to Zelor's tunnels. Uselya came to the mouth of the tunnel. It was very dark inside, and this only heightened her terror.

"Are you sure he's here? Maybe he's gone hunting," she suggested.

"If he was hunting, he'd have come back by now. If you're coming, hurry up."

"OK, I'm coming," she said. "But I still don't know your name."

"You're right. My name is Orfin."

They walked through the tunnel. She wondered what they were hoping to find.

What does this dawrf have to do with Ayzer? Uselya wondered.

After they walked awhile, Orfin stopped. "We should rest. I'm not young anymore," he said.

She agreed.

"Where does this road go?" she asked.

Orfin didn't answer. He pulled some dried fruit from his pocket and offered some to her.

"Eat some; you won't be hungry for a long time."

Uselya thanked him and took the food.

"You're not from Ador, right?" she asked.

"No, I came from very far away. You probably haven't heard the name of the place I'm from."

Orfin continued eating.

"Do you like gold?"

Uselya was surprised.

"What woman doesn't?" she said, smirking.

"You're right. Women deserve all the beauty in the world. The flowers and jewels."

"And love. We deserve that, too."

Orfin was surprised.

She wanted to say, "love is more important than all the others," but she didn't.

"You didn't tell me your name, yet. I'm not curious about it since we won't see each other later on," Orfin said. Though he was old, he still looked strong.

"Come on, let's go," he said.

They began to walk again.

After a long walk, they arrived in a big forest. The trees had scary shapes. They kept walking.

"This road has taken many things from me," Orfin said.

The dwarf was walking in front of her. He looked very short. She looked carefully and saw that he was actually shrinking. Uselya then fainted...

When she recovered, she saw the dwarf's face.

"What happened?" he asked. "There's nothing to hurt you here, nothing to scare you."

She stood up with his help.

"How do you feel now? Are you okay? If you want, we can rest."

"No, no," Uselya said.

When they saw a pond, they forgot how tired they were. This pond fed into a lake. The light and the colors spreading on the pond were very attractive.

***

"Stop, don't do it!" Orfin screamed.

Zelor looked at Orga's body. Zelor kicked Orga. Orga was on the ground. Orfin was begging.

"Zelor, don't do what you're trying to do!"

Uselya didn't understand what was going on.

"Who are you, old man? And why do you mingle in my affairs? Tell me, or I'll kill both of you," Zelor demanded.

"I beg you Zelor; it's not a monster. Let me take it and go. It can't harm you. It's wounded."

"You say so, dwarf? I don't believe it."

He lifted the axe he held.

"Zelor, don't do it! This is a father's wish. You know the tie between father and son."

Uselya approached. Zelor lowered the axe again.

"If you don't tell me what you mean, I'll water this ground with your blood."

"Just like you and your father Ridar; there's a tie between me and Orga."

"What does that mean? Tell me."

"Zelor, please. Let him speak."

"Uselya, what's going on here? What are you doing here? With this sinister man!"

"He is my road friend. He showed me the way to find you."

"Okay, then. Tell me, you two: what's going on here."

"First, pull this axe away from my throat," Orfin said.

Zelor pulled the axe away.

"That's my son."

Zelor was shocked.

"I don't get it."

Uselya was happy to learn that the one Orfin was looking for and the one she was looking for were different people.

Orga and Orfin

"Father, I decided to go."

"Orga, Orga, Orga! There are many things you should learn from me. You should stay with me. Where do you think you will go?"

Orga was angry. Huge Orga looked nothing like his father.

"Please, come with me to this city. You don't realize the power we have. With our whispers, we can guide people to hell."

Orga turned his back.

"Could you tell me exactly what you're looking for?"

Orfin moved in front of his son. They were on the hill from where the city was easily seen.

"Here are people, the reason for our existence. The day has just begun. They'll wake up and go to their jobs. And we will break them down, and steal their good things, with our breath. What is insufficient for you? Some might think you aren't proud to be my son."

Orfin stopped for a while.

"What do you want?" he screamed.

"Father," said Orga, stretching his left arm towards the city.

"People do those kinds of things anyway. Even if we don't exist. They kill each other, steal from each other, lie... They worry about their own interests. They don't care about morals."

"What did you say? Did you learn nothing from me? What you're saying disrespects our ancestors. Disrespecting your heritage is dangerous, even for the Fire Creatures. Don't forget that!"

"You and our ancestors are cowards," Orga roared. "Not even one of you could go to Ador."

Orfin was trying to stay calm.

"Orga! The place you talk about is written only in books. Yes, nobody from our clan could go there because there is no such place. Now, stop all this nonsense and come with me!"

"We all know that you're lying to me, father. You told me that everything Tubar wrote was real. And I found that book which you hid from everyone. And I read it."

"I shall go to Ador, father."

Orfin was trying to figure out how to persuade his son, but nothing came to mind. Finally, he decided to tell the truth.

"If you go there, you can't come back. You'll disappear there. Your ambition is too great, even for the Fire Creatures like us."

The War of Ridar and Orga

*R*idar was sitting in the smallest cell of the temple, all alone. This was the place he would come whenever he wanted to be alone. It was about midnight. The Ador community was slowly falling into sleep. He was thoughtful and alone.

Ridar was thinking of the emptiness that was trying to take him from there. He was in a mood as if he received an invitation. All of a sudden he saw a line of light in the middle of the room. The purple light expanded and thickened. Then appeared the noble Workers of Ador's history. Ridar greeted them and bowed in front of them. The souls who were there told Ridar to lift his head.

"Our great veteran of Ador's guardian. You're the pride of all of your ancestors! Do you know why we're here and why we called you?"

"I can only know what's taught to me."

"We came here to meet you with your fate. In a short time, Ador will face a great danger. We came here to give you the rules that will help you to defeat that danger. However, you'll make the choice. Because to fulfill this duty will cost the one you love the most."

"All of Ador's people would like to sacrifice anything for this city. No one can escape their fate. We only have one choice all the time. At the end, we get one result; either happiness or regret."

The souls looked at each other. The one who was speaking approached Ridar, putting its hand on his shoulder.

"Then, you must stop Orga, who will come here soon and try to spread evil. He's the son of Orfin. He thinks he can overstep the rules we made for his father. We sacrificed our most beloved ones in the past. Because you accepted this duty, you'll get what you deserve."

The soul extended a bottle with its other hand.

"In this bottle, there are lots of animal essences. Use them against Orga. If even one drop touches him, he will be destroyed."

They greeted Ridar and then disappeared.

***

Zelor's eyes narrowed as soon as he closed the book. Ridar finished his preparations and wached his son, who fell into a deep sleep. He fought back tears. He kissed his forehead, folded his hands gently and watched his face for a long time.

He then departed. He began to pray; he wanted God to help him. The Fire Creatures would use the passage to come to the land of Ador. It was the only way for them to come. He waited some, but Orga didn't appear. Then he began to walk through the passage. It was very dry, which concerned him.

When he saw Orga from far away, his mind went blank. Should he attack or hide? He couldn't decide yet. However, Orga was approaching.

When Orga saw him, it stopped. Ridar was waiting. Without losing his courage, Orga walked towards Ridar. All of the sudden, Orga attacked. Ridar tired to counter-act. Orga was squeezing his throat. Ridar had to do something or else he was going to die.

All of the sudden he poured the bottle on Orga's face. Orga's eyes began to burn and it began to scream. It carried on screaming and after awhile it disappeared. Ridar found himself in the passage. He couldn' resist anymore, and he fainted.

***

When Zelor saw his father lying on the floor, he knelt down and he embraced his father. He tried to wake him up, but couldn't. He hugged his father, picked him up and began to walk towards Ador. The holy wall that surrounded the city had a small hole in it. It was made to protect the city from Orga. He laid his father on his bed. He told people that his father was tired and sleepless. He needed to go to the temple and wanted some help. He wasn't feeling good because of lying to people about his father.

When he was walking through the streets, the Worker Emol called him.

"Zelor, my dear, what are the things that we are told? Where is your father and how is he?"

Zelor responded with moist eyes.

"Sir, I don't understand anything. My father fainted and now he's lying on the bed."

"My dear, let's go home now. I want to see your father."

Zelor turned back to the house with Emol.

"I found him in the passage of Ador. He was lying on the ground. There are no wounds on his body, but he can't open his eyes."

"Nothing to fear for. He's just asleep. He got tired. When he gets some rest, he'll be okay. Now, I have to go. When he wakes up, make him eat some light things. We shall come to visit him later."

He touched Zelor's heart a few times.

"My dear, you get some rest, too. I'll come later."

Then he left the house. Zelor then went to bed to get some rest.

***

When Ridar left the temple, he preferred to walk towards the meadows instead of his house. As he walked, he saw the little Sagun.

"What are you looking for here, little butterfly?"

Sagun was looking after the cattle. "I'll look after the cattle today. My uncle's son is ill. My uncle didn't want me to come here, but I insisted. When will my family understand that I grew up, sir Ridar? I can overcome everything."

Ridar was bored. Before, he was feeling love when he saw the little kids, but now there was a serenity in his heart. He didn't know the reason... He touched Sagun's shoulder.

"Don't think such things! As far as I see, you're doing very well."

"Yes, I grew up. Right?"

"Sure, you did. It's not easy to look after this many animals. If your family didn't trust you, then they wouldn't send you here. Do you have salt in your bag?"

"Yes, I do. Here."

"Then let's go and give these animals some salt. See, they begin to lick the rocks. Just foraging is not enough for cattle; they also need minerals in the salt to stay healthy."

Sagun looked at the animals. "How did I not notice this?" he said.

"Okay, no need to hurry up. Let's go together."

Sagun began to run towards the animals. As Ridar was watching him, he was thinking of his son. He had no idea even where he had been going in the last several days. He would come in late at night and go to sleep immediately. He would then be up very early in the morning, leaving home without saying anything. Indeed, no one in Ador knew what he was doing and where he was going nowadays. He had to hide it. He couldn't even participate in the prayer this morning.

"Put the salt on a wide rock."

"Nice idea."

"This way, the animals can eat easily; salt will also increase their appetite and milk yield."

"I never gave salt to the animals before, sir. Thanks for your help."

"It's fine, but please don't call me 'sir' anymore. Okay?"

Walking was good for him. He was feeling better.

He carried on walking back to the house with a hope in his heart. He called out to Zelor, but there was no answer. When he checked his room, he saw some mud on the floor. He scraped the dried mud and tidied up the room. As he was making his bed, he recognized the piece of gold he found under the pillow. This was one of the sizable pieces of gold placed on the bottom of the doorway of the temple so that people would step on them as they walk into the temple. This was done long ago, to raise the awareness that they should never put gold in their hearts.

Now Ridar understood how his son was sacrificed. He decided to put the gold piece back in its place that night, without anyone noticing it and before Zelor returned.

But Zelor never came back to Ador after that day. He was gone to the Gepose Hill, digging within it to extract more and more gold. Though Zelor realized how this greed for gold was engraved in his heart, he could still feel some pure spots. He did not fully surrender himself to it; he was going to strive against it. He thought of his father and how sad he was.

"Here," Orfin said all of sudden. "Part of your fate has already been sealed," he continued.

"What do you want? Why do you wish ill-fate to befall good people?" Zelor asked. "Do you think you'll win a victory against God? Why this ambition?"

"In this universe, every creature walks towards the purpose of its creation."

"You'll never achieve this."

Orfin came next to Orga. It was obvious that he was poisoned. He watered the ground and then treated his wounds.

"I know that."

"Then why?" Zelor asked.

Orfin approached Zelor. "Loneliness," he replied.

***

The three of them were sleeping in the rock cavity. Ayzer and the snakes in his hands... When Ayzer woke up, the animals would bring fruit from the forest for him. In their eyes, he was truly a hero, saving them from the monster. They were always taking care of him and talking about him. According to Monse, the snakes were the fate of Ayzer.

A monkey came near Monse and told him that two people were coming to see him. Monse had a few wolfs with him, and they went to look for these people.

Zelor and Uselya had come a long way to see Monse in order to find Ayzer. After all Uselya told him about Ayzer on the way, Zelor took pity on him and decided to help this poor man who had been sent to the Blue World in his place. Zelor was walking deep in thought of what he could do to help Ayzer, who was waiting there helplessly, just like himself. They carried on walking without speaking for a little more.

"Worrying is forbidden, Uselya. In this world, the burdens that people can carry are much more bigger than we thought. Believe me," Zelor said, breaking the silence.

"And we must live with these heavy burdens?"

"Yes. We live in a world of probabilities, where only the occurring probabilities are realized out of endless probabilities. And this is what life is. Each moment has only one probability realized. In other words, everything happens only in one place and at one time. This is the realization of a specific probability. Very few people can go beyond this."

"I don't get it. How?"

"I mean, very few people can live at different places at the same time."

Uselya didn't want to think much about this.

"Do we have far to go, Zelor? I want to find him very soon."

"Not far."

"Let me complete my words. What I will say is really important, and it may have happened to Ayzer."

"You mean being in two places at the same time?"

"Yes."

"This kind of thing scares me," Uselya said.

"Somebody is coming," Zelor said.

"It's a wolf pack," he said as they came into view.

"They won't attack us. Right?"

"I don't know, but stay next to me."

Zelor pulled out his axe. It was the place where Ayzer and Orga fought together. When they were waiting in silence, Zelor saw another wolf pack behind them.

Then came Monse. "What are you two doing here?" he asked.

"Greetings to you, Monse. Me and Uselya came to see you. As we trust your friendship, we want help from you."

"I feel like you're looking for someone. Am I wrong?"

"You're right, Monse. We're looking for Ayzer. You must know where he is. Uselya is worried about him."

"You know his fate as much as I know. Nobody can interfere in this."

"We don't know Ayzer's fate. How can you know the fate awaiting him?" Uselya asked.

"It has to be like this. There are Ador's rules and a few rules that very few people know."

Uselya knelt down. Zelor looked into Monse's eyes, pleading. The old wolf couldn't resist anymore and approached Uselya.

"There's not much time left. He'll be back soon."

"No!" she screamed. "Take me to him now!"

Monse finally agreed.

***

When Uselya found her lover, he was lying in a tree cavity. Ayzer's hands were tied up and he had bruises on his arms.

"What happened to him?" she said and then she embraced him.

Uselya burst into tears and hugged him. When she calmed down a bit, Monse told her what had happened to him.

"If I had accepted his offer, this wouldn't have happened."

"What offer?" Zelor asked.

"To escape from Ador to the Blue World," Uselya said.

"Yes, things would be different."

"The fate we live and our choices are never in vain. There is nothing you can do for the things of the past. The best thing to do now is to regret what happened, because every thing in the past has half sides."

Monse called Zelor to him. He took Zelor to a place where they could talk more comfortably.

"Look, if I'm saved then he may also have a chance. We have to find a way to solve this problem."

Monse didn't say a word.

"Do you mean that he'll always be like this?"

"I can't know that much. However, I have a small hope."

"Please share it with us, wise Monse. The lonely nights in Gepose, Ayzer came to see me many times. He also brought me some basic stuff I needed. I can't forget the day he brought some oil for my candle so that I could read books during my lonely nights. Ayzer was a good friend of mine."

"Nobody ran away from you and you didn't run away from anyone. The curtain had dropped on your eyes and heart. So, for you and the ones you loved. It was only a curtain."

"It doesn't matter. I'm relaxed now. Now tell me, how will Ayzer get rid of this?"

"I'm not sure. Next morning or the morning after, I'll be more sure about the solution."

"What will happen to Ayzer during this time? He doesn't look good."

"For now, there is nothing we can do. No more new pains shall come," Monse said. "Now, you go next to Uselya. To stay alone with Ayzer may hurt her."

"I wait for good news from you, my father's fateful friend."

"I hope," said Monse. "Come on, hurry up."

"Okay, I will go."

They said farewells and Zelor left the place. The old wolf was anxious.

***

Zelor came next to Uselya.

"How do you feel, Uselya?"

"I'm okay."

"Everything will be all right. Because we believe in this. Come on, you too, get some rest. Ayzer needs strong people who will raise his hopes more than he needs the desperate, weak people."

He waited until she fell asleep. Then, Zelor sat near Monse and started talking about Ayzer's situation.

"Yes, old wise man, is there any good news for us?"

"I'm not sure this news is considered gospel for you. However, I have a big hope."

"Did you find a solution?" Zelor asked with a pitch of excitement in his voice.

"Don't get too excited. For Ayzer's salvation will take some time. There's nothing we can do now. We didn't commit this offense and we'll not be judged. There will be a bargaining between Ayzer and the Adjudicating Will. That's why, all we can do is wait. However, this will not be a vain expectation."

"Do you have an idea how much time we have to wait?" Zelor asked.

"Time is different in the presence of the Adjudging Will than for us. A day with Him can be like a thousand days in our reckoning, and a duration of time which we see as being long can indeed be very short in His sight. He has put all the alternatives in front of Ayzer and given him the inspiration to do the right thing. One thing's for sure: Ayzer will need to make the choice."

Zelor finally yielded to what Monse said.

"Is Uselya sleeping?" the old wolf asked.

"Yes, she got really tired. She didn't want to leave his side. I insisted, so she could get some rest."

"It is quite natural for her to behave like a compassion-ate mother toward her Ayzer after she saw him collapsed with exhaustion and with all those deep purple bruises on his arms. Let's go look at our friend now," Monse said.

Ayzer was sleeping and looking very anxious.

"He's sweating too much. He needs to drink more water."

"Is it good or bad for him?"

"It's good. It means he's struggling inside. He didn't give up yet."

"What about the snakes in his hands? Did they harm anyone?"

"No, his hands will be his fate. They're waiting now. I hope that those hands will take Ayzer to salvation."

The sun had risen. They all fell into sleep.

In the morning, Uselya approached the baby squirrel who put blackberries next to Ayzer.

"Where did you find those, you cute little thing?" she asked.

"We picked them up with my mother. Then, I brought them to Ayzer."

"How sweet. Thank you very much, on his behalf."

"He saved me from dying."

"You're too little to think about such things."

Uselya caressed the baby squirrel's head.

"Why is he sleeping so much? Do you know when he will wake up?" he asked.

"He began to get better. He shall be up soon," she replied.

"I want to ask him things."

Uselya smiled.

"If you want, you can ask me. Maybe I can answer them."

"Okay then. How did he defeat Orga? I was there with him."

"You're very brave. I'm sure your mom is proud of you."

"Sure. I bring her too much food. If you want, I can bring some more for him tomorrow."

Uselya took the baby squirrel in her arms.

"Come on, go back to your nest. Your mom shall be worried."

She slowly put the baby squirrel on the gorund.

"Bye bye. I'll come tomorrow again."

Then the baby began to run towards its mother.

***

They were in the forest, a little ways from the lake. Uselya was worrying about Ayzer. He might be better compared to the old, but he still had a ways to go. She wanted to find Zelor and talk to him...

"How is Ayzer? Did he wake up today?" he asked, anxious.

"I need to talk to you."

"Did something bad happen?"

He approached Uselya.

"No, nothing bad happened. But if we wait here, no good thing will happen. You see how he looks. Let's take him to Ador."

"You know that we can't do this. To take him to Ador is impossible. Don't you see, he's getting better."

"Really? Look at his hands and face. Look carefully. He could have found salvation just like you did, in a stroke. But Ayzer is still in this situation."

"It will not happen in an instant. Don't forget how I explored the entire Mount Gepose for gold. Be patient. He'll get better."

"Please, let's take him out of here."

"Please, be much more patient."

"Even if you don't help me, I'll do it by myself."

She ran to Ayzer and tried to lift him. Zelor prevented this.

"Uselya!" he screamed. "Be patient a little more. Trust me, he'll be okay. Believe me."

Uselya took a deep breath and was very angry.

"I shall wait some more. However, I tell you this. If it takes too much time, I'll do whatever is in my mind. I hope that day doesn't come. You should not stop me, because it will not work. Yes, I'll do what I believe."

"Okay, Uselya. I'm sure Monse knows something. He's my father's old friend and very wise. Did you eat anything?"

"No, I'm not in the mood to eat."

"But you must eat, especially if you're to look after an ill man. You must take care of yourself."

***

Uselya fell into sleep next to the man whom she loved the most... It was a silent night. Ayzer awoke and started to move toward the dark part of the dense forest.

"I need to find Rogamp. My shadow is already on the road. I need find him before my shadow."

His sudden loud voice awoke Uselya as well. Squinting through bleary eyes, she said: "Ayzer, you got well. You woke up!"

She threw her arms around his neck. However, Ayzer stepped back.

"There's no time. I need to find Rogamp. I should go now and alone. My shadow is on the road."

"I guess you had a dream. Sit down here. First calm down a bit and then tell me everything. What is Rogamp? Tell me."

"There's no time," he screamed and then plunged into the forest. She followed him. Uselya was worrying he might lose his mind. Ayzer stopped all of a sudden.

"You shouldn't come with me. This is very dangerous for you. Please, go back and wait me there."

"No. If you don't tell me where you're going, I won't go back. What is Rogamp? Tell me, please. Did you have a dream?"

"No, I didn't have a dream. You should go back."

"I'm coming with you."

Ayzer didn't care for this, but they continued walking. Ignoring all the danger, she followed Ayzer. Ayzer was stopping and looking around and waiting to hear which way he should go. He looked as if he was trying to get the directions to a place he'd seen before.

After taking a direction, he would walk a while more, and then repeat the process. After passing through ten or twelve turns in this way, Ayzer turned back to her.

"Come near me. They must be very near. I can feel it. As though I feel their hands on my back. We should find Rogamp before the shadows find us. Do you hear the voices?"

"What voices? I don't hear anything."

"They must be away from us. I hope they are not ahead of us. Come on, let's go."

Then they began to walk again.

"Where are we going?"

Uselya didn't get an answer to her question.

"We still have the chance to find it before the morning. We have to hurry."

She thought of many things as they were walking. Maybe it would be better to wait, just like Monse told them. Uselya was very tired when they came to a cliff.

Uselya looked down from the cliff. Then she stepped back. She suggested they go back but Ayzer didn't listen to her. He insisted that it was the place where they should be.

"I know the road will go on from here."

"Don't you see? There is a cliff in front of us and at the end of the cliff there's water and there are only rocky places around us."

Ayzer thought for a time.

"Yes, there should be a Rogamp tree."

"What is a Rogamp tree? As far as I know, it's not a tree name."

"It's as black as a pitch tree. It has no branches and leaves. It is only a trunk. It's round like a turtle back."

Then, he jumped up.

"The sun is on the opposite side of the shadow. They said something like this."

"Who said that?" Uselya asked, but he didn't hear her. He carried on walking towards the sun's light.

"This way Uselya; we found the way."

Together, they went down this rocky road. The wind was blowing very hard. They could hear the sounds of the birds. This solitude was drawing them closer together, but Ayzer kept a minimum space of safety between Uselya and his hands, which were still snakes . Even if she didn't know where they were going and what they were looking for, she was next to her lover in devotion.

They passed a flat area. They carried on walking. They looked around. And then they climbed down a steep hill. The road turned right again. A few steps away, they saw a temple's front, which was very high. Ayzer thought of walking around the temple. The walls and the door were very big and high.

"Uselya," he said. "We should go inside, because that is where the road goes."

"Okay."

Before they went inside, they checked behind, but they could not see anything familiar; even the rocky road they came from vanished without trace.

"We shouldn't wait any longer. I worry about having you here. It makes me anxious."

"Then I can wait here."

Ayzer approached the huge door and pulled it. Uselya was near him. When they saw the darkness appearing, Ayzer shouted: "Here it is. Rogamp."

He looked at Uselya.

"Do you see how black it is?"

She was very surprised at what she saw.

"What shall we do? It has closed the road."

"We shall go over it, Uselya. If we can make it..."

He held out his hand. Uselya was praying inside. Ayzer made the first step and then the second. He turned and looked at Uselya. He wanted to go forward, but he got stuck on something. He lifted his feet but couldn't move. He didn't want Uselya to know this. He tried very hard and at last he made it.

"It's almost finished, Uselya. In a minute I'll be able to see behind the tree."

"May I come too?" she asked.

"When I reach the other side."

With aching feet, Ayzer reached the hill on the other side.

"Here, I'm coming."

Ayzer was surprised because she didn't have a problem while walking. As they went forward, their view was getting clearer. All of the sudden the silence was gone.

"Hurry up, the big prayer will start soon. Everyone write their name on the rock." The words were repeated, again and again. Then, out of nowhere, a dwarf-child ran up and hit Ayzer.

"Stop! Who are you?" Ayzer shouted.

However, the dwarf ignored him and carried on his way. Afterwards, they saw many dwarfs running around. Ayzer was trying to call to them.

He then turned to Uselya.

"I don't understand what is going on. Why don't they talk to us?" she asked.

"Don't worry. They are blind. If they wanted to harm us, they would have done so easily."

A young man spoke to them. "What are you waiting for? Write your names on a stone. Didn't you come here to reach salvation?"

They looked at this young man, who was middle-sized.

"Come on, hurry up. Write your names and then join the big prayer. You only need a small stone."

Ayzer bent down to get a stone but he couldn't find any. He kept searching.

"There are stones everywhere. The ground, the ceiling, the wall ... Come on, find one!" the man said.

"Ground, ceiling and wall? But I don't see them. The only thing I see is the toughened ground under my feet. This place must be very big. But I can't find a stone. Uselya, can you find one?"

The two of them couldn't see even one stone.

"Here. Write on this," said a dwarf and then left.

"What do we write with?"

"You can take one of these," said the young man.

Ayzer took a pen and wanted to write Uselya's name first, but the man wouldn't let him.

"No, you can only write your name. She isn't invited here."

"But in my hard days she was always with me and I want to write her name. I can give up my name."

"The prayer will be performed by the wise Arut. He will call everyone's name. She is not the one we wait for."

For a while they discussed this subject. At last, Uselya and Ayzer's names were written and sent to the wise Arut.

They joined the big prayer. They knelt down and began to pray. After a long wait, the young man came near them.

"Ayzer and Uselya, we thank you for sincerely joining our prayers. With the kindness in your hearts, the power of our prayer is increased. Welcome!"

"We're happy to be here, too. However, we don't know you as much as you know us."

"You're right. My name's Hirb. I'm the servant of this temple of Old Shadow Creatures."

"The temple of Old Shadow Creatures? Do Old Shadow Creatures live here?"

"Sure. The people you see around me are the members of the Shadow Creatures community."

Uselya was really surprised.

"I didn't know Shadow Creatures would be this short. Only you look different."

Hirb smiled.

"This is the nature of Shadow Creatures. As we get older, our height gets shorter. My duty here is provide peace for our old people on their last days."

"How did you know that we would come?"

"Don't worry friends, you're in a place where you'll find the answers to your questions. However, please don't rush."

They went to a guest house. Ayzer and Uselya got some rest for a while. When they got hungry, they went out of the house and looked for something to eat. They came to a stream. They saw different colors spreading over the stream. Uselya was really impressed with this wonderful reflection. Ayzer saw some strange fish who were standing still as if they were fixed to the rocky wall of the waterfall flowing down into pond.

"Look at them! How are they hovering horizontally in the water? What do you think about getting some?"

"No, let's get some fruits. That seems dangerous to me."

Ayzer stayed indecisive for a while. Uselya went towards the flowering pond. She took some fruit, which looked like an apple.

"They're enough for us."

"No," Ayzer said. "They're not for us. Let go of the ones you're holding."

"Why? They look very nice. They need to be washed."

"Then wash them."

Uselya put them into the water and when water touched them, they turned black and hairy. Uselya screamed.

"Water uncovered the truth!"

Uselya began to cry. Ayzer ran to her and took the fruit, throwing them aside.

"Come on, let's get our food somewhere else."

They went to another pond. Ayzer entered into the water. This time, big fish were moving all around him.

"This is incredible. The fish are everywhere. Come here, if you want."

Uselya was scared, staring at the lions.

"You forgot the lions. Please be careful."

"Don't worry, they won't harm us."

However, one lion roared and then began to move towards Ayzer. He could barely notice the shadowy lion jumping over his head, Uselya screamed and closed her eyes. The lion rolled into the water.

"See? They're harmless."

When she heard his voice, she opened her eyes. Then they got some fish.

"There's a stove outside of the hut. We can cook there."

"I caught one," she said proudly.

"We have plenty. You don't need to catch more."

When Hirb came to the guest house, he found Ayzer and Uselya talking with each other.

"Did what you see shock you?" Hirb asked. "Surely you had seen such scenes before. You've come from very far away."

"Which long way do you mean? I came here from Ador."

"I'm talking about much earlier. Nevermind. There isn't too much time left for all these questions now. Master Arut is awaiting to see you before sunset."

"Is there a reason for us to hurry?"

"Yes, Ayzer, you are right. There are things we need to do before your shadow is set free. Let's go now."

The three of them went to a house at the end of the village.

Book of Arrogance

"Yes Asha, you're the most beautiful girl."

The young princess was looking at her green eyes in the mirror and telling herself these words.

"No one like you has ever lived. Some might even consider you unlucky, because who could possibly deserve your love?"

The princess watched her body in front of the mirror. Then someone knocked on the door.

"Come in."

"You look very beautiful this morning – as always, princess. All the nobles are waiting to leave everything they have just for you."

"I've heard this plenty, Eshni. Stop telling me this nonsense."

Eshni flushed deeply and lowered her black eyes.

"I only tell you what I see, my lady. Please forgive my mistake."

Then she bowed her head.

"Your father is waiting for you in the dining hall."

Asha went to the dining hall very quickly. Eshni was now alone in the luxuriously furnished bedroom of the princess. She began to look at herself in the mirror. She touched her body and then she let her hair free.

"Arrogant lizard," she said very slowly.

She dreamed that she was using these essences and oils for her body. She woke up with the coming of the old royal servant who ordered her around.

***

"I have a son and daughter but still don't have grandchild. This makes me sad," King Sodu said.

"We're not as lucky as you are, dear father," responded Asha. "You found the most beautiful woman. Since there's no one whom we can give our hearts to, what can we do other than wait for someone who is suitable for us? Also, I don't know about my brother, Sorve, but I won't marry until I find someone like you or my brother."

"I must tell you that I'm not able to wait too much longer."

Then King Sodu called his assistant.

"Is everything ready?"

"Yes my lord, everything is done just like you wished."

"Then, we shall start off."

Then he turned to his children.

"I must go to a village. I guess there's a problem there and I need to learn what's going on. You wait for me here."

"Sir, please don't approach the villagers too closely. I don't want any village odors to come to our palace."

As Sodu heard these words, he got very angry. He thought of his wife, who was very kind and generous to the public. He headed for the door.

Eshni was giving orders to the gardeners about where to put the flowers.

"These roses look very nice! The princess likes buds. Please cut them. One of you cut those yellow flowers among the grasses. Or else, she will send you to the dungeon. Come on, hurry up."

The weather was very nice. Eshni began to dream...

"Eshni! You should be next to the princess, shouldn't you? Why are you here?"

All of a sudden the dream vanished; that was her mother's voice...

"No, mom. This morning, she'll be reading. She won't need me. She sent me here to look after the garden."

Her mother spent her life serving the queen. As her mother began to walk through the parts of the palace, she stomped angrily. Eshni could hardly go out and see her Sorve as she had to accompany Asha, helping her all day. But now she headed towards the door resolutely. She left the palace and walked into the forest. She came to a fountain and she took off her shoes and stepped into the water. She was really excited. She then walked on the grass with bare feet. She saw a fresh oak sapling. Dreaming that it was the prince, she started talking to it.

"Sorve, Sorve. My dear lover, give me your hands. I'm the one who shall make you the happiest man..."

She stretched out her hands. But there was no one to hold them.

"You're just like your sister. You two have bigheads. You don't deserve anything beautiful."

She bowed her head to the ground. She clenched her fists and began to cry... For a while she cried and then sat down next to the fountain. She washed her face and hands. She then turned to the direction of the sound she heard in the distance. After awhile, she realized an old man was among the trees. This old dwarf was approaching her. She felt a bit anxious.

"We should get rid of whatever is making our Princess cry," he said.

When she heard the word "Princess," she began to feel good. All of a sudden this man looked like a very sweet old man to her.

"You're wrong, old man. I'm neither princess or queen," she said, smiling.

"For some princesses, there is no need to wear a crown. Even these uncrowned princesses are much more impressive than others."

"You think so, old man?"

"Sure. Do you think that there can be lies in an old man's words? If I were young, maybe I could lie to intrigue you, but I'm old."

Eshni thought of this old man as young, which made her anxious.

"You say that I look like a princess, then have you ever seen a princess?"

"Many princesses admire their beauty in my mirrors. They wear my silks. Many years ago, I was a very rich merchant. However, now I travel with my poor mule and sell hair ornaments, bracelets and necklaces to the villages' girls. Back then, when they said, 'The merchant Orfin is here!' everyone would run to me."

"Your name's Orfin, then."

"Yes, everyone calls me this. Orfin – it's easy to say."

"I'm Eshni. I would like to talk to you, but I have to go back to palace," she said.

Then she began to walk towards the palace without looking behind her. She hurried up and went into Asha's room.

"You're failing at your duty, Eshni. Don't ever make me look for you again!"

"I'm sorry, my lady! I took the weeds out. Otherwise, they grow up and ruin the garden."

"Aren't there many gardeners who can take care of that?"

Eshni suffered under her words. Her hands were very cold, her eyes filling with tears.

"I'm really sorry, my lady. It will not happen again, you can be sure."

"Anyway."

Asha wanted a new dress and now she was trying the dress on.

"We have guests for dinner tonight, you know that, right?"

"Yes, I know. Preparations have started," Eshni replied.

"I hope you don't embarrass me. Please prepare the bathroom for me now."

Asha was complaining about the tailor working on the dress slowly and with meticulous care.

"It's almost finished," the tailor said.

Eshni hastened to make all ready for the bath.

"I hope a nice bath will take all my worries away," the princess said.

***

It was nearly dark.

"Your hair is fine, my lady."

"Yes, now I'm ready. Did all the guests arrive?"

"Yes. They're looking forward to seeing you and your brother. You'll enthrall everyone with your beauty."

"Don't keep telling me the same words. I want to have a happy face for my guests. Do you hear me?"

She didn't say anything. She bowed her head.

"Now, go and call Sorve. We will go down."

"Yes, my lady!" Eshni said.

Asha watched herself in the mirror for the last time. She had a blue dress on. She didn't see any defect.

Someone knocked on the door. It was Sorve.

"Are you ready, my sister?"

"Despite Eshni's big mouth, yes, I'm ready."

"What mistake did the poor girl make? She's hovering around you."

"Let's not talk about her."

Sorve invited his sister to take his arm.

"Kindly step this way, Princess."

Eshni was watching the guests from the corner of the hall. She watched them eating. Then she looked at Mr. Arki's daughter, Saya, and her cousin, Osli, sitting next to her. The two of them were frail and tall, just like the other members of the family. Right behind them, there were the King's right hand Humer's son, Fisman, and his daughter, Ucze. These children had innate nobility. Eshni was analyzing the guests.

Asha and Murse didn't like each other at all. This might have been becasuse of Sorve's visits to Tsol's manor house. At the beginnig, Murse liked Asha just like the others did. As the Princess grew to dislike him, he returned the favor.

There was a curly haired, brunette girl next to Murse. She was Paos's daughter, Sossa. Alko was sitting in front of him and was the son of the commander of the army. In the palace, people were talking about Asha and Alko. They wanted them to get married. However, for Alko, Asha was a little girl.

Eshni was watching Sorve. She couldn't keep her eyes from him. After a while, Eshni couldn't resist watching anymore. She went back to her room. She laid down on her bed. At midnight she was called to help the princess.

After that night, a few weeks passed. Eshni and Orfin saw each other a few times.

"So, you live here?" she asked, looking at his empty hut.

He nodded.

"It's really hard to believe that you were a rich merchant once."

"You should not be fooled by appearances, Princess," Orfin said.

Eshni approached Orfin.

"Never mind. Where are the things you told me about?"

"Here they are, Princess."

He handed her the silk fabrics.

"Take them. They're yours. You deserve to wear these."

She was about to faint with excitement.

"They're so nice."

"They're nothing. There are more."

He handed her lots of jewelery with diamonds, gold, silver, and rubies.

Eshni couldn't believe her eyes. She was about to faint.

"Now, I hope you believe how rich I'm."

Eshni didn't answer.

***

"All of them are mine, right? You promised me."

The old man was sitting on a chair.

"At this age, what can I do with these? I don't have a wife to give them to as a present, or a child to leave them to. Take them all; they're yours."

Eshni was stunned.

"However, I don't think these will make you happy."

The girl paused for a moment.

"These have made me very happy. Very happy … However, if I could see that Asha was in trouble, I would be the happiest girl in the world. I wish that stupid princess could be in love with that hustler, Arusan. That ugly hustler…"

Orfin had found what he was looking for.

"Do you think there is a possibility? Could a princess be in love with that hustler?

"Of course, not."

"I see. You think that she doesn't deserve what she has?"

"Yes. She doesn't deserve anything."

"Do you know what? I had many friends when I was rich. When my work began to go bad, they all left me. However, I took appropriate measures and I thought about my senility. I saved something." He stopped, looking into the soapbox.

"But you were very kind and became my friend. We're friends, right? Or else like father and daughter?"

"Yes Orfin, we're friends. Maybe even like father and daughter."

"Then, your problem is mine."

He took a mirror from the soapbox.

"Do you see this mirror?"

"This can't be. Asha has the same one."

"That's true. Her mom must have given it to her. I sold it to her mom."

"What's going on? I don't understand."

"Sit down. If you listen to me, then the ambitious fire in your heart may go out."

They sat down and Orfin began to tell her.

"This mirror doesn't look like other mirrors."

Eshni was a bit thirsty.

"Asha's mother bought the same mirror, just because it went nicely with the color of her eyes. She was a noble woman."

"Okay, tell me whatever you want to tell me."

"This mirror is a 'love mirror'."

"What?"

"It means that whoever looks in the mirror falls in love with the next person to look into it. This could help you achieve your goal. You can gain Sorve and get rid of Asha at the same time."

"It's really hard to believe this, Orfin. Can such a thing happen?"

"Poor little thing! Why do you still have suspicions in your heart about me? Hasn't everything I've told you been true?"

Eshni took the mirror in her hands.

"Be careful," Orfin said. "Don't open the tulle veil yet!"

***

"Are you ill this morning, Eshni?" Asha asked. She asked her this question only to make fun of her silence, not because she was interested in her. "You're usually not this boring. Are you okay?"

"I'm okay, my lady. Thank you for caring about your servant."

She was going to change the mirror when Asha was in the bathroom. The princess wouldn't notice the switch.

"Eshni! Did you leave the soaps in the bathroom?"

Eshni said,"yes."

Then Eshni quickly took Asha's mirror and tied it to her ankle and replaced it with the one she brought with her. She began to feel anxious. She wanted to leave the room.

"My lady, I forgot to bring you new towels. Before you leave the bathroom, I'll bring them quickly."

"Hurry up! I can't wait on you all day long."

"Going right now, my lady!"

She left the room. She needed to drink some water. The head cook saw her in the kitchen.

"What are you doin' here?"

"I just need some water. That's all."

"Here you go."

Eshni drank the water in one swig.

"You're very thirsty."

Eshni did not answer. When she came to the hall, Sorve was leaving the princess's room. Eshni quickly moved away from him without uttering a greeting. When Eshni came inside, the princess spoke to her.

"The towels were here. You've gone blind."

Eshni didn't say a word. After Asha got dressed she looked into the mirror that was her mother's heirloom.

"Is breakfast ready?"

"Yes, my lady."

Eshni was relaxed because she didn't understand anything. Now, she began to make plans for Arusan to look in the mirror.

The next day, conjuring an exuse, she went to see the hustler. Arusan saw the mirror she was holding in her hands.

"Where did you find that? Very nice mirror. Or did you steal it?"

"No," she said. "This is a present from my mother. The queen who isn't with us gave it to mother when she was still alive."

"Could you let me take a look at it?"

"No, it's really precious to me. Your ugly face doesn't fit this mirror."

"Give that to me."

He took the mirror forcibly from her hands. He began to look at his face in the mirror.

"It's a really nice mirror. Now, it's mine."

She pounced on him.

"It can't be yours."

They began to pull the mirror from both ends and at last the mirror was broken.

"No, Arusan! Look what you have done! You broke my most precious gift. You won't get away with this."

Arusan looked behind her. He felt sorry.

***

Prince Sorve woke up early that morning and got dressed for hunting. He was practicing with his bow. There was a knock at the door.

"Come in, Ughulte."

Ughulte came in.

"My fateful friend. Welcome. How do I look?" Sorve asked.

"As always, you're under a lot of strain. You're fresh as a spring and as agile as an arrow."

"Today seems to be the first day of good hunting; what do you think?"

Ughulte was older than the prince. He was broad-shouldered, medium-sized, and a bit plump. He used to be a good warrior in the army. He then left the army and devoted himself to training the prince.

"I'm ready to leave immediately."

"I should remind you that there's a send-off ceremony."

Sorve bridled his horse, which Arusan brought. He caressed the horse's black mane. He had grown up with this horse.

"Arusan, you deserve an award because you look after Tirfi very well."

"This is your kindness, my lord."

"Ughulte, both our horses were born from the same mother and father, but why does yours follow one step behind?"

"My lord, it's because Kavi is older than Tirfi. Also, Tirfi is your horse and Kavi is mine. The two of them are smart enough to know where to stay."

Sorve thought about these words for a while.

Eventually, they left. A fire had been lit in the palace's garden, and a cavalcade moved towards it. Sorve was in the front, but he spoke to his mentor.

"I don't understand why my father has stayed this long. Could this problem be that big?"

"Don't worry, my lord. This morning, your father's reporter came. He'll be back within a few days. The reason for his delay is that he dealt with the problems of the surrounding regions."

"I don't worry about anything, Ughulte. These lands won't see a king like my father again..."

Tirfi and Kavi slowed down when they approached the crowd. The oldest wise man of the palace, Narune, welcomed the horses.

"Sefar's horses, country of Sefar's wings, dust clouded eagles, have a safe journey!"

The riders pulled their swords and greeted the crowd.

Narune said a short prayer in an old language.

"Now, give us your entrusted things, Sefar's horses."

"Asha isn't around. Do you know why, Ughulte?"

"I sent a man, my lord. They'll be here soon. Here they come. See!"

"What's wrong, Asha?" Sorve asked.

She wasn't looking well.

"I don't know. I really don't know. However, there's a big sorrow inside me. I don't want you to join this hunt."

Sorve took Asha's hands.

"Sadness does not fit with your emerald eyes. No need to worry. This is not a war, only a hunt. Nothing to fear. I'll come back to you within a few days."

"Your words do not calm my heart."

She was about to cry. She bowed her head and took her brother's hands. Sorve pulled out the ring, which was their family's symbol, from his pocket. He handed the ring to Asha.

"I'll come back to you. We'll always be together and love each other."

He then jumped on his horse. He called to the riders waiting for him: "In order to get the ones given us, move forward!"

After the crowd was gone, Asha could not move for a long time. Eshni wasn't trying calm her down; she was justing waiting.

"Come on Eshni, let's go. I don't feel well."

***

It had been ten days since Sorve left. Asha had barely left her room or eaten. Except for emergencies, she did not want visitors. In her room, she watched the stars or lay on her bed and cried.

She was in her room, as always.

"Call Eshni," she told her servant. "I want to visit my mother's grave. Call her now!"

"Yes, my lady!"

When they arrived at the grave, which was very far from the palace and over a hill, Asha ordered Eshni to wait at the entrance.

"I need to be alone," she said.

Asha didn't look at the decorations on the columns or the triangular stone. She prayed inside and began to walk towards her mother's grave. On her grave, there were star shaped holes on the columns; in the middle of a marble crown there were many small and big stars. Her mother, Ayulke, liked everything about the sky. Asha touched the purple violets on the grave. She looked at the grave, crying.

"Mother, can you hear me? It's your dear daughter, Asha. Since death took you away, I have been the loneliest girl in the world.

"When you were alive, I was proud of being the daughter of the most beautiful woman in the world. Even in your breath, there was nobility."

Then she closed her eyes.

"Mom, do you remember? Your little daughter loved to watch you while you combed your hair. Your little daughter learned everything from you. Your daughter never stepped on a place where you did not walk. Mom, I fell in love. I know that you see everything. My heart burns with this love. My dear mom! I'm too weak to withstand this love. Do you see how weak I am? My love is shameful for our lineage... But I have no power to withstand this. I don't wish to be forgiven, because I know this is impossible. I choose my love, mom."

Then she stood up and came to the entrance of the grave.

"Eshni, we're going. Hurry up."

Then, they returned to the palace.

***

Eshni ran into the room: "My lady, the riders are coming."

Asha looked through the window and saw the riders. The princess quickly ran to the entrance of the palace.

"Thank God, you came back Sorve. You don't know how much I missed you."

She could not see Sorve yet.

"Why isn't he in the front? Sorve, where are you? There Ughulte is, but I don't see Sorve."

The riders approached the princess. Ughulte came near princess and bowed his head.

"Where is Sorve? Why isn't he among you?"

She asked Ughulte again: "I asked you where Sorve is!"

Ughulte could not say a word.

A young rider dismounted from his horse and knelt down: "My lady, we lost prince Sorve in Tuda forest. After two days, his horse returned."

"And he wasn't on it, right?"

She looked far away and all of a sudden she fainted. The crowd gathered around her with fear. The palace's doctor came and medicine was prepared. The night passed in crying jags. Then she woke up with a groan, yelling "Sorve." Doctor Rutu, who was waiting beside her, stood up.

"Please, don't make yourself tired. Your body is exhausted."

"Where's my father? Didn't he return? Why don't they go and search for Sorve? Do these people have this little loyalty for their prince? Oh, Sorve!"

"Please drink some."

Eshni came in. Doctor Rutu had a bad feeling about her. He didn't know the reason, but he thought that there was something they didn't know about her.

Eshni was thinking of her love; why was he sent to that forest? As Rutu was leaving the room, he gave instructions.

"She will wake up towards midday. I need to go prepare the medicine. This may last until night. I know that you're sorry, too, but do not let her tire herself and try not to talk too much."

Inside, he kept telling himself that nobody could be able to return from that forest. Then, he left the room. He went to his room and sent his assistants to different places to look for the materials he needed for the medicine.

***

Although two days passed, Asha could not come to life. Eshni was worried that this tragic event would prevent her love from emerging.

***

Sefar's people suspected that it was the beginining of bad days... The palace people began to fear sleeping. People were hopeless.

Late one night, somebody was in the palace's garden. Only Ughulte realized this black shadow. He followed this shadow but unfortunatelly he lost it. He went downstairs and listened to the rooms, one by one. However, he didn't hear a voice.

Then he went upstairs. He heard some voices from Asha's room. As he put his ear to this door, the door opened. When he saw Sorve holding Asha's hands, he was shocked.

"Sir, you're here."

All of a sudden Sorve, punched him in the face. He fell down.

"Get out Ughulte! We're going."

Ughulte was watching him from the floor and was really surprised to hear these words.

"Where are you going? Could you please tell me what's going on? Are you okay?"

He looked into Asha's eyes.

"Asha and I, we love each other. We're running away from here, my friend. We were made for each other."

Then he hit Ughulte's head with his sword. Ughulte fainted.

***

King Sodu was listening to his assistants in the crown room.

"Markun, you're saying that my son and daughter left the palace. However, you don't say anything about the reason."

"Sir, if I had any information about this, I would have told you. But I know nothing more. Please forgive me!"

"Now, explain the reason. Where are my daughter and son?"

The blue-eyed Purila answered.

"The answer to this question is only known by Ughulte."

"Didn't you tell me that he was injured?"

"Yes, but he has woken up. He is in a position to answer your quesitons."

King Sodu went to the palace's doctor.

When the king came into the room, the injured man tried to sit up. However, the king did not care about this behavior. He came near Ughulte.

"I have entrusted my son to you. I never saw you make any mistakes up to now. Both my son and daughter are gone. Tell me Ughulte: what happened? Where are they? If you don't tell me where they are, I'll kill you now."

"They're gone," he said and tried to hide his face.

"I know that," Sodu yelled. "Now tell me everything!"

"They were in love with each other. Not like a sister and brother; like a woman and man... They run away from here and then they'll get married."

Sodu's eyes got bigger.

"Do you realize what you're telling me? Is such a thing possible? They're siblings, they're my son and daughter, they're my heirs, they're the hope of our people, the future of their kingdom's lineage..."

He suddenly stopped and looked at Ughulte, who was crying.

"I tell the truth, my sir! I heard these words from Sorve. I could not prevent them. They injured me and ran away."

Sodu knelt down.

"How could this happen? My God, what kind of disaster is this? Oh, the Merciful God! Please help us."

He folded on his knees. The old assistants lifted King Sodu up. The king was sent to his room for treatment, too.

***

King Sodu rode towards the rider in silence.

"We heard that they're on the Lumen road, my lord."

"Soldiers come with me," the tired king said. "Others stay here."

"Riga, Parkut! Ready our horses; we'll go to Lumen. These men are enough for us."

The Lumen City was established upon a range of high mountains, and it never accepted the power of the Sefar country. It never accepted the existence of the Sefar country and had always been problematic. They would not hesitate to use Asha and Sorve against King Sodu. They knew that Sodu would kill them in order to save his children. Priests with evil intentions would like to bless this marriage. Now, the king had to find them before they got married.

***

Eshni was trying to put the pieces of the mirror back together. Since King Sodu was gone, there was a big sorrow in the palace. Nobody understood that there was a link between Eshni and this disaster. She wanted to see Orfin because she couldn't overcome these difficulties by herself. She secretly went to this dwarf's house. He wasn't there. She knelt down and began to cry. Would the kingdom end this way? She was feeling regret. She was thinking of this disaster... Her love was now with his sister. According to their plan, Asha was going to fall in love with Arusan. However, it didn't end that way.

***

As King Sodu and his soldiers were going towards Lumen, they learned from the villagers that Asha and Sorve were going to the west of Lumen. Even though Ughulte was injured, he was with them. The king turned to Ughulte.

"Do you think they want to go to Ador?"

"I don't think so. It's not possible for our people to pass through Ador; unless they get help from the Shadow Creatures..."

"The Shadow Creatues are faithful to their words. But it would be a mistake to trust them. While we thought that Lumen would be a problem for us, now we have bigger problem."

The weather was very hot. Ughulte was trying not to lose hope... However, he knew that as soon as King Sodu found them, he would end their lives.

***

"You still didn't tell us where you're taking us, Orfin."

Sorve looked very tired. Orfin stared at him.

"Do you want to be saved and be happy together? I take you to that place and I don't want anything from you for doing this favor. Now, do you want to come with me or wait for your father? You decide that."

Sorve pulled Asha's hand.

"Let's go Orfin. We shall do what you want."

"What you're doing is a huge sin. However, you go very well with each other and I respect your love. I will help you because I'm the most precious person for you in the world. There isn't anyone else who can help you. To have been born as brother and sister is not your fault. It's really nice for me that the king's children want help from me. I'm proud of myself for helping you."

"I'm thirsty," Asha said.

"Orfin, we should find water now. This way, we can get some rest."

"We must walk a little more. I told you that this journey would be hard. Do not tire yourselves by speaking too much. When we reach the water, we will have come to the end of road. Until we get there, do not ask me any questions."

"No," Asha said. "I can't walk anymore. I shall rest here, you old man."

"We will rest," Sorve said.

"I just want you to reach your freedom. Do not be angry, my Princess. If you're tired, then we will rest."

The three of them sat down under a tree.

"Sorve, I want to drink water, please. Please find me some," Asha begged.

"You stay here, make some fire. I will try to find some water and something to eat. I'll be back soon."

"You get some rest, Princess. I will deal with the fire. As far as I know, Sorve is a good hunter. So, he'll be back with something."

Asha didn't care about what he said. She wanted Sorve beside her. She wanted him to love her always. To be sister and brother was not their fault.

"Did you sleep?" said a voice.

"Asha, come on drink some forest fruit juice," she heard another voice.

Sorve laid down beside Asha, who was under the tree.

"We stay here for tonight, then we will continue our journey tomorrow morning," Sorve said.

"If we respect the old man's experience, we should respect the young man's courage," Orfin said.

"Then you should pick some more wood for the night, Orfin."

"Yes, sir," said the old man and then he left to collect some wood for the campfire.

When Orfin came back with the wood and put it in the fire, the princess turned to Orfin.

"Why do you help us without expecting anything?"

"I explained this, my Princess. Since I am the only one who can help you, I feel a responsibility to do so. Please don't be suspicious."

Silently, Sorve vowed to keep an eye on the dwarf.

"I don't know what you know and this makes me feel anxious," Sorve said, eying him warily.

"Your words hurt your servant, sir. Let's listen to our stomach's words..."

Sorve stripped the skin off the rabbit and handed it to Orfin.

"You cook it."

Orfin stood up in order to cook the meal. The prince sat down under a tree.

"If we don't meet trouble tomorrow, I'll take you to the temple where the Shadow Creatures live. You can live there, if you want. Nobody will know who you are, and none of your people can cross that border. You'll be safe, but you'll have to serve the Shadow Creatures."

Sorve was trying to understand the situation.

"If our people cannot pass through that border, then how shall we pass it?"

"Leave that part to me. This is not that hard for me. After taking you there, I'll go on my way."

"Well, where will you be going, Orfin?"

"You better not ask too much. Also, knowing where I am going will not make you gain anything. I was just looking for a good company for my journey."

"Good company? Didn't you ever have a family?"

Orfin didn't want to answer the question.

"Let's eat something," he said.

Sorve checked Asha and made sure that she was good. He turned to Orfin.

"We should extinguish the fire now. Or else they'll find us very easily."

"You know better," Orfin said.

"You seem very comfortable. This makes me worry that we are moving towards disaster. My heart feels this way. You should prove that it'll be good for us to trust you."

Orfin looked into the prince's eyes:

"Could you prove everything you know and everything you're sure about, Sorve? Now, get some rest."

Prince Sorve looked at Asha. He remembered Ughulte's words.

"When you feel sad, distressed, watch the most distant point. Watch distant mountains and forests, the sky... They will help you forget your problems. When the time comes and you need to listen to your heart, then retreat into a place that resembles the *kurgan* (or burial chamber)."

He then slowly fell into sleep.

***

"Tie them up!" King Sodu said with a loud voice echoing through the darkness.

Asha and Sorve woke up with a start, looking around and trying to understand what was going on.

Sodu dismounted and stood in front of them with anger, "How dare you do this! You two will bear the consequences of this disaster!"

He squeezed his son's throat. Bristling with rage, he yelled at both of them: "You have brought shame on your family and the whole of your country."

Brother and sister sat there gaping at Sodu, too shocked to speak.

"Tell me that this isn't true. This is impossible. You can't see each other as lovers."

He stopped for a while.

"Ughulte!" he screamed. "Burn these two trees. But before, make sure that these two are tied to the trees tightly."

"My lord," Ughulte said. "You're making a rash decision. There are things to tell you. Please, make your decision after you have listened to me."

"What are you talking about?"

***

"Come next to me, Ughulte."

King Sodu was sitting on a log. Ughulte preferred to stand up while listening to the king. He knew that the king was badly in need of speaking to someone. So, Ughulte waited for him faithfully, keeping still.

"Where are they now?" the king asked.

"We put them into different tents, my lord" he said. "They were very tired from this journey. However, we can depart tomorrow morning."

"Is there any news about that dwarf?"

"He must have run away when he saw us coming. The men I sent to look for him returned a minute ago; unfortunatelly, he is nowhere to be found. As Sorve tells it, they don't know who he really is; he only told them that he would help them. But obviously he knew whom he was helping."

The king sat in silence.

"Ayulke," he finally said. "The only woman I loved in this world. The woman who made me proud of being a king and a father... While you were in my life, we were all under your light. You completed our weak sides. You entrusted our children and our country to me. I love them very much. I know what I'm doing right now is wrong, but I don't know if I would love them this much if you weren't their mother. I want to punish them for staining your memory."

Ughulte couldn't look at his King's face.

"Now, they need your love more than our anger."

The king closed his eyes. He was about to cry.

"I was almost going to kill my children, Ughulte. What kind of father am I? During these years, maybe I couldn't love them as I should have loved them. Maybe that's why this curse happened to me. Am I being punished?"

The king cried in silence. Ughulte could not answer any of his questions.

"This is the game of traitorous people in Lumen. Don't you think so?" the king said. "They kidnapped hundreds of our people. They plundered our lands. They did not accept living with us nor did they give up the bad things they did to our people and country. The only thing they wanted from us was blood and sorrow. They're making fun of us by harming our people. Yes, no doubt. This is their game!"

"I suggest you not to think this way, my lord. Even if they caused many problems, Lumen would not want our end to be like this. This is a different problem."

"What? You think that dwarf did this by himself? I'm sure those traitorous people showed him the way."

"We agree that Lumen is our enemy. However, they don't have the courage to destroy us. If we don't exist, then they won't have places to plunder. So, this problem comes from somewhere else."

"If we say that you're right, what kind of people thought that we deserved such a disaster?"

"I don't know. This won't be easy to solve."

Ughulte relaxed, for the king had not understood his last words. "For now, I have a solution, my lord. As soon as we return to the palace, we should invite Sennemur to visit."

"Why would we want help from this old magician?"

"If we use our common sense, I think we can be rid of this curse, my lord."

The king thought about this proposal. "Even if you're right, how would we convince that old magician?"

"I shall find a way, my lord. Leave the most difficult work to me. Stay calm, and keep your common sense. Any mistake now might be the end of our country."

"You are worth too much to our country. You and your children will always be the most trustful men. You should get some rest. We have a long journey ahead of us."

"Good night, my lord."

Sodu began to think about his children again. He was blaming himself for not loving them enough. What are a mother and father but their love? How should children be loved? His mind was very busy. All of a sudden he heard a voice.

"Who's there?"

He looked around.

"Hurry up. Show yourself, I am the king of this land."

A loud laugh could be heard everywhere.

"Sefar's powerless king?"

"Who are you? Won't you show yourself, you coward?"

The king circled and looked around.

"Why don't you call your powerful soldiers to help you? Brave Sodu, the King of Sefar!"

"You can meet my anger without my soldiers, you coward."

"You looked in the wrong places during your lifetime. You are still the same, poor Sodu."

The voice was coming from behind him. The king turned back and was shocked by what he saw.

"Sennemur!"

She showed up in a fabulous long white dress; her face seemed ageless in the dark. Sennemur stood there in silence for a while, then she said, "I know the truth. You wished to speak with me. And here I am."

"How did you find me? How did you I know I wanted to speak with you?"

"I guess time has stolen most of your memory. You once knew the extent of my power."

Sodu knelt down on his knees.

"I want help from you, Sennemur. My children, my country, my throne are about to be taken from me. Will you help us?"

"The situation of your children is very sad, you noble king. You, Ughulte, and all of Sefar's people are in serious trouble."

"Please help us, Sennemur. If you do that I promise, I'll give you whatever you want."

"A king should not kneel down, Sodu. No matter how much trouble a king is in, he shouldn't compromise his nobility. However, you don't have that heart."

"As a father, I beg you. Save my children. For this to happen, I can kneel down and put my head on your feet. I only want my children to be saved..."

"I may be able to do this, I may not."

"What do you want for this? Please, tell me."

Sodu was about to cry.

"You owe me a lot, Sennemur. Now, I want you to save my children in return."

"Is that so? Do I owe you a favor?"

"Yes," the king said. "I raised Ughulte. I looked after him just like he was one of my children. Now, he's the one whom I trust the most and Sefar is proud of him. I entrusted my son to him. Do all these things soften your heart a bit?"

"Your children's tragedy tears my heart out, but I remember very sad things about the past. You sent me and my husband—my Ughulte's father, into exile, just because he didn't help you to attack the perverted people of Lumen. Then, you took my son into your palace's army to be a talented soldier and watched him grow up without a mother and father. This is the price of your fate to pay. I must say that I'm sorry, wise king."

Her words left Sodu totally dismayed and aghast. He tried to defend himself.

"What happened in the past is not my fault. You know that very well, but you still blame it on me. That was a decision of the council and it wasn't possible to break their decision. You know that very well. However, you had enough information to destroy Lumen, but you didn't share it with us. You didn't stay next to your people in their hard times."

"You still do not understand me, do you?"

Sennemur did bent towards Sodu, and whispered in his ear: "Ughulte would be a better king than you."

Then she moved swiftly away. Sodu panicked, because he thought she was leaving. As he was about to run after her, Sennemur turned her back. The king stopped where he was.

"Sefar is where the sun rises and Lumen is where the sun sets. This is the fate made by the Creator. Lumen was always jeaolus of Sefar's favorable position. They thought that your having upper hand on them was an exclusive right given to Sefar by the Creator. They wanted to end this and decided to take advantage of the richness of your country with continuous raids of plunder."

Sodu was listening to Sennemur.

"Thus, they found a way to stay alive. However, they have nothing to do with your current problem. You can't control your children's fate. Everything happened without you and it'll end that way.You only describe the way. With your silence, King Sodu … With your silence."

The king stood up in anger.

"Never! I'll never be that weak. With or without you, I'll save my children and my country."

Sennemur disappeared in one swift movement. The king was surprised and very angry.

"Did you hear me, Sennemur?"

Hearing his yelling, some of the soldiers came to him.

"Are you okay, my lord?" they asked with fear.

The king turned to them, "I'm fine. Go back to your duties, now."

"Yes my lord."

***

"We have to hurry up; we don't have much time."

Orfin grew angry because of Rtambuse's indecisive behavior.

"What are you waiting for? They're near the border of the passage. If they return to the palace, it will be difficult to take them back here."

"You forget I'm an exile. If I let them go through the passageway into Gelpagoren without Arut's rod, I die. And

I haven't seized the rod yet. According to our agreement, I will go into action tomorrow, remember?"

"Rtambuse!" Orfin yelled to the Shadow Creature dressed in black cloth. "You can cheat your king and everyone. But not me! I know well all of your games. If you really want to get rid of this severe punishment and take the Gelpagoren throne, you'll help me to reach my goal. I will tell you again, if we cannot reach them before they return back to the palace, just forget about the throne. You, Shadow Creature; you cannot even imagine how ruthless I can be, stopping at nothing to make your exile worse."

Orfin relaxed a bit when Rtambuse nodded.

"I'll return to the land of Sefar and take them to the border. You find a way to get the rod," he said.

"I'll get it at the most opportune time during the big prayer tomorrow. We must wait until then," Rtambuse replied.

"I will have them brought here by morning. Let's move now."

The Shadow Creature looked him in the eye.

"Why do these poor two people mean so much to you?"

"Your people wouldn't understand," Orfin answered.

"I don't think there's a major difference between your race and mine, except that your race has much arrogance and evil. We are both made from fire."

Orfin stretched towards Rtambuse.

"Yes, we are made from fire. But we have difference. You're made of flame, and we're made from the essence."

Orfin turned away, saying: "I'm going. There is no time for nonsense, Rtambuse. Do not disappoint me."

When Rtambuse reached the temple, he heard the voice everywhere.

"The big prayer is beginning. It's beginning. Sir Arut is inviting all of you to join."

Rtambuse stood up.

"Dear Gelpagoren's old people, pray until the day any weak creature wouldn't deserve to live."

Old Ozak was the last one to enter the temple. There were huts at both the right and left sides of the temple. The oldest people were staying there. The temple resembled a small village. Arut was waiting for Rtambuse, who went inside to see him.

"Your soul does not want to improve. We can still see its unregenerate nature. You're late again."

"I was helping Ozak, sir."

"You know how important time is for those people who live their last days in this world."

"I beg your pardon, sir. It will not happen again."

Arut wasn't looking at him. Everyone was waiting for him.

"You can go now. Preparations for the prayer have already been completed."

When the ceremony began, Rtambuse waited for the right time to swing into action. As the ceremony was going on, the old ones held their hands together and began to pray. After a while, they began to go into a trance. Rtambuse came near a very old Shadow Creature who had fallen into a very deep trance. He took the ring from his finger swiftly. After some time, Rtambuse quickly left the temple. He just needed to find the rod...

***

He was very happy because he had found the ring that would guide him in the Kalsor labyrinth. He went towards the Gasra waterfall, full of hovering fish.

There was a pond, and over it, a bridge. He was on the bridge. He put the ring onto his finger and looked at the water for a long time.

"Now, it's time," he said and then put his hand that had the ring into the water.

He began to wait. His hand began to heat up. A vibration appeared over the water. Then the water began to foam. All of a sudden, the water went still. Rtambuse was very excited by the emerging sight of the blue tree in the water. It was first the lock of the door that opened to Kalsor labyrinth.

In the distant past, those trees were planted and grown in Gelpagoren. There was a connection between these trees and the ufis birds. The wise man named Atarcat unraveld the mystery of this connection for the first time. When the birds left the tree, the blue tree was locked by itself. And chaos would surround everyone and everything. This would end when the birds returned to the tree.

Atarcat collected and put these birds over a large signet ring when they were mere spots. These little birds saw the first daylight when they were still spots on the ring. They were tied to this ring, but they were always faithful to the blue tree, thus continuing their relations with it.

The Shadow Creatures used these trees as a lock when they wanted to hide something. As some of them began to share this secret with human beings, King Kalsor had forbidden the tree. The rod that Rtambuse was looking for was made from this tree. When Rtambuse saw a blue tree, he was very impressed. The tree looked like a blue glass. Rtambuse felt the ring begin to spread vibrations.

Now, the door will open, he thought.

All of a sudden, four ufis birds came out of the water. The birds flew and then settled on the branches of this tree. As they sang, a blue light spread. The light spread everywhere. At last, the non-flowing water of the Gasra waterfall turned blue.

The shadowy lions that were the guardians of the blue tree were waiting in silence. Rtambuse walked towards the pond. He walked through the pond as it became solid. He reached the waterfall. There it was. The famous labyrinth of Kalsor... It was very hot. He watched the scene for a while.

"Lofty King Kalsor... You cannot stop the one who has power over you."

He lifted his hands.

"You cannot stop..."

He waited for birds to come. As he waited, ufis birds came and settled on the tree. The only thing Rtambuse had to do was to follow the birds. Since the rod was made from blue tree, the birds would fly towards it.

"Come on, Ufis. Show me where the rod is."

So, he followed the birds. He passed through many bridges. He kept on following them. As he had overcome many difficulties on the way, he began to think of his death...

"I'm not afraid of my death. I'm afraid that our people will lose their true leader. That's why I'm the one who has to be the most careful. If I don't change this path, maybe our people won't ever find the leader who would carry them to where they should be."

He kept on following the birds. They passed a pit of lava. He was scared. He thought that the birds were flying faster. He began to walk faster. He was scared of being unsuccesful. Thinking of failure brought him deeper sorrow than thinking of death. He looked at the birds, then fell on his knees and rolled on towards emptiness. Just a few steps down...

***

When Rtambuse woke up, he found himself on the highest step of forty-step ladder. The ladder reached a bridge. He was watching the scene. He realized that the ufis birds were impatient. Thus, Rtambuse remembered why he was there. There was a nice odor in the air. He began to follow the birds. He realized the rod was on the circled-pyramid. He passed the bridge and walked forward. He looked around. There was no one here. He raised his head and watched the blue light of the rod.

"At last, I have reached you.This would be the price for Gelpagoren to end my exile."

He waited, carried on speaking to himself. "Then, it's time to answer the questions."

He approached. He climbed the steps of the first half-circle. After he took seven steps, he reached the first half-circle shaped pond. The color of the water was black. One of the ufis birds stayed on the ground and the other three settled on a higher step.

"Here, I'm opening the last locks, Kalsor. Your labyrinth could not prevent me." The Ufis staying on the ground dived into the water, and the pond turned into blue.

Rtambuse passed the last pond. He was very calm. Now, he was in front of the rod. He approached it.

"Now, ask your question, *the Rod of Possibilities*," he yelled.

A voice reverberated everywhere: "King Kalsor's lock opened, one by one. The rod wants to hear the answer that will free itself."

Rtambuse shouted with happiness: "I'm ready to answer Kalsor's question."

"Then, the one who wants the power of rod, 'what is the answer that has no question?'"

The Shadow Creature was certain of his answer. "Existence," he shouted.

The walls lightened. Rtambuse took the rod. First, he was happy to have the rod but after a while, he began to feel anxious. He didn't know if it would harm him or not.

Orfin was approaching him.

I wish I had another way to reach my goal. I hate to work with this old man. But when it's time, this evil man will know how far one can go, he said inside.

"I see that you succeeded. Now, come with me. We have no time to lose."

"I did what you told me, Orfin. I might lose my life by using this rod. I may lose my life. I take too much of risk for this duty."

"If you call what you're living life, I have nothing to tell you. I can handle this without you. But you can't posses the things you want without me. So stop speaking nonsense."

They were very far away from the temple. When they reached the border, Orfin again began to give orders that made him angry.

"You open a corridor from here by using the rod. I'll take them to the forest."

Orfin went to the forest. As he disapperared, Rtambuse looked at the rod in his hands. The was the most powerful rod in all of Gelpagoren.

***

"Here, Orfin's coming," Asha said. Sorve stood up quickly.

"He seems calm. I hope everything's okay. Come on."

They quickly ran to Orfin.

"Didn't I tell you? We have come to the end of the road. Happy days are waiting for you. We'll talk about other details after we pass the border. Do not get scared by the things we'll see in a minute. This border is a bit different from others."

Asha was feeling a bit tired and was scared. If Sorve didn't trust this man, she wouldn't take one step.

"Let's walk towards the forest," Orfin said.

Then three of them began to walk towards the forest. When they reached it, it was very foggy. They looked at the huge trees.

"In a minute, a corridor will be opened here. You can't pass this forest otherwise."

"But you pass it all the time," Asha said.

Orfin got angry because of her words.

"This poor old man had some privileges during his long lifetime. This shouldn't make you angry, dear Princess."

The Sefar King would find them soon. He was after them. Orfin waited for the corridor to be opened. *I hope that Rtambuse didn't give up doing this. No, it could not be. Maybe the prayer did not finish yet.*

Asha and Sorve were waiting with curiosity. All of a sudden, they heard something. King Sodu appeared, riding his horse towards them. Asha and Sorve didn't know what to do. Orfin very quickly ran into the forest at the border.

Orfin found Rtambuse thinking by himself at the Gelpag-oren side.

"What are you doing here? Everyhing is about to be ruined. Now, stand up and bring them here. Or else, I'll end your life right now."

Rtambuse was shocked. He looked at the rod.

"If this is really that important, then let's do it. You go to Sefar and tell them to go into the forest."

Orfin ran to the other side of the border. Sodu was really approaching.

"Come on, we must go into the forest."

When the prince and princess saw Orfin, they calmed down a bit. When they went through the forest, Sodu was very close behind. Orfin stopped. At last, Rtambuse opened the corridor. There came a helix coiling around. They went into that helix.

"Do not be frightened by what you see," Orfin said. "They aren't real. They are only possibilities. Don't be scared. Just walk."

They were really scared, because the possibilities they saw were terrifying. Asha was holding Sorve's hand, but even this wasn't helping her fear. She was trying to be strong. Sorve began to run and he passed Orfin. He looked behind him for a while; he thought that they would have passed a great distance but they hadn't gone far at all. This was the place where people would lose their real personalities.

All of a sudden Orfin yelled.

"Rtambuse!"

At last, they reached the end of the corridor.

"We're almost done," Orfin said. "Close the corridor, Rtambuse. Close it now!"

The Shadow Creature lifted the rod up. Using the rod was making him very tired. He requested it, and thus the corridor began to slowly close. Asha and Sorve were watching with astonishment. The circle was shrinking, the corridor was about to be closed in a minute. All of a sudden, Sodu jumped inside the circle and stood up very quickly. He attacked Asha and Sorve with his sword. They could not move even one step. Orfin hounded Rtambuse.

"Take us away! Use the rod or we'll all die."

Rtambuse was trying to understand what was going on. He realized that things were really bad. Orfin and Rtambuse grabbed the rod. There came a blue light and then the two of them disappeared. However, they couldn't take the rod and the ring with them. The rod and the ring fell down to the place where they were last.

Meanwhile, the big prayer was finished. As those in the temple realized that the ring was lost, they began to look around. Arut was very calm. He was watching the king and his children from the other side of the corridor. The king and his children did not realize the ring was missing. Arut extended his right hand forward and the ring came into his hand from the place where it was. As Arut got the ring, he had the power to control the rod. As this was happening, Sodu stuck his sword into his children's hearts. Arut tried to decide what to do. When he approached them, he lifted the rod.

"Wait until your fate comes to you."

And then he straightened the rod towards them. A blue light attacked them. Arut waited until the three of them turned into blue sculptures.

***

Uselya and Ayzer were far from the temple and small village. Hirb was with them. They had accepted Arut's invitation. Uselya seemed relaxed. Her only love, Ayzer, was with her.

"There sir; Arut is waiting."

Arut was on top of the hill waiting for them. The cloth that was covering his old and small body was waving in the wind. He looked thoughtful.

As they were approaching him in silence, Ayzer thought of the old days. He thought that maybe he had had enough of sorrow and his punishment was finished.

Ayzer turned to Uselya, smiling.

"How are you?"

Uselya shook her shoulders and winked. The was Ayzer's favorite answer. He felt happy.

"We can learn the meaning of life only from the one who gave this life. Not only from the ones who live this life," Arut said when the three of them came near him. He turned to them.

"So, you came. I was waiting for you. I hope you rested well. You came very far. Sure, you came here to have answers to some of your questions. However, I must warn you that the answers will cause new questions in your minds."

"Can we start in a minute? As you said, we came a very long distance."

"Yes, we can. However, we're waiting for someone else."

Ayzer and Uselya looked at each other.

"Could our first question be who we're waiting for?"

Arut was very calm. He smiled.

"Your trip was very long, Ayzer. I hope your patience got stronger."

"We won't wait long," Hirb said. "There he comes."

They looked behind them.

"What is Zelor doing here?"

"You're not the only one who wants to solve the knot that refuses to come undone," Arut said.

Zelor approached and greeted them.

"Let's go," he said.

They reached a flat place. There were three human sculptures. They got a bit anxious.

"Here, this is the place where all of your questions will be answered."

"You, Ayzer. You were born in Ador and then sent to Blue World. There you were defeated by your weakness and thus you were called back to the place where you were born. Then you were sent to the Ralka lake to live out your punishment. From there, you got rid of the shadows and reached here. Is that right?"

All of them were shocked.

"Yes, everything is right," Ayzer said.

Arut was smiling. He turned to Uselya.

"You, Uselya. You sent the person whom you loved the most to the Blue World, according to your traditions. You sacrificed your dream of being a mother and having a family. You didn't show any sign of weakness then. However, when Ayzer returned back with his failure, you hesitated to forgive him for a while, but then you listened to your heart and ran to help him. Right?"

"You're right."

Then Arut turned to Zelor.

"You, Zelor. You're the son of Ridar, who is the Worker of Ador. You have been sacrificed by your father for your country. Even if you felt what was going to happen, you did not run away and you did what you had to do. You never stepped back from what you believed. Right?"

"You're right, wise Arut."

"I'll tell you all very slowly and you listen to me with patience. This is not a thing that is easily understood. First of all, I want you to know that you did not contact with us by conscious. You only knew Ador and the Blue World. However, you learned that in this universe there are creatures like us—I mean Shadow Creatures and Fire Creatures."

Ayzer asked a question at this point.

"We knew your existence as information, at least. However, you say that you, Fire Creatures, meet us in a dimension where we can perceive you. Can you explain this?"

Arut smiled.

"I understand your curiosity. Because you have never met a Fire Creature. Uselya and Zelor had experienced us before. They met Orfin."

He turned to the two of them, saying, "Right?"

Then Arut carried on: "Well, this is mostly about Orfin. He played a role in your coming here. However, I should tell you the story of these blue sculptures. It will make you understand much easier."

Ayzer looked at the sculptures and asked, "They're alive, right?"

"Sure," Arut said. "They're like you when you first woke up in emptiness. Time is stopped for them. When they came here, their father attempted to kill them, stabbing them in their hearts.

With the help of Rtambuse, Orfin returned here, taking them with him.

"Do you know why?" Zelor asked.

"He had a clear purpose. He wanted to have a child."

"Why did he want to have a child this way? We all know that Fire Creatures can have children," Zelor further asked.

"Yes, that's true. However, Orfin is different from other devils. His capability of having a child is obstructed by his leader. I mean, he was sentenced to not have any child. That's why he wanted to have a child born from arrogance. When he returned here, he put together Asha and Sorve's blood and Orga was born."

All of them were shocked.

"The monster Ayzer attacked in Ralka lake was Orga. Orga was imprisioned in the lake by Zelor's father Ridar, to prevent it from coming into Ador city. It was Orfin who whispered about the greed and put it into your heart, Zelor. He even asked you to forgive Orga's life, remember?"

Arut was a bit tired. Hirb understood that and went near him.

"If you are tired, you should get some rest, sir. We can finish later."

Arut looked at his assistant. He was twice his size. Hirb's strong appearance made him feel safe.

"No, I'm not that tired. There is nothing to worry about. What were we talking about?"

"Ayzer forgave Orga's life. This was where we stopped talking," Zelor said.

"Yes, he achieved that. But all his works will make him sorrow more."

"Why do you say that?" Ayzer asked.

"Because Orga is about to die and you're the one who will kill him.

"Asha and Sorve caused Orga's birth without wishing to do so. We kept them here. If we let them return to Sefar, their father would have killed them. We gave them another opportunity and seperated them from time. And by time, their existence joined with their fathers. There became a will that would destroy Orga. That will helped you in your fight against Orga. Didn't the snakes in your hands poison Orga when you were fighting with him?"

"Now I'm beginning to understand better."

"When you were in the Blue World, you harmed your heart much and that would end in your destruction in the future. We prepared roads for you to return back to Ador and we made it easier for you. If we weren't there, you would have lost yourself in that emptiness. In your journey, you should have seen a young woman who looked after many old women and children."

"Yes, I met that woman, but she never spoke to me."

"She didn't, because you're not the one whom she waited to speak with."

"Who was she waiting for then?"

"This is their business. It's not necessary you know this."

The word "young woman" made Uselya cough, and she lowered her gaze, pulling her forelocks in a smooth, reflex action.

"How is it possible for me to kill Orga and why is Orga's death this important for you?"

"Orga is not an ordinary devil. He's Orfin's strongest weapon, and the best way for him to take his revenge against his own people. We are created from flames just like the Fire Creatures, who are created from its essence – the ember. This little difference makes them superior to us, Orfin claims. This is the reason behind their arrogance. Their arrogance is born from this fire. If he stays alive, all of the Fire Creatures will be in serious danger."

"All these things have happened and will happen to the Fire Creatures?" Uselya asked.

"It's not that simple. The real danger is for us and for people. That's why we're helping you."

Arut touched Ayzer's shoulder. Ayzer was remembering his struggle with Orga.

"What's going to happen now? What do you want from me?" Ayzer asked.

"The thing I want from you is the same thing you want, Ayzer. To untie your hands and get rid of the snakes, thus giving Sorve and Asha their hearts back. You can't carry this trust anymore. This is the only way to kill Orga."

"I have a question," Uselya said. "Ayzer and I went into the pond. There, I saw a black ball. What did it mean?"

"Ayzer wanted you to trust him, but there wasn't much trust in your heart. At last, it chose the right way."

"It was only a hallucination?"

"No. That was the most true moment for your two hearts."

"How can you be certain that we trust you?" Zelor asked.

"I don't know that."

After they spoke for sometime, they approached the blue sculptures.

"Ayzer! The snakes on your hands did not come to you with your wish. However, your will can make them leave. If you really want to do this, then you can be rid of them. They are in the hearts of these two people."

Then he looked into Ayzer's eyes.

"When you're ready, stand up and go next to these young people and extend your hands towards them."

Ayzer took a deep breath.

"I'm ready."

Zelor and Uselya were watching. Ayzer slowly walked towards the scupltures. As he was walking, he felt like the snakes were moving. He began to think about these two young people and their father. He untied his hands. When the snakes saw the daylight, they tried to hide. Then they began to wait without moving. When nothing happened, Ayzer looked at Arut.

"They want to touch the ground. Put your hands on the ground," he said.

Ayzer slowly knelt down. As the snakes touched the ground, he felt a heat spreading through his body. His body began shaking. He was about to cry. He pressed his hands upon the ground very strongly. He could feel the snakes' desire to go into the ground and mix with the sculptures. He closed his eyes and took a deep breath. Very thin splits appeared on Ayzer's hands. They began to get bigger and much more blood was coming out. For a moment he opened his eyes and wanted to see Uselya. However, he could not do this now. The snakes were trying to mix with the ground by hissing. When they left Ayzer's body, Ayzer felt very cold. This coldness ended the sorrow in his body; he was relaxed. After awhile, his body was turned upside down.

Zelor and Uselya wanted to help him, but Arut prevented them.

"Let them renew themselves," he said.

Ayzer was breathing very slowly. Uselya approached him. Arut smiled at him. Then, Uselya and Zelor's hearts filled with trust.

***

The first snake moved towards Asha's wound made by her father. Then the snake turned back and went towards Ayzer with the other snake. They touched his feet. One of the snakes went into Asha's wound just like water. The other one went into Sorve's wound in his head. The two snakes disappeared. The wounds in which the snakes went through began to heal. Arut understood that everything was going well. He took a deep breath. The wind began to blow from Tuda forest.

"You bring news of great importance," Arut said to the wind. "Be next to us."

The wind continued to blow and began creating an eddy. Asha began to turn around Sorve and Sodu. The circles that was drawn in the air had shrunk. The color blue appeared everywhere and the wind blew faster. First, Asha's hair appeared. With the power of the wind, Sorve and Sodu got rid of their blue covering. Arut watched in silence.

When the wind stopped, the three of them began to breath slowly. The people who were watching them ran to help. Zelor held Asha, he carried her to a room for rest, putting her head on his chest. Arut and Hirb helped the others to their rooms. Ayzer sprang to action a bit.

"We should wait for them to come to life," Arut said.

"How long will this contine?" Zelor asked.

"We did what should have done."

"So everything is fine?"

King Sodu couldn't move well, but he looked around as if trying to understand. He still couldn't hear.

"Yes, that's it," Arut said.

**

"Please, try not to stand up. Get some rest. You should sleep well, Princess," Uselya said. She had made Asha's bed and helped her put on her gown. She looked lost. When finished with Asha, Uselya ran to Ayzer. Before she could find him, Arut stopped her.

"Dear Uselya," he called. "Don't be afraid. It's me. I was wondering how the Princess is?"

"She's fine. Sleeping."

"I wanted to thank you for your help and devotion. You should know that your favors have reached much farther than just this country. Even if it was really hard, you all chose the right path. Be careful about your feelings for Ayzer. He had to be here, in this situation. Most of the things were not in his control. You should always be at his side. You should know that in his heart, your place is as fresh as the first day. If that weren't the case, we couldn't have overcome this difficulty."

"I'll always keep your words safe," she said.

The old man smiled: "Good night, dear Uselya."

When she came into the room, Ayzer was watching the ceiling. He ran to her and held her.

"Let our mornings and night be bright. One breath with you raises a thousand suns."

"Do you realize what's going on, Ayzer? The things we've been through are like magic. However, I just realized that we can be the architect of our own experiences. What we lived through might be called a fairy tale by others."

"When I left Ador, I never thought that we could be next to each other again.Now, we're together. We solved our problem and I fully trust Arut," Ayzer said.

"Yet you feel different beside me ..."

Ayzer laughed.

"You're right. The Ayzer you knew when you left is different from this Ayzer."

"You'll always be the same as the first day I met you. My feelings for you haven't changed."

They both fell into silence.

"Now, how do you feel? You saved a dynasty. You must be tired," Uselya asked after a time.

"I didn't save them, Uselya. They helped me realize my salvation."

"You saved them and you saved yourself. Come here, let's eat our meal together."

***

Zelor looked at the meal on the table and didn't eat anything. He kept thinking of Asha. He darted an embarrassed glance over Sorve's shoulder at Asha's face.

Her breathtakingly beautiful green eyes, her stunning face and her exquisite manners... His feelings towards her were different. He began to see Asha's face everywhere. The only think he could think of was Asha.

I've been through just as much as Ayzer. This must be my fate, he thought.

As he was thinking of his meeting with Asha, he fell into a deep sleep.

***

As Arut was on his way to his house to sleep, he met Hirb.

"Did the old ones sleep, dear Hirb?"

"Most of them, yes. Don't worry, they did not ask many questions. I only informed them about the visitors' health."

"I hope you didn't talk to them much about today. Right, Hirb?"

"Please, relax sir."

"This isn't about a lack of trust or privacy. It's just that I don't want them to be unnecessarily curious. They'll meet them tomorrow morning, anyway."

"Yes, sir. I never had doubts about your decisions. You know this as much as I do."

Arut held his young assistant's hands.

"Your loyalty is very deep. Your loyalty is a good example for our people."

"Do you want me to accompany you to your home?"

"No, there is no need. After checking those who are very ill, I'll go to my home. Good night," Arut said.

As he was about to leave, he remembered something and turned back.

"Do not forget to send clean clothes to our guests. Madda will help you with this."

Hirb was surprised.

"All this time, didn't we wait for them?" Arut said with his usual smile.

Hirb left to finish his duties. Meanwhile, Arut went to check on a house on the edge of the village. He knocked quietly, but there was no sound coming from inside. So he went it.

"Didn't you sleep yet?" Arut asked when he saw Notan.

"Come in, my sister's son. Did you come for a visit or do you want to talk to me?"

"I only wanted to check whether everyone was doing okay."

"Let me ask you: who is worried about your health?"

"Hirb is a very devoted assistant. As long as he's beside me, you don't need to worry about me."

Arut sat down next to the wall.

"Thank you for your help today."

"Do not exaggerate. I just want my last days to be peaceful. I won't ask about them."

"I know that you know everything."

"I am afraid I can't pass any comment on this issue," Notan said. Then he continued, "When you were a child, you didn't speak much either. But you were always certain of what you were doing. You believed in yourself. This always surprised us, which you liked. I don't think you'll do anything wrong now."

"Thank you for trusting me. I always followed in your steps. Maybe you're right. Speaking too much does not suit me," Arut said.

"I don't know what's right or wrong, and I can't say whether time will move quickly or slowly. I don't control what happens; I just act according to the events."

Notan laid down on his bed, saying: "I better sleep, instead of speaking more."

He fell into sleep quickly. His bed was made of Gelpagoren clay. This clay minimized the amount of *Ziz* and water his body lost.

When Arut saw that his uncle fell asleep, he left the house and began to walk towards his own house.

***

Asha opened her eyes. The daylight touched her face. Then she covered her face with a cloth that was covering her body. Where was she? Where were her brother and father?

There was a knock on her door. Outside was a young woman's voice:

"May I come in, Princess?"

Asha didn't say a word. The door was opened very slowly.

Uselya smiled at her.

"Good morning, Princess."

Asha lay in silence.

"How do you feel this morning? I hope you're feeling better."

Asha still didn't say a word.

"It's normal that you're surprised. However, there's nothing to worry about. You're safe here."

Asha moved the cloth from her face,

"Where am I? And who are you?"

"You're in Gelpagoren," Uselya said.

"Where are my brother and father?"

"They stayed in another room last night. Arut set aside a special room for you to help you feel comfortable."

"I have no idea who Arut is. Are my brother and father well?"

"They are fine. It's time to wake up, Princess Asha."

Uselya came near the bed.

"Is everything okay?"

Asha shook her head.

"Then, let's get ready now."

"Get ready?"

"Yes. There will be many gentlemen who will accompany us. We can't go out like this, right?"

"You're very beautiful," Uselya said.

"What kind of preparations must you do?" Princess Asha said, behaving as if she didn't hear her compliment.

"I'm talking about you. A girl this beautiful should look after herself."

"No," Asha said. "I'm okay like this. Please tell me if I'll see my brother and father."

"Sure, Princess. They'll come to the breakfast, too."

Asha understood that she could trust Uselya. She did not have another choice... At least she looked more friendly than Orfin. She also needed a new dress.

"Would you like to know my name?" Uselya asked.

"Please forgive my behavior. I'm just a bit shocked."

"Haven't you heard anything about Gelpagoren before?"

"I kind of remember some things. But they're fearful things. I guess they're the tales I heard when I was a little child."

"Those tales should stay in childhood."

She took a dress in her hands.

"This is a very nice dress. It'll be perfect on you."

Asha was a bit embarrassed. While Asha and Uselya were talking to each other, there was another knock. Uselya opened the door. It was Hirb, who brought a mirror. He greeted Uselya, gave her the mirror, and left the room.

"The bathroom is on this side. Now, I have to go, but I'll come back in half an hour. When I return, we will go to breakfast."

After she left, Asha felt very relaxed. She looked into the mirror. She didn't see what she was searching for.

After half an hour Uselya came back. She was impressed when she saw Asha.

"All the things I heard about your beauty were real. You're gorgeous!"

In the past, Asha would have been very disrespectful towards this kind of compliment. However, this time she was really embarrassed hearing Uselya's compliments.

"If you're ready, we can go. The gentlemen are waiting for us."

"Yes, I'm ready."

The two of them left the house and they stopped in front of a house near the waterfall.

"You'll see your brother and father in a minute."

Hirb welcomed them in front of the house. They went inside. When Asha saw her father, she ran to hug him. Sorve ran to them, too. They cried silently. Sorve held his sister's hands.

"The bad days are over. Now, there is nothing to worry about."

Sodu turned Asha.

"We're with friends here. You already met with Uselya. The wise man Arut is the leader here. The man next to him is Ayzer. He's from Ador city and Uselya is his lover. And here is Zelor. He is the son of Ridar, who is the leader of Ador."

Asha greeted them with love. Then she sat down. After Hirb came in, they all began their breakfast. The house was very peaceful.

Hirb served the the guests wheat paste.

"Welcome, everyone. We can start," Arut said.

They all began to get to know each other and had a lovely time during breakfast. Zelor found Ayzer very courageous. While they were speaking to each other, Asha turned to her father.

"When will we return home?" she asked.

The guests were shocked by the question.

"Sir Arut, please do not misunderstand me. I'm not judging your hospitality. However, I want to be in my home and make up my mind. I feel like I can't make it up while I'm here. I hope my words do not hurt you."

"Dear Asha, we know that you're very emotional right now and that you never want to hurt us. It's really natural that you miss your home. Going into Tuda forest made you cross the border from your home. I'm sure, staying here and getting some rest will make you feel better. As long as you stay here, you'll find the help you need. Be sure of this."

Asha seemed to be convinced after these words. Zelor was listening and he still could not look into her eyes. After he heard that she would delay going home, he felt very happy and began to eat more. Arut wanted to change the subject and he turned to Uselya.

"How do you find our food? Are our breads as delicious as in Ador?"

"In Ador, everything has a diffeent taste. However, yours taste is delicious as well."

"Zelor, you're very quiet. Don't you like the table?"

"No, everything is well prepared. However, as far as I know, Shadow Creatures do not eat such things. I wonder where you found these."

"You're right. We have many things that differ from what you have. However, this doesn't mean that we don't share similar tastes, too. Everyone deserves to taste this delicious apricot jam, don't you think?"

They laughed together.

"See, Shadow creatures learn some things from human beings, too."

"I hope you only learn nice things," Ayzer said.

All of a sudden, Arut grew serious.

"Badness is everywhere in this universe. Every creature learns it naturally."

Arut was making plans in his mind for the next few days. Breakfast would not be enough for them to get to know each other. He knew that. He needed to find other ways. Hirb would help with this. However, he needed Uselya's help, too.

"Can we take a walk after breakfast," he said to her.

"Yes, that would be great. We can watch waterfall a bit."

The others were surprised by her answer.

After having breakfast, Zelor, Asha, and the others went to the Gasra waterfall near the Ralka lake. Uselya remembered the things that had happened a few days ago. So did Ayzer. Uselya and Ayzer realized that the fish and the lions weren't there anymore. Uselya went near Ayzer.

"The fish and lions aren't here. Did you notice?"

"We'll learn this later. But I don't think Arut wants his visitors from the Sefar country to learn many things. They would want to remember their past, just like me."

They all began to walk towards the flower garden.

"There are many things I want to know, Arut," Sodu said.

"I know."

"This magic mirror controlled the fate of my children and my county. You've helped me a lot. But how will I explain this to my people? Even if I had solved this, there is a possibility Asha and Sorve will remember what happened, right?"

"How long have you been on the Sefar throne?"

"Thirteen years whileQueen Ayulke was alive and twelve years after she passed."

Arut didn't say anything more, so as not to make him worry.

"Everyone missed the past's happy days, right?" Sodu said.

"Not everyone has nice days to remember from the past. I'm sure you appreciate it that you do."

"Well, let's return to our subject. Including me, you're the person whom everyone trusts here. Would you guide the way for us?"

"I can't guide the way for you. I can only help you as you go. And I promise I will do anything I can."

"I don't want my children to remember what happened. Or else how would they look into their eyes again? It would be like entering the tomb alive."

"I can help you. It would be more accurate for them to meet face to face with this problem and to remember it. However, you know that we have a rod that controls possibilities. If you want, I can make it so your people and you do not remember anything. Everyone can forget the events that happened after Princess was lost."

Sodu was shocked.

"How could this possible? Everyone in a big country will not remember anything?"

"Isn't this what you wanted?"

"Does the rod have such power?"

"It would be truer to say that this is a special condition in Sefar."

"Could you be clearer, please?"

Arut looked behind him to check what the others were doing. They were far enough away that no one could hear them.

"It's not that complicated, King Sodu. However, it's not that simple, either. We'll meet you after sunset at my home. Then, I promise you that I'll tell you everything I know."

Sodu didn't have another choice.

"Then, let's go and have a look at what the young ones are doing."

***

Arut and Sodu were not terribly interested in the waterfall. After finishing speaking, they began to walk towards the temple. They walked through the small streets of the town. They first encountered the old shadow creature,

Mende. Mende greeted Arut and the guests. Afterwards, Arut took them into the kitchen where lunch was prepared.

"Here is where we cook meals for our guests in Gelpagoren."

"What does the sand in these boilers do?"

"Our eating habits are different from your habits, as I told you before. We don't like much variety, especially when we get old. In these boilers, our main meal is being cooked, and it is made from Nashi fruits."

Then, he greeted Kalnu.

"Dear Kalnu, what did you prepare for lunch for our guests?"

"We tried to cook meals that would appeal to their taste buds."

"Then, we wish you luck."

"Thank you, sir."

***

They carried on walking around. King Sodu admired the temple from outside and was very impressed.

"It must be hard to sustain such a dome. Who built this place?"

"It's an ancient building. The name of the architect is kept alive in the name of our town. Goren... Gelpagoren means the miracle of Goren."

"Gelpa-Goren, Gelpa-Goren..." Zelor repeated. "It really deserves this name."

***

It was time to have lunch. They all went into the large living room where the Shadow Creatues were having their meals. The place looked like a kitchen. There, they saw wizened old men, Ozak and Sizida. The old Shadow Creatures formed two rows to welcome the guests.

They began to have their meals. Hirb and Ayzer spoke to each other. At the beginning, Asha was a bit scared, but then she realized she liked these people. Deasher and Naferis were talking with each other.

"You always liked the world. You were such a punk," Deasher said and then laughed.

"You lived like you were already dead, just like today. I'm happy that among the young people in Gelpagoren, nobody takes you as an example."

Deasher got angry.

"I should have beaten you up."

Naferis imitated him.

"See, he wanted to beat me. I wonder how you could do this..."

Then they began to talk to each other in a more friendly way. They were close friends.

Kotahe asked the guests a question.

"Who can lie to me by looking into my eyes?"

This question disturbed Arut.

"It's not time for this, Kotahe. Let's not disturb them. I'm sure they'll play this game another time," Arut said.

"What kind of game? I'm curious about this," King Sodu asked.

"It's an old game. I'll tell you later."

"Okay, then. We shall talk later."

***

That night, King Sodu and Arut met each other. Arut began to tell him the story of Sefar. King Sodu listened in silence.

Hirb took Ayzer, Zelor, and Sorve to the meadow. They were going to play Gelpagoren's game. Hirb explained the rules of this game.

"Attention and balanced power should be used together. Whomever does this best wins this game."

Each team built two castles. Each team had to destroy the other team's castle. They all enjoyed playing this game.

***

At night, Sorve and Asha spoke to each other when they were alone.

"I want to ask you something but I don't want to hurt you," Sorve said gently.

"Nothing is like we knew or thought before. You know that, right, Sorve?"

"Yes, I know that."

"Come on, ask me. I wonder what you are curious about."

"Do you remember?"

Asha didn't answer.

"Yes, Sorve. I remember everything. The poison poured into our hearts. I remember everything..."

"However, we were saved by the good people."

Asha had been rubbing his shoulders, and she stopped.

"You've really started to look like our mother," Sorve said.

"How do you know that? You were only a child when she died."

"You weren't that much older."

"But I remember better than you."

After a while, Asha left the room and went to see Uselya.

***

Zelor was trying to control his intense feelings for Asha. "I should be decisive and courageous," he said to himself. He kept talking to himself. He called his inner voice a "fantastic clown."

He was walking through a field of purple flowers. He thought of some drawings in his mind. He saw Asha everywhere he looked. As he was walking around, he suddenly saw the *real* Asha.

"I hope I'm not disturbing you," she said. "I was just out walking."

"No, not at all. I was wandering around, too. I didn't realize that you came here."

Asha sat down and this made Zelor feel much more comfortable. The two of them talked about the sights. Then, Asha asked him a question.

"Did I weigh too much?"

"I don't get it."

"Don't you remember that when I woke up, you were carrying me?"

"Of course, I remember."

Asha smiled.

"Did I weigh too much? Did you get too tired?"

"No, you weren't heavy at all. I only was trying to help you and your family. Besides, there was no time to think of anything else."

"I didn't have an opportunity to thank you before. Now, I want to thank you."

Zelor only smiled.

***

Arut was looking out the window. Hirb came in.

"You look very tired, sir. You rest today. I can finish everything."

"Is the rod in its old place?"

"Yes, sir. I put it there as you ordered."

"Is the ring with you?"

"Yes, sir."

"I guess you're right, I should go now and get some rest. However, I'm not comfortable with the placement of the rod. Rtambuse reached there and I'm anxious that he could again. Do not forget to bring the ring to me tomorrow morning. We can go and check together, to see if we can find a safer place.

"Yes, sir."

Right after Arut left the temple, Hirb saw Sennemur coming in.

"Welcome. Sir Arut just left to go home."

"It would be better not to call him sir for a while."

Hirb didn't like this answer.

"Did he want the ring from you?"

"Yes, tomorrow morning he wants to change the rod's place. He wanted my help."

"Poor Orfin. His first plan was more impressive. The afflictions he has suffered must have made him absent-minded. But what can people do about it? Everyone pays the price of their choices, after all. Poor Orfin, poor Orfin," Sennemur said and laughed up her sleeve.

Then she turned to Hirb, the young Gelpalian next to her.

"You must be cold-blooded. This is easy for us."

Hirb said he will do his best.

"Tonight, we have to change the rod's place. We can't take any chances."

"Are you scared that Arut will take it tonight? He seems very tired today. I don't think he'll be able to wake up."

"If I know him, he'll try for it."

"But he wanted me to bring the ring tomorrow morning?"

"He doesn't need your help on this subject. He spoke to you about this because he didn't want you to suspect him."

"How could he learn where the ring is?"

"For now, we proceed like he doesn't know. However, as I told you before, we can't take any chances. Now, let's go and change the place of the ring. Then, if you want, you can follow Arut and see whether I'm right or not."

Sennemur looked at Hirb, who understood that he had to shut up.

"Where is the ring now?"

"In my room at the back of the temple."

"They gave you room, then. Now, I understand your sensibility towards Arut."

"It's nothing to do with the things they afforded me. I always try to do my duty as well as I can."

"I can see your excitement. Now, take me to the room."

Then they went to his room.

"Here's my room."

"It's not very safe here. You must have taken special precautions," she said.

Hirb handed her a box he hid behind a secret wall. Sennemur quickly opened the box and saw the thing she was looking for.

"For now, we have no problems. We can solve the other part tomorrow. You stay here. I'll be around. If Arut comes here tonight, you should be awake. If he insists on taking the ring and changing the place of the rod, we shall have no option but to get rid of him," Sennemur said.

"Will you kill him?" Hirb asked in a state of shock.

"I told you at the beginning. If you want to help me with this business, you have to be cold-blooded. Never forget the reason of your guests being here. We will need to kill Arut if he insists on it. If I see you doing anything wrong, you will have the same ending."

Hirb clenched his teeth. He wasn't scared for himself, but for Arut.

"Don't worry, this likely won't happen."

Then Sennemur left the room to check out everything and then find a nearby place to hide for herself. Hirb lay down on the bed but could not fall asleep. He kept thinking about Arut.

It was well past midnight. Hirb felt fine, because Arut didn't come to his room. Sennemur came in instead.

"Now, you can sleep. I checked Arut's home, and he's sleeping."

"Let me show you a place where you can sleep," Hirb said.

"Don't think of me. See you in the morning. And do not tell anyone about our meeting in the morning, especially your guests."

"Won't you inform sir Ridar about your coming?"

"Not now. Stop worrying about all this now."

***

In the morning, the three of them were in Hirb's room.

Arut pretended that he was happy with Sennemur's abrupt visit.

"It's very nice to see you. It's been a long time. You didn't tell us that you'd come here. Anything wrong?" he asked.

"No, everything is fine. Thank God. However, after you stopped time in Sefar, there's nothing left to do for me there, so I decided to visit you. How is Gelpalian doing – and how are your guests?" Sennemur asked.

"If we couldn't get the rod on time, they wouldn't... Whatever, everything is fine here."

"They all have become good friends. They really got used to it here," Hirb said with an irritatingly fearful tone of voice.

Seeing how fearful Hirb was, Sennemur decided to swing immediately into action. She said, "I would like to see them. Especially, I would like to speak to Asha. But unfortunatelly, I can only do it later on."

Then she turned to Hirb.

"Do you not consider me as a guest? Come on, run quickly and bring us some food," she said with a gurgle of laughter.

Hirb rushed to the kitchen unwillingly and brought some food. When he came back, the plate in his hand fell to the ground. Sennemur was checking Arut's dead body. She had choked him while Hirb was gone. When Hirb finished crying, he saw that Sennemur was wrapping Arut in a black shroud.

"If you're done crying, could you help me a bit? You're younger and stronger than me."

"Why do you do this? What does the black cloth mean?"

"You just do what you're told. We don't have time to talk."

After they finished wrapping the body, Sennemur turned to Hirb.

"Now, we have to protect him from sunlight for a week and make sure the others suspect nothing. Can I trust you on this?"

"Please understand me. This is really hard for me, but I always do my best for my duty. I'll do the same now."

"Tell them that Arut has left for the palace where he'll meet the king and will not come back for a week. They should not suspect anything."

**

Hirb told the guests that Arut had gone to speak to the King of Gelpagoren. Hirb also told them that in Gelpagoren, the king consults with Arut on many issues. For a week Hirb would be looking after the guests.

"If you need anything, just let me know. For the week, I'll be able to fulfill all your needs."

King Sodu was bothered that Hirb talked about another king. He was now in an unknown land where he was welcomed by its frail old people, instead of the king himself. Zelor and Uselya were not concerned. After he informed them, Hirb went to the temple.

**

"Shall we send this message tonight?"

"Yes, tonight. Even now..." Sennemur said.

"Are you sure no one suspects us? Everything is alright so far, right?" she asked.

"Everything is on the way, do not worry. While I look for some firestones, you can write the message."

Hirb went outside to bring some colorful firestones. Sennemur sat on a table and began to write the message. Then she began to wait. Hirb came into the room. He had a few little stones with him.

"Put them here. Remove the lamp."

Hirb brought a box that was kept under the bed and then put it on the table.

"I haven't done this before. You better open it."

"There's a first time for everything. You might have to do this in the future."

Hirb was very helpless. He went near the table and looked at Sennemur.

"Come on. Don't be a coward. It's only a simple box. I never thought you'd be this scared."

Hirb opened the box. A messenger lamp came out of the box all of a sudden. Sennemur was able to catch the lamp jumping up into the air. Then, Hirb handed the little stones to Sennemur. She took one of them and settled it into the lamp and took a deep breath. She then blew strongly towards the lamp. The lamp started to glow.

"I want you to know that this is one of the stones we use to communicate with each other. Everyone has a different color of stone. Blue is my color."

Then, she took a yellow-colored stone.

"This is Arut's stone. When you light the lamp with this, your message goes to Arut. The blue ones, however, bring me messages."

"It's good I learned this. Maybe, one day, I'll have it, too."

Sennemur took the paper from the table and brought it closer to the light of the lamp. The paper began to darken. Then, it strangely turned pure white and began to flow into the lamp as bright light. The lamp soaked up all the light. Then the lamp burned out.

"Unless something goes wrong, he will be here at the expected time."

***

"Come on, Hirb. Wake up. The time is near."

"Sir Ridar! Welcome."

Ridar only smiled.

"Don't we need to do something to finish our duty?" Sennemur asked.

"You're right, Sennemur," Ridar said. Then he turned to Hirb.

"Could you please take us to Arut?"

"Please follow me, sir. This way."

They went to the room where Arut's dead body was. Hirb opened the soapbox. It was the seventh morning since Arut's death.

"Well done," Ridar said.

Ridar and Hirb took the dead body out of the soapbox.

"We must carry the body of the shadow creature to where the sun first reaches."

Hirb took the dead body on his shoulder.

"I will carry him, Sir Ridar."

The three of them climbed up the hill. When they reached the top, he set the dead body on the ground very slowly.

"Take off the cloth, young shadow creature," Sennemur said.

Hirb got a bit angry, but he took off the black cloth from the dead body.

"The seven days are up. Arut, you must return now," Ridar said.

Then he turned to Sennemur. "Could you give me the yellow stone? The sun is about rise," he asked.

Sennemur handed the yellow stone to Ridar. Ridar put the stone on Arut's nose. With his other hand, he closed Arut's mouth.

"Arut will wake up with the sun's light. His first breath should be yellow stone dust."

Hirb could not wait and asked him a question.

"What if his first breath is different?"

Sennemur smiled.

"I don't think that will be a problem. You can't see Arut's shadow anymore."

Hirb didn't like this joke. Ridar didn't care about it. After a while, Arut opened his eyes.

"Thank God, you returned."

Arut seemed a bit tired.

"I returned, but it wasn't Orfin who stole my shadow. It wasn't Orfin," he whispered into Ridar's ear.

Arut and Ridar didn't say anything more. They carried him to the temple so he could rest. Ridar didn't say anything to the others about what he heard. He waited for Arut to rouse. He would talk to Arut.

***

"I told the others that you'd return tonight. They began preparations already."

"Nice," Arut said. He was lying on the bed and watching the ceiling. They were in Hirb's room with Ridar.

"Where is Sennemur?"

"Last night, she said that she couldn't sleep well. In order to get some rest, she went to one of the next rooms, sir."

"I hope there wasn't any problem while I was gone."

"Everything went well, sir."

"You can go now."

Hirb left the room.

The two old friends looked at each other.

"How are you? You look tired," Ridar said.

"Yes. Many things that we didn't anticipate happened."

Ridar approached him. "What kind of uncertainty is this? It upsets you greatly," he asked.

"You know that I sent a message to you and Sennemur when I realized that my shadow was captured. I guessed that Orfin would want to capture the rod, and that he would use my shadow to do so. However, this time things were worse than we thought."

"What happened?"

"You know Orfin has his own way of capturing a shadow. In his method, whoever has their shadow stolen cannot see or remember anything."

"I know this."

"This time, I witnessed something new. It was not him who wanted to capture me."

"Are you sure?"

"I didn't tell you the worst part, yet."

"What could be worse than this?"

"Somebody in the Blue World convinced Arin that Oen could be cured. This mysterious person is healing the body of our Ayzer."

"This is terrible. Ayzer has exerted too much strenuous effort to mature, and we are threatened with losing him at a time when he has shown the progress we expected from him. The enemy we have now proves himself to be worse than Orfin."

"Don't lose hope. Together, our peoples have surmounted many hurdles over the centuries. This is difficult to handle, but we can solve it."

Ridar began to walk around the room.

"What do you think?" Arut asked.

"I think that if Ayzer is getting well, then we have to send someone anew from Ador. The other students aren't ready yet. The only name that comes to mind is Zelor, but it's impossible to send him now. He is not fully prepared for this journey."

"We talk about this later, when you feel more relaxed. Be with us tonight. You can meet with the guests of Sefar and at the same time, see your son."

"You think that I still have a son?"

"You should be proud of your son and he should be proud of his father."

Ridar didn't respond.

"You can meet us at dinner, thus you can speak with Zelor. Also, when everything is finished, you can take Ayzer and Uselya with you and bring them to Ador."

"No, it's not good for me to do this," Ridar said. "This wasn't in our plans. My son has a journey to finish."

"I'm not sure whether growing older is good for us."

"I thank God for being old."

"You're right, there are things that can only be done by old people."

"After you see Sefar's people and Zelor off, me and Sennemur will come here and get our things. Then, I'll take Sennemur to Ador."

"I don't think she'll come with you," Arut said. "She doesn't like to be far away from the land of Sefar."

"I know that. A woman's heart is a bigger grave compared to a man's. I believe that I'll convince her."

Arut called Ridar next to him: "I want a small favor from you, my friend. The secret I whispered to you this morning better stay between us."

"I would like to know what worries you this much."

"We can take care of this. There is really no need to share it with you or anyone else for now."

***

After dinner, Azyer asked the others to take a walk. Asha and Sorve asked for permission and then left with the crowd.

"What do we have to do with Kotahe? At this time?"

"Let's be quiet. I want to see how serious the old man was about what we told us," Sorve said.

"I saw him coming home after dinner. He must be there."

Sorve could not object to his sister anymore. They went to Kotahe's home. He was in the garden.

"I guess you came here to play the game."

"Yes, we came here to learn that game you told us about," the Princess said.

"I see. If you're ready, we can start."

"Yes, only her," Sorve said. "I've had enough of games. You can start. I'll be waiting here in silence. Or else I can go outside."

"This is the Princess's choice. If she wants, you can stay. Either way is okay with me."

Asha looked into Sorve's eyes.

Sorve left.

Kotahe and Asha were alone.

"Why did your friend react when you told us about this game for the first time?" the Princess asked.

"His reaction is widespread in Gelgaporen. We don't share everything with people. This is because we have different tastes than humans. Thus, reality appears in different ways to us and human beings. Human beings generally don't understand."

"I see. However, why did you accept to talk to me? Now, I'm curious. I'm a human being and I may not understand."

"Possibly. However, in this game you'll give the answers, I'll ask the questions. This much is easy."

"This game doesn't seem logical."

The old man looked into her eyes.

"You have deep valleys in your pupils. Birds are flying. Some are hopeful, some are worried, some decisive. However, none are happy."

"What else do you see there?"

"Walls. There are many walls in your eyes. Also in your heart. Whomever has the courage to destroy the walls in your heart is the real hero."

"I thought you'd ask me questions. However, you're talking about me."

Kotahe smiled.

"The questions must have scared you a bit."

"That's not true."

"Questions scare everyone. There are many questions we can't answer, even in our hearts. We sometimes have to tell lies in order to hope..."

"I believe that I can respond to every question asked of me," she said confidently.

"This is impossible. I'm lying to you now; there is no such game, and it never existed. Maybe you will forgive me, or maybe not... But the thing I will tell you now is important. You should let your heart decide. You can't control it all the time. It does not beat only for you."

Asha was a bit upset. However, she was impressed with his last words.

"Thanks for taking the time. I shall think about what you told me."

From Sefar to Valmeniar

Asha was looking out the window, choked with grief. She remembered everything she'd been through with her brother.

The people of Sefar wanted to celebrate their return. King Sodu was anxious for his daughter, who was remembering everything. He wished she would not remember anything...

King Sodu accepted Sennemur's help. Sennemur was with them. However, Sennemur left the palace on the second day of her visit. No one knew where she went. Zelor and Asha were not as close as they had been before. This was difficult for him. Asha was trying to look strong. When she got bored looking out the window, she wanted to take a walk.

"Eshni, could you come here?"

Then she realized that she badly needed to grow out of calling Eshni all the time, as she was already sent to exile. Eshni had left a deep mark in her heart. Indeed, she had determined her fate. But was this really all Eshni's fault?

She kept thinking about her past and what she should do now. Then, she heard King Sodu's order.

"My lady, our King wants you to meet a guest. He's waiting for you in the garden."

Asha was surprised. *Could it be Zelor?* she thought.

"Do you know who the visitor is?"

"I do not, my lady."

"Then, could you help me to get prepared? I would like to know who the visitor is."

***

As Asha began to walk towards the garden, she thought of the guest. Who could the guest be? She saw her father and a woman talking to each other.

Asha was not well enough to receive any unexpected visitor, but Sodu insisted. He hurried away, saying: "I leave you alone."

The old woman waited for the king to go away.

"How are you Princess Asha, my sister's beautiful daughter?"

Asha was struck dumb with what she just heard. The woman really looked like her mother. She was totally lost for words.

"Thank you. How are you?" she could say at last.

"You look more beautiful than your mother. If she were here, she'd be proud of you."

"Yes, she could only be proud of my beauty... Because I wasn't worthy of being her daughter."

All of a sudden, Sennemur's face changed.

"I know what happened. There is no reason for you to feel this guilty. I also know this!"

Sennemur suggested they take a walk through the garden.

"Can we sit down here? You know that I'm not as young as you," Sennemur asked when they reached the roses.

"Sure. As you wish."

They sat down.

"I don't know how to talk under such conditions…" The princess trailed off.

"Is there anything special you have to tell me? Is this why you're so anxious?"

"I have many things to tell you, but I'm not anxious. It's just that I'm a bit undecisive. My inner voice tells me to stay quiet. But I don't think one can hush her inner voice all the time. My inner voice always provided me a path. Nothing has meaning without this voice."

They talked to each other for a while. Asha was beginning to feel better about her coming .

Asha was in a good mood now. One morning, she wanted to see Zelor and she sent him a message that she would like to talk to him at lunch. Zelor received the message while he was spear training with Ughulte. He tried to hide his excitement.

At lunch Zelor was anxious, but Asha was happy. They didn't speak much. Asha went to her room very quickly when they finished. Zelor was trying to understand what was going on. Then, after hearing the servant's message, he felt happy again.

***

"We've had such a good time in Gelpagoren. Remember?"

Zelor didn't say a word. Asha realized that he was excited, so she carried on talking.

"There is one difference. Remember when you wrote a name on a tree with a pocket knife? Now, it's me who is doing that."

Zelor looked at the body of the tree. He felt his heart go out to her."

"This is my name! How did you learn to write it in Adorian script?"

"Never mind how I learnt it. Tell me if it is right"

"Perfect. You wrote it very well. Who did you learn it from?"

"That's not important. Two names are written on two different trees and they're in two diffferent countries."

Asha's words made Zelor's heart ascend. He held her hands and looked into Asha's eyes.

"Are our hearts as big as two countries? Are they enough for two countries?"

"Our love doesn't have to be enough for anything. Ours is real and will last forever in spite of everything."

They kept seeing each other more often. Sodu was very happy for his daughter recovering from trauma with such a great man.

A few weeks later, Asha and Zelor's wedding preparations began. Even Sorve seemed to be glad about this. Sodu visited his daughter one night before the wedding. He began to cry as he entered her room. Asha hugged her father.

"What's wrong? What happened, my dear father?"

The king tried to smile.

"You can't know how happy you make me, my dear daughter."

"Then, why all these tears?"

Asha began to cry, too.

"That's enough, father. Please stop crying. You seem as if you're going to leave. I can't handle this much."

Sodu understood this was too much for her, so he said "goodnight" to her and then went to his room. Later, the two of them spent the night at Queen Ayulke's grave...

After the wedding reception at the palace, Sennemur was waiting for Sorve in another room.

"My child, there are things that I should talk to you about. Could you please allow some time for me tonight?"

"Do you want me to marry someone?" Sorve asked in jest.

"No, my dear. I want to speak about other things. It was a nice wedding and your sister seemed very happy."

"Yes," Sorve said.

"Men may lament such situations. A little trip with this old woman would be good for you. If you want, come with me."

"In fact, I feel a bit broken. I don't want to leave my father alone here."

"It won't be a long trip. He has a groom who will help him."

"Okay, then."

Sennemur was very happy.

"Then, we'll depart tomorrow morning. Be ready very early in the morning. Now, there is one more thing to do. Send me Zelor. I want to speak to him about your sister. He has to know how to protect our trusts."

"I'll send for him."

After awhile, Zelor came in.

"Congratulations. I'm very glad to see you happy."

"Thank you, ma'am. Your approval is really precious to me."

"You should not be embarrassed anymore; you're part of this family."

"I'll try, ma'am."

"I want you to take care of Asha. Always be next to her."

"Hereafter, I'll live only for her. Don't worry about this."

"I don't want to take much of your time tonight. Good night."

"You, too, ma'am," Zelor said and he was about to leave the room. All of a sudden, Sennemur, pulled out a handful of dust from her pocket. The room was lightened in a strange way. As the light touched Zelor's eyes, he fainted. She opened his shirt and looked at the black moles on his back.

"I am surprised to see that you have grown this much?"

She put her thumb and forefinger on one of the two moles and took off a white bug under the skin and threw it into a jar. She did the same for the other mole. Then she put medicine on his wounds. Then Zelor's wounds closed. As the light disappeared, Zelor came to life. He left the room as if nothing had happened.

The next morning, Sorve and Sennemur departed. They reached Malvo through the Gushe mountains; then they arrived at Nassan village, which was situated on the foothills of the Sudol mountains. Some hospitable villagers welcomed them. Sennemur did not tell them who they were.

The villagers didn't ask many questions to these strangers. After dinner, Sennemur asked for permission, and then Sorve and Sennemur went to the room that was prepared for them. Sorve laid down on the bed and after awhile he heard a voice. He looked around but could not see anything. Then he jumped to open the door. There was a young boy looking at him.

"Why were you watching me? Is peeping a common practice here? Why are you here? Why are you curious about who I am?"

"I know who you are," the child said.

Sorve was surprised.

"How do you know me?"

"I don't know, but I know you."

"Then tell me: what is my name?"

"I know your name in a language that you don't know yet."

Sorve was surprised.

"A language that I don't know and my name in that language?"

Then he laughed.

"Whoever told you a fairy tale, well done. Now, leave me alone. I need to sleep. It's not kind to disturb guests."

"I know this," said the child, who seemed about five or six. "However, no one tells me fairy tales."

"Okay, then. Tell me my name in that language."

The child quickly ran to the stairs and answered his question. Sorve began to get some rest.

In the morning, they thanked the villagers and left the village. They walked for a while.

"We have finally arrived, my dear nephew. This is the place where your heart shall be at peace."

Sorve looked around. There was only a big forest.

"Here?"

Sennemur didn't answer. She turned back and lifted her hands towards the sky. Four falcons settled on her arms. Sennemur whispered something to them. They flew away immediately. They disappeared and after a while they returned. She did the same. Then they flew away again.

"I don't want people to know where I live."

"Are you afraid of the Lumen barbarians?" Sorve asked.

"Maybe," his aunt said. "Maybe I'm just obsessed with privacy."

"This doesn't seem like a comfortable place. Especially for a woman."

"Do not hurry up to decide, my nephew."

She looked at the ground and then hit her right foot three times on the ground. After, a wind began to blow. The wind was growing in intensity. Leaves began to fall in front of Sorve and Sennemur.

"Would you like to take my hands?"

Sorve held out his hand. After each step, Sorve realized that they were rising from the ground.

"Don't be scared."

"I'm not scared."

"There is my home," Sennemur said, pointing. "These trees are my friends and they always protect me. Besides, all creatures around here are under my control. As I told you before, privacy is really important for me."

She showed him her house.

"See, that's my house. It's also your house now."

"My father told me about some of your powers, but I didn't expect this much. I'm impressed."

Sennemur's house was even more beautiful than it was from a distance. Two servants welcomed them. Sorve decided that this place would be good for him. They went to the guest room on the first floor. Servants brought them fruit juice.

"I thought you were living alone. I mean, without no one around you."

"Nevermind. These people and this city have nothing special. It is good to have some people around; they do chores around the house. That's all. There is nothing to talk to them about."

Sorve was silent for his first few days there. His aunt didn't ask anything of him. She wanted him to get some rest. After dinner, Sorve was in the garden. Sennemur thought that the time had come...

"Don't you think now would be a good time to discuss and share our problems?"

"I'm not sure. It's been a long time since I have shared my grief with anyone. I even forget how to do this."

"Since you came, you have been very quiet and absent-minded, Sorve. Don't you like it here? If you want, we can walk around the city tomorrow."

"I have no problem with you or your city. However, as I was coming here, I hoped to find something, but I haven't found it... I think this place is one of the stations of my journey, not the destination."

"If I say that I don't understand much, will you get angry?"

Sorve took a deep breath.

"You and I. I mean, there are many things that you don't know about my family, dear aunt. It's like we just met each other."

"If you tell me those things, then we'll have opportunity to get to know each other better."

"It's about love. I fell in love for the first time. So far, I haven't shared this with anyone and I don't think I can share it. However, now I want to share this and find a way out for my heart... In Sefar, Eshni and I were in love. The last time I saw her, I knew she still was in love with me."

"Do you still love her?"

"I can't say that I am still having a passionate feeling for her. It's kind of like a period that comes after love. It's a demand for a wife, a child and to feel responsible for them. And to do anything just to make her happy. I caused everything; I'm the responsible one. I left her helpless. She had no one with her..."

"Even if I don't know the details, it's good to feel affection for someone. And to understand your mistake. If you don't really love her, then how will you make her happy?"

Sennemur stood up.

"Think until the morning. I'll ask you again in the morning whether you truly love her or not. Then, I'll give you a choice. The Creator has created many paths for us. I'll show you another option. Now, I better go to my room."

Sorve felt better. He could not wait for the morning. At midnight, he knocked on his aunt's door. She invited him inside.

"Couldn't you sleep, Sorve?"

"I want you to inform me about my way after this. Could you forgive my impatience?"

"The best thing for a boy who wants to do something for others is to open his way immediately. Take off your shirt. I want to see your back."

"What for? What's going on?"

"You'll see in a minute. I hope you're not fond of comfort."

Sorve took off his shirt and turned his back. Sennemur approached him. All of a sudden, he felt a burning on his right shoulder and then smelled burning flesh. He turned back immediately.

"What was that? Are you torturing me?"

Sennemur laughed.

"No, this is only a sign for your journey. You'll benefit from it when the time comes. I hope you know that your journey is not an ordinary ride."

Sorve was deeply embarrassed.

"I'm sorry. I didn't want to say anything wrong. I guess it was because it hurt."

"It doesn't matter. Well, I better tell you some more things."

She applied an ointment to his wound and the wound healed quickly. She made him sit down in a chair.

"It's only a seal which will help you on your ardous journey to unknown worlds where the modes and principles of life are totally different from ours. Your journey will not come to an end when you find Eshni. You will still have to do some things to save her from exile. This seal will make you breath in those worlds... I'll give you this seal, because Eshni will need it as well."

Sorve was very serious.

"When I find her, how will I know the places to go? Do you know the way?"

"Don't worry. Eshni knows about this. You only have to reach her unharmed."

"You speak as if you're not sure about that..."

"I only speak about what I know. Do not interrupt me. I still have things to tell you."

She stood up, went towards the library and took a little jar from one of the shelves. Then, she showed it to Sorve.

"Do you see these two?"

She showed him two cocoons at the bottom of the jar.

"Here it is. It's your sap. Before they become butterflies, you must find Eshni. Together, you will need to do certain things in order for her to be saved from the punishment of exile. If you find her in time, you must impress this seal on her back. Then, wait for the butterflies to leave cocoons. They'll know the seal and you'll be able to breath during your journey. Thereafter, Eshni will tell you what to do. You, the Prince of Sefar, are you able to take all these risks?"

Sorve felt very decisive.

"I'll find her and we'll be happy in Sefar."

"Then, go to your room and sleep well. Tomorrow I'll give you other things that you'll need and then I'll see you off, my dear nephew, Prince Sorve."

Sorve lay down on the bed and began to think about Eshni. He thought of the times when he was nineteen and Eshni was seventeen. He thought of those days again... He was seeing Eshni's black eyes...

The first time they understood that they were in love, it was raining. Sorve was going to look for his horse, Tirfi, but all of a sudden he saw Eshni and the rain began. They walked together that night. After that night, they both knew that they were in love.

Eshni had to work a lot more for Asha. Thus, Sorve and Eshni could not see each other much. As he was thinking of those days, he could not sleep. He turned right and left and at last he stood up. He went to the window. He began to speak to himself...

"God knows how much I hurt you..."

He took a deep breath.

"Whatever happened in the past, I know what I should do and I'll do my best, my darling."

Afterwards, he began to feel relaxed, as if he had seen Eshni's face. He turned back to bed and fell into a deep sleep...

***

"You're earlier than I thought, Sorve."

"Why did you think that I'd wake up late, dear aunt?"

"Whoever falls asleep late cannot wake up early. Nevermind."

They came to the barn at the back of the house. There he saw his horse! He was shocked.

"Tirfi! My friend! It's you!"

He caressed its mane. Then he turned to his aunt.

"When did you bring it here? And how did it happen?"

"It's not important. Stop paying attention to your horse and come with me."

Then they went to the front of the house.

Sennemur handed him the bag she had prepared.

"I don't like goodbyes... I don't believe that people who have ties can leave each other. In this bag, you'll find things you need. Enough food and water. Protect well the seal and the cocoons. The only thing you must know is that whatever you do, do not dismount from your horse. Never. If you do, then you will be lost and no one will find you. Now, go on and find what you're looking for, my nephew."

"I'll come to visit you my aunt, after everything is finished. And I'll take you to Sefar. There, you'll live with us forever."

He rode his horse and tried to control it.

"Do not control it. Your horse knows where to go."

***

Sorve mounted his horse and charged at full gallop; he was now far away from the city. He came to a steep hill and turned back to watch the city from a distance. It was a place he hadn't been before…

He thought of his aunt. He said to himself, "Dear aunt, you're a perfect woman." Then, all of a sudden he thought of Eshni. When was the last time he saw her? Where was she? And how was she now?"

Riding off for long hours, Sorve felt very hungry. He took out some food from the bag and began to eat on his mount. He wished that Tirfi could talk to him during this journey. He remembered the first day, when Ughulte brought him Tirfi…

Tirfi galloped down the hillside as if flying. Sorve said, "No one would believe me that I was on such a road."

The rain became stronger. Tirfi was galloping without any pause, never wearying. "Tirfi! When will you stop? If you go on like this, we'll both be exhausted."

Tirfi wouldn't listen to him.

"God! When this journey is finished, I want to do many things… Please be with us, O the Owner of the earth and the sky."

He struggled through the blinding rain for hours, telling Tirfi, "Try hard, my friend; we'll make it!"

When the rain stopped, Sorve could see clearly. They descended to a plain where he saw a lake.

"The water seems to be drinkable."

He extended from the horse and tasted the water.

"Very delicious water!"

He drank a great deal, but he was still thirsty.

"My friend, what kind of place are we in? What kind of water is this? You drink and then it makes you more thirsty... We have to be patient."

Then he decided not to drink. The water was very strange. Tirfi was good, but Sorve was sweating and losing so much water... He couldn't think of anything but getting a drink. He fainted. When he came to life, they were moving forward in the water. He looked around. He looked for Tirfi's body. Then he saw Tirfi two steps ahead, feeding itself.

"No, this cannot be!"

"So, you woke up!" said a nice voice.

Sorve turned his back and saw Eshni.

"Eshni! It's you. At last, I found you."

Eshni didn't say a word at first. She was looking into her lover's eyes.

"Are you okay?" Sorve asked.

She bowed her head, saying: "I have waited for this day. You came to me."

"Now, we have years to live together."

He held her hands. They stayed like this for a long time.

Then, all of a sudden, Sorve realized something.

"Where is the jar?"

"Do not panic! They're all here."

She handed the jar to Sorve.

"Do you what this is?"

"Yes, I know. Sennemur gave it to you, right?"

Sorve was surprised.

"You know?"

"Nevermind. It's a long story. We better speak about this later. Sennmeur must have told you about what happened."

"I can't exactly say that I know everything. But Sennemur told me that you knew everything."

"Then, impress that seal on my back. Meanwhile, I will tell you what's going on here."

"I want you to know that every mistake I've made towards you was because of my love. I could not prevent this love from turning into an ambition. Thank God that He gave me a second chance for this love. During those black days, Sennemur found me. She told me my fate and the way to get rid of it..."

"I had to twist in the wind because of my sin of ambition. My punishment was to be a mother to my weakest conditions. Sennemur showed me a hut where I would be a mother to my childhood and old age. I had to not to complain about this. Because for each complaint, the number of child Eshnis and old Eshnis would increase. At the beginning, I was strong. I behaved with affection. But as time passed, my patience decreased. To feed and clean them began to be difficult for me. Now, I am the keeper of six child and six old Eshnis. Sennemur told me that they're not human beings, they're not even creatures like us."

"What are they then?"

Sorve touched her hair.

"Sennemur told me that they're residual spirits."

"Residual spirits?"

"In order to learn exactly what they are, we have to go to Valmeniar."

Then he impressed the seal on Eshni's shoulder and then applied the medicine his aunt gave him. All the wounds healed.

"Now, we have to open the jar."

"The cocoons and the butterflies seem ready to hatch."

"Okay, then let's go to where we have to go."

"Stop, Tirfi. Where are you going? Tirfi, Tirfi," Sorve called as the horse walked away.

"Let it go," Eshni said. "It finished its duty."

"Will it go to Sefar?"

"It'll go where its home is."

Sorve hopelessly watched his horse leaving.

"Do not worry for Tirfi anymore. See, the butterfiles came out of their cocoons. We do not have much time left. We need to go to Valmeniar."

Two butterflies landed on their seals, which hurt. Suddenly, a door appeared near them.

"Here is Valmeniar's door. You cannot pass through this door if you don't put a handful of soil on your forehead and assume a humble attitude. Valmeniar is the country from where life is distributed. And towards life, one always has to be modest."

"What is it behind this door waiting for us?"

"This is an easy question. We'll want freedom for the children and the elderly who are tied to me."

"Who are we asking for this?"

"Belis and Belia. They're old siblings who devoted themselves to the universe's balance. And there is a stone we must take from them. I don't know what kind of property it has. We shall learn the rest from them, if we can take the stone from them."

"Then, let's not waste time."

They put their foreheads on the ground. And Sorve touched the door; it opened. The two of them went inside and passed through a corridor. Afterwards, they saw a woman and a man waiting for them.

"The ones who are unbalanced have come," the old woman said.

"They came here to re-stabilize," the old man said.

"Is this the right time?"

"Yes, it is."

Eshni and Sorve looked at each other. Sorve greeted the man and woman.

"Hello."

The man and woman responded in kind.

"It's time for the woman to speak," the woman said.

"Yes," said the man. "Who are you?"

"We were sent here by Sennemur," Eshni said.

"She is the Worker of the Council of Serenity," the man said.

"Now it's your turn, young man," the woman said. "Where did you come from?"

"We came here to get the help Sennemur told us to seek."

"Everyone should speak when their turn comes," the man said impatiently.

"If balance is broken, everything is turned upside down," the woman added.

"Serenity is balanced by serenity."

"The ones who are unbalanced, have come to get the stone."

"Why should we give them the stone?" the man asked.

"The stone belongs to their fate."

"You're right."

"Then, they have to give us something that replaces the stone – so that the balance is not broken."

The woman turned to them, saying: "Now, come with us."

The old man had long white hair down to his shoulders. They were walking towards a house. The house was in a big garden. There were two fountains in front of it. The two of the them sat in chairs in the garden.

"Come closer. Slowly," said the woman.

Sorve and Eshni did what they were told.

"Who ruined the balance first?"

"It was Orfin," the old man replied.

"Orfin caused a great chaos. He had a child born of arrogance. Orga," the woman said.

"Orga was killed where it was born," the man said.

"Orfin fell into a deep sorrow at his son's death."

"Two tears fell from Orfin's eyes. Normally, Fire Creatures never cry," the woman said.

"Those tears landed on a stone," the man said.

"Because of those tears, other residual spirits were released."

"Sennemur knew that the stone hid those tear drops; thus, she looked for the stone but could not find it."

"We gathered the stone when we saw it broke the balance," the woman added.

"Sennemur is a very self-sacrificing Worker and is an important member of the Council of Serenity."

Sorve and Eshni were listening to them. The woman stood up.

"You want a very important thing from us."

The man stood up, too.

"Then, what will you give us in order to protect the balance?"

Sorve answered, "I'm the prince of Sefar. My fate has been planned for me. I've embarrassed the ones I love and my country. The same things happened to Eshni, too. You, the Guards of the Balance! We came here to askhelp from you. Do you want to help us or find reasons to refuse us? If you won't help us, this means that our fate is sealed already. Give us the thing we need, and then we can go our way."

"You spoke well, young prince. To specify that fate is not in the hands of one person."

"You never come to the end by ignoring the great artist and his work."

"In order to see him, you should not be unbalanced. That's why, you must give us something."

"You can't take anything from here, unless you replace something with another."

"Don't you have the butterflies?" the woman asked.

"If you leave the butterflies, we will give you what you want and tell you what you should do."

"They make us breath. How can we give them to you? Besides, they're within us," Sorve said.

"You can give them to us when you leave," the man said.

"We can remove them from you and you won't get hurt," the woman added.

Sorve stood up.

"Then, they're yours. If you keep your promise."

Woman smiled mockingly.

"Prince excellency, don't get angry."

"Anger is the biggest enemy to balance."

The two of them stood up and came near to Sorve and Eshni. They took out the stone from the little pond of a fountain.

"Here's the stone you're looking for."

"Take it."

"To the Balance Garden."

**

Belia and Belis made Eshni and Sorve meet Lork, an old giant, who would accompany the visitors on their difficult journey to the Balance Garden.

Lork was one of the residual spirits in Valmeniar.

"Follow me," said Lork. "Sir Ilshuba is waiting for you."

They began to climb the stairs. They followed Lork without saying a word. When they reached the Life Garden, they saw a young man who looked like Sorve next to a spring in the distance.

"I can go no further. Sir Ilshuba is waiting for you there," Lork said.

"Welcome you noble people of Sefar. You brought light and peace! Come here, please," sir Ilshuba said.

Sorve and Eshni were were impressed by the beauty of the garden. It was full of colored flowers and trees.

They went next to Ilshuba standing by the spring.

"We're the ones that Sennemur sent. We came here to ask for help."

"I know why you came here, Eshni and Sorve. And I'm glad to see you at the end of the way. Let me introduce myself."

He smiled.

"I'm Ilshuba, the Worker of the Life Garden."

"Then, please could you tell us why there's a country called Life Garden?" Sorve asked.

"First, we drink a bowl from the fountain of life. So that our life will be freshened. This garden is a very special part of Valmeniar. It doesn't resemble the Blue World or Ador, Gelpa or Sefar. Earth is a place for those created from soil to live, Gelpa is for Shadow Creatures. And this is a place for Light Creatures. This is where the people on Earth get their life from. Anyway, in a minute you'll see how life is sent from here to Earth."

They saw some animals in the distance.

"It's beginning. Today is the day life is shared. See, they're coming. Watch them."

Various kinds of birds appeared in the sky. Similarly, one representative from every species in the land was coming to the spring en masse.

"Look at the vibrations on the water. Every species has a representative here. The representatives drink an elixir from the water of life and thus extending the life of their own kind for another year on Earth. The representatives, whose real bodies are destroyed, stay here as "residual spirits." Here, we give them different kind of duties.

The two of them were listening quitely. They didn't realize time was passing.

"Just like human beings, their representatives are free to make choices. If you look carefully around you, you'll see many precious stones here. The representatives of human beings, just like human beings, have ambitions. Because of their ambitions, the way of their getting the water of life is different from other creatures. They do not drink water. They have to take it to the earth."

"Why do they have to put in so much effort?" Eshni asked.

"This is the result of having strong will. To sustain life laboriously is the fate of humanity. It has been like this since the first human being was created."

Ilshuba stood up.

"Here comes the representative of humans."

A tall man was coming towards them. He had dark brown eyes and was carrying a large basket on his back. He came near to the spring.

"If you want, you can come closer. Maybe you'd like to see what he's carrying."

"We don't want to disturb him," Sorve said.

"Don't worry. He can't see us."

Then, Eshni and Sorve accepted Ilshuba's offer. This human representative took the basket from his back and sat by the water.. He rested for a while and then he took a bowl out of the large basket.

"See that bowl?" Ilshuba asked.

"Yes, it's really nice," Eshni said.

"It's nice and heavy."

"At the beginning, three bowls were offered to him so that he could carry the water to the earth. They were made of wood, soil, and gold. He chose the heaviest and the most beautiful one. Whereas, it was easier to carry the others and they carried more water."

The human representative bent over the water to fill the bowl. He paused for a while. He dipped his hands into the water and took as much jewelry as he could and filled the bowl with them.

"See, he put the jewelry into the bowl. This means he could not fill part of the bowl with the water of life."

Sorve seemed sorry. He held Eshni's hands.

"What does that mean? Why did he do such thing?" she asked.

"It's really clear. Due to material ambitions, many people on Earth will be killed this and every year. Because of the greed of some people, innocent people will be killed. By breaking the rules of the Creator and then by deciding on behalf of the Creator, they'll find justifications for their crimes. This is self-destruction of the race. But it was determined like this at the beginning due to their haughtiness. Indeed, the human representative was also offered to drink this water of life here just like the others. But he found it bestial because of his arrogance, and then he was offered to carry the water to the world with a bowl. Then he accepted.

"Even if he's just a human representative, he feels all the spiritual responsibility that a human being feels... I don't like this, but there's nothing we can do about it."

The human representative put the bowl into the large basket and then began to walk, almost bent double. There was a smile on his face, but this was not because of the duty he was fulfilling. It was a greedy smile because of the gold he was carrying. It was difficult for Eshni and Sorve to watch his suffering and exhaustion while carrying the water of life to the Earth. They felt hopeless.

"I'm sorry for all this grief. You came here for my help. We have things to do, right?"

They shook their heads "yes."

"Then, give me the stone you brought."

They handed him the stone.

"This is not an ordinary stone. It will be decisive for many fates. Orfin's trap will be hoisted by his own petard. This shows us how fate works in its own way. Orfin's tears will end all this suffering.

They were watching him very carefully.

"Eshni, you got rid of those residual spirits and came to the end of the journey. And you now have a pure spirit. You should protect this pure spirit until the end of your life. I'll offer you two choices. You may either go back to your world and time, or stay here as my guests for a while and get to know each other better."

They were indecisive. In order to impress them, Ilshuba made them an offer.

"Maybe you'd like to see our Earth library."

They still were indecisive.

"You shouldn't be indifferent to this offer. The things you'll see may interest you."

Then, they accepted.

"Here is the country of Light Creatues. Here, you don't need to eat and sleep. We don't get tired. We can make your transition here very easy."

Then, Ilshuba called the residual spirits and gave orders to them. Some of them were giants and some were dwarves. They prepared a place for Eshni and Sorve, a house on a hill that had a nice view and a nice garden.

Eshni and Sorve stayed in that house for some time. They didn't want to return to their country. Sorve was curious about the library that Ilshuba told them about. One night, a residual spirit named Hayuba brought them a message that Ilshuba wanted to see them. They went to see him.

"There's something I want to show you," he said.

"Shall we go to the library?" Sorve asked.

"No. However, I'll show you something that will make you understand the existence of the library better."

They walked together for a while and came to a garden. They went inside.

"Here's the record garden of Valmeniar. It's the place where the information of the library is recorded. However, I want you to look at the horizon. To where the sun goes down. They're about to come."

"Who?"

"The record carriers. If you want, we can sit on these thrones."

Ilshuba took a deep breath and then began to explain: "We record everything that happens in the World."

Sorve's eyes widened.

"To record everything that happens in the World? How is that even possible?"

"This is one of our duties. Let me explain it to you from the beginning...

"Every morning, two Light Creatures go to the World. One goes to the South Pole and the other goes to the North Pole. At a determined time, the one in the North opens the register sphere there and points it toward the South. When the rotation of the earth around its own axis is done, in other words when one day is finished, this register sphere is closed from the South and collected. Then, it's brought here by two Light Creatures. I'd tell you more, but just look at the horizon."

When they looked at the horizon, they saw two record carriers who were flapping their wings. They left the sphere in the garden and then flew away.

"They don't need eyes to see like us. And every Light Creature fulfills this duty only once in a life time. That means, you can't see them here again."

"Where are they going then? Do they die?"

Ilshuba laughed.

"Your heart is full of affection, Eshni. Don't worry, they don't die. They go to some other worlds in order to carry the records."

"Why can't they see, Sir Ilshuba?" Sorve asked.

"It's simple. This information is very precious. Including me, no one here has a right to see these records. Their eyes see what they need to see. It's not like how we see, but it's enough."

"This is all very strange."

"Would you like to see more?"

"What could possibly surprise us at this point?"

They waited for the sphere to shrink. Then, a child appeared. This child was familiar to Sorve. Then, the child took the sphere and went away.

"Here's where the records of the Earth are translated into the real language of the universe. The children do this duty. The translation is written on the Preserved Leaves and then sent to the library."

"Rendering into the real language of the universe? I don't understand."

"Yes, Sorve. This language is not understood by humans. They cannot read or write it. Any creature that has free will cannot learn this language. This is why children, and those who are weak-willed, are chosen to translate. These children are the ones who were killed unjustly. They live the life they could not live and by this duty they complete their lives. They never grow up; they always stay as children."

"Why is it impossible for a human being to learn this language?"

"In fact, it's not impossible. Only that to achieve it would be shocking. They have to widen their viewing angle. Sennemur, Ridar, or Arut can do this. You seem like you want try to do this, Sorve?"

"Maybe."

"Your courage is impressive, but such dreams will exhaust you."

Then, everyone fell quiet. They began to watch the child. The child gazed at the sphere for a while. When the child went into a deep trance, he began to write something on a grean leaf. Not much, just a few lines. When he came out of trance, he stood up and went near a tree. There, he attached the leaf to a tree. Then he ran over to Ilshuba.

"Now, may I go and play some games?"

Ilshuba handed the child a candy.

"Sure, you can go. Thank you for your work. You do it well; right and fast."

The child looked at Sorve and smiled, then ran next to the other children.

"So many trees," Eshni said.

"Yes. There is one tree for every year of the Earth in this library. When the record is completed, it will be given to its owners. Come on, let's go to the library."

Eshni was very calm. However, Sorve wasnt; he kept thinking many things. He thought of learning the Real Language. It didn't seem hard for him...

After they walked through the library of trees, they went back to their houses. Sorve was the only one who felt tired, even though no one in Valmeniar was so supposed to get tired.

In the morning, he left Eshni in the Life Garden to go and visit Ilshuba. He got permission from Ilshuba to visit the library. He began to look for that child. He passed some time sitting there. As he stood up to return back to the house, he heard a voice.

"Are you looking for me, Sorve?"

Sorve was surprised.

"Yes, but how do you know my name?"

"Here, everyone knows your name, Sorve. Here, all of the children know more than anyone in the world."

"I know that. You're right."

"Did you come here to learn what we know?"

"No, I'm not trying to learn something. I just want to remember where I saw you first. Your face seems very familiar to me."

"This is normal. In the universe, even if things are different from each other, they look like each other.

"Yes, but I'm sure I saw you before."

"Then, to remember is your duty, not mine."

The child ran to his friends. Sorve returned to Eshni.

That night, he could not sleep well, either. In the morning, he went to the Record Garden again. Then, he began to wait for the child. When the child came, he ran towards the child.

"I remembered where I saw you. You're the one who watched me in Nassan village. Am I wrong?"

The child didn't care. At last, he could not resist Sorve's words.

"Yes, I think so. If you think that you can learn this language, then you can try. I'll help you, okay? Now, I want to play a bit, if you'll let me, Prince Sorve. Okay?"

"What do you mean? I don't want that."

"Do not lie to yourself! Otherwise, you can never learn your Real Language. I'll take care of you. Now sit down here and wait for me. Okay?"

Sorve didn't know what to say. At last, he did what the child told him. After a while, the child came.

"Let's go."

Together, they went to the library.

"Sit down and look around," the child said.

Sorve did what the child told him.

"There are trees everywhere, and the sky."

The child hit his feet on the floor and seemed very angry.

"Now, you'll wait here until you hear someone calling for you. A sound that you have never heard before... You'll be hungry and thirsty. However, before hearing that sound, neither food or water will be given to you. Is this too much for you? Could you overcome this, noble Prince Sorve?"

Sorve seemed very decisive.

"Yes, I can make it. And I'm neither prince or a noble anymore. My name's Sorve; just Sorve."

"My name's Agaman. I'm your teacher."

After these words, the child went away. Sorve stayed there. He took a deep breath.

"Of course, I can make it."

The next morning, Agaman came near him.

"Not this way. If you behave with too much ambition, you'll fail. Just try to wait and listen."

And then Agaman went away. Even if things were meaningless to Sorve, he did not give up. He tried to relax. He fell into sleep. When he woke up, the stars were shining in the sky.

"Where is Agaman?" he asked himself. Then, he fell into sleep again. When he woke up, someone was yelling and this was Agaman's voice.

"Do you think by sleeping this way you'll find it? I told you not to be ambitious, but you chose to be lazy, instead. Are you sure that you'll be able to learn this?"

"It seems really hard."

The child disregarded him and left.

"Hearing your voice is much more enjoyable, Agaman," Sorve yelled after him.

Then he lay down on the ground. At midnight, Sorve woke up to Agaman's voice. He could not move but he could hear.

"This is not a thing that you can understand. This is a kindness, a favor. And if you want to attain it, you must start simply from a *point*, or *dot*. Its meaning is never known and but it is inside of everything. It is the primal point, as in the first creation of existence from a dot. Maybe it's as small as nothing, but without it, nothing can be read. And a *dot* is the starting point of any letter you will write. You cannot learn it unless you understand the *point* that makes things start and finish."

Then Sorve fell into sleep again. While he was sleeping under a tree, he had good and bad dreams. A few days passed like this. Agaman came to the library in the morning.

"At last, you made it," he said.

Sorve was moaning. The child called Ilshuba. He took some residual spirits with him and then carrried Sorve to his house. He gave Eshni some advice and then left them alone.

Eshni did not leave his side for a few days. As she was told, she gave him the medicine. At the end of the third day, Sorve came to life, but Eshni was not there. He got anxious about all his dreams. He ran to Ilshuba.

There he found Agaman working for Ilshuba. "You better not ask him anything about all those things you have dreamt and all the strange sounds you have heard. He can't explain them in any language. Do not bother asking," Agaman advised.

Sorve greeted them and turned to Agaman.

"I don't know whether I made it or not."

"You're right. You did not exactly make it. You only passed the first part. However, that was the important one, just like learning how to swim. Once you learn how to swim, then you can swim in any water."

All of a sudden, the child inside him began to move.

"Can I take another child swimming with me?"

Ilshuba smiled, saying: "You're good at bringing the subject to the point you want, Agaman. But this is not good for me."

"I didn't do anything bad. I only thought that I'd have a good time with other children."

"Okay, then," Ilshuba said. "But first finish your work, then you can go."

Agaman shouted with joy and held Sorve's arm.

"Come on then. Let's go and fulfill our duties. There's much you need to learn."

***

Agaman came into the library. Sorve was still waiting outside.

"Why don't you come in? There's nothing to fear. No sorrow. You're just like before. You won't feel hungry and thirsty anymore. Come on, come here."

Sorve wasn't afraid of going inside, but he was irritated.

"There's nothing for me to fear, my little teacher."

"That's not true. You should never say it again. Every human has to be afraid of something. The real courage is to touch the things that you're afraid of."

"If you say so."

Sorve went inside.

"Now, it's time to read, not to get rest. Come next to me. Do you remember what I told you while you slept?"

"About the points?"

"Yes."

"Sure, I remember. Your voice is resounding in my ears."

Agaman laughed.

"I whispered those words."

"Well, it sounded loud."

"Okay, then. Now, I want you to look at this leaf."

There were just a few signs on it.

"Is it one of the leaves that you wrote on?"

"Stop gazing around and look at it carefully. And tell me what you see."

"There are only some scars on it. That's all. How can I read this?"

"I told you to look carefully. Without being possessed by greed. Try to see the points there. Then, everything will come to you."

"Points, points... This makes me remember my old teacher, Hunder. The things he liked in mathematics were the points. Points on the leaf... The points hidden on the lines. Points that make a beginning and points that make an ending; points that determine our limits."

Agaman approached Sorve very slowly.

"What is there in those points?"

Sorve was lost in his thoughts.

"I see the Mediterranean. Two big crowd are getting closer to each other. There will be a big war."

"Where does the crowd come from?"

"From both North and South."

"Who is the old man coming from the North, at the end of the row?"

"The one who is walking strangely?"

"Yes, tell me who is he."

"He is a hustler."

"Where's his family; could you tell me?"

"They're in a city settled near the river. All of them are sorry. Men have gone to the war and the women and children are in big trouble. The children begin to cry. They're crying. People die."

Agaman pulled at Sorve. Sorve, who was crying, fell on the ground.

"It's okay. Eveything is finished. That was one of the recorded events. A page from the past. They're all in the past."

Sorve regained his strength and stood up.

"You've made it! My first and only student. Would you let me proud of you?"

Sorve was trying to breathe normally again.

"Now, go and tell everything to Ilshuba. I'm going to go swimming. Do you know how to swim?"

"Sure, I know how. Why?"

"Do you think you could teach me?"

The Council of Serenity

A group was gathered in a big salon. It was late at night. They sat in silence, and there was a knock at the door.

"Come in," Sennemur said.

Two people came inside. With papers and pens in their hands, they went to a table.

"Since the clerks are here, we can start," Arut said.

"Yes," said Ridar. "Let's start. We have too much work to do."

"You're the landlady, so you'll preside over this meeting," Arut said to Sennemur.

"Then, I'm opening the meeting of the council of serenity. The first thing we must do is to record the things done so far and to keep them for the members who come after us. When clerks finish their work, the celebration of serenity will start."

Ridar seemed thoughtful and Arut seemed tired.

"Wise man of Ador, Ridar. The first word is yours. Speak for the record."

Ridar walked to the window.

"I am the Worker of Ador, Ridar; I used the power given to me and opened a corridor for Ayzer. I sent him to a determined path and I prepared the conditions for him, so that his mind and emotions would behave the way we wanted. At last, Ayzer's spirit matured and he can now serve us. I did what was necessary."

"I am Arut, the Worker of Gelpa. I opened a corridor for Zelor. I sent him to the Gepose mountain, where he could feel like he was at home. I sent many men to work beside him. They looked for gold all day and night. In order to overcome Orfin's tricks, I made him stay there and gain power. Then, I brought him and Uselya here."

"I am Sennemur, the Worker of Sefar. In order to fulfill the duty given to me, I opened a corridor for Sorve. I sent him to Valmeniar after he was done with Arut. I gave him opportunities to learn the Real Language. Sorve learned it. At last, all three of these men reached a mature spiritual level and can now serve us."

When the clerks finished writing all the records, the ritual ceremony began at night. For three days, they kept constant a vigil, did not eat and drink, but lost themselves deep in thought.

After three days, when the ceremony finished, the three Workers were together. They ate and drank herbal tea.

"What do you think of our goals from the three days of Serenity?" Sennemur asked.

"First, we need to find a solution for this unlooked-for event of keeping Ayzer in the world. We must block Orfin and his evil assistant Hannas' plans over Ayzer's body. Or else, there will be serious trouble," Ridar said.

"The purpose of Hannas' slave, Dr. Feyn, is clear: to capture Ayzer," Arut said.

"Then, we must solve this problem with Ayzer."

"I don't think it would be a good idea. We should not forget that we used our power to open corridors. These corridors may not be in our control, so this could cause more problems," Ridar said.

"You're right, my brother. I have an idea. We need to seize the initiative from Hannas and reach the goal before him. Thus, we can disable Hannas through our man. Let him think that Ayzer is under his control."

"This seems possible in theory, Arut. However, I'm not sure if it will work in practice," said Sennemur.

"I think it's our only solution."

Sennemur stood up.

"Then, we must try. I'll help you all."

"Then, we must find someone very soon and send him. For this journey, let's use the White Waterfall. Let's pray for everything going right."

"Let's pray together."

"Let's pray."

***

"Is there any place more beautiful than you, Ador? You're the light of my heart," Ridar said as he watched the river from the window.

There was a knock at the door. "Come in," he yelled down from upstairs.

Ayzer and Yasev came in and greeted him.

"It's so good to see you again, Sir Ridar," Ayzer said.

"Your arrival is just like your departure; they're all in silence. I hope there is no problem," Yasev said.

"We have the same problems. With time, we get used to it. I'm really happy to see you, too. Especially, you

Ayzer! You're with your friends here. We'll always be happy that you open your heart to us. I hope now you can be at peace with us."

"Sure, I know this and it makes me feel stronger."

"Have you chosen a day for your marriage? I don't think Uselya wants to wait too long."

"We didn't want to choose a date until you were here."

"See, Yasev. Fate takes us where. Do you remember him when he was a faithful student?"

"Of course, sir."

"I called you both here to discuss an important matter. Please don't be anxious. I don't want to go into details. We must find someone from our city to send to the Blue World. Who would you recommend?"

"May we speak directly?" Yasev asked.

"Your opinions are very precious for me. There is no need to repeat this."

"The students are not ready yet," Yasev said.

"I agree with you, Yasev. However, we have to hurry up; we don't have much time. We must decide very soon."

"I would choose Nagun. He seems to be ready. He passed much time in the library and the years have matured him. I think he can handle this. What do you think?" Yasev asked.

"We should resolve this before your wedding, Ayzer. I'll speak to Nagun."

"There's a possibility that Nagun may reject this, my sir," Ayzer said.

"I don't think this will be a problem. Nagun is faithful to our teachings."

"Then, it's time to pray for Nagun."

"Yes, we must pray with our words and deeds."

***

When Nagun heard the decision, he didn't know what to say. He could not sleep for a few days. He would need Ayzer's advice. The people of Ador appreciated this. When the departure date came, the people gathered together next to the waterfall to send him off. With Ridar's signal, they fell into silence and began to pray. When the prayer was finished, Nagun approached to Ayzer.

"Your wedding gift is in the purple rock, where your name is written," he told his friend.

Nagun approached Uselya.

"I'm sorry I'll miss your wedding. My fate has determined this ..."

"Make us proud."

Nagun smiled.

"You have done too much for me. I'm really grateful and thank the Creator that I have you people. As you know, I must leave to fulfill this duty. Everyone of you will be in my heart, wherever I go."

Then Nagun fell silent.

"It's time to go, my child. God's help be with you always. You're always in our hearts and minds. And we'll be there, wherever you go," Ridar said.

Ridar whispered something to him. Nagun closed his eyes. A blue colored fog rose from the waterfall. Ridar waited until the fog spread everywhere. Nagun moved his hands up and down and through the fog, and a white road appeared. The road stopped in front of Nagun's feet.

Without looking behind him, he began to walk very slowly. They watched him into the blue fog.

Uselya approached Ayzer and began to cry.

"He's going for us, right?"

"No, don't think this way! Just like us, he goes to his fate."

Ayzer began to think about the time he spent with Nagun...

The blue fog disappeared.

"Time to return, my sir," Yasev said.

"I'd like to stay a little while. If you're at the temple, I'll join you soon."

***

With lots of questions in his mind, Ayzer began to walk towards the library. He was feeling Nagun's absence. He thought of the days they spent in the library...

He approached the books. He was looking for a purple covered book. At last, he found it.

"Here are the words!" he said. Why did he feel so much sorrow, such a big absence? He began to read the book. As he was looking through the pages, a paper fell to the ground. It was written by Nagun and Ayzer began to read it:

"I want to ask something. Is the respect we show other creatures real? Or is it just a responsibility? We are proud of our favors, and we smile in the mirror of existence. Why don't we think? Have we found the truth? I know that when God created us, He didn't want anything from us. He gave us the gift of existence. I have so many questions, and I don't expect to answer them. When one pays the price for his mistakes, he should get a gift. I've already prepared my gift."

The First Node

For months, Arin's days and nights blurred together. After Oen tried to kill himself, she could not sleep well. She had been thinking of the times she had with Oen. She even forgot to speak because she prayed too much... She was visiting the hospital every day and waiting to see him again. She was feeling very lonely.

One day, she came to Oen's room, and Oen was sent to another place for some examinations. A nurse gave her this information.

"Thank you. Is it okay if I wait here?"

"Of course. We're all used to seeing you. You're like one of us."

"Without any knowledge."

"Maybe you don't have knowledge, but you're giving power to Mr. Oen Atara. I'm sure he'll make it and return to us."

Arin was about to cry. She held the nurse's hands.

"Thank you for believing as much as I do."

The nurse smiled, "I'm sorry, I have to go."

Times passed by. Arin approached the door, but at that moment, it opened.

"Is that you, Miss Arin?"

Arin looked at a man, who was about thirty years old and had a doctor's uniform. She hadn't seen him before.

"Did you come to see Oen? Oh I'm sorry. Let me introduce myself first. I'm Dr. Feyn, and I will be in charge of his treatment after this stage."

"Nice to meet you, Dr. Feyn," Arin said.

"I have good news for you, Miss Arin."

"I felt it this morning. You won't believe me, but I felt it this morning."

"It's normal. You have spent much of your time here with him. Even if Oen thanks you, it won't be enough for the things you've done for him. However, very soon he'll be able to thank you."

Arin could not believe what she heard.

"My God, please tell me I'm not dreaming! When can I see him?"

All of the sudden doctor's face changed.

"Let's go to the cafeteria now. We have to be patient."

***

"As you know, Oen has been in a coma for months. Two days ago, he spoke to us. He said two words. This is really good. However, we must be provident. The time he stayed in a coma may have created a problem in his perception. We think we need to give it some time before he sees those who are close to him."

"I assumed that in his condition, it would be good for him to see those he loves."

"You may be right, but Oen's been through a lot. We can't leave it to chance."

"I see, Dr. Feyn. We must be patient."

"I hope it won't be too hard for you."

"I can wait. But I want you to promise me that he'll be as good as before."

The doctor smiled, "I'll do my best. I promise. Now, I must go."

"Thank you so much, Dr. Feyn."

"Goodbye, Miss Arin."

***

A few weeks passed. Dr. Feyn stated that Oen was ready to speak. She ran to the hospital, where she saw a little boy, Yuri. She began to cry. Then she caressed the child:

"At last we can be happy! Oen is better."

"I know. That's why I'm here."

Dr. Feyn was waiting for her.

"Are you ready?" he asked.

Arin began to cry.

They went inside. There he was. Oen looked better than before. Oen extended his right hand to Arin, who held it.

"Is that you Oen? Did you return to me? Are you real?"

"I'm more real than I've ever been. I had a headache last night. It was a real pain."

"I'll leave you alone," Dr. Feyn said.

"The doctor told me everything, Arin. Please forgive me for what I've done to you."

"We talk about it later. Don't worry. Get some rest."

She smiled. "I was so scared I'd lose you," she said.

Oen didn't say anything.

"Who is this gentlemen, Arin? Will you introduce us?" he finally said.

"Oh, yes. This is Yuri. He's that old man's son. He got well before you."

The child approached Oen.

"I'm glad to meet you, sir. I'm happy that you're fine. I prayed for you every night."

Oen looked at Arin.

"I'll tell you later," she said. "You know Oen, when you were sleeping, Yuri came to see you every time he had an opportunity to come. He was reading books to you."

"I thought it wouldn't bother you, since you were sleeping."

"I don't remember, but I'm sure it didn't bother me," Oen said.

"If you want, I can carry on reading..."

A few hours later, the car that would take Oen home pulled up in front of the hospital. When Oen was saying goodbye to Dr. Feyn, the doctor leaned to his ear.

"Rtambuse, from now on, you're Oen Atara! Try to get used to this. Do not forget what I told you."

Feyn heard Arin's voice.

"What are you whispering to him?" she asked.

The doctor approached her.

"I told him how lucky he is. You really love him and few men are lucky enough to meet a woman like you."

Arin was embarrassed.

"And you're a perfect doctor, Mr. Feyn. I thank you so much for everything."

They got in the car. It was long, black car. It turned left from the hospital's garden and then disappeared. The other doctors went inside. Finally, Feyn walked into the hospital, following them.

Cómo entender y superar la bulimia

Lindsey Hall
y
Leigh Cohn

Cómo entender y superar la bulimia
Primera edición

© 2001 por Lindsey Hall y Leigh Cohn

Gürze Books
P.O. Box 2238
Carlsbad, CA 92018
(760) 434-7533
www.gurze.com

Diseño de cubierta por Abacus Graphics, Oceanside, CA
Diseño de la tela original por Dorothy Turk
Traducido por Kiser y los asociados

Library of Congress Cataloging-in-Publication Data

Hall, Lindsey, 1949-
   [Bulimia, a guide to recovery. Spanish]
   Cómo entender y superar la bulimia / Lindsey Hall y Leigh Cohn.
   p. cm.
   ISBN 0-936077-38-7 (alk. paper)x
   1. Bulimia--Popular works. 2 Eating disorders --Popular works.
I. Cohn, Leigh.
RC552.B84 H35 2001
616.85'263--dc21
                    2001023707

Nota:
Las autoras y el editor de este libro tienen el objetivo de proporcionar información veraz en él. Se vende en el entendimiento de que su propósito es complementar los servicios de un(a) profesional de la medicina y/o la psicología, y no de sustituirlos.

1 3 5 7 9 0 8 6 4 2

Contenido

Introducción

Estoy bien despierta y salto de inmediato de la cama. Pienso en la noche de ayer, cuando preparé una lista nueva de lo que deseaba hacer y cómo quería estar. Mi esposo está atrás de mí, no muy lejos, camino al baño, preparándose para ir al trabajo. Quizá pueda escabullirme hacia la báscula antes de que me vea. Ya estoy en mi mundo privado. Me lleno de júbilo cuando la báscula dice que conservé el mismo peso de anoche y siento esa leve sensación de hambre. Tal vez eso acabe hoy, quizá este día todo cambie. ¿Cuáles eran los proyectos que quería llevar a cabo?

Tomamos el mismo desayuno, salvo que yo no pongo mantequilla en mi tostada, ni crema en mi café y nunca repito un plato (hasta que él sale por la puerta). Hoy me voy a portar bien de verdad, lo que significa comer ciertas raciones preestablecidas de alimento y no tomar un bocado más de lo que pienso que me está permitido. Me cuido mucho de no tomar más de lo que él toma. Puedo sentir que la tensión se acumula. Quisiera que se apresurara y se fuera, ¡para poder comenzar!

Tan pronto se cierra la puerta, intento ocuparme de alguna de los cientos de responsabilidades de mi lista. ¡Pero las odio todas! Sólo deseo arrastrarme y meterme en un agujero. No quiero hacer nada. Preferiría comer. Estoy sola, me siento nerviosa, no sirvo para nada, sea como sea, siempre acabo haciendo todo mal. No tengo control. No puedo terminar bien el día, lo sé. Ha sido lo mismo por tanto tiempo ya.

Recuerdo el feculento cereal que tomé en el desayuno. Estoy ya en el baño y sobre la báscula. Mi peso es el mismo, ¡pero no quiero seguir igual! ¡Quiero estar más delgada! Me miro en el espejo. Pienso que mis muslos son feos y se ven deformes. Veo un pelele lleno de bultos, torpe, con forma de pera. Me siento frustrada, atrapada en este cuerpo y no sé qué hacer al respecto.

Floto hacia el refrigerador sabiendo exactamente lo que hay adentro. Comienzo con los bizcochos de chocolate de anoche. Siempre comienzo por los dulces. Al principio intento que parezca que nada falta, pero mi apetito es enorme y decido hacer otra tanda de bizcochos de chocolate para reponer la que estoy devorando. Sé que hay media bolsa de galletas en la basura, que tiré la noche anterior, así que las saco y las limpio. Bebo un poco de leche para que el vómito salga con más facilidad. Me agrada la sensación de hartazgo que me invade después de tomar un vaso grande. Saco seis rebanadas de pan y las doro por un lado en la parrilla, les doy vuelta, las cubro con mantequilla y las pongo de nuevo bajo la parrilla hasta que burbujean. Me llevo las seis en un plato hasta el televisor y regreso por un tazón de cereal y un plátano. Antes de terminar con la última tostada, ya estoy preparando la siguiente tanda de seis rebanadas más. Podría comer otro bizcocho o cinco del nuevo lote, más un par de tazones grandes de helado, yogur o queso cottage. Mi estómago se ha expandido y es una bola enorme bajo mis costillas. Sé que pronto tendré que entrar al baño, pero quiero posponerlo. Estoy en la tierra de nunca jamás. Espero, siento la presión, camino y entro y salgo de las habitaciones. El tiempo pasa. El tiempo pasa. Ya casi es hora.

Camino sin rumbo, una vez más, por la sala de estar y la cocina, ordenando, dejando la casa limpia y con todo en su sitio. Por fin, doy vuelta hacia el baño. Afianzo los pies, tiro de mi cabello hacia atrás y me introduzco el dedo en la garganta, frotando dos veces. Sale un chorro enorme de comida. Tres veces, cuatro, y otro chorro de alimento parcialmente digerido. Veo cómo regresa todo. Me alegro de ver esos bizcochos de chocolate porque engordan tanto. El ritmo de la descarga se interrumpe y empieza a dolerme la cabeza. Me pongo de pie y me siento mareada, vacía y débil. El episodio completo ha tomado cerca de una hora.

Durante nueve años comí hasta hartarme para luego vomitar incluso cinco veces al día. Aunque había algunos días en que no lo hacía, los pensamientos estaban siempre ahí, aun cuando soñaba. Era doloroso y terrible. Nadie sabía de mi bulimia, porque la mantenía perfectamente oculta tras una fachada de competencia, felicidad y peso corporal medio. Sin embargo, cuando mi salud y mi matrimonio comenzaron a deteriorarse, una serie de coincidencias me enfrentaron con la recuperación y me dediqué a intentar librarme de mi obsesión por la comida.

Trabajé duramente y de buen grado, y experimenté una transformación asombrosa. A medida que los pensamientos y la conducta bulímica amainaban, pude ver para qué me habían servido todos estos años. Fueron una eficaz herramienta de supervivencia física y emocional en una época en que no conocía otra mejor. Habían sido una amiga, un amante, un escondite, una voz, una búsqueda de significado y de amor. Eran una manera de enfrentar el crecimiento en un mundo aterrador e incierto. Pero lo que comenzó como una dieta inocente se convirtió en un monstruo que amenazaba con devorar mi vida entera.

Mi curación no ocurrió de la noche a la mañana. Durante año y medio abandoné poco a poco la conducta bulímica, examinando el significado y el propósito de cada comilona. Al cabo de otro año conseguí comer algo más que sólo mis alimentos "seguros" y, por último, empecé a sentirme a gusto viviendo en mi cuerpo, en vez de sentirme atrapada. También dejé de juzgar el cuerpo de las demás personas, sin importar su forma o su talla, algo muy difícil de hacer en una cultura que fomenta el prejuicio del peso.

Una de las revelaciones más profundas que tuve en la recuperación fue que no sabía quién era yo o qué sería sin la bulimia. De modo que, para poder conocerme en un nivel más profundo, enfoqué mi atención primero a lo que pensaba y sentía en mi interior y después a mi aspecto externo. Esto lo hice meditando, escribiendo diarios y cartas, haciendo largas caminatas y entablando conversaciones profundas. Descubrí que era una persona buena y amorosa, con altas y bajas como cualquier otra y, una vez que establecí la conexión con esta vida interior, todo comenzó a cambiar. Ahora estoy sana, soy feliz y me he librado por completo de la bulimia. Así me he conservado durante más de 20 años.

En 1980, cuando mi esposo, Leigh Cohn, y yo escribimos mi historia en un folleto titulado *Eat Without Fear* (Come sin temor), no había otras publicaciones disponibles que tratasen exclusivamente de la bulimia. La respuesta fue extraordinaria. El pequeño folleto inspiró y motivó a muchas personas que intentaban dejar la bulimia; y, a medida que aprendimos más acerca del síndrome de comilona y purga, comprendimos que había más que decir al respecto.

En los años siguientes dimos muchas charlas en Estados Unidos y me convertí en la primera persona en exponer la historia de su bulimia en la televisión de cobertura nacional. Escribimos varios libros, entre ellos *Cómo entender y superar la bulimia*, con más de 125,000 ejemplares impresos en diversas formas. Además, creamos una pequeña compañía editorial especializada en libros sobre trastornos de la alimentación, escritos por autores respetados. Esta versión es resultado de nuestra experiencia personal combinada y puesta al servicio por más de 20 años de todos los que padecen trastornos de la alimentación, así como de sus seres queridos, de los terapeutas, educadores e investigadores involucrados.

Este libro se divide en dos partes principales. La primera responde las preguntas que se formulan más a menudo e incluye mi propia historia, "Come sin temor". La segunda parte ofrece motivación, apoyo, inspiración, sugerencias específicas para la recuperación, cosas que hacer en vez de atiborrarse de comida, y consejos para los seres queridos.

En el libro hay un buen número de citas en itálicas. Muchas son de bulímicas que se han recuperado o están en vías de recuperación, así como de terapeutas de trastornos de la alimentación que respondieron los cuestionarios que les enviamos por correo. Asimismo, se incluyen citas de las numerosas cartas que hemos recibido de lectoras que han querido compartir sus experiencias de recuperación, o bien agradecernos nuestro apoyo. Las personas que ofrecen sus citas han pasado por diferentes circunstancias; el único elemento aparentemente común en todas es que entienden la bulimia en virtud de sus experiencias directas con ella. Estas personas han compartido su percepción con nosotros y nosotros se la transmitimos a ustedes.

Gran parte de este libro se dirige a ti o a "ustedes", las lectoras con bulimia; y, puesto que la mayoría de las personas bulímicas son mujeres, empleamos pronombres femeninos. Sin embargo, la información y las herramientas prácticas de autoayuda sirven igualmente a los varones. Por otra parte, aunque "yo" soy la "oradora", Leigh contribuyó por igual a la redacción, las ideas y la publica-ción de este proyecto y en ocasiones "nosotros" dos hablamos en el texto.

Por más de 20 años ya, Leigh y yo hemos trabajado tiempo completo en el área de la capacitación y la edición de publicaciones sobre trastornos de la alimentación. Hemos llegado a ser reconocidos en el campo, trabajamos con la mayoría de las organizaciones estadounidenses relacionadas con estos trastornos, asistimos a convenciones nacionales e internacionales y continuamos escribiendo y hablando acerca de la recuperación.

Cuando escribí "Come sin temor" en 1980, lo hice como una forma de dar por concluida mi recuperación de la bulimia. No esperaba ni me proponía tener que ver más con este asunto. Sin embargo, compartir mi experiencia sigue siendo parte integral de mi vida, por el efecto que ha tenido en otras personas. Quizá tú muy pronto puedas formar parte de este grupo.

CAPÍTULO 1

Preguntas más frecuentes acerca de la bulimia

¿Qué es la bulimia?

La bulimia es una obsesión por la alimentación y el peso que se caracteriza por comilonas que se repiten, seguidas de una conducta compensatoria, como el vómito forzado o el ejercicio excesivo. Para un número de mujeres y hombres que alcanza proporciones epidémicas, la bulimia es una adicción secreta que domina sus pensamientos, menoscaba su autoestima y amenaza su vida. Los síntomas fueron descritos por los egipcios y se reseñan en el *Talmud* hebreo; la bulimia (del griego: "hambre de buey") era casi una práctica cotidiana en tiempos de los griegos y de los romanos. Sin embargo, en la segunda mitad del siglo xx se ha identificado a los trastornos de la alimentación como un fenómeno cultural generalizado. La bulimia también se conoce como bulimia nerviosa y bulimarexia.

En 1980, la American Psychiatric Association reconoció formalmente la bulimia. En su cuarta edición, el *Diagnostic and Statistical Manual of Mental Disorders* (Manual de diagnóstico y estadísticas de trastornos mentales) enumera los criterios bajo los cuales a una persona se le puede diagnosticar bulimia:

a. Episodios recurrentes de comilonas, que se caracterizan por: 1) comer en un determinado periodo, por lo común de menos de dos horas, una cantidad de alimento significativamente mayor que la que la mayoría de las personas comerían durante un lapso similar y en circunstancias parecidas; y 2) una sensación de carencia de dominio sobre el acto de comer durante el episodio, como la sensación de que una no puede dejar de comer, por ejemplo.

b. Conducta compensatoria inapropiada y recurrente, que tiene por objeto evitar el aumento de peso, como vómito autoinducido o uso incorrecto de laxantes, diuréticos o enemas (tipo purgante); o bien, la práctica del ayuno o el ejercicio excesivo (tipo no purgante).

c. Estas conductas se presentan como mínimo dos veces por semana durante al menos tres meses.

d. En la autoevaluación influyen demasiado la forma y el peso corporales.

e. La conducta no se presenta sólo durante episodios de anorexia nerviosa.

La lista anterior se creó para ayudar al médico a diagnosticar y tratar este complejo trastorno. Sin embargo, muchas personas, calificadas como "subclínicas", satisfacen sólo algunos de los criterios. Estos casos también son perjudiciales para la vida y es necesario que se les tome en serio.

Aunque los síntomas manifiestos de la bulimia giran en torno a las conductas relacionadas con la alimentación y con el temor de aumentar de peso, en realidad se trata de una manera de hacer frente a las aflicciones personales y al dolor emocional. Las comilonas toman tiempo y desvían la atención de problemas más perturbadores, y las purgas son un medio eficaz para recuperar el control y la sensación de seguridad perdidos durante la comilona. Asimismo, pese a que la conducta bulímica pudo haber surgido como un recurso aparentemente inocente para perder peso, el ciclo de comilona y purga suele convertirse en un escape adictivo de problemas de otro tipo.

La mayoría de las personas con bulimia son en extremo reservadas acerca de su conducta, y a veces hacen enormes esfuerzos por aparentar que comen de manera normal ante otras personas. De cierta manera sienten vergüenza de su conducta y de lo que este trastorno ha provocado en su vida. Muchas admiten ser como dos personas distintas: una que desea renunciar a la bulimia y sentirse sana, y otra que sabotea constantemente sus esfuerzos. Las mentiras y el disimulo son rasgos comunes. Algunas confiesan haber robado alimento que saben que pertenece a otros o haber escarbado en la basura durante episodios particularmente desesperados.

Aunque una comilona típica representa una gran cantidad de alimento, habitualmente entre 1,500 y 3,000 calorías, con predominio de altos carbohidratos en ellas, cada persona que la ingiere la define a su manera. Incluso una comida "normal" tal vez parezca "demasiado" a quien le aterra la posibilidad de engordar.

Son muchos los factores que pueden desencadenar una comilona: números altos en la báscula, comer algo que normalmente está prohibido o comer un poco más de lo permitido; sentimientos difíciles; un acontecimiento traumático, o algo tan inofensivo como hablar acerca de la comida. Hay quienes describen que durante las comilonas las invade un descontrol total, un impulso y un deseo desesperados de sentirse aunque sea un poco mejor. Aunque quizá se sientan feas, indignas, desesperanzadas e impotentes antes y durante un episodio de comilona y purga, después pueden sentir una mezcla de vergüenza, disgusto, mareo, agotamiento, alivio, dominio y determinación. Parte del ciclo suele incluir la promesa de que cada ocasión será la última.

Es difícil saber cuántas personas tienen bulimia. Es probable que las estadísticas no reflejen la realidad de las cifras totales, pues, como ya mencionamos, por lo general las bulímicas ocultan su conducta. De hecho, un estudio mostró que las estudiantes universitarias respondían los cuestionarios con más sinceridad cuando se les indicaba que pusiesen un toque de su saliva en el papel de la encuesta, ¡pues pensaban que se analizaría químicamente para determinar si eran bulímicas!

De las investigaciones realizadas acerca de la frecuencia de los trastornos de la alimentación, las estadísticas más confiables indican que alrededor de 5% de las mujeres en edad universitaria satisfacen los criterios clínicos estrictos de la bulimia. Sin embargo, algunos estudios presentan cifras mucho más altas. Uno realizado con estudiantes de bachillerato y universitarias informa que 15 por ciento satisfacen los criterios de bulimia y algunos expertos sugieren que quizá hasta una de cada tres mujeres han practicado ciertas conductas de este tipo. Los varones representan al menos 15 por ciento de los casos, aunque parece ser que esta cifra ha aumentado en años recientes. Asimismo, hay indicios de que, a diferencia de la anorexia nerviosa, que se ha conservado razonablemente constante en las últimas décadas, la incidencia de bulimia creció de manera significativa a principios de los años 80. Sean cuales fueren las cifras reales, un número importante, de mujeres y de varones, practican esta conducta autodestructiva.

¿Por qué enferman de bulimia las personas?

No es fácil responder esta pregunta. Así como la vida de cada persona es única, así también lo son las razones por las que enferma de bulimia y los caminos que debe seguir para superarla. En general, se considera que la bulimia es un trastorno psicológico y emocional, que a veces coexiste con otros trastornos psiquiátricos, como la depresión o el trastorno obsesivo-compulsivo.

Estudios muestran que está relacionada con un trastorno afectivo mayor y, por tanto, en ella influyen la herencia y los desequilibrios químicos del organismo. (Consulta la sección "¿Pueden los medicamentos ayudar a la recuperación?" en este capítulo.) Por consiguiente, en ciertos casos los medicamentos pueden moderar la conducta de comilona y purga o la depresión y ayudan a que la psicoterapia y otros recursos resulten más eficaces. Otros estudios han vinculado la bulimia con una reducción de la función cerebral de la serotonina. Sin embargo, las razones de fondo con las que la mayoría de las personas explican su trastorno de la alimentación son una compleja mezcla de baja autoestima, conflictos de la infancia y presiones culturales.

En general, las personas se vuelven adictas a sustancias y a conductas para evitar sentimientos dolorosos, del pasado y del presente. Algunos de estos sentimientos se originaron en la infancia; por ejemplo: sentirnos no queridas e indignas de ser amadas, avergonzadas, temerosas o incompetentes. Otros provienen de la presión para comportarnos como el resto de nuestras congéneres o ser aceptadas por ellas. Los más devastadores son los que se asocian con la baja autoestima: sentir que no valemos nada, que nuestra vida carece de valor o propósito, y que nunca nos sentiremos realizadas ni felices.

Paradójicamente, en sus primeras etapas un trastorno de la alimentación puede elevar la autoestima cuando proporciona una sensación de triunfo: en este caso, por alcanzar el ideal cultural de la delgadez. De hecho, muchas personas recurren a la purga cuando han fracasado con una dieta y temen que no exista para ellas otra manera de bajar de peso. Sin embargo, una vez que se inicia el ciclo de comilona y purga, los desequilibrios metabólicos resultantes y el escape habitual se convierten en un pozo cada vez más profundo y terminan por erosionar todo sentido inicial de la propia valía y de control. Es importante para ti, que lees este libro, recordar que las recompensas de la delgadez son sólo implícitas y, no obstante que las dietas y un cuerpo esbelto prometen una vida más feliz, ¡la promesa no siempre se cumple!

Sigue en pie la pregunta de por qué es la bulimia el escape elegido, y al parecer hay similitudes en cuanto a los antecedentes, la personalidad y las experiencias de los pacientes que ayudan a responderla. No todas estas características son aplicables en general, pero sin duda algunas lo son.

La mayoría de las mujeres bulímicas provienen de familias en las que, de alguna manera, no se satisfacen las necesidades emocionales, físicas o espirituales de sus miembros.

En algunos de estos hogares los sentimientos no se expresan y falta comunicación. Puede haber antecedentes de depresión, alcoholismo, toxicomanía o trastornos de la alimentación; es posible que la hija reconozca de manera inconsciente que el escape es la actitud más correcta. En este contexto, la comida se convierte en una droga "buena", algo que no tiene las connotaciones negativas del consumo de alcohol o de estupefacientes.

Las bulímicas suelen ser consideradas como hijas "modelo", y hacen hasta lo inimaginable por complacer a los demás. Ofrecen una fachada aceptable —aparentemente extrovertidas, seguras de sí mismas e independientes— cuando los sentimientos de angustia hierven bajo la superficie.

Quizá se las aprecie por no necesitar atenciones, por cuidar de sí mismas y por madurar pronto. La bulimia es una forma de expresar lo que no se puede decir directamente con palabras, en este caso, algo como: "Quiero que alguien me cuide" o "¿Me amarás tal como soy?"

Son muchos los casos en que se utiliza la bulimia para posponer la madurez. La hija que ha recurrido a otros para obtener aprobación y sentimientos de autoestima, y que ha asumido el papel de la "niña perfecta" porque funciona en casa, puede experimentar un miedo formidable al tener que confiar en sí misma y hacer frente al mundo exterior ella sola. A veces, esta inseguridad se ve reforzada inconscientemente por los padres, que tampoco están dispuestos a dejar en libertad a los hijos.

A menudo padres e hijos asumen papeles que limitan las relaciones y el crecimiento personal al interior de la familia. Quizá la madre refuerce la idea de que para las mujeres es importante ser delgadas. Los padres pueden verse relegados al papel de sostén económico y encargado de la disciplina, en vez de participar en la vida emocional de su hijo o hija. Las chicas, en especial, pueden adquirir inseguridad acerca de su apariencia, su competencia y su capacidad para ser amadas si no se las valora por sus propios y singulares talentos. En una sociedad donde el papel de la mujer está cambiando, las relaciones firmes con los progenitores, fundadas en la singularidad del hijo o hija, le darán la confianza y la capacidad de tomar decisiones inteligentes y negociar relaciones sanas en el futuro.

Las mujeres con bulimia tienden a ser en exceso críticas de su persona y de los demás; se les dificulta expresar sus emociones mediante el lenguaje; temen a la crítica; evitan las desavenencias, y tienen baja autoestima. Y todos estos rasgos tornan difíciles las relaciones con otras personas. De hecho, muchas de las 392 bulímicas recuperadas y en recuperación que participaron en nuestra encuesta señalaron que se sentían incómodas con las relaciones íntimas y que la bulimia era una aliada predecible, confiable e incondicional. Muchas habían sufrido abuso sexual o maltrato emocional en su infancia y a duras penas podían confiar en otras personas. Los rituales y pensamientos bulímicos las protegían de lo que podría convertirse en rechazo, abandono o algún otro posible dolor. La bulimia llegó a ser la única relación —si bien vacía— y que además les impedía experimentar un amor profundo... descrito en la respuesta de una mujer como el "Gran satisfactor".

Las participantes en nuestro estudio identificaron diversas causas de su trastorno. Muchas recordaban las razones específicas de sus comilonas iniciales, y también la utilidad subsiguiente de su conducta. Pocas pensaron que podría llegar a ser adictiva. Además de las causas originales, que persistían, enfrentaban sentimientos de culpa, reserva, efectos físicos secundarios y un número creciente de razones para querer escapar. Las mencionadas con más frecuencia fueron: aburrimiento; influencia de los medios de comunicación y la cultura; dinámica familiar; "entorpecimiento" mental; gusto irresistible por la comida; presión para bajar de peso; "euforia" experimentada después de la purga; episodios abrumadores de ansiedad; liberación de la tensión física y sexual.

A la mayoría de las bulímicas les han preocupado la comida y la dieta durante años, pero los episodios iniciales de comilona y purga pueden ser desencadenados por acontecimientos específicos, como: cambios traumáticos (graduación, mudanza a otra ciudad, matrimonio, muerte de un ser querido), aflicciones no resueltas, cambios profesionales, una dieta fallida y rechazo por parte de un amante, real o deseado. En la encuesta se registran razones específicas para iniciar el comportamiento bulímico:

Comencé porque a los 15 años un chico me rechazó. Pensé que el único aspecto importante malo en mí era mi peso.

Adquirí mi trastorno de la alimentación la noche anterior a mis exámenes finales en la universidad. Mi padre había muerto un mes antes y me sentía nerviosa por los exámenes y por la idea de regresar a casa sin él.

Empecé a vomitar durante mi cuarto mes de embarazo, cuando no pude enfrentar los cambios que sufría mi cuerpo y era imposible eliminar las calorías haciendo dietas.

No importa cuáles sean las razones de fondo, la bulimia "funciona" en muchos niveles diferentes. La comilona ofrece un alivio instantáneo. Toma el lugar de todos los demás actos, pensamientos y emociones. La mente cesa de pensar en otra cosa que no sea la comida y cómo engullirla. Los sentimientos quedan en suspenso. Incluso el vómito puede ser placentero cuando es el contacto más íntimo que le permitimos a nuestro cuerpo. Al concluir todo el episodio de comilona y purga, la bulímica recupera el control durante un breve instante. Sin sentirse ya culpable por haber ingerido tantas calorías, se encuentra agotada, relajada y eufórica.

Debido a que la bulimia falsamente se percibe como menos peligrosa que el alcoholismo o la toxicomanía, resulta en especial insidiosa y cautivadora.

Siempre hay comida disponible para una "dosis", y comer en público, así sea sobre la marcha, es algo aceptado y no causa extrañeza.

Asimismo, nada pone en evidencia a la bulímica, pues habitualmente su peso parece normal. La alimentación da vida, sana, nutre y significa amor. La seguridad, el alivio, la disponibilidad, el placer y la compañía que la comida representa parecen compensar todo inconveniente inmediato.

La bulimia se convierte en un remedio de corto plazo para el dolor, lo que a la larga puede ser desolador.

Es importante que tú y todas las personas que lean este libro comprendan que un trastorno de la alimentación es una enfermedad dolorosa y agobiante. Todo aquel que la sufra merece una gran compasión y comprensión. Juzgar a estas personas como derrochadoras, egocéntricas, vanas o mimadas invalida sus sentimientos, ignora problemas de fondo e intensifica la vergüenza que sienten.

Recuerda, un trastorno de la alimentación no tiene que ver sólo con la comida.

¿Por qué quienes padecen bulimia son mujeres en su mayoría?

En términos simples, vivimos en una sociedad que resulta fundamentalmente insatisfactoria para un número enorme de mujeres y los trastornos de la alimentación son un símbolo de este vacío interior. Muchas de nuestras instituciones, empresas, sistemas y estereotipos se basan en una estructura jerárquica orientada al varón. Este tipo de ambiente, que favorece la independencia y la competencia, margina a las mujeres, que se sienten más a gusto en contextos caracterizados por la cooperación y la interdependencia. Se explota la sexualidad de la mujer, se cuestiona su inteligencia y se limitan sus funciones, que suelen ser confusas. Se las bombardea con promesas de ser "mejores personas" merced a las industrias de las dietas, la moda, los cosméticos y el combate al envejecimiento. Muchas se sienten carentes de apoyo con una cultura cuyos valores son tan huecos. Desean y merecen algo más: algo que otorgue significado a su vida de una manera más profunda.

Es este papel dentro de esa sociedad lo que en diversos momentos resulta limitante, confuso, estremecedor y poco satisfactorio; es lo que empuja a muchas mujeres a refugiarse en la seguridad y el aturdimiento de los problemas con la alimentación.

• Las mujeres aprenden a tener trato social de formas específicas.

En términos generales, a las mujeres se les enseña, a lo largo de su vida, a relacionarse y a comportarse de ciertas maneras específicamente características de nuestra cultura. A esto se le llama "socialización" o "aculturación". Aunque es mucho lo que se ha avanzado, aún prevalece un buen número de ideas arcaicas. Cuatro de las lecciones más nocivas que pueden contribuir a los trastornos de la alimentación son las siguientes:

1. Las mujeres deben desconfiar de su espontaneidad y energía, y ser, en cambio, cuidadosas y recelosas, en especial respecto a sus propias capacidades. A los chicos se les permite, incluso se les alienta, a tener una libertad física mucho mayor y a asumir más riesgos.

2. Las mujeres no deben tener demasiadas necesidades, y las que tengan deben satisfacerse en último término. Asimismo, deben prever las necesidades de los demás, tal como las madres prevén las de los bebés y los niños.

3. Las mujeres deben hacerse a un lado y dejar que otros tomen la iniciativa, renunciando por tanto a sus opiniones y colocándose en posiciones subordinadas y auxiliares.

4. A las mujeres debe preocuparles su apariencia, porque se las juzgará en función de ella. Al mismo tiempo, su cuerpo será tratado como objeto y sexualizado en escala masiva.

Estas lecciones les enseñan que tienen "limitaciones" culturales. Llegan a sentir miedo de expresarse libremente y niegan sus propias necesidades, talentos, opiniones y belleza intrínseca. La bulimia puede ser una distracción de la sensación de estar desconectadas de su propio ser.

- **Las mujeres adolescentes son particularmente vulnerables.**

El mensaje de que las mujeres deben preocuparse por su aparien-cia se comunica a ambos sexos desde el momento del nacimien-to, durante toda la infancia y adolescencia, y hasta la misma edad adulta. Cuando los chicos entran a la pubertad y comienzan a ser más independientes de su familia y a enfrentar la cultura en la que se desenvuelven, las jovencitas se ven abrumadas por una llu-via de imágenes de cuerpos femeninos que son objeto de un escrutinio implacable. Toman también conciencia de los rasgos "femeninos" estereotipados, como la limpieza, la docilidad, la generosidad, la cortesía y la actitud provocativa en determinadas situaciones. Al llegar el momento en que se inician los juegos se-xuales, la mayoría ya sabe que su cuerpo es una herramienta para alcanzar popularidad y poder, y que hay conductas correctas e incorrectas relacionadas con el hecho de ser una chica.

Por otra parte, a las jóvenes de esta edad les ocurre algo extraño: su seguro sentido de identidad, sus enérgicas opiniones y su desenfadada participación ceden el paso a la impotencia, la inseguridad y las dudas respecto a su apariencia. Dejan de ser lindas chiquillas y se convierten en mujeres sexuales en ciernes.

Desde la perspectiva de una joven, esto la coloca en una po-sición vulnerable en relación con los varones y en competencia con las mujeres. En los momentos en que se está forjando una identidad, moldear su cuerpo para adecuarlo a las expectativas de todo el mundo, incluso las de su cultura, parece ser un medio razonable de complacer a todos. Muchas adquieren trastornos de la alimentación si fracasan en sus intentos iniciales de hacer dieta y enfrentan el temor de que nunca podrán ser una mujer "ideal".

- **En esta sociedad, tener un cuerpo femenino puede ser aterrador.**

A los varones, en su mayoría, los impulsa más el sexo que a las mujeres, ya sea que este rasgo sea una herencia biológica o algo aprendido de su ambiente. A ellas las mueve mayormente un deseo profundo de mantener vínculos con los demás. Estos dos factores han creado una atmósfera de maltrato y hostigamiento sexual generalizado contra las mujeres, tanto jóvenes como mayores, a la cual apenas comenzamos a hacer frente.

Las estadísticas recientes de maltrato sexual y violencia contra las mujeres son pavorosamente elevadas. Un trastorno de la alimentación es un medio para habérselas con el dolor de esa experiencia: "Mi cuerpo es mío; yo decido lo que entra y sale de él". Puede ser una recreación inconsciente del maltrato original o una forma de castigar al cuerpo, que es "el culpable" del ataque. También puede ser una forma de tomar distancia respecto al propio cuerpo o de adormecer los sentimientos asociados con el maltrato u hostigamiento. En último término, un trastorno de este tipo es un lugar seguro para esconderse del dolor y el temor al maltrato.

- **La sociedad contemporánea niega la diversidad y la función natural del cuerpo de las mujeres.**

"Convertirse en mujer" es, para muchas, un asunto embarazoso e incómodo, que demanda el cotidiano escrutinio de una misma. Incluso quienes han vivido el milagro de parir se sienten obligadas a recuperar rápidamente su vientre plano, ¡como si el parto nunca hubiese ocurrido! La negación de la verdad biológica más profunda de la mujer hace de su vida algo trivial. Un trastorno de la alimentación puede aliviar el dolor de sentirse desconectada de esta fuente interior de fortaleza y significado.

- **Se espera que las mujeres controlen sus emociones.**

Muchas mujeres con bulimia dicen sentir temor ante la intensidad de sus sentimientos reprimidos. En consecuencia, tienen escasa experiencia en cuanto a sus emociones o sus apetitos relacionados con la sexualidad, el alimento o la vida. Algunas afirman ser incapaces de distinguir un sentimiento de otro, o bien oscilan repetidamente entre la euforia y la depresión extremas. Dejar salir sus emociones significaría ser consumidas por ellas o consumir a otros. De las mujeres se espera que mantengan su ira bajo control... ¡que ni siquiera hablen demasiado! El control de su cuerpo, específicamente respecto al consumo de alimentos, se convierte en un medio concreto para sentirse señoras de esta inestabilidad interior. La delgadez llega a ser una medida del control emocional, y la bulimia un recurso para asegurarla.

- **Las mujeres se sienten frustradas en el trabajo.**

Aunque el movimiento feminista brindó nuevas oportunidades a algunas afortunadas que lo han aprovechado, la mayor parte de las que trabajan hoy día, continúan siendo víctimas de discriminación en el mercado laboral y en el escenario político, ambos dominados por los hombres.

Aquellas que consiguen ocupar puestos en sus áreas de interés y pericia suelen recibir un sueldo menor que el de los varones y se ven sometidas a una presión enorme para lograr un buen desempeño. Por otro lado, como ya señalamos, los puestos que exigen un alto grado de competencia y supervisión pueden ser poco satisfactorios para muchas de ellas, quienes tienen más posibilidades de prosperar en una atmósfera de cooperación y reciprocidad.

En estos casos, la bulimia puede ser síntoma de una vida carente de significado, creatividad o trabajo gratificante. Asimismo, este padecimiento ayuda al desahogo y ofrece una forma de autosabotaje que permite evitar el fracaso o la intimidad en el lugar de trabajo.

* **Los medios de comunicación y el dinero perpetúan los valores tradicionales.**

La amplia influencia de los medios de comunicación es incuestionable. La imagen de la mujer como objeto sexual se ve interminablemente reforzada por los anuncios espectaculares, el cine, la prensa, la televisión, y los productos de consumo, que transmiten a *ambos* sexos la idea de que las mujeres deben ser delgadas, bonitas y sexualmente atractivas.

Muchas grandes empresas dependen de que ellas se sientan inseguras acerca de su apariencia. Si bien una fotografía de una modelo de portada o un anuncio de cosméticos no es causa de una comilona, estos recordatorios constantes de que ser más esbelta es mejor, establecen valores que generan modos deformados de contemplar la alimentación y la propia identidad. ¿Cómo puede una mujer sentirse bien respecto a su interior si todos los demás parecen concentrarse en lo exterior? Irónicamente, muchas de las actrices y modelos esbeltas, a quienes se les pagan sumas enormes por su *look* y su delgado cuerpo, enfrentan trastornos de la alimentación a causa de sus esfuerzos por conservar su atractivo comercial.

¿Qué problemas especiales enfrentan los hombres con bulimia?

Aun cuando las cifras reales de varones bulímicos se desconocen —las cuales, sin duda, son menores que las de las mujeres—, en la actualidad muchos más padecen bulimia en comparación con lo que se pensaba a principios de los 80, cuando comenzó a surgir información acerca de este trastorno. Se estima que al menos 15 por ciento de las personas con bulimia son hombres.

Sin embargo, gran parte de las investigaciones más recientes sobre su frecuencia se basa en estudios muy limitados y no ofrecen datos concluyentes. También los varones pueden padecer anorexia nerviosa; por otra parte, y a diferencia de las mujeres, algunos se obsesionan con ser más grandes y musculosos, afección conocida como anorexia inversa o dismorfia corporal, la cual también puede llegar a ser adictiva.

Si pensamos en los problemas relacionados con la bulimia, como el sentimiento de culpa, la vergüenza y la baja autoestima, es de entenderse que los hombres sientan estas emociones incluso con mayor intensidad si sufren algo que suele considerarse como una "enfermedad de mujeres".

Por esta razón, muchos varones bulímicos se muestran reacios a solicitar ayuda profesional. En términos generales, quienes utilizan la adicción al ejercicio como un tipo de purga niegan tener algún problema con la comida. Los perfeccionistas que consumen sólo alimentos "bajos en grasas" ocultan su obsesión tras una fachada de salud y buena condición física.

En gran medida, los hombres parecen hacerse bulímicos por el mismo tipo de razones que las mujeres. Ciertos atletas masculinos, como los luchadores, los jockeys y los gimnastas, utilizan la bulimia para conservar su peso o reducirlo y se tornan adictos a ella, de igual manera que las mujeres atletas. Aunque el modo de pensar contemporáneo sugiere que hay más mujeres que hombres con bulimia —debido a que, tradicionalmente, la sociedad ha puesto más énfasis en la apariencia de aquéllas—, a ellos se les presiona cada vez más a ajustarse a una gama reducida de tipos corporales. A la comunidad homosexual le preocupa en particular mucho su apariencia, y aproximadamente la mitad de los varones bulímicos pertenecen a ella. Los modelos rollizos son tan poco frecuentes como las modelos de figura redonda y se les alienta a hacer dietas, modificar su cabello, y someterse a cirugía plástica tanto como a ellas.

Los hombres también se sienten presionados a parecer fuertes, con dominio de la situación e independientes; como tales, sus papeles en nuestra cultura tienen limitaciones y desventajas, del mismo modo que los de las mujeres.

A muchos les resulta difícil expresar sus sentimientos, y su experiencia en cuanto a relaciones emocionalmente íntimas es escasa. Experimentan una presión enorme por estar al mando, cargar con las preocupaciones financieras, ser los cimientos de su familia y asumir otras responsabilidades. Pocos desearían que se les calificase como seres obsesionados por su apariencia.

Todas estas situaciones pueden hacerlos más susceptibles de utilizar la bulimia como un mecanismo de defensa, así como sumamente renuentes a buscar ayuda. Al comparar a hombres y mujeres con bulimia, casi todas las investigaciones concluyen que son más las similitudes que las diferencias. Además de nuestra inquietud cultural generalizada por la dieta, otros factores, como la disfuncionalidad familiar, el abuso sexual, la baja autoestima y la carencia de significado de la propia vida contribuyen a las causas del padecimiento, independientemente del género. Los resultados de la recuperación en cada caso también son similares.

La búsqueda de una terapia adecuada plantea inquietudes especiales a los varones. Las opciones de tratamiento para sus contrapartes femeninas son abundantes y variadas, en tanto que los programas disponibles exclusivamente para hombres son de reciente creación. Por consiguiente, para encontrar apoyo profesional quizá requieran investigar mucho y tengan que conformarse con un grupo de apoyo general, varonil o mixto, contra la bulimia. Tal vez tengan que apartarse de los papeles que han definido para sí mismos e interpretar las publicaciones feministas de recuperación para satisfacer sus propias necesidades. Por ejemplo, un aspecto del feminismo consiste en valorar las relaciones entre las personas, en vez de mantenerse apartadas de ellas. Esto podría muy bien aplicarse a los hombres, a quienes se alienta a ser tan independientes y competitivos que se sienten aislados de los demás y atraídos hacia la bulimia.

Como sociedad, hombres y mujeres perpetúan estereotipos negativos, y corresponde a ambos sexos aprender a relacionarse de maneras satisfactorias y enriquecedoras. Como ya señalamos, en este libro nos dirigimos principalmente a las mujeres, pero la mayor parte de los mensajes implícitos y las actividades sugeridas son también valiosos para los hombres.

¿Cuál es la relación entre la bulimia y los traumas sexuales?

Los estudios clínicos no coinciden en las cifras publicadas en cuanto al número de pacientes con trastornos de la alimentación que han sido víctimas de abuso sexual, y hay cierta controversia al respecto. Las cifras de mujeres bulímicas con estos antecedentes van desde un asombroso 7 por ciento hasta un 70 por ciento, observándose que la tendencia imperante es de alrededor de 60 por ciento. Puesto que estas cifras no incluyen a las personas que han reprimido el recuerdo del maltrato, es indudable que la incidencia real es mayor de lo que las investigaciones muestran.

Es importante estar consciente de la naturaleza extremadamente delicada de tal situación y de que un libro de autoayuda como el presente no constituye una "terapia" adecuada para curar estos problemas. Dado que las víctimas necesitan trabajar con un terapeuta calificado, con experiencia en el tratamiento de personas que sufren trastornos de la alimentación y traumas sexuales a la vez, aquí presentaré sólo una perspectiva general del tema. Asimismo, aunque utilizo el pronombre "ella", el incesto y el abuso sexual presentan una incidencia sorprendentemente elevada entre los varones, con consecuencias similares.

Sufrir un ataque sexual, en especial de un adulto "de confianza", un padre o un(a) hermano(a), es una experiencia aterradora, desconcertante y horrible para cualquiera. Es un acto de violencia y de traición tan intenso que su solo recuerdo es terriblemente doloroso. Para sobrevivir, no sólo al trauma mismo, sino además a su recuerdo, puede ocurrir que la víctima se disocie del suceso y de las partes de sí misma que estuvieron presentes en ese momento. Incluso puede llegar a considerar que la persona violada es distinta de ella misma, porque el dolor resulta insoportable. Su supervivencia emocional y física depende de que consiga olvidar los acontecimientos o los sentimientos relacionados con lo que sucedió.

Un trastorno de la alimentación consigue proteger, reprimir, completar, desviar, adormecer o confundir estos sentimientos y recuerdos. Es indudable que no está dentro de las posibilidades de la niña culpar al abusador por lo que ocurrió, pero incluso una mujer adulta tiende a culparse a sí misma del ataque y a hacer de su cuerpo el objeto de su odio y su necesidad de control. Al atiborrarse de comida consigue ahogar la ira y silenciar la voz que exclama: "¡No me hagan esto!"

Proyectar y llevar a cabo una comilona logra adormecer ansiedades y negar necesidades físicas, como las de alimento o de afecto. Estar a cargo de lo que entra y de lo que no entra a su cuerpo es una forma de recuperar simbólicamente ese control que se perdió durante el trauma original.

La relación con la alimentación dificulta tener relaciones plenas con otros y de esta manera se elimina el riesgo de una nueva traición. Según las herramientas de supervivencia internas con las que cuente la persona, ser sumamente gruesa o delgada, o incluso percibirse como demasiado gruesa o demasiado delgada, es una manera de mantener a distancia al abusador en potencia. Por último, el doloroso y violento acto de vomitar es una forma de expresar y dar salida a la ira y al odio por una misma.

Muchas víctimas de abuso sexual se tornan promiscuas, masoquistas, o incluso tienen fantasías de violación durante las relaciones amorosas que sostienen con pleno consentimiento, sin comprender que están enganchadas a la "droga" del alivio que experimentan al borrar de su mente el ataque que sufrieron.

De igual modo, pueden repetir esta "euforia prohibida" a través de comilonas y purgas. Algunas mujeres bulímicas siguen de manera compulsiva rituales que quizá reflejen incidentes repetitivos, como, por ejemplo, el abuso de un(a) cuidador(a) de niños cada sábado por la noche o las visitas de un(a) hermano(a) estando los padres fuera de casa. La ingestión de comida y el vómito forzados también pueden ser un remedo de un acto sexual oral obligado. Estas conductas repetitivas quizá sean un intento, por parte del inconsciente, de completar el abuso original en el presente. Un método de alimentación aun más perturbador acaso sea consecuencia de rituales satánicos, que pudieron haber incluido la ingestión de excrementos o de sangre. Dadas las atroces posibilidades de traumas sexuales en este contexto, es evidente que un trastorno de la alimentación se convertiría en un mecanismo crucial de supervivencia.

Pese a que aquí definimos el abuso sexual en términos de conductas más extremas, de hecho casi todas las mujeres han sufrido humillaciones sexuales de una forma u otra. Alguien ha rozado "accidentalmente" sus senos, su virginidad ha sido objeto de murmuraciones entre varones, y personas desconocidas les han silbado o se han burlado de ellas. En todos estos casos, se justifica el maltrato hacia la mujer con la frase de cajón: "Ella se lo buscó". No es coincidencia que un número impresionante de mujeres sufra también algún tipo de conflicto entre la comida y el peso, el más común de los cuales es hacer dieta. Vemos con tristeza que el cuerpo de la mujer se ha convertido en su enemigo, en vez de la maravilla natural que es.

Los traumas sexuales deben ser tratados en un ambiente de seguridad y confianza. Aceptar la experiencia, reprimida o no, y hacer que el niño interior regrese a una experiencia de amor y aceptación incondicionales, es una empresa de enormes proporciones. Son necesarias mucha comprensión y paciencia afectuosas por parte del terapeuta y del paciente por igual. No olvides que eliminar la conducta de comilona y purga sin introducir destrezas defensivas saludables puede provocar una resurrección del horror original. La mejor manera de hacer las paces de algún modo con la pesadilla que yace debajo de la superficie bulímica, es valerse de la orientación de un profesional capacitado y hábil.

El acto de trabajar y poner al descubierto la verdad acerca de mi familia, así como el hecho de que fui víctima de incesto, ayudó a que todo tuviera sentido. Comprendí que la motivación de mi trastorno de la alimentación era mi arcaica necesidad de proteger a mi familia y que en realidad estaba recreando el abuso.

Cuando tenía 12 años, mi hermano comenzó a abusar sexualmente de mí. Me sentía terriblemente confundida, y pensé que si engordaba, él me dejaría en paz. Creo que aumentar 18 kilos en tres meses era también mi modo de decir: "Atención, algo anda mal aquí", sin tener que expresarlo con palabras.

Tenía un problema para engullir por haber sido forzada a tener relaciones sexuales orales. Escupía toda la comida, incluso los líquidos. Me sometieron a todos los exámenes médicos habidos y por haber, pues los médicos pensaban que tenía un problema en la garganta. Al cabo de cuatro años de terapia, mi trauma por fin ha desaparecido; sin embargo, regresa a veces en momentos de mucho estrés o cuando los recuerdos se hacen presentes.

Es importante que los padres, los terapeutas, los médicos y el público en general sepan que las mujeres que han padecido abuso sexual sufren un gran dolor. Su trastorno de la alimentación es una forma de hacer frente a todos los sentimientos: cólera, enojo, miedo, sigi-

lo, traición, impotencia y muchos más. Un trastorno de la alimentación es un trastorno de los sentimientos porque ayuda a manejarlos.

¿Cómo afecta la bulimia mis relaciones?

A veces se describe a la bulimia como un trastorno de las relaciones porque, en gran medida, altera las relaciones normales y sanas. Las personas con bulimia se retraen poco a poco de los demás, hasta que su obsesión por la comida prácticamente se convierte en la única relación. Asimismo, el concepto que tenemos de nosotras mismas, por ejemplo, si somos buenas personas o si debemos ser delgadas para ser amadas, proviene de nuestras relaciones más importantes. El trastorno de la alimentación funciona como un dispositivo protector que asegura que las heridas pasadas que tienen que ver con estas experiencias no se recuerden ni se repitan en el presente.

En la infancia, la manera como nos tratan nuestros padres, otros adultos, nuestros iguales y la comunidad en general nos dice algo acerca de nuestra persona. Estas relaciones constituyen los cimientos de nuestros sentimientos de importancia, competencia y capacidad de ser amadas. Por desgracia, muchas hemos sufrido maltrato emocional y físico de manos de las propias personas que están a cargo de nuestra vida. En nuestra mente infantil, no podemos creer que la culpa es de quienes se encargan de cuidarnos; por tanto, nos culpamos a nosotras mismas. Incluso nos resulta muy difícil creer que nuestra cultura, la familia más grande de todas, tal vez no sea tan buena al fin y al cabo.

Lo anterior no implica que los trastornos de la alimentación se presenten sólo en los hogares donde hay violencia o maltrato físico. No ser tomada en cuenta o ser subestimada repetidamente puede resultar tan nocivo para la imagen que una niña tiene de sí misma como ser víctima de incesto. Las niñas que no se sienten amadas ni seguras en una familia, del tipo que sea, no confían en sus propios actos. En esas condiciones, buscan fuera de sí mismas las pautas acerca de cómo deben comportarse. En consecuencia, sus relaciones estarán "orientadas hacia los demás" y fundadas en una baja autoestima.

La bulimia, que suele comenzar como un intento inocente de ser más delgada y así agradar a los demás, es un ejemplo de esta conducta orientada hacia otros. La persona bulímica no sigue los dictados de su corazón, sino que reacciona a lo que sucede a su alrededor. Aunque la bulimia parece protegerla al sostener un frente falso y una sensación de seguridad, también mantiene a la gente a distancia. Las bulímicas interactúan con los demás sabiendo que pueden retraerse en cualquier momento hacia sus conductas conocidas y repetitivas. Incluso cuando parecen estar presentes en la conversación, puede ser que su mente esté a años luz de distancia, pensando en la última o en la próxima comilona.

Ciertos aspectos de la bulimia son especialmente dañinos para establecer relaciones honestas y satisfactorias. Es evidente que mantener una fachada de felicidad y competencia en lo exterior, cuando en lo interior una se siente angustiada o deprimida, es un esfuerzo y una distracción. Las conductas de comilona y purga se practican en secreto, por lo común bajo una capa de sentimientos de culpa y vergüenza. Los cambios de humor y las mentiras son características comunes.

El robo, mencionado por 3 por ciento de las personas que respondieron nuestra encuesta, refuerza la baja autoestima y la tendencia a esconderse. La concentración en la delgadez alienta la competencia entre las mujeres, en vez del mutuo apoyo, y hace hincapié en la naturaleza sexual de las relaciones con los hombres y no en el afecto o el respeto.

Con el tiempo, la relación de la persona bulímica con la comida termina por sustituir a todas las demás relaciones. Como una de ellas respondió en nuestra encuesta: "La bulimia es una amiga que no critica, ni juzga, ni compite, ni rechaza". Sin embargo, la conducta bulímica no puede amarnos como necesitamos que nos amen. No nos nutre, ni nos apoya, ni nos satisface en el nivel interior más profundo, como sin duda puede atestiguarlo cualquiera que se haya atiborrado y purgado una y otra vez. Se trata de un remedio muy tenue y de corto plazo para un dolor oculto y de largo plazo, y por ello crea soledad y aislamiento a su paso.

Renunciar a la conducta bulímica es algo que causa alarma en quien la padece. Significa correr el riesgo de un rechazo y enfrentar sentimientos de inutilidad, pero los beneficios son obvios: honestidad, confianza, alegría, intimidad y amor.

Como destacamos en la sección en la que hablamos de cómo obtener apoyo, una relación abierta y confiada, así sea con una sola persona, puede ser un factor crucial para la recuperación. Muchas personas han encontrado esta confianza en la terapia; otras la han hallado en sus padres, amantes, cónyuges y amistades.

La naturaleza misma de un trastorno de la alimentación impide el cultivo de las relaciones. ¿Cómo podría tener una relación con alguien, fundada en la honestidad y la verdad, si constantemente mentía acerca de cuánto comía, cuánto no comía, si hacía ejercicio o si me purgaba?

Cuando estoy enamorada o trabajo en la intimidad, mis hábitos de alimentación se normalizan, pero cuando no tengo relaciones estrechas ni nada que ver con los demás, siento que me muero de hambre. La comida reduce la angustia y enmascara los sentimientos. Sólo cultivando la intimidad consigo poner alto a este patrón de conducta. En mi opinión, la formación de relaciones es indispensable para la recuperación.

Mis relaciones con mis familiares se deterioraron cuando me pillaron en muchas mentiras. No podían confiar en casi nada de lo que yo decía. Llegué a creer de verdad que la razón por la que mis hermanas me seguían por toda la casa, tratando de impedir que siguiese vomitando, ¡era que estaban celosas porque al fin había conseguido ser más delgada que ellas!

Cuando salía con amigas, estaba tan ausente de lo que ocurría que lo único que podía hacer era calcular cuán rápido necesitaba llegar al baño para vomitar. No me interesaba en absoluto en las personas que me rodeaban; sin embargo, gracias a la terapia, todo eso está cambiando.

He aprendido a decir "no" a los demás, y me he ganado su respeto por ello. Siempre me aterraba lo que podría ocurrir en caso de no estar de acuerdo o de querer que algo fuese diferente. Ahora siento que merezco tener una opinión.

¿Es la bulimia lo mismo que la anorexia nerviosa?

Durante muchos años se consideró a la bulimia como un tipo de conducta anoréxica. Sin lugar a dudas, en ambos casos la relación con la comida es un síntoma de otros problemas serios y existen muchas otras similitudes. Sin embargo, al reconocer en 1980 a la bulimia como un trastorno diferente, la American Psychiatric Association identificó un grupo mucho más grande que el de aquellas mujeres que podían clasificarse desde el punto de vista clínico como estrictamente anoréxicas.

La cuarta edición del *American Psychiatric Association's Diagnostic and Statistical Manual of Mental Disorders* (DSM-IV) (Manual de diagnóstico y estadísticas de trastornos mentales) cita cuatro criterios según los cuales a una persona se le puede diagnosticar anorexia:

a. Mantiene un peso corporal que está alrededor de 15 por ciento por debajo del normal de acuerdo con la edad, la estatura y complexión.

b. Siente un intenso temor de aumentar de peso o de engordar, no obstante que está por debajo del normal. Paradójicamente, perder peso puede aun empeorar el miedo a engordar.

c. Tiene una imagen distorsionada de su cuerpo. Algunas sienten que tienen grasa por todas partes; otras reconocen que en términos generales están delgadas, pero consideran que partes específicas de su cuerpo (en especial el vientre y los muslos) son demasiado gordas.

Su sentimiento de valor personal se basa en las dimensiones y la forma de su cuerpo. Asimismo, niegan que su bajo peso deba ser causa de preocupación.

d. En la mujer se produce una ausencia de al menos tres ciclos menstruales consecutivos. También satisface este criterio si su periodo se presenta sólo cuando toma píldoras de hormonas (incluidos los anticonceptivos orales, aunque sin limitarse a ellos).

El DSM-IV también establece una diferencia entre dos tipos específicos de anorexia nerviosa. El "tipo restrictivo" es indicador de personas que pierden peso principalmente por reducción de la cantidad total de alimento ingerido mediante dietas, ayuno o ejercicio excesivo. El "tipo de comilona y purga" describe a quienes hacen comilonas con regularidad (consumen grandes cantidades de alimento en periodos cortos) y se purgan mediante vómito autoinducido, ejercicio excesivo, ayuno, abuso de diuréticos, laxantes y enemas, o con alguna combinación de estas medidas.

Aunque algunas anoréxicas también se purgan después de comer, la anorexia nerviosa se caracteriza, en términos generales, por la inanición autoinfligida. Por lo general, las anoréxicas rechazan la alimentación, tienen bajo peso corporal, suelen comenzar más jóvenes y son menos maduras social y sexualmente. En cambio, el peso de la mayoría de las bulímicas parece acercarse más al normal, casi todas comienzan a purgarse poco antes o después de los veinte años (muchas anoréxicas se convierten en bulímicas) y son más extrovertidas en el aspecto social. Asimismo, como ya señalamos, los criterios del DSM-IV incluyen amenorrea, algo poco frecuente entre las bulímicas; sin embargo, éstas suelen informar de menstruaciones irregulares.

Las anoréxicas por lo general requieren hospitalización y presentan una tasa de mortalidad mayor: entre 5 y 20 por ciento mueren por complicaciones relacionadas con su enfermedad. No hay datos definitivos en cuanto a estadísticas de mortalidad por bulimia, pero la impresión clínica es que son bajas, mucho menores que en el caso de la anorexia nerviosa.

Como ya señalamos, existen similitudes en lo que se refiere a los problemas subyacentes a la anorexia nerviosa y a la bulimia. Las personas que padecen estos trastornos comparten una preocupación excesiva por las dimensiones de su cuerpo y por lo que han comido o dejado de comer. Su atención se concentra en un lugar interior vacío, que puede contemplarse en términos físicos, emocionales, sociales o espirituales. Ambos tipos de personas utilizan el control de la alimentación para manejar sentimientos intensos de diversa índole, como depresión, enojo, sensación de rechazo, soledad, egoísmo, temor a ser independiente o dependiente y amor. Asimismo, todas usan la comida para evitar situaciones en las que pueda haber conflictos, reprobación o fracasos. En última instancia, todas emplean la alimentación para expresar algo que perciben como inaceptable, o que no consiguen expresar directamente.

Sin embargo, aunque una comilona y la purga consiguiente dan a la bulímica el valor para enfrentar el mundo, el hecho de no comer confiere poder a la anoréxica. No obstante que algunas anoréxicas se someten a purgas si comen más de lo que consideran prudente, no comer sigue siendo su herramienta principal de autoconservación. Para ellas, la recuperación no es tanto cuestión de evitar una comilona, sino de comer lo suficiente para estar sanas. Pero, para ambas, lo esencial consiste en ser capaces y estar dispuestas a cuidar de sí mismas con cantidades adecuadas de alimento (sin inanición ni atiborramiento) de una manera saludable y favorable a su desarrollo.

¿Qué es una comilona típica?

Lo "típico" depende por completo de la persona. La magnitud y la frecuencia varían, al igual que el tipo de purga y la duración del intervalo entre sesiones. En realidad, una comilona provoca sentimiento de culpa. Sin embargo, las comilonas típicas tienen dos características: el consumo de una cantidad excesiva de alimento y la sensación de haber perdido el control de la situación.

Muchas bulímicas han afirmado que pueden "identificarse" con mis comilonas, una de las cuales describí en la Introducción. En muchas ocasiones inicié una comilona en el transcurso de lo que me parecía una comida "buena" o "segura". Por ejemplo, quizás en una barra de ensaladas me servía con cuidado una ración moderada. Al comerla, comenzaba a sentirme culpable por las calorías del aderezo o por haber tomado cuadritos de pan frito. En algún momento decidía que había comido un poco más de la cuenta. En vez de dejar de hacerlo, pensaba: "¿Cuál es la diferencia? Ya he ido demasiado lejos. Haré una comilona y todas esas calorías me importarán un comino después de vomitar". Nunca se me ocurrió que había "problemas" que inducían esta extraña conducta.

Si tenía la opción, prefería comer dulces y carbohidratos refinados. Una sola comilona podría incluir un litro de helado, una bolsa de galletas, un par de tandas de galletas de chocolate, una docena de rosquillas y algunas barras de caramelo. Sin embargo, cuando estaba desesperada me atiborraba de lo que fuera: avena, requesón, zanahorias o panecillos del día anterior que rescataba de la basura, para lo que iba a ser mi última comilona, ahora sí.

Mi estómago se hinchaba tanto que parecía embarazada y habitualmente posponía el vómito durante unos 30 minutos de aturdimiento. Después, metía los dedos en mi garganta hasta vomitar todo lo que podía. El episodio entero duraba alrededor de una hora y muchas veces me sentí débil y mareada al terminar. No abusaba de laxantes, enemas ni diuréticos, aunque algunas bulímicas sí lo hacen.

¿Cuáles son los peligros para la salud?

La bulimia rara vez causa la muerte, pero sí puede ocurrir. El vómito excesivo provoca un desequilibrio de electrólitos. Los electrólitos, que son sustancias químicas del organismo como el potasio, el cloruro y el sodio, ayudan a regular los latidos del corazón. Cuando estas sustancias se agotan debido a las purgas o la deshidratación, suele presentarse arritmia cardiaca, esto es, un latido irregular del corazón. A veces esto no es grave y se corrige cuando se vuelve a tener una salud y nutrición apropiadas, pero en ciertos casos puede provocar la muerte por paro cardiaco. La insuficiencia renal es otro posible efecto colateral de la escasez de potasio, que pone en peligro la vida. El vómito puede ser mortal cuando provoca asfixia o si el esófago o las vías bronquiales se rompen.

Entre los problemas de carácter médico más comunes en las bulímicas se cuentan el estreñimiento, las caries, la hinchazón y otros trastornos digestivos, glándulas infectadas o inflamadas conocidas como "mejillas de ardilla", ampollas en la garganta, manos y pies helados y pérdida de líquidos.

Otras complicaciones potencialmente graves, aunque poco frecuentes, por lo general, son las anormalidades de los sistemas endocrino y gastrointestinal, anemia, sangrado interno, hipoglucemia, periodos menstruales irregulares o amenorrea, osteoporosis, miopatía e irregularidades en la formación de imágenes en el cerebro.

Algunas bulímicas emplean jarabe de ipecacuana, detergentes u objetos extraños para inducir el vómito, todos los cuales son en extremo peligrosos. La ipecacuana, un líquido de muy mal sabor, se utiliza para tratar a las víctimas de intoxicación y su abuso puede producir debilidad muscular o paro cardiaco. El abuso de los laxantes irrita las terminaciones nerviosas intestinales, lo cual puede inhibir su función de desencadenar contracciones.

El uso intensivo de laxantes o enemas elimina la mucosidad protectora de la pared intestinal, lo cual provoca infecciones intestinales. El intestino grueso puede perder tono muscular, quedando flácido e incapaz de producir contracciones. Se presentan deshidrataciones y desequilibrios de líquidos, con los mismos efectos colaterales ya señalados. Asimismo, quienes abusan de los laxantes padecen dolor en el recto, gases, estreñimiento o diarrea (o ambas cosas) y tumores intestinales.

Aunque sin una vinculación directa, las personas con trastornos de la alimentación tienden a tener otros padecimientos de carácter médico, entre ellos, diabetes mellitus, fibrosis quística, afecciones inflamatorias del intestino, como la enfermedad de Crohn, y problemas de la tiroides. Las diabéticas con bulimia suelen hacer mal uso de su insulina, lo que pone en riesgo su vida.

Es difícil, si no imposible, saber cuáles bulímicas corren más riesgo de adquirir alguna de estas afecciones específicas. Sin lugar a dudas, cuanto más tiempo padece bulimia una persona, más probable es que experimente problemas de salud asociados a esta enfermedad. Sin embargo, incluso quien apenas ha comenzado a purgarse enfrenta la posibilidad de padecer graves consecuencias físicas o hasta la muerte.

A muchas bulímicas les inquieta la posibilidad de embarazarse o de estar embarazadas. Algunas temen que el vómito dañe al futuro bebé o les preocupa engordar demasiado. Aunque la información disponible sobre el embarazo y los trastornos de la alimentación es limitada, lo que sabemos es lo siguiente:

1. No obstante que las mujeres con trastornos de la alimentación tienen más probabilidades de dar a luz bebés pequeños, ni la bulimia ni la anorexia nerviosa originan defectos congénitos de consideración.

2. Puesto que el sistema digestivo de una madre que se purga es independiente del feto, por lo general la criatura no sufre daño. Sin embargo, la nutrición deficiente y la actitud mental negativa son poco saludables para la madre y para el hijo.

3. Con las mujeres en tratamiento, pueden emplearse ciertos antidepresivos, pero hay otros que será necesario evitar. En todo caso, la paciente debe consultar a su médico acerca de los medicamentos específicos que está tomando.

4. Un alto porcentaje de bulímicas experimenta una disminución notable de sus síntomas mientras están emba-

razadas. Quizá sienten que su cuerpo pertenece a su bebé durante este periodo y ello las hace desechar las conductas poco saludables. Sin embargo, es probable que durante el periodo de posparto regresen a su bulimia, en especial al enfrentar el hecho de que han aumentado de peso.

5. El nacimiento de un hijo saca a relucir otros aspectos emocionales de las mujeres bulímicas: cómo afecta el trastorno de la alimentación la crianza de los hijos; las relaciones madre-hijo, la sexualidad y el atractivo; los conflictos de separación y las preocupaciones sobre la alimentación adecuada para el bebé. Es necesario prestar atención a estos aspectos, por el bienestar de la madre y del hijo.

¿Qué pensamientos y sentimientos se relacionan con la bulimia?

Los trastornos de la alimentación son trastornos de los *sentimientos*. Las rígidas reglas y rituales de la conducta bulímica son un medio definido para distanciar el propio ser de ciertos sentimientos que parecen incontrolables, abrumadores o simplemente aterradores. Estos sentimientos pueden ser pavorosos como el miedo que nace del recuerdo del abuso; calmados, como el dolor de no ser amada o no ser considerada importante; o sentimientos de la vida diaria que subyacen en acontecimientos del pasado o recientes. Una comilona hace a un lado todos los sentimientos al ofrecer algo más en que fijar la atención.

Tarde o temprano, las bulímicas terminan por no emplear otro medio para manejar sus sentimientos *salvo* la comilona y la purga. Esto es lo que describen cuando afirman que se sienten impotentes. Lo que es más, la enfermedad trae consigo toda una serie de nuevas complicaciones que enmascaran los viejos sentimientos y suelen hacer que empeoren. Por ejemplo, una persona que teme a los demás puede utilizar la bulimia para mantener su distancia, ocultando sus bochornosos pensamientos y rituales. O bien, alguien que se siente incompetente perfecciona el arte de vomitar, sin intentar mucho más. De esta manera, niega efectivamente aquello, sea lo que fuere, que desencadenó la conducta de comilona y purga y, a la larga, lo entierra bajo nuevos sentimientos de vergüenza y culpabilidad.

La mayor parte de las primeras lecciones acerca de los sentimientos se aprenden a una edad temprana y dejan una huella profunda. Ciertas familias no expresan o no saben cómo manejar una gama irrestricta de emociones, en especial las "negativas", como la ira, el desengaño o incluso el desacuerdo. Otras tienen reglas estrictas respecto a las emociones que se pueden expresar y cuáles son los modos de expresión permisibles. Los hijos de las familias de este tipo aprenden que deben vigilar y proteger sus sentimientos, y en muchos casos los niegan por completo. Carente de experiencia en cuanto a identificarlos y a hablar de ellos, es posible que la bulímica no sepa siquiera con exactitud *qué* es lo que siente, o quizá suponga que sus sentimientos son malos y que ella lo es también por tenerlos. Tal vez tema asimismo los sentimientos de los demás, y se esfuerce por asegurar que nada los altere.

Con el tiempo, estos sentimientos ocultos encuentran expresión de otras maneras, por ejemplo, mediante un trastorno de la alimentación. De hecho, muchas bulímicas malinterpretan una amplia gama de emociones como hambre. Casi todas afirman sentirse deprimidas, desconectadas e impotentes la mayor parte del tiempo. La naturaleza cíclica de las comilonas bulímicas se aplica igualmente a los sentimientos que, en cuestión de horas, pueden pasar de la *falta de valor* (baja autoestima) a la *impotencia* (no tengo control sobre mi vida), a la *eficacia* (puedo librarme de estos sentimientos), a la *euforia* (por la liberación que la purga ofrece) a la *esperanza* (de que esta comilona pudiera ser la última) y, por último, el regreso a los sentimientos de *falta de valor.*

La bulimia es un trastorno del *pensamiento,* en cuanto a que quienes la sufren están atrapados en métodos de pensamiento nocivos. Un ejemplo es el "pensamiento en blanco y negro", en el que todo se divide en categorías extremas. Por ejemplo, los alimentos son "buenos" o "malos", los cuerpos son "gruesos" o "delgados", y no estar al mando significa haber perdido totalmente el control. Otros modelos consisten en la exageración de los problemas, el pensamiento mágico y dramático, la comparación constante de una misma con los demás, y el hábito de tomar los comentarios o situaciones de un modo demasiado personal. Algunas bulímicas también parecen tener una actitud negativa, en términos generales, hacia la vida, lo cual influye en todos los aspectos de su experiencia. La mayoría piensa que no valen, a juzgar por las dimensiones de su cuerpo.

Es característico de las personas bulímicas albergar ideas centrales profundamente arraigadas, de las cuales se deducen otras conclusiones dañinas. Por ejemplo, la creencia de que estar gorda es malo también significa que la comida es mala, que tener un cuerpo grande es señal de fracaso, y que permitirse un capricho es signo de debilidad. Pensar: "Soy una mala persona" —cosa que muchas bulímicas hacen—, fomenta ideas como: "No hay razón para cuidar de mí misma" y: "Es imposible que alguien me quiera". Esto conforma todo un sistema de valores: ideas a partir de las cuales ellas se vigilan y juzgan constantemente a sí mismas, y en ocasiones a los demás. Su mente hace lo que se describe como "girar sobre sí misma", esto es, repasar una y otra vez los mismos pensamientos negativos. Estas interminables "cintas" automáticas de la mente les impiden escuchar cualquier otra cosa, mucho menos su sabiduría interna. En la recuperación, es necesario sacar a la luz y cuestionar todos esos sentimientos y pensamientos. Esto puede ser, al mismo tiempo, una experiencia atemorizante y rejuvenecedora, agotadora y gratificante, por lo que la mejor manera de vivirla es con la orientación de un terapeuta.

Puedo ver sin dificultad cómo, en los momentos difíciles de la vida, uno busca algún tipo de consuelo. Yo lo encontré en la comida. Otras lo hallan en las drogas y el alcohol.

Antes de iniciar la terapia, nunca asocié mis emociones con mi deseo de hacer una comilona. Siempre sentí que era un deseo incontrolable de ingerir cantidades enormes de alimento. Ahora entiendo que la comilona toma el lugar de la decisión de permitirme sentir cualquier emoción.

¿Qué otras conductas comparten las mujeres bulímicas?

Las personas que padecen trastornos de la alimentación tienen personalidades compulsivas; los rituales que ellas crean son lugares seguros y conocidos en los cuales poder residir. Muchos de los rituales giran en torno a la comida y a la imagen corporal, como la tendencia a acomodar la comida en el plato, el ejercicio excesivo, comer de forma sistemática, verse en el espejo y contar calorías de manera obsesiva. Ciertas conductas no guardan relación con la alimentación, como el hecho de saber dónde está el baño más próximo, evitar a la gente, mentir, guardar secretos, cleptomanía y compras compulsivas.

La mayoría de las bulímicas toman medidas exhaustivas para ocultar sus síntomas. Durante los cinco años iniciales de mi primer matrimonio, mi esposo nunca descubrió mis secretos celosamente guardados. ¡Nadie los sabía! Ocultar mi rastro era parte de mi rutina diaria. Mentir acerca de la comida era ya un acto reflejo. Por ejemplo, si iba dos días seguidos a la misma tienda de abarrotes a comprar grandes cantidades del mismo alimento para mis comilonas, le decía a la cajera que era maestra de un jardín infantil y estaba comprando bocadillos para los niños. Mis rituales incluían la preocupación por las básculas, los espejos y probarme prendas de vestir. Acostumbraba pesarme antes y después de las comilonas para estar segura de no haber aumentado de peso. (En un momento determinado de mi recuperación, ¡llegué con un martillo a la báscula!) No podía pasar por un espejo sin juzgar cualquier protuberancia insignificante o cabello fuera de su lugar.

En nuestra encuesta, 37 por ciento de las bulímicas mencionaron la cleptomanía como síntoma. Es obvio que robar es un medio para compensar el costo de la comida, pero la cleptomanía tiene que ver con algo más que la simple economía básica. Tanto las compras compulsivas como el robo son formas de "llenarse" sin comer, así como de satisfacer de manera simbólica necesidades emocionales no saciadas. Asimismo, robar a otras personas puede ser una manera de comunicar sentimientos negativos sin emplear palabras.

En mi caso, me sentía indigna e incapaz de darme el lujo de comprar cosas "bonitas", no obstante que gastaba grandes cantidades en comida. Quería amor y atención y, no sabiendo cómo conseguir esas recompensas emocionales, me conformaba con la satisfacción temporal. A veces sólo buscaba la excitación de hacer algo indebido. Las mujeres de nuestra encuesta tuvieron experiencias similares. Sus hurtos iban desde barras de caramelo hasta artículos más grandes y costosos. La mayoría de las que robaban también señalaron que no era muy difícil cambiar este modelo de conducta. Algunas mujeres fueron arrestadas, y dejaron el hábito de inmediato, como ésta:

¡Dejé de robar cuando me descubrieron con un pollo en mi bolsa!

¿Qué se siente hacer comilonas y vomitar?

Para responder esta pregunta, es importante recordar que la bulimia cumple un propósito para la persona que la padece. En otras palabras, las bulímicas no harían comilonas ni se purgarían si ello las hiciese sentirse peor, no mejor. En especial en las etapas iniciales, cuando se justifica la purga como una forma de perder peso o conservar un peso bajo, la bulimia proporciona un falso sentimiento de autoestima, competencia y control. En las etapas más tardías, renunciar a ella significa entender lo que es real y verdadero y lo que no lo es. Asimismo, significa optar por lo que es real.

El "aturdimiento" mental y la "euforia" física son razones importantes para explicar por qué la conducta misma de comilona y purga llega a ser tan adictiva. De hecho, muchas participantes en nuestra encuesta, que eran compulsivas respecto al alimento, también eran alcohólicas o provenían de familias con antecedentes de abuso de sustancias. Son varios los estudios que se han realizado sobre la conexión entre los trastornos de la alimentación y otras adicciones, y se ha demostrado que entre 9 por ciento y 55 por ciento de las bulímicas son también alcohólicas o consumen drogas. Estas personas también se hacen adictas a las píldoras para adelgazar, a los diuréticos y a los laxantes.

Los amigos y los seres queridos de estos pacientes deben saber que vomitar después de una comilona no es lo mismo que vomitar cuando una está enferma. La persona con bulimia no se siente enferma, sino desesperada y empujada. Las comilonas y purgas eliminan temporalmente el estrés, como una droga. Todo se centra en el ciclo, desde tratar de evitar una comilona, ceder al impulso, organizarla y ejecutarla. Después de una purga por vómito, también se experimenta una "euforia" física debida a la presión de tener la cabeza hacia abajo y al agotador esfuerzo físico.

Son comunes las sensaciones de limpieza, renovación y relajamiento subsiguientes o también de indiferencia y aturdimiento emocional. Puede haber sensaciones sexuales causadas por el surgimiento, la excitación en privado, la entrega total, la plenitud, la fricción y la liberación repentina.

En mi caso, en la calma posterior a la tormenta de la purga, me prometía que nunca haría otra comilona, con lo cual añadía sentimientos de esperanza y renovación al ciclo. Empero, poco tiempo después empezaba de nuevo, sin remedio. Durante más de cinco años hice comilonas y vomité cuatro, cinco o más veces, prácticamente todos los días. Varias de las mujeres encuestadas comentaron acerca de la semejanza de la bulimia con las drogas:

Me gustan la euforia y el aturdimiento que vienen después. Una vez que inicio una comilona, no hay forma de detenerme.

No importa lo decaída y deprimida que te sientas, piensas en la comida como una satisfacción o "euforia" temporal. Encuentra algo permanente, porque, después de purgarte, te sentirás igual o incluso peor. ¿Por qué perder el tiempo?

¿Cómo sé si tengo bulimia?

¿Hemos estado hablando acerca de ti? Yo hice comilonas y vomité todos los días durante nueve años sin pensar que tenía un problema, aunque eso ocurrió antes de que se le diera nombre a la bulimia. Me topé con el mismísimo primer artículo de revista acerca de la "bulimarexia", y quedé estupefacta al descubrir que había otras personas que se comportaban respecto a la comida igual que yo.

Ya sea que hagas comilonas y te purgues diariamente o sólo de vez en cuando, o si comes en exceso y después haces ejercicio de modo compulsivo o te sometes a dietas estrictas, en todos los casos estás abusando de tu cuerpo de una manera bulímica.

De hecho, incluso si eres obsesiva sólo con el pensamiento respecto al peso, la dieta y la comida, aun así tienes un problema con la alimentación, aunque no corresponda a la definición clínica de anorexia o bulimia.

Para tratar los problemas de las personas que no cubren los criterios estrictos, la American Psychiatric Association estableció una nueva categoría en el DSM-IV: "Trastornos de la alimentación sin otra especificación" (EDNOS, por sus siglas en inglés). Algunos síntomas de los EDNOS son: las comilonas sin purga; satisfacer todos los criterios de anorexia, excepto que la persona tiene menstruaciones normales o su peso es casi normal; tener síntomas bulímicos menos de dos veces por semana o durante un periodo menor de tres meses; purgarse después de comer raciones relativamente pequeñas, o masticar y escupir la comida en vez de deglutirla.

Casi todos disfrutamos de una comida abundante ocasional (¡las comilonas de las festividades!), pero una obsesión es un escape. Si tienes constantes pensamientos negativos acerca de la comida y de tu cuerpo, tienes un problema, cualquiera que sea su clasificación clínica, y te exhorto a hacerle frente.

¿Cuánto tiempo toma mejorar?

Eso depende de ti. La conducta no se interrumpe de improviso sin esfuerzo. Es lo suficientemente adictiva para continuar como una obsesión de toda la vida.

La recuperación comprende algunos pasos necesarios. El primero es reconocer que uno tiene un problema y tomar la decisión de cambiar. Para ciertas personas es necesaria una terapia prolongada, incluso hospitalización.

En general, vencer la bulimia toma tiempo y un compromiso firme, e invertir más tiempo, esfuerzo y determinación hará que ello ocurra más pronto.

El tiempo que toma dejar de hacer comilonas varía con cada persona. He oído de algunas que han "parado en seco", de manera instantánea, y de otras que han reducido el número de comilonas poco a poco a lo largo de meses o años, mientras trabajaban en los problemas de fondo. Detener la conducta de comilona y purga es como abrir la caja de Pandora. En su interior están las razones por las que la bulimia comenzó y echó raíces, así como las nuevas que ha creado. Es necesario resolverlas todas.

A menudo me preguntan cuánto tardé en recuperarme. Pasé un año y medio trabajando para detener las comilonas y las purgas. En cierta etapa del proceso una sola comilona al día parecía un objetivo imposible de alcanzar, pero los días se convirtieron en semanas, y con el tiempo mi meta fue no hacer comilonas durante un mes. Deshacerme de mis pensamientos obsesivos acerca de la comida y de mi cuerpo fue más lento pues debía confrontar los problemas que desde un principio me llevaron a la bulimia.

Parar la conducta, no obstante, fue sólo un aspecto de la recuperación. También tenía metas relacionadas con mi vida emocional: mejorar mi relación con mis padres, hacer más amistades, manejar los conflictos, saber lo que necesitaba y poder hacérselo saber a las personas más cercanas a mí. Además, tenía metas en cuanto a mi imagen corporal; quería ser capaz de amar el cuerpo con el que nací, cualquiera que fuese su tamaño o forma, y dejar de criticar el de otras personas. Tuvieron que transcurrir tres o cuatro años para que me considerara capacitada para hacerlo. Pocos años después, había dejado por completo la conducta bulímica y me había convertido, de una persona fundamentalmente negativa, en otra feliz en lo esencial. No esperaba volver a ser jamás como había sido, y me consideré totalmente "curada".

Así pues, mi recuperación tuvo múltiples aspectos. Cuando me preguntan cuánto tiempo me tomó mejorar, respondo que siempre estoy trabajando en mi "mejoramiento", sobre todo en mi vida espiritual. Sin embargo, no he tenido síntoma, pensamiento ni sentimiento bulímico alguno durante muchos años. Ahora me resulta difícil recordar siquiera mi batalla contra la bulimia. No he hecho una comilona en algo así como veinte años, y nunca pienso en regresar a eso. Hay momentos, especialmente durante la menstruación, en que se me antoja comer más de lo habitual, y lo hago, sobre todo chocolates, pero esto en nada se parece a las comilonas que hacía cuando era bulímica, ni en términos de contenido ni de calidad.

Por otra parte, hace poco me diagnosticaron hipertiroidismo. Al principio, no sabía por qué mi cuerpo estaba acelerado ni por qué perdí algo de peso y tenía hambre todo el tiempo. Simplemente sobrellevé la situación, haciendo con frecuencia cinco comidas al día, hasta que por fin se descubrió mi afección.

Después del tratamiento, estoy recuperando mi peso y me siento eufórica de volver a estar en lo que siento como mi "viejo y conocido" cuerpo. Sé cuando tengo un peso saludable (no uno determinado), y me siento bien.

No todos concuerdan en que una puede "curarse" de un trastorno de la alimentación. Algunos expertos piensan que la bulimia es una adicción y que la abstinencia es la única forma de evitar recaídas. Resaltan el carácter adictivo de ciertos tipos de alimentos que desencadenan respuestas que llevan a las comilonas. Al igual que en el caso del alcoholismo, la cura total es imposible porque siempre estamos propensas a la bulimia, incluso si ya no repetimos la conducta de comilona y purga. Estos expertos dirían que una está siempre "en recuperación".

Sé que esta estrategia de abstinencia funciona para muchas, pero, en lo personal, yo quería *reducir* el poder de la comida sobre mí.

Quería ser totalmente libre para comer lo que se me antojase. Por ello, mi recuperación se concentró en lo que se conoce como la actitud "legalizada" hacia la alimentación. En vez de restringir, los partidarios de este método destacan la importancia de distinguir el hambre estomacal del hambre emocional, y satisfacer ambas en consecuencia. Insisten en que debemos obtener satisfacción del acto de comer lo que nuestro cuerpo nos pide y sugieren que, cuando desaparece la preocupación por la comida y el peso, las comilonas también se detienen.

Pese a mi experiencia personal, yo recomiendo muchos terapeutas y centros que fomentan el método de abstinencia, así como otros que no lo hacen. La información de este libro se aplica a las mujeres bulímicas interesadas en su recuperación, cualquiera que sea su postura en este sentido. No soy partidaria de alguna modalidad específica de tratamiento: lo que sea que funcione en tu caso, ¡hazlo! Puede ser necesario depender de otra conducta, por ejemplo, de las conversaciones telefónicas programadas con regularidad con amistades, o acudir a reuniones de grupos de apoyo para aliviar la tensión o distraerse. Siempre existe la posibilidad de simplemente cambiar una compulsividad por otra. Sin embargo, si te preguntas continuamente si las medidas que estás tomando te encaminan en una dirección más positiva, poco a poco conseguirás renunciar a toda conducta compulsiva. Llegará un momento en que los días pasen sin sentir temor alguno por lo que comes o por tu apariencia. Recuerda: eres un alma valiosa e importante cuya bulimia ha sido útil en muchos sentidos. Sé paciente y comprensiva, trabaja duramente, y renuncia a ella.

¿Pueden los medicamentos ayudar a la recuperación?

Incluso los partidarios más decididos de la terapia con fármacos no recomiendan un tratamiento basado exclusivamente en ellos. Ninguna "píldora mágica" puede resolver cabalmente los problemas emocionales y espirituales que están en la raíz de la conducta bulímica.

Pese a todo, los datos científicos recientes apoyan el uso de antidepresivos para el tratamiento de ciertos pacientes, como parte de un programa completo administrado por un equipo de tratamiento. Una conclusión consistente en muchos estudios es que la psicoterapia cognitivo-conductual, por sí sola, es mejor que el uso exclusivo de antidepresivos, y en ocasiones la combinación de medicamentos y psicoterapia resulta aun más eficaz.

Este tema causa controversia entre los profesionales clínicos. Casi todos coinciden en que las personas con trastornos de la alimentación tienen perturbaciones del humor, y muchos argumentan que la bulimia guarda relación con el trastorno afectivo primario, es decir, la familia psiquiátrica dentro de la cual se clasifica la depresión primaria. Los datos también sugieren que la causa de los trastornos de la alimentación podría encontrarse en factores hereditarios, genéticos y biológicos, incluso en anomalías del hipotálamo, una glándula del encéfalo que regula muchas funciones corporales.

La fluoxetina (nombre comercial: Prozac®) es el antidepresivo de uso más extendido para la bulimia, y muchos pacientes y terapeutas informan que han obtenido buenos resultados con este medicamento y con otros, como los tricíclicos (TCA) y los inhibidores de la monoaminooxidasa (MAO). Sin embargo, ni los antidepresivos ni ningún otro tipo de tratamiento funcionan con todos los pacientes. En términos generales, los estabilizadores del humor, como el carbonato de litio, los ansiolíticos y los antagonistas opiáceos, no han resultado eficaces en el tratamiento de la bulimia.

Algunas bulímicas han respondido bien al tratamiento farmacológico y han reducido las ansias de hacer comilonas en cuestión de semanas. Muchas de estas pacientes tienen antecedentes de depresión, aunque, sin duda, el hecho de ser descubiertas en el ciclo de la conducta bulímica también puede causar depresión. A ciertas bulímicas les son provechosos estos medicamentos en razón de los cambios químicos que ocurren en su organismo y que están relacionados con el hambre y la saciedad. Saca tus propias conclusiones luego de consultar a un profesional capacitado en el tratamiento farmacológico de la bulimia.

Muchas de las encuestadas han tenido experiencia con la terapia farmacológica. Cerca de 60 por ciento de quienes usaron antidepresivos los encontraron provechosos para la recuperación. Varias mujeres indicaron que la terapia farmacológica redujo sus ansias de hacer comilonas y permitió que los problemas que alimentan la conducta de comilona y purga saliesen a flote.

¿Cómo aprendo a comer correctamente?

Así como no hay un camino único hacia la recuperación, tampoco existe sólo una forma de comer correctamente. Cada organismo es diferente y, a final de cuentas, la decisión de qué y cuánto comer está en tus manos. Sin embargo, en las primeras etapas de la recuperación, cuando las emociones son intensas y las ideas dan vueltas en la cabeza, las decisiones respecto a la comida son sumamente difíciles, a veces paralizantes. Es muy útil contar con algún plan con el que te sientas a gusto en el momento de emprender la búsqueda de nuevas pautas de alimentación. Un dietista o nutriólogo calificado, en colaboración con tu terapeuta, puede ayudarte a elaborarlo. (Consulta el Capítulo 6: "Alimentación saludable y peso saludable".)

Como ya señalé, existen dos maneras principales de abordar las conductas respecto a la comida en la recuperación de la bulimia. Las personas que utilizan el método de abstinencia eliminan diversos alimentos de su dieta y se apegan a un plan de alimentación. Esto les permite evitar los alimentos que podrían desencadenar temores acerca del aumento de peso o las comilonas, como son los dulces y los alimentos procesados o fritos. Una práctica común consiste en hacer tres comidas bien planeadas cada día y tomar hasta tres bocadillos saludables.

La otra orientación alienta a las personas a ingerir el alimento que deseen, en raciones moderadas, cuando están físicamente hambrientas. Ésta es una táctica más espontánea, y por ello puede resultar muy difícil para alguien que apenas se inicia en la recuperación, pues demanda una nueva conciencia de los indicios de hambre y la autorización para comer lo que antes se consideraba "malo", sin sentimientos de culpa ni pérdida del control. Casi todos los terapeutas recomiendan un plan de alimentación con mayor estructuración externa al principio, y una introducción más gradual a un plan guiado en mayor medida desde el interior.

En estos tiempos es difícil elegir, incluso para quienes comen normalmente. Los cuatro grupos de alimentos parecen ser los rápidos, los congelados, los grasosos y los fritos: ¡malas opciones para cualquiera! Muchos restaurantes sirven raciones abundantes de alimentos grasos, azucarados y procesados. Salvo raras excepciones, las frutas y las verduras reciben tratamientos químicos, a las aves de corral y al ganado se les inyectan hormonas de crecimiento y buena parte de nuestros mariscos nadan en aguas contaminadas.

Por último, se gasta muchísimo dinero en la promoción de planes de dieta con sustitutos de comida en polvo o alimentos procesados de marcas comerciales. Lo que se considera saludable una semana incluye advertencias de riesgo la siguiente. Las bulímicas en recuperación tienen problemas para abrirse paso entre toda esta basura y aprender a consumir alimentos nutritivos.

Es obvio que comer correctamente significa no hacer comilonas ni sentirse mal por lo que una ha comido. Significa seguir una dieta lo más saludable y nutritiva posible, permitiéndose la libertad de darse gustos ocasionales sin sentimientos de culpa o de temor.

Una dieta sana y bien balanceada incluye carbohidratos complejos, proteínas, grasas, vitaminas y minerales. Los carbohidratos son la fuente principal de energía del organismo y son cruciales para el funcionamiento de los glóbulos rojos, del cerebro y del sistema nervioso central.

Por consiguiente, los granos enteros son una fuente excelente, al igual que la pasta, el arroz y las hortalizas que contienen féculas, como las papas. Las proteínas también suministran energía y, si se ingieren suficientes carbohidratos, las primeras se utilizan para construir y reparar tejidos y para ayudar a mantener el buen funcionamiento del sistema inmunológico. Los productos animales suministran proteínas "completas", pero los granos y las leguminosas (como el arroz y los frijoles) se pueden combinar de manera adecuada dentro de un periodo de 24 horas para formar proteínas "complementarias", que son indispensables para las dietas vegetarianas. El organismo también necesita grasas para obtener y absorber vitaminas liposolubles (solubles en grasa) y ácidos grasos, así como para retrasar el vaciado del alimento del estómago, lo cual proporciona una sensación de saciedad. Son buenas fuentes las semillas (como las de girasol) y los aceites insaturados. Una dieta balanceada y variada proporciona las vitaminas y minerales que se requieren, aunque puede ser apropiado tomar complementos. Si deseas más información, consulta a un profesional o buenos libros sobre nutrición (no sobre dietas).

Las personas con problemas de alimentación suelen estar enteradas de esta información nutricional básica, pero tienen dificultades para actuar en consecuencia. La causa de esto es que el alimento representa mucho más que un combustible y el acto de comer simboliza cuestiones más profundas. Modificar tu conducta relacionada con la alimentación puede exigirte que recurras al método de ensayo y error a lo largo del tiempo para encontrar los cambios que estás dispuesta a hacer en las diferentes etapas de tu avance.

Comer normalmente significa disfrutar lo que como. También significa amarme lo suficiente para alimentar mi cuerpo con una nutrición sana y adecuada.

Ya no hay más alimentos "buenos" o "malos". Como cuando me siento físicamente hambrienta, y dejo de hacerlo cuando me siento a gusto y satisfecha. Puedo consumir los alimentos que me gustan siempre que siento apetito por ellos, y estoy más consciente de su sabor y su textura. Ya no hago más comilonas como consecuencia de las privaciones.

Si dejo de purgarme, ¿aumentaré de peso?

No hay una respuesta única a esta pregunta que sea válida para todo el mundo. Algunas personas aumentan de peso cuando dejan de purgarse, otras lo pierden o permanecen como antes. La interrogante es de obvio interés para la mayoría de las bulímicas, pero hace surgir otra, más pertinente: ¿por qué te preocupa? Ganar o perder peso no es tan importante como llegar a aceptarte a ti misma, cualquiera que sea tu peso o tu forma. (Consulta el capítulo 6: "Alimentación saludable y peso saludable".)

En la actualidad, el nocivo mensaje de que la delgadez tiene un valor intrínseco se permea en todos los niveles de la sociedad, aunque no siempre ha sido así. Aun cuando han existido normas sociales de belleza en todas las culturas y épocas, en los países occidentalizados se ha puesto cada vez más énfasis en la delgadez desde finales de los años 60, en particular respecto a las mujeres. Las actrices y modelos contemporáneas, que representan la mujer "ideal", son entre el 5 y el 10 por ciento más delgado de la población en general. En consecuencia, el 90 o 95 por ciento de las mujeres se sienten presionadas a perder peso. Tan arraigado está el valor de la delgadez, que hacer dieta ha llegado a ser una parte aceptada de su vida. Un estudio estadounidense mostró que el 42 por ciento de las niñas de primero a tercer grado quieren ser más delgadas. Otro mostró que el 51 por ciento de las niñas de nueve y 10 años se sienten mejor respecto a su persona cuando hacen dieta; el 9 por ciento de las de nueve años han vomitado para perder peso; el 81 por ciento de las de 10 años tienen miedo de ser gordas.

Un cuerpo esbelto se ha convertido en una panacea, con recompensas tanto implícitas como reales. Pedimos a las personas que han tenido problemas con la comida que enumerasen sus reacciones viscerales ante las palabras "delgada" y "gorda". "Delgada" se asocia con bondad, poder, éxito, glamour, comodidad, dominio, felicidad, aprobación, atracción, amistad, amor y perfección. "Gorda" indica lo contrario: ¡pánico, ira, odio a sí misma, inferioridad, infelicidad, falta de valor personal, soledad, frustración, repugnancia, desesperación, pereza, rechazo, falta de control, fealdad, descuido y fracaso! Ya no somos capaces de distinguir el valor intrínseco de una persona sin fijarnos en la significación que connota el tamaño de su cuerpo. Esto crea prejuicios, cuyo resultado final es la discriminación contra las personas de cuerpo grande. Como es natural, ¡a ti te preocupa la posibilidad de aumentar de peso!

El hecho es que los cuerpos son de todas las formas y tallas, y que cada persona tiene un peso "natural", genéticamente programado, que es el más saludable para ella. A esto se le llama "punto de equilibrio", y es el peso en el que una se siente mejor, sin comer en exceso ni demasiado poco, y tiene un metabolismo balanceado. Este peso ideal es muy diferente del que aparece en una tabla estandarizada. Es característico de cada persona. En realidad, nuestro punto de equilibrio tiene un intervalo de variación de entre dos y cinco kilogramos. (Consulta el Capítulo 6: "Alimentación saludable y peso saludable".) Incluso un cuerpo grueso puede estar en buena condición física cuando se encuentra en su punto de equilibrio, recibiendo alimentación sana y haciendo ejercicio moderado con regularidad.

Cada mujer puede encontrar su cuerpo en su árbol genealógico, ¡y no es mucho lo que puede hacer al respecto! Las investigaciones han demostrado consistentemente que la gente gruesa, en promedio, no come más que las personas delgadas. Los hijos adoptivos biológicamente esbeltos que viven en hogares de padres adoptivos obesos no engordan al crecer, ni viceversa. Las personas genéticamente esbeltas que son sobrealimentadas no engordan. En las familias adoptivas no hay relación entre el peso de los padres y el de los hijos. Los estudios realizados con gemelos también demuestran que la herencia explica alrededor del 70 por ciento de la obesidad.

En respuesta a la pregunta original, por atemorizante que pueda ser, muchas mujeres bulímicas que vuelven a comer de manera normal ganan algo de peso, mientras tanto su organismo se ajusta a la normalidad y se repone su provisión de agua celular. *Con el tiempo, se estabilizan en el peso genéticamente correcto para su cuerpo específico.* En forma simultánea hacen el compromiso de lograr felicidad, serenidad mental, sentimientos de unidad e integridad, y también de cuidar de sí mismas en lo emocional y en lo físico. Resulta interesante que muchas de las participantes en nuestra encuesta descubrieron que, cuando renunciaron a hacer dieta y a la necesidad de ser esbeltas, su cuerpo encontró el equilibrio en pesos que resultaron aceptables, cómodos, hermosos y singulares, sin alcanzar necesariamente la delgadez.

Solía pesarme al menos 25 veces al día. Ahora, no me he subido a una báscula en más de dos años. Las personas con trastornos de la alimentación, como yo, estamos obsesionadas con los números. Lo que cuenta es cómo se siente una, no un número en una báscula. Es difícil romper con el hábito, pero mi consejo para todas es: ¡no te peses!

Nada me dolía más que me llamaran "gorda". Es sólo ahora, con pasos definidos hacia la recuperación, que he logrado entender cómo utilizaba la comida y los problemas de peso para ocultarme de los verdaderas dificultades: problemas de relación, soledad y timidez. Sólo cuando tomé la recuperación como asunto serio conseguí entender que no todo en la vida gira en torno a ser obesa o esbelta.

¿Cómo elegir un terapeuta?

Para la mayoría de las bulímicas es recomendable pensar en someterse a terapia profesional. Con frecuencia la gente me pide que le recomiende terapeutas, y en una conferencia recomendé a un psiquiatra considerado como experto en trastornos de la alimentación en todo el país. Desde la parte posterior del salón, una mujer exclamó de inmediato: "¡Oh, no, ese hombre es horrible!" Enseguida describió sus experiencias con él, que fueron de verdad terribles. Sin embargo, sé que ha ayudado a otras. Es importante encontrar el o la terapeuta más conveniente para una. ¿Comprarías un auto sin hacer un recorrido de prueba? Algunas personas se toman una hora para decidir qué helado comprar en el supermercado. Sin duda, la elección de un terapeuta amerita más consideración que ésa. Dedica tiempo y esfuerzo a encontrar uno capaz de ayudarte.

El término "terapeuta" se refiere por lo general a un o una psiquiatra, psicóloga o consejera matrimonial y familiar, pero puede referirse a otros profesionales, como dietistas, trabajadoras sociales tituladas o nutriólogos. Asimismo, ciertas enfermeras registradas, clérigos, acupunturistas, quiroprácticos o practicantes del contacto terapéutico pueden brindar servicios muy valiosos. Una estrategia multidisciplinaria combina varios profesionales en un equipo

de tratamiento. Si se considera la posibilidad de una terapia farmacológica, es necesario contar con un médico calificado como parte del equipo.

Consulta el directorio telefónico y haz algunas llamadas para
pedir referencias. Las recomendaciones son un buen punto de partida, pero es conveniente investigar. Llama a su consultorio y pide
una cita breve para conocerlo. Coméntale que estás entrevistán-
dote con otros terapeutas; así apreciará tus esfuerzos.

Acude preparada con una lista de preguntas. No será una
sesión terapéutica, de modo que pueden ser hipotéticas o directas, eso depende de ti. Algunas de ellas podrían ser: ¿Cuál es su
estrategia para el tratamiento de la bulimia? ¿Con qué frecuencia
tendré que acudir al consultorio? ¿Cuán rápido piensa que podría-
mos ver resultados? ¿Cuánto espera que dure la terapia? ¿Cuál será
el costo? ¿Tiene escala móvil de honorarios, con base en los in-
gresos y necesidades? ¿Acepta mi seguro?

Para evaluar las entrevistas, aplica criterios que tengan sentido para ti. Se trata de medidas subjetivas. Probablemente el aspecto más importante que debes considerar es cómo te sentiste
durante las entrevistas. Si estuviste a gusto con el o la terapeuta y
sentiste que podrían trabajar juntos honestamente, sería un buen
indicio. Otras cosas que deberás observar son: ¿Te agrada el consultorio? ¿Parece amable el personal? ¿Te responde directamente
el(la) terapeuta y te invita a expresarte?

Por último, siempre se puede cambiar de terapeuta. Una vez
que hayas elegido uno, prueba al menos durante algunas sesiones. Dale oportunidad a la terapia de probar sus bondades. Tú y
el terapeuta podrían acordar un periodo razonable antes de evaluar sus avances. Si tu primera elección resulta poco satisfactoria,
¡busca otra persona!

¿Qué puedo hacer para ayudar a una persona bulímica?

El apoyo de un cónyuge, padre, hermana o amiga es una de las herramientas más valiosas que la persona que padece un trastorno de la alimentación puede tener. Si alguien cercano a ti tiene bulimia, pueden enfrentarla juntos de diversas maneras, pero recuerda que, a fin de cuentas, ella o él es quien encara el problema. Los seres queridos pueden investigar opciones de tratamiento, leer libros adecuados, asistir a conferencias, hablar con expertos y apoyarla escuchándola con simpatía, pero sólo la bulímica puede hacer el trabajo. (Consulta el Capítulo 8: "Consejos para los seres queridos".)

No olvides que la bulimia es una forma de sentir que una tiene dominio sobre su propia vida. A veces, lo que pretende ser útil y considerado puede interpretarse como un intento de control por la persona que padece el trastorno. Comunícale que estás disponible para ayudarla, pero que no te corresponde vigilar su conducta. Tú estás ahí para apoyarla y alentarla en su lucha por sanar, pero sólo si eso es lo que ella desea.

La bulimia es un dispositivo protector que se utiliza para manejar el dolor. Si fuera fácil renunciar a ella, la persona ya lo habría hecho. Alguien que usa la comida como un mecanismo de defensa necesita comprensión y compasión. Es posible que la realidad de la bulimia te cause horror y repugnancia, pero procura separar a la persona de su conducta de comilona y purga. Ella merece amor y aprecio por lo que es, aparte de la bulimia, y compasión por el dolor que la ha empujado a la enfermedad. Si un ser amado quedara incapacitado o estuviera enfermo, permanecerías a su lado. La bulimia es también incapacitante y pone en peligro la vida.

Si es tu caso, no permitas que te manipulen ni te mientan por causa de las comilonas. No "posibilites" el trastorno haciéndote de la vista gorda o fingiendo que el problema no es grave.

Si abasteces el refrigerador de comida sólo para que ésta se vaya por el excusado, sé honesta y firme respecto a tus derechos y necesidades. No debes permitir que una bulímica abuse de tu confianza o de tu billetera; tener bulimia no justifica tratar a los seres queridos de mala manera. No conviertas las comidas en batallas: el alimento no es el problema.

En especial, los padres de las bulímicas necesitan estar conscientes de sus limitaciones si se trata de ayudar a sus hijas. La relación suele ser demasiado estrecha para hacer una evaluación objetiva. Dejen que su hija les exprese abiertamente sus sentimientos y, si no logra avances con su ayuda en un plazo corto, aliéntenla a recibir terapia.

También sería conveniente que busquen consejo profesional o un grupo de apoyo que les ayude a manejar sus propios sentimientos de frustración e impotencia.

Por lo regular, los padres desempeñan un papel en el desarrollo de la conducta de su hija y, en muchos casos, pueden verse en la necesidad de encarar problemas y hacer ajustes por su cuenta. Eso no quiere decir que ellos sean la causa del trastorno de la alimentación, sino que quizás han contribuido a él de alguna manera y es necesario que lo reconozcan. Tal vez deban reevaluar sus valores, sus formas de comunicación, las reglas familiares acerca de la comida, sus modelos para manejar los sentimientos, sus funciones en la crianza de los hijos y el proceso de toma de decisiones de la familia. Son probables los sentimientos de culpa, ira, frustración, negación y cinismo.

Pese a lo duro que esto parece, la terapia familiar ha probado ser uno de los modelos más satisfactorios para vencer los trastornos de la alimentación. Con mejor comunicación, más conocimiento de sí mismos y la aceptación mutua de lo que ha ocurrido en el pasado, padres e hijos pueden concentrarse en la importante tarea de la recuperación en el presente.

CAPÍTULO 2

Come sin temor
Una historia de la vida real del síndrome de comilona y purga

Lindsey Hall, a los 3 años de edad
(fotografía de LeMoyne Hall)

El comienzo

Crecí en una familia acomodada que vivía en una casa colonial de tres pisos. Mi padre era banquero inversionista y mi madre se encargaba del hogar. Tuve tres hermanas mayores que me dedicaban poca atención, salvo una de ellas que me fastidiaba sin piedad. A todas ellas las fueron enviando una por una a un internado a la edad de 14 años, y a partir de entonces las vi sólo en las vacaciones. Tenía siete años cuando nació el quinto bebé, y mis padres contrataron a una pareja que vino a vivir a la casa para cuidar de mi hermanito y de mí.

La impresión general que tengo de mi infancia es la de estar sola y con miedo de haber hecho algo malo. Nunca me propuse meterme en dificultades; por el contrario, siempre traté de ser una niñita perfecta. No obstante, tenía la impresión de que constantemente arruinaba las cosas, como la vez que puse los animales de juguete de mi hermana en una funda de almohada para mostrarlos a alguien, sin comprender que eran de porcelana delicada y se romperían.

Una de mis peores equivocaciones fue encerrarme accidentalmente en el armario donde mi madre guardaba su ropa. Ahí me quedé todo el día, llorando y con miedo de los zapatos, que parecían serpientes debajo de mi cuerpo. Nadie escuchó mis gritos, ni el ama de llaves ni mi nana, y me encontraron hasta que mi madre regresó a casa cerca del anochecer. Pese a que me rescataron, sentí que la vida en esa casa podía continuar sin mí y nadie lo advertiría. No era ni la más inteligente, ni la más bonita, ni la mayor, ni la menor, ni siquiera un niño, cualidades, cualquiera de ellas, que yo pensaba me habrían conferido cierta importancia en el hogar.

También recuerdo claramente la atmósfera de nuestra casa, que podría describir con facilidad como "tenue". Mi padre se irritaba con facilidad y todos hacíamos lo posible por no interponernos en su camino. En la mesa, durante la cena, lo escuchábamos narrar anécdotas de su día en el trabajo o bromear acerca de personas con las que se había encontrado en la ciudad, y nos preguntábamos por qué siempre parecía mucho más feliz cuando estaba lejos de nosotras. A veces menospreciaba a mi madre por no interesarse lo suficiente en su trabajo o por no tener la inteligencia suficiente para entenderlo. Cuanto más crecía, más me enfurecía esto, y muchas veces me interpuse entre ellos para desviar sus ataques verbales.

Mi madre era una mujer de voz suave, muy educada, que provenía de una numerosa familia católica. Participaba activamente en causas ecológicas, jugaba tenis cada semana y era aficionada a la fotografía. Tenía un cuarto oscuro en el sótano de la casa y recuerdo haber pasado horas enteras con ella bajo la tenue luz, mirando cómo las imágenes surgían de las malolientes bandejas con productos químicos. No recuerdo haberla visto perder los estribos una sola vez, aunque eran pocos los problemas que se comentaban. A partir del momento en que contrataron a la nana, pasé cada vez menos tiempo con ella.

Por lo regular yo permanecía a solas en mi habitación, en el cuarto de juegos del desván o en los graneros vacíos. Tenía algunas amigas que vivían cerca, pero evitaba ir a sus casas por temor a sus padres. Una de las madres acostumbraba reírse o gritarme cuando yo no quería comer. Otra amenazó con golpearme con una cuchara de madera si no me sentaba a la mesa a terminar mi almuerzo. Me aterrorizaba la posibilidad de regresar a ese lugar: ¡me hizo comer tomates!

Cuando tenía 10 años, en un examen físico anual, alcancé a escuchar que el médico le decía a mi madre que yo pesaba demasiado. No me lo dijeron a mí, pero después de eso cobré conciencia de mis imperfectas dimensiones. Las vendedoras de la tienda de ropa donde mi madre y yo comprábamos los vestidos para la escuela de baile siempre mostraban simpatía por mi "problema con mi figura" y me recomendaban faldas de "línea A". Pese a mi apodo en la escuela primaria —la "piernuda"—, no era fea ni deforme. A la edad de 13 años pesaba 61 kilos y medía 1.63 metros. Era una chica activa, atlética y, de hecho, tenía una figura similar a la que tengo ahora.

A la edad de 14 años me enviaron a un prestigioso internado. Todas mis compañeras de grupo de la escuela primaria se fueron también a escuelas particulares, porque se consideraba a la escuela pública local como de "clase baja". Sin comprender cuánto miedo tenía y sin saber cómo comunicar mis temores, salí de casa bañada en lágrimas. Durante meses lloraba a la primera provocación. Nunca había compartido mis problemas emocionales con mis padres ni hecho confidencias a mis amigas. Ni siquiera sabía, en realidad, qué era lo que me molestaba. Todo lo que sabía era que me sentía desesperadamente infeliz y terriblemente sola.

Las demás chicas de la escuela parecían todas hermosas y distantes: uñas largas, ropas elegantes, cabello rizado y cuerpo *esbelto*. Desde el principio, fue obvio que ser delgada estaba de moda. Yo tenía piernas gruesas, lo que para mí era la forma más desagradable de estar "pasada de peso", y senos pequeños, lo que resultaba "indeseable" según los dictados de la moda. Tener un cuerpo con forma de pera era un pecado tácito. A partir de entonces, comencé a ver el mío como la fuente de mi desdicha, y a cada bocado que entraba por mi boca como una complacencia fea y egoísta, todo lo cual hizo que cada día me viese con más desagrado.

Había otras chicas de quienes sospechaba que tenían problemas con la comida. Una de ellas, que se alojaba en una habitación vecina a la mía, compraba todo el tiempo litros de helado y los escondía en su cuarto. Después, proclamaba orgullosa que iniciaría una dieta que demandaba ayunar durante los dos primeros días. Otra chica bajó tanto de peso que sus músculos ya no podían sostener su cuerpo de 1.75 metros de estatura y caminaba encorvada con su escuálida pelvis echada hacia adelante para mantener el equilibrio. La sacaron de la escuela, víctima de anorexia nerviosa, y se rumoraba que había estado vomitando para adelgazar. Ese rumor fue la primera noción que tuve de alguien que vomitara por la fuerza. Incluso la otra chica de mi pueblo natal que asistía a la escuela hizo la "locura" de no comer otra cosa que naranjas durante varios meses. Cuando la visité en la enfermería, a donde la enviaron para hacerle pruebas de azúcar en la sangre por su bajo peso, no supe qué decir. En secreto, envidiaba su fuerza de voluntad y sus marcadas costillas, y sentí como si hubiera perdido nuestra amistad.

Al llegar a mi último año, había dejado de llorar en público, y ya no daba muestras de sentirme infeliz. Hacía deporte, cantaba en el coro y tenía una buena amiga. Ella sabía que yo me consideraba fea y solía tranquilizarme diciendo que la apariencia no importaba, pero en mi fuero interno yo pensaba que ella me seguía la corriente, como lo hacían mis padres. Evitaba las situaciones que me habrían hecho sentir como una fracasada. Supliqué que no me incluyeran en el cuadro de honor de matemáticas; rehusé ser postulada para cargo alguno; rara vez asistía a los bailes, y sentía temor de hablar en clase. Me complacía sentir cólicos menstruales una vez al mes para refugiarme en la seguridad de la enfermería. No buscaba a otras amigas y prefería pasar el tiempo sola o cuidando de los animales en el laboratorio de biología.

Comencé a acumular alimentos en el refrigerador del dormitorio y a veces me ocultaba en el armario durante la hora de la cena, comiendo a escondidas mis reservas particulares de yogur. Guardaba una lata de dos kilos de mantequilla de maní, y sacaba cucharadas a escondidas cuando no había nadie cerca. Solía pensar mucho en la comida, aunque no había comenzado aún con las comilonas y purgas.

Con frecuencia me probaba ropa ante un espejo de cuerpo entero para ver si me quedaba más suelta o más apretada. Comparaba mi cuerpo con el de las modelos de revistas y el de mis compañeras que hacían dietas. Temía nunca llegar a ser suficientemente delgada. ¿Quién me querría? Me dio por fumar cigarrillos en privado, lo que a mi modo de ver era algo malo, pero era mejor que comer. Recurría a la goma de mascar, a veces hasta cinco paquetes al día. Con todo esto, me las arreglé para conservar un peso constante.

Al término de mi último año, estando en casa de vacaciones, una amiga de la escuela primaria me habló de un médico que le había dado una dieta con la cual bajó cinco kilogramos en una semana.

Restándole importancia a mi desesperación, conseguí que mi madre me llevara con él. El médico me entregó un folleto donde describía la dieta y regresé al internado pensando que ahora sí, mi vida iba a cambiar; perdería los nueve kilos que se interponían entre mi persona y la felicidad. Iría a la universidad como una mujer nueva, delgada, confiada, amada. Pero la dieta era terrible.

Las instrucciones eran que debía beber dos cucharadas de aceite vegetal antes del desayuno y de la cena, comer sólo alimentos ricos en proteínas y beber dos litros de agua cada día. Perdí cuatro kilos en una semana, pero me sentía hinchada, nerviosa y deprimida. Débil y enferma, dejé la dieta, pensando que era una fracasada, segura de que nunca podría lograr lo que consideraba como algo muy importante para una mujer: una apariencia esbelta. En esa época tenía novio; pero, cuando la dieta fracasó, dejé de verlo. Asimismo, recorté y pegué en un muro de mi habitación, en letras de medio metro, la palabra *"cambio"*, aunque ya no esperaba que llegara a producirse.

Comencé a husmear en las habitaciones de otras chicas para examinar sus pertenencias. Puesto que disponía de poco dinero para ropa, no podía comprar más de lo necesario. A veces "robaba" algunas prendas y las guardaba varios días o semanas hasta que perdían su novedad, para después intentar devolverlas sin que me vieran. Muchas veces se daba parte de que un objeto se había perdido y se hacía mucho escándalo acerca de lo baja que como persona debía ser la ladrona, y yo me veía obligada a manipular las circunstancias de manera que pareciese que la víctima simplemente había extraviado el objeto faltante. No quería que se me considerara una ladrona; sólo pretendía ser como todas las demás durante un corto tiempo.

Sin embargo, los pensamientos más abrumadores eran que las demás podían comer y yo no. Miraba a la chica más delgada y preciosa poner azúcar morena y mantequilla en sus tostadas cada mañana sin engordar jamás, ¡sin la menor apariencia de culpabilidad! ¿Cómo sería vivir en un mundo como ése, donde una no *pensase* que es fea? Comencé a retraerme de la gente y me ponía celosa de todas las que eran más delgadas que yo.

La primera vez que pensé en meterme los dedos en la garganta fue durante la última semana de clases, después de ver a una chica salir del baño con la cara roja y los ojos hinchados. Pese a que su cuerpo estaba realmente bien formado, ella siempre hablaba de su peso y de que debería hacer dieta. Me di cuenta al instante de lo que había hecho, y me gradué sabiendo que vomitar podía ser la solución a mi "problema de peso". No imaginaba siquiera que mi peso no era un problema. *Cómo me sentía acerca de mí, ése era el problema.*

Sorprendí a todos —incluso a mí misma— al ser aceptada en una universidad situada a cinco mil kilómetros de casa, y partí haciendo gala de independencia y valor. Pero, una vez a solas en mi dormitorio individual, frente a frente con mis conocidos sentimientos de soledad y desprecio por mi persona, me refugié en la comida para adormecer mi angustia y perfeccioné el arte de vomitar.

Comencé por los desayunos, que se servían al estilo *buffet* en el piso principal del dormitorio, y pronto aprendí cuáles eran los alimentos que salían con facilidad. Al despertar por la mañana, solía atiborrarme durante media hora para después vomitar antes de ir a clase. Había cuatro compartimientos en el baño del dormitorio, y debía asegurarme de que nadie me atrapase en el acto. Si había mucha gente, ya sabía cuáles baños podrían estar desocupados en el camino a clases. En ocasiones una comida no bastaba para satisfacer el ansia de comer, así que comencé a comprar comida adicional. Podía comer una bolsa entera de galletas, media docena de barras de caramelo y un litro de leche para rematar una abundante comida. Una vez que la comilona comenzaba, no me detenía hasta que mi vientre parecía el de una embarazada y no podía deglutir un bocado más.

Ése fue el comienzo de nueve años de comidas obsesivas y vómito. A nadie le dije lo que estaba haciendo y no intenté dejar de hacerlo. Me atraía sentirme aturdida más que ninguna otra cosa y, aunque el hecho de enamorarme o desenamorarme —u otras distracciones—, mitigaban las ansias, siempre regresaba a la comida.

Estaba convencida de que hacer comilonas era simplemente una manera de hacer dieta. Por otra parte, no pensaba que hubiese algo de malo en ello, aunque lo hiciera todos los días. No establecí una conexión entre mi extraño comportamiento y los problemas de fondo, ni me consideraba una adicta, pues estaba segura de que podía parar en cualquier momento.

Muchas veces me prometí que "Esta comilona será la última", y que, mágicamente, me transformaría en una persona "normal" tan pronto vomitara "por esta última vez".

Mis cartas a la familia fluctuaban entre el cuestionamiento de por qué estaba en la universidad y vagas quejas acerca de mi salud.

Carta tras carta decía las mismas cosas: "Tengo miedo, pero no se preocupen por mí". "Me siento enferma, pero soy fuerte y estoy mejorando." "Probablemente estoy pasando por alguna especie de etapa." Solicitaba su atención y enseguida los tranquilizaba diciendo que no la necesitaba; y, pese a lo mucho que deseaba que me preguntasen cómo se sentía estar sola y atemorizada, habría negado esos sentimientos. Lo sé.

Era una chica inteligente, había estado en las mejores escuelas, provenía de una familia de banqueros, abogados y profesionales. Era atlética, aparentemente independiente y "centrada". ¿Cómo podía admitir que estaba vomitando para ser delgada?

Cómo vivir con un hábito

En mi segundo año me mudé fuera del campus porque no soportaba la presión de estar siempre rodeada de gente. Pensé que se veía como lo que una "mujer liberada" haría, y nadie me cuestionó. Organicé mi vida para dar cabida a mi hábito, fingiendo ante todos, incluso ante mí misma, que era más adulta de esta manera. Me juré que cuando me estableciera en el nuevo lugar dejaría las comilonas y el vómito porque no habría gente a mi alrededor que me pusiera nerviosa. Comenzaría un programa de ejercicio, me llenaría de fuerza de voluntad, adelgazaría, y el mundo sería mío. El único problema fue que, tan pronto estuve a solas, las comilonas y las purgas tomaron el mando una vez más.

Decidí que lo que en realidad necesitaba era una meta de peso específica. Elegí 50 kilos porque pensé que con ese peso me veía como una modelo.

Conservé esta meta como una obsesión que duró ocho años, y sólo la alcancé un día en que estaba totalmente deshidratada a causa del vómito. Incluso entonces, con los 50 kilos, mi imagen corporal permaneció sin cambio; pensaba que me veía igual... y eso significaba que estaba obesa. También me sentía de la misma manera cuando me veía en el espejo. Distante, fría. ¿Había sentido esta clase de autodesprecio cuando era más joven? ¿Qué me había ocurrido?

Si me iba a casa en bicicleta después de la escuela, llevaba galletas y rosquillas para comerlas mientras pedaleaba.

A veces llegaba y vomitaba todo, sólo para sentirme abrumada por la tensión una hora más tarde, y entonces partía otra vez hacia la tienda de abarrotes, en un frenético recorrido cuesta arriba. Después, podía deslizarme cuesta abajo en el camino de regreso, llenándome la boca de galletas todo el camino, sabiendo que al llegar me esperaba la liberación total.

Si tenía la opción, compraba siempre los mismos alimentos: un paquete de panecillos, medio kilo de mantequilla, un paquete de rosquillas congeladas, una bolsa de galletas, leche (de preferencia con chocolate) o helado, y quizá cinco o seis barras de caramelo para iniciar la comilona.

Comenzaba a comer en la fila y le decía a la cajera que estaba haciendo compras para una escuela de párvulos, para que no sospechara que eran para mí. Podía comer todo ese alimento en una hora, más o menos. Si no lograba terminar algo, lo tiraba a la basura, convencida de que ésta era la última vez y prometiéndome que así sería.

Si no había comprado suficiente comida en la tienda, o si no podía ir a ella, comía cualquier cosa: un par de tortillas de huevo, un lote de masa para galletas dulces, o tazones llenos de avena. No importaba.

Todo era diferente ahora que ya vivía sola. No había por qué preocuparse de si el baño estaría desocupado o de si a alguien le parecería extraño que yo entrase a mi habitación con una bolsa llena de los mismos alimentos todos los días. Ahora, la adicción estaba al mando.

Comencé a quedarme sin dinero. Mis padres me enviaban la colegiatura y una pequeña asignación, y participaba en un programa de trabajo y estudio en el que hacía pruebas a niños con retraso mental. Estaba contenta con el trabajo porque ayudar a otros me hacía sentirme bien y el empleo me mantenía lejos de la comida durante unas horas. Pero siempre gastaba todo el dinero que ganaba.

Me encontraba en este punto cuando comencé a hurtar comida. Sentía una tremenda oleada de triunfo cuando lograba salir con una bolsa de galletas o medio kilo de mantequilla. Era parecido a lo que sentía cuando robaba en el internado; quería lo que no era mío y lo que, a mi modo de ver, se me negaba. Pero había una importante diferencia: no tenía intenciones de devolver lo robado.

Unos seis meses después me descubrieron en el supermercado con medio kilo de sustituto de azúcar en la bolsa, y el gerente me amenazó con enviarme a la cárcel. Prometí corregirme, y lo hice, pero las comilonas continuaron a todo vapor.

Un matrimonio con vida secreta

En ese año tuve muchas relaciones de corta duración que fueron agradables, pero no lo que yo consideraba como la auténtica. Entonces, un amigo de un amigo, llamado David, comenzó a visitarme. Me gustaba estar con él. A medida que pasábamos más tiempo juntos, pude darme cuenta de que era en verdad una buena persona. Talentoso, entusiasta, inteligente, seguro. Avergonzada, decidí no hablarle acerca de mis hábitos de alimentación porque estaba segura de que, de cualquier manera, iban a cambiar "mañana". Tenía 20 años y era agradable estar enamorada. Debido a su servicio militar, pasamos separados gran parte de nuestros dos años de cortejo. Cuando estábamos juntos los fines de semana, solía quedar libre de mis obsesiones con la comida.

Mis padres le tomaron afecto a David de inmediato, lo que me hizo sentir que había elegido acertadamente. ¡Escogerlo a él era al menos una cosa que había hecho bien! Sin embargo, durante las visitas a casa, cuanto más se integraba él a mi familia, más me retraía yo. Acostumbrada a sentirme inadvertida, pero sin saber cómo manejar ese sentimiento, me dedicaba a comer. Me comportaba y me sentía como una persona ajena a la familia; metía a escondidas mis emparedados y galletas y vomitaba en un baño con el ventilador trabajando al máximo para que nadie oyera lo que hacía.

Cuanto partíamos, siempre era con los mismos sentimientos de desconexión que experimenté al dejar mi hogar años antes. Aferrada a la estabilidad y seguridad de mi relación con David, el matrimonio me pareció el paso lógico siguiente. No pensé que tuviese importancia el hecho de que mi mente solía estar en otra parte, soñando en comida, porque al parecer me sentía amada y enamorada.

Durante los cinco años que estuvimos casados, los rituales cotidianos y mis problemas con la comida se tornaron cada vez más rígidos. Aprendí a aplicarme polvo facial en los ojos para ocultar su color rojo, debido a la fuerza que hacía al vomitar en el excusado, y en los nudillos, que se ponían en carne viva por el roce con mis dientes. Como rutina, hacía correr agua en el lavabo para ahogar los sonidos de mi vómito. Me pesaba en la báscula siempre que entraba al baño, al igual que antes y después de cada comilona. Me probaba mi ropa metódicamente ante un espejo de cuerpo entero, con la esperanza de que colgara más suelta que la vez anterior.

Me convertí en un ama de casa meticulosa, especialmente cuando no tenía empleo y "trabajaba" en casa. A veces detenía el vómito mientras pasaba la aspiradora y lavaba los platos, comiendo todo el tiempo y preparando el escenario para la "limpieza" de mi cuerpo.

Hacía, en promedio, de tres a cinco comilonas al día, para lo cual necesitaba ocultar mis huellas con cuidado. Entre comilonas, corría a la tienda a reabastecerme de alimentos. Hubo días en que tuve que hornear dos lotes de pastelillos de chocolate. Lavaba platos y a cada rato limpiaba bien el excusado para asegurarme de no dejar rastro alguno. Quería que todo estuviera ordenado y limpio. ¡Lo único que no estaba perfecto era yo misma! Y estaba atrapada en una pesadilla de la que no podía hablar con nadie.

Aunque con mucha frecuencia comíamos fuera de casa, me sentía nerviosa y preocupada en los restaurantes. Nunca ordenaba un plato principal porque temía perder el control. En vez de ello, ordenaba platos de acompañamiento y sugería que tomáramos helado después de la cena, para así poder deshacerme de lo que había comido. Siempre pedía leche entera, porque era espesa y tersa, y hacía que la comida saliera con más facilidad. Incluso sabía cuáles restaurantes tenían baños privados.

Para los demás yo parecía una fanática de la alimentación saludable. En público, me aseguraba de comer sólo alimentos con pocas calorías y grasas.

Leía libros sobre nutrición y salud, en la creencia de que serían una influencia positiva. Tomé un curso de anatomía y fisiología porque pensé que, si podía ver lo que me estaba haciendo a mí misma físicamente, quizá dejaría las comilonas. En determinado momento, incluso asistí a un curso llamado "Sueños creativos", impartido por una mujer llamada Patricia Garfield, pensando que quizá mis sueños me revelarían la clave de mi infelicidad.

Qué ignorancia la mía.

Fui sorprendentemente productiva durante esos cinco años en los que mi bulimia empeoró. Obtuve mi título, tuve dos empleos estimulantes y llevé a cabo proyectos creativos por mi cuenta.

Inicié un negocio que aún está en marcha, y mantuve relaciones con mi familia y mis amistades, aunque a cierta distancia. Sin embargo, pese a que conseguía aparentar una vida externa normal, en lo interno caminaba por una cuerda floja emocional. Durante los últimos cinco años, comía y vomitaba varias veces al día. Podía sentir que me estaba derrumbando.

Al cabo de nueve años, comenzaron a ser preocupantes ciertos efectos físicos colaterales. Mi vista solía ser borrosa y padecía intensas jaquecas. Lo que antes eran mareos y debilidad pasajeros después de las purgas se convirtieron en un caminar inseguro, en golpearme con las paredes y en agotamiento. Mi cutis se deterioró, y con frecuencia sufría estreñimiento.

Casi siempre estaba deshidratada, pero no me gustaba tomar agua porque me hacía sentir hinchada. Mis dientes eran un desastre. Mis uñas formaron grandes ampollas de sangre en la parte posterior de mi boca. Aun así, me negaba a reconocer que tenía un grave problema, pese a que las señales eran evidentes: una adicción delirante, mala salud, un matrimonio cada vez más distante, aislamiento, baja autoestima, ataques de depresión y sigilo.

Un cambio de enfoque

Pese a la intensidad de mi bulimia y al sigilo en torno a ella, David y yo tuvimos muchos momentos felices y llenos de amor. Nunca cuestionamos abiertamente nuestra vida en común, pero él estaba comprometido con muchas otras actividades y yo tenía mi comida.

Para darme una sorpresa, a mediados de aquel invierno mi padre me invitó a ir con él a una pequeña isla de las Indias

Occidentales por dos semanas. No obstante que la idea me puso sumamente nerviosa, tomé la oportunidad al vuelo. Quizá el asunto de encadenarme a un baño durante nueve años comenzaba a sonar a viejo. No lo sé con exactitud. Lo que sí sé es que hice un viaje con mi padre, a quien temía intensamente, y con este hecho se inició para mí la marcha hacia la recuperación. Durante todo el tiempo que estuve ahí, la bulimia me dejó por completo en paz.

Eso, por sí solo, ya era un milagro, pero en ese viaje ocurrió algo aun más inesperado. En cierta ocasión me desperté a media noche y anoté en mi diario de sueños: "Conocí a una mujer cuyo nombre era Gürze. Tenía cabello de visón y en ella habitaban siete animales". Por la mañana, leí de nuevo esta frase y examiné el dibujo que había hecho de una curiosa mujercita de piernas largas, cabeza grande y labios rojos con forma de corazón. No pensé mucho en ello en ese momento, y pasé los últimos días de mi viaje aprendiendo un extraño procedimiento de *batik* que me enseñaron unos artistas del lugar.

Cuando regresé a casa, comencé a experimentar con motivos de batik, claveteando marcos de dos metros y medio para la tela y pasando horas inclinada sobre toneles de cera caliente y tintes. Por capricho, sin embargo, también hice una muñeca de metro y medio de estatura, con la mujer de mi sueño, Gürze, como modelo, y la vestí con mis coloridas telas de batik. Después, le hice un novio, Dash, y finalmente todo un grupo de amigos, todos de metro y medio de estatura y vestidos como personajes cómicos.

Durante un año conseguí hacer un espacio para mi arte entre las comilonas y, cuando hube acumulado un buen número de obras, me llevé mis batiks y dos de las muñecas a una ciudad cercana para venderlas. Pensaba quedarme con unos parientes a quienes no conocía muy bien. Estaba decidida a hacer mi mejor esfuerzo y programé citas con varios diseñadores. Intenté reunir la confianza suficiente en mí misma para aceptar las críticas de buena gana, pero sentía una presión abrumadora. Regresar al departamento me daba miedo. Fueron muchas las noches en las que me detuve en un mercado camino a casa para comprar montones de comida que devoraba en mi habitación cuando ya todos se habían ido a dormir. Una noche, preocupada por una comilona, dejé unos papeles importantes en un lugar donde me detuve a comprar pizza y helado. Regresé corriendo por calles oscuras y poco transitadas, por completo ajena al peligro. Mi obsesión por la comida me había privado de la capacidad de pensar racionalmente.

Fue durante este viaje que me topé con un artículo en una revista en el cual se hablaba de personas que tenían problemas con la comida similar al mío. Dicho artículo fue uno de los primeros que se escribieron acerca del ciclo de la comilona y el vómito. La autora, Marlene Boskind-White, consideraba que la enfermedad que ella denominaba "bulimarexia" estaba relacionada con la anorexia nerviosa, un padecimiento que se caracteriza por la inanición autoinfligida, pero diferente en virtud de la repetición de las comilonas y purgas.

¡Me quedé impresionada! Ella dirigía grupos de terapia a cinco kilómetros de donde yo vivía.

Por añadidura, y por increíble que me pareciera en ese momento, en una esquina un caballero me preguntó por las dos muñecas que colgaban de mi mochila y me las compró. Los batiks despertaron poco interés, pero dondequiera que iba la gente me preguntaba de las muñecas.

Mi mundo dio un vuelco de improviso. Mi trabajo parecía haberse vuelto de cabeza porque a la gente le gustaban las muñecas y no podía dejar de pensar en ese artículo acerca de la bulimarexia. Cuando regresé a casa, pasé una semana haciendo fuertes comilonas y después llamé a la doctora Boskind-White, quien me indicó que fuera a verla de inmediato.

En el camino, me detuve a introducirme el dedo en la garganta por si aquélla fuese la última vez. ¿Qué tal si ella me curaba hoy mismo? ¡No estaba preparada!

Durante la entrevista, resté importancia a mi falta de control y a la gravedad del problema. ¡Era la primera vez que hablaba con alguien acerca del asunto! No sé si ella adivinó que le ocultaba cosas, pero me invitó a unirme a uno de sus grupos de terapia permanente que se reuniría en unos pocos días. Le dije a David que había decidido resolver un antiguo problema de una nueva manera, y no agregué más detalles, salvo que recurriría a ayuda externa.

Lejos de sentirme aliviada, seguí inquieta en casa, pensando en que tendría que hablar ante un grupo de extrañas acerca de mis comilonas.

Cuando llegué a la primera reunión, presenté mi fachada habitual de confianza en mí misma, pues me avergonzaba reconocer que abusaba de la comida de una manera tan insólita.

No quería admitir exactamente con cuánta frecuencia hacía comilonas, cuánto comía o que estaba a solas buena parte del tiempo, pero lo hice. Decir en voz alta: "Vomito cinco veces al día" fue sumamente difícil. Pero las mujeres del grupo estaban dispuestas a ayudar y se mostraban receptivas, pese a que cada una de ellas luchaba contra sus propios problemas con la alimentación. Todo el tiempo yo había pensado que era la única que mantenía una relación tan extraña con ella, pero el grupo me ayudó a ver que no estaba sola en absoluto.

La doctora Boskind-White subrayaba también la importancia de poner en práctica acciones como hacerse oír, reconocer los sentimientos con honestidad y llevar un diario. Comencé un diario que llevé durante varios años, y ese simple paso significó una gran diferencia. Estaba aprendiendo a expresar con palabras lo que había estado diciendo con mi bulimia. Poco a poco, conseguí posponer las comilonas por un día o dos, y comencé a adquirir confianza en que me pondría mejor.

Había asistido a cinco sesiones cuando a David lo transfirieron a otra ciudad. Aunque el propósito de recuperarme de la bulimia se estaba convirtiendo en el foco de mi atención, aún tenía miedo de decirle algo a mi marido. Por otra parte, sometido a la tensión de mi vida secreta y a la dedicación de él a sus estudios de posgrado, nuestro matrimonio se había convertido en una distante camaradería. Decidí que debía vivir sola por un tiempo. Le dije que me mudaría con él, pero que quería mi propio espacio. Pensé que necesitábamos un cambio para que pudiésemos mejorar como pareja. El problema era mío, y más tarde regresaría a él limpia, pura, libre e independiente, cuando todo hubiera quedado atrás. No era necesario que él se enterase.

Cuando nos mudamos, nos fuimos a vivir a lugares separados, lo cual era doloroso y desconcertante para ambos. Nunca esperamos vivir cada quien por su lado. David alquiló un departamento en la ciudad, y yo una habitación en una casa en el campo. Nos veíamos prácticamente todos los días, pero siempre resultaba incómodo. Pese a que había comenzado a experimentar cambios en mi interior, cuando estábamos juntos era incapaz de describirlos o expresarlos.

Susan, la mujer que me alquilaba la habitación, me agradaba, y esperaba poder abrirme con ella y contarle mis problemas. Pero extrañaba la seguridad de mi grupo de apoyo, y reanudé las comilonas casi de inmediato. Seguí llevando mi diario, pero me sentía asqueada de mi forma de comer y escribía sólo acerca de las cosas de la vida diaria, sin describir cómo me sentía.

No obstante haber dado algunos pasos audaces hacia mi propia curación, aún me aferraba a la mágica promesa de mejorar "mañana".

En dos meses se instalaría una feria artística y decidí vender mis batiks y mis muñecas en ella. Aunque me estaba quedando sin dinero, seguí comiendo en exceso y vomitando, suponiendo que las cosas cambiarían cuando llegase la feria. Podría pasar buenos ratos con David, que ofreció llevarme en su auto. Pero hasta ese momento dejé de trabajar en mí misma. Una vez más, mi bienestar no era prioritario, y me atiborré y me purgué sin parar hasta que llegó la feria.

El momento decisivo

Había confiado en que la feria sería un momento crucial para mí, y lo fue, pero no de la manera como esperaba.

En términos monetarios fue un fracaso, pues no conseguí vender nada. Al término del tercer día, estaba hecha un manojo de nervios y me solté llorando con David y su madre, con quien nos estábamos quedando. No estaba dispuesta a decirles que mis mayores preocupaciones tenían que ver con la comida, así que no pudieron ayudarme. Me esperaba el regreso a mi habitación, a mi aislamiento, sin un trabajo "real", incapaz de confiar a nadie el problema con la comida que dominaba mi existencia.

Pero no fueron estos aspectos los que hicieron del viaje un momento decisivo, sino mi encuentro con un hombre llamado Leigh Cohn, quien también vendía en la feria. De inmediato me sentí capaz de identificarme con él, y pasamos horas conversando en los ratos en que había poco movimiento. Nunca me había sentido tan a gusto con alguien; hubo intimidad en nuestra conversación desde un principio, algo diferente de mis otras relaciones. Sentía su presencia incluso cuando estábamos separados y, cuando la feria terminó, a nuestro pesar nos dijimos adiós. Intercambiamos cartas y llamadas telefónicas tan pronto como pudimos, e hicimos planes para vernos una semana después.

Cuando por fin tocó a mi puerta, la atracción fue increíblemente intensa. Durante las tres semanas siguientes pasamos casi todos los días juntos, en lo que sentíamos como una unión perfecta.

Para sorpresa de todo el mundo, incluso mía, Leigh, que había pedido un año de permiso para ausentarse de su trabajo de enseñanza, dejó su casa, que estaba en venta en Los Ángeles, para venir a vivir conmigo en mi habitación de la casa de Susan.

Cuando David se enteró, reaccionó con incredulidad y tuvimos muchos enfrentamientos. A mis padres les causó disgusto nuestra separación, pero lo que les pareció más incomprensible fue que yo estuviese viviendo con un hombre al que había conocido sólo durante un mes, estando aún casada. Hasta a Susan le pareció mal. Todos estaban en contra nuestra, ¡y no podía culparlos!

A pesar de todo, sentía que, en un nivel muy profundo, por una vez estaba haciendo lo correcto y comencé a sentirme mejor, tratando de sobrellevar las presiones. Era increíble, la bulimia desapareció durante esas primeras semanas. Leigh y yo estábamos juntos casi todo el tiempo y la repentina diferencia en mi rutina diaria me causaba una sensación maravillosamente saludable y refrescante. Ésta parecía ser la cura instantánea y mágica que siempre había deseado.

A medida que los días comenzaron a volver a la rutina, sin embargo, mi recién descubierta fortaleza comenzó a disiparse. Me preocupaba el dolor que estaba causando a mis padres y a David. Me sentía culpable por ser tan egoísta. Temía no poder renunciar a la bulimia. ¿Quién sería yo sin ella? Comencé a dudar de si realmente actuaba bien y si sabía lo que hacía. Después de todo, había comido y vomitado durante nueve años, sabiendo a ciencia cierta que hacía una locura; ¡quizás aún estaba loca!

Con la tensión en aumento, comencé a sacar comida a escondidas mientras Leigh dormía y cuando me encontraba a solas en el estudio que había alquilado. Sentía cómo se acumulaban la desesperación y la soledad —como había ocurrido en el pasado—, y me sentía frustrada al reconocer que estar tan enamorada no me curó totalmente, a final de cuentas. Supe entonces que no habría una salida fácil. Tenía mucho trabajo por delante si quería vencer la bulimia alguna vez, y si no tomaba la iniciativa en ese mismo instante, corría el riesgo de recaer en mi adicción de forma permanente.

Anhelaba que todos los aspectos de mi vida fueran tan maravillosos, llenos de afecto y libres de bulimia como lo habían sido esas primeras semanas con Leigh. Los recuerdos de aquel tiempo libre de bulimia con mi padre estaban aún frescos en mi memoria.

Decidí correr el riesgo y contar todo a Leigh; de lo contrario, habría sólo secretos y ocultamientos. Ahora deseaba honestidad y amor.

El fin del comportamiento

En un arrebato emocional, con lágrimas en los ojos, describí mis comilonas y mis vómitos. Al principio, él pensó que no era un problema serio, porque nunca había oído hablar de la bulimia. Además, había sido fanático de los dulces toda su vida, y era capaz de comer cantidades enormes de rosquillas y pasta de galletas sin sentirse culpable, aumentar de peso ni padecer caries. A su familia le encantaban las grandes comidas y las cajas de caramelos, en especial a su madre. Él supuso que yo era simplemente una fanática de los dulces, como él, y que vomitaba porque me sentía culpable por ello. Sin embargo, a medida que le describía la magnitud y la frecuencia de mis comilonas, pudo darse cuenta de que el asunto era algo más profundo y que no se trataba de un problema ordinario.

Me escuchó con mucho amor y compasión y dijo que trataría de ayudarme.

Antes, siempre esperé que mejoraría "mañana", "después de esta última comilona". Pero ahora sabía que necesitaba comenzar a tomar medidas concretas. Me hice dos propósitos. Sería totalmente honesta, le contaría a Leigh acerca de todas mis comilonas, y haría cualquier cosa para recuperarme, incluso internarme en una clínica si fuera necesario. Esta promesa evocaba imágenes terroríficas y melodramáticas que a toda costa quería evitar. Leigh prometió apoyarme en tanto mantuviese mi compromiso de luchar por mi recuperación. Él me ayudaría a idear las medidas que yo podía tomar y estaba dispuesto a escucharme, a ayudar, a reír y a amarme; empero, admitimos que entender y dominar la conducta era mi responsabilidad.

Fui a ver a un psiquiatra debido a la tensión y al sentimiento de culpa que sentía por vivir con Leigh estando casada con David. En un principio, no mencioné mi bulimia pero cuando le hablé de ella, me recomendó ver a una psiquiatra que había tratado a anoréxicas. Me reuní con ella en una ocasión, pero no me sentí a gusto. No obstante, comprendía la importancia de poder confiarme a alguien, y decidí continuar haciéndolo con Leigh.

Sin una guía, nos dedicamos a pensar cómo podría yo recuperarme. Comencé a meditar con regularidad y a cumplir con el compromiso de escribir en mi diario.

Procuré establecer un marco mental positivo observando constantemente lo que pensaba y lo que decía, y, conscientemente, reformulaba mi "autodiálogo" negativo para adquirir una perspectiva más positiva. Quería sentirme más relajada, así que comencé a hacer caminatas y a escuchar mi música favorita. Decidí beber una cantidad fija de agua cada día, pero tuve dificultades para hacerlo, así que modifiqué mis expectativas en vez de sentirme fracasada. Por otra parte, mi negocio de muñecas, al que puse el nombre de Diseños Gürze, comenzó a marchar bien y requería horas de costura con mucha concentración, durante las cuales hablaba conmigo misma acerca de mi recuperación: ¡era una especie de autoterapia!

Hice listas: metas inmediatas, metas futuras, listas de "pobre Lindsey" y "afortunada Lindsey"; lo que me agradaba y lo que me disgustaba de mí misma; razones por las que deseaba recuperar la salud; cómo me sentía acerca de mis padres, mis hermanos, mi vida; formas de manejar los sentimientos difíciles, y muchas cosas más. Elaboré otra lista de cosas que podría hacer si estaba a punto de iniciar una comilona, por ejemplo, hacer ejercicio, coser, arreglar el jardín, tomar un largo baño caliente, y hablar con Leigh o con alguna amiga acerca de mis sentimientos. A menudo la lucha era difícil, pero cada vez con mayor frecuencia conseguía vencer el ansia de hacer una comilona.

Tuve que abordar la alimentación de una forma nueva. De hecho, ella se convirtió en mi maestra, porque el modo como la trataba se asemejaba mucho a cómo me trataba a mí misma. Si la comida era poco importante, prescindible, si no valía la pena tratarla con amabilidad, entonces, pensaba, así era yo. Por tanto, en vez de rotular los alimentos como "buenos" o "malos", lo que les confería poder sobre mí, quería aprender a comer cualquier cosa sin temor. Deseaba escapar de toda prisión en la que pudiese estar. Con miras a esa meta, decidí permitirme un gusto "prohibido" cada día sin experimentar sentimientos de culpa. Era una orientación por completo distinta para mí, y fue sorprendentemente fácil. Comencé a apreciar ese gusto, que era algo muy diferente de las comilonas. Ciertos alimentos me agradaban y otros me desagradaban, y aprendí a decir "no" diciéndolo a ellos. Comencé a poner atención a mi modo de comer y procuré hacerlo con más calma. A veces ponía música apacible de fondo durante las comidas, y afirmaba en silencio que comer en forma saludable era un acto de amorosa atención hacia mi persona. Esto era fundamental, pues me había tratado muy mal durante mucho tiempo.

Di un paso inusitado, el cual tuvo un efecto enorme en mi confianza en mí misma, pero que no habría intentado sola. *Nadie que esté en proceso de recuperarse de la bulimia debe intentar algo como esto sin apoyo y supervisión.* Lo que hice fue emprender una comilona de todo el día, previamente planeada, con la intención de no vomitar. Quería saber, en lo más profundo de mí, que podía comer cualquier cosa, es decir, que podía tener poder sobre la comida.

Llegado el gran día, Leigh y yo iniciamos la mañana con una bolsa de dulces de leche malteada en la mesita de noche. Compramos medio kilo de caramelos, una docena de rosquillas, manzanas con caramelo, maíz acaramelado, una tanda de galletas hechas en casa, pastelillos de chocolate y bebidas, todo eso para llevarlo con nosotros mientras entregábamos muñecas en las tiendas. En el transcurso del día, también comimos hamburguesas y papas fritas, licuados y una grasosa comida de pescado y papas; además, consumimos trozos de chocolate blanco.

A la hora de ir a dormir, estábamos agotados y atiborrados. Leigh se sentía mal, pero a mí me preocupaba la apariencia de mi cuerpo y cómo me sentía: embarazada e incapaz de yacer acostada a gusto en ninguna posición. Leigh no me perdía de vista por razones obvias.

Nunca habría intentado esto sin una persona que me apoyase; sin duda, habría vomitado. Pese a los cólicos estomacales, al final me sentía orgullosa de mí misma y me reía de lo que había logrado. Éste fue un momento clave y decisivo para mí: sabía que podía alcanzar una meta, y tenía control sobre la comida, en vez de que ella me dominase a mí.

Durante muchos meses consumí sobre todo alimentos que consideraba "no peligrosos", como yogur y plátanos, o requesón y jugo de piña, pero procuraba hacer tres comidas al día con pequeños refrigerios entre ellas. Comer tan a menudo me parecía mucho al principio, pero estaba decidida a apegarme a mi plan aun si con ello empezaba a aumentar de peso. De hecho, destruí mi báscula con un martillo después de escribirle una nota de despedida. Nunca más me gobernaría un número.

Intenté adaptar lo que consideraba que "debía" comer a lo que mi organismo realmente ansiaba, haciéndome consciente de los indicios internos de hambre a los que había dejado de atender durante muchos años. Comencé a probar alimentos nuevos. Éste fue uno de los pasos más difíciles que tuve que dar, pues tenía mucho miedo de perder el dominio de mí misma. Lo que descubrí fue que, cuanto más restringía mis comidas a ciertos alimentos específicos, más ganas sentía de hacer comilonas. Cuando me daba el tiempo de hacer un autoanálisis y descubrir qué era lo que de verdad tenía deseos de comer, experimentaba satisfacción y saciedad. ¡A veces lo que ansiaba no era siquiera comida! En ocasiones, hacer trabajos artísticos, decir algo que era necesario comentar, o simplemente sentarme en paz conmigo, era justo lo que necesitaba.

En otros momentos, necesitaba gritar contra una almohada hasta quedar ronca o llorar durante horas enteras. Daba salida a sentimientos reprimidos, en especial al enojo, luchando con un gran colchón de espuma plástica en el piso y peleando agotadoramente contra murciélagos del mismo material. Nos poníamos guantes de boxeo y Leigh me dejaba golpearlo. Siempre detenía a tiempo sus golpes, pero se acercó mucho a mi rostro en varias ocasiones. Tomaba prolongados baños sauna. Todas estas cosas tenían un efecto calmante también sobre mi mente.

Comencé a explorar cuestiones espirituales porque me sentía aislada de la iglesia a la que asistí cuando niña. Leí libros sobre diferentes religiones y descubrí muchos maestros espirituales estupendos, cuya vida me inspiró a mostrar más amor hacia mí misma y hacia los demás.

Tenía una fotografía mía sobre mi tocador, con una vela y flores, con el fin de recordarme constantemente que era una buena persona a la que valía la pena cuidar. Aprendí ejercicios específicos que me hicieron ver con claridad cómo influían en mis valores y convicciones mis padres, mi infancia y la cultura en la que vivía. Tener en cuenta todas estas cosas me permitió descubrir la verdad de mi corazón, y al fin poder vivir en armonía con quien yo soy en lo más profundo de mi ser. Ésta sí que era una nutrición verdadera.

El compromiso más difícil que hice fue el de decir la verdad en todo momento. Comencé por compartir mis secretos acerca de la bulimia con las personas con quienes menos deseaba hacerlo. David, quien finalmente había aceptado que nuestra separación era permanente, se quedó atónito, pero el que le confiara mis problemas le pareció un acto de genuino afecto. Comentó que no sabía la razón por la que nunca me preguntó por qué pasaba tanto tiempo en el baño, y le entristeció enterarse de todas las dificultades que tuve que sortear. Aunque después de eso nos separamos, pienso que estuvimos más cerca el uno de la otra de lo que estuvimos en años.

Un mes después, empecé a escribir cartas a diferentes personas; algunas las enviaba y otras no. Les escribí a mis padres acerca de cómo me sentía cuando estaba cerca de ellos. Les describí mi recuperación, pero no les pedí, ni esperé ni recibí mucha participación.

Hice confidencias a mis amigas, quienes en su mayoría se mostraron interesadas y comprensivas y me brindaron apoyo, aunque unas pocas desaparecieron de mi vida. Escribí lo siguiente en una carta a una amiga de mi infancia, aquella que comía tantas naranjas en el internado: "Por fin puedo hablar con la gente respecto a las comilonas y el vómito. No sabes lo avergonzada que me he sentido todos estos años, pensando que era anormal y repugnante".

Poco a poco me sentí más cómoda de ser simplemente yo misma. Siempre había estado ansiosa por mostrar una imagen de perfección e independencia a toda prueba, pero ahora dejé de ocultar mi timidez, mis opiniones, mis temores.

A medida que fui comprendiendo quién era y por qué, también entendí lo útil que la bulimia había sido para mí. Fue mi amiga, mi colchón, mi seguridad y mi expresión cuando no conocía otras.

Fue un medio de anestesiar mis abrumadores sentimientos, un vehículo para afirmar mi lugar en mi familia, y un sitio para esconderme cuando no deseaba participar en la vida. Como adicción, sin embargo, no me permitió otra conducta que no fuera ésa y me había consumido por completo. ¡Combatí duramente para rescatarme!

Durante los primeros meses de recuperación hice muchas comilonas, pero estos deslices se hicieron cada vez menos frecuentes hasta que, al cabo de un año, fueron escaseando llegando a uno cada dos meses. Cuando ocasionalmente hacía una comilona, procuraba considerarla una forma de aprender, en vez de pensar en ella como en un retroceso. Al fin y al cabo, después de cada desliz, Leigh y yo sosteníamos largas sesiones en las que conversábamos y hacíamos planes. Gradualmente, conseguí aceptar que una sola comilona no me hacía volver al punto de partida. Por el contrario, era una bandera roja de alerta para examinar las razones por las que había recaído y pensar qué podía hacer la próxima vez para evitarla.

Este nivel de aceptación compasiva, aunada a un compromiso firme, fue exactamente la estrategia que necesitaba. Los episodios dejaron de presentarse por completo al cabo de un año y medio. Han pasado casi 20 años desde que dejé la bulimia, y casi los mismos desde que pensé por última vez en hacer comilonas o purgarme.

Una recuperación duradera

Terminar con la conducta de comilona y purga fue sólo una parte de mi recuperación, pues la bulimia se había infiltrado en todos los aspectos de mi vida. Poco a poco, he sufrido una transformación en mi modo de ver y de experimentar cada situación, desde una simple conversación hasta una crisis urgente.

El cambio más evidente se advierte en mi relación con la comida. Ya no como para escapar, ni estoy obsesionada por mi peso. Reconozco las señales de hambre y me alimento en consonancia. No evito alimento alguno y disfruto de todo, desde las comidas nutritivas hasta los postres sibaríticos.

Dejo de comer cuando estoy harta, y no siento remordimientos por servirme una segunda porción o por dejar algo en mi plato. No sigo reglas y he abandonado mis rituales compulsivos. Cuido mucho mi cuerpo y, en términos generales, sigo normas de conducta saludables. En efecto, ¡como sin temor!

Por fin comprendí que mi trastorno de la alimentación tenía menos que ver con la comida que con los sentimientos. En vez de estar aturdida todo el tiempo, ahora experimento la vida de una forma totalmente diferente.

La mayor parte del tiempo en que estoy despierta me encuentro en paz y llena de confianza en mi persona, aunque a veces me siento feliz, nerviosa, orgullosa, frustrada, satisfecha, preocupada o triste. Tengo una gama completa de sentimientos, pero, por encima de todo, procuro mantener un estado de amor, que es mi favorito.

Haberme liberado de la bulimia me ha puesto en contacto con un ser interior que nunca supe que existía. ¡Nadie me había dicho que muchas de mis propias respuestas ya estaban en mí! Esto lo comprendí al ser honesta y confiar en mis instintos. Una vez que hice el compromiso de practicar la honestidad, dejé de preocuparme por lo que pensaba que los demás querían, y pude concentrarme en mis propias necesidades. Conforme aprendí a confiar en que podía tomar las mejores decisiones, descubrí que mi ser interior siempre me guiaba en la dirección correcta. Llegué a respetar y a honrar a ese yo interior, a permitirle expresarse en el mundo. Él me ha servido de guía en todo lo que he hecho desde entonces.

Por extraño que pueda parecer, mi bulimia es responsable de quién soy y dónde me encuentro ahora, porque sin una enfermedad tan grave nunca habría trabajado tanto para ser feliz. Tuve que superar todas las barreras que había en mi camino para vivir y amar con plenitud, con mi propio bagaje de valores e ideales. Comer sin temor me enseñó a vivir sin temor, y eso me ha hecho verdaderamente libre.

CAPÍTULO 3

Cómo comenzar

La decisión de detenerse

Los pensamientos y las conductas bulímicas continúan de modo indefinido, y por lo regular empeoran, a menos que se tome la decisión de terminar definitivamente con ellas. Yo recomiendo optar por no hacer comilonas por muchas razones: vivir una vida más larga, saludable y llena de afecto; tener relaciones sinceras; hacer realidad la creatividad potencial; disfrutar de la comida; experimentar tranquilidad de espíritu; ahorrar dinero. La lista es interminable.

Sin embargo, en realidad no importa cuáles sean sus razones: lo que importa es que hay algo que tú deseas *más que* la bulimia; por tanto, a partir de esa decisión brotarán tu determinación, tu valor y tu disposición.

Ciertas personas tienen menos dificultades para superar su trastorno de la alimentación que otras, pero la cura nunca es instantánea. Recuperarse de un trastorno tan complejo como la bulimia es un proceso de triunfos, reveses, percepciones y decisiones propios de cada individuo y sin un final bien definido. Sin duda, es importante detener la conducta de comilona y purga, pero esto sólo es una parte de la recuperación cabal. Es necesario hacer frente a las causas que están en el fondo de esa conducta para no recaer en ella en momentos de estrés. La tarea es enorme y no se puede tomar a la ligera. Decidirse a parar no significa prometer que uno va a mejorar "mañana", pues éste es un pensamiento bulímico, sino hacer cualquier cosa que sea necesaria en este preciso instante para conquistar la libertad.

Incluso la conducta que pone en peligro la vida es difícil de cambiar si sirve para protegernos de sentimientos dolorosos, como tristeza, ansiedad, aburrimiento, vacío espiritual, miedo o recuerdos de un pasado traumático. Renunciar a esa protección causa pavor; si nuestra confianza en nosotras mismas o nuestra experiencia es poca, carecemos de armas para enfrentar un futuro incierto. Muchas bulímicas se limitan a esperar la llegada de una cura ansiada que las transforme mágicamente, sin tener que aportar esfuerzo ni trabajo. Sin embargo, en última instancia, ellas deben tomar la decisión de terminar con la bulimia.

La razón de cada quien para tomar esa decisión es propia de sus circunstancias particulares, como lo indican estas experiencias:

Comprender que soy la única persona que puede detener mi conducta me ayudó a iniciar mi curación. Todo dependía de mí.

Diecisiete años es mucho tiempo para estar en la cárcel. Ya he cumplido mi condena y me he ganado la libertad. Para mí no existen acontecimientos, ni siquiera actitudes concretas en mi curación, sino una decisión existencial en favor de la vida, la cual afirmo constantemente.

En realidad, la decisión de detenerme fue lo que me permitió lograrlo. En ese momento, tuve que ser muy indulgente conmigo y renunciar a la necesidad de ser perfecta. Comer mejor era contagioso: cuanto más lo hacía, más deseaba hacerlo. Me tomó dos años terminar con las ansias.

Varias bulímicas mencionaron que las complicaciones físicas las indujeron a cuestionar su conducta. Sin embargo, el simple conocimiento de los efectos colaterales no es garantía de que una bulímica renuncie a su conducta. Algunas señalaron que eran "expertas" en nutrición, salud y psicología, y entendían en un nivel intelectual que sus comilonas eran poco sanas, pero aun así se resistían a asumir el compromiso de cambiar. Una enfermera describía sus problemas físicos en términos médicos muy específicos; no obstante, ocultaba esta información a médicos que eran además sus amigos. Una mujer de 38 años, que gastó miles de dólares en tratamiento dental durante 15 años de vómitos repetidos, se sentía afortunada porque su cuerpo no había sufrido daños peores.

El 22 por ciento de las bulímicas que respondieron a la encuesta habían sido hospitalizadas a causa de sus síntomas, como la que escribió lo siguiente:

¡Miedo! Mi hospitalización de emergencia por problemas cardiacos debidos a falta de potasio no fue premeditada ni planeada. Después de ella, renuncié a la bulimia "de un día para otro" y nunca más recurrí al vómito, pero fue muy difícil desde el punto de vista psicológico.

El embarazo motivó a algunas a dejar la conducta bulímica, gracias a un recién descubierto respeto por su cuerpo y al amor por el hijo por nacer:

Mi conducta bulímica/anoréxica ha cesado casi por completo porque estoy embarazada. Siento tanto amor por este bebé, que quiero amarme también yo misma. A veces, un profundo sentimiento de afecto hacia otros puede ponerte en el camino hacia la recuperación.

Establece metas razonables

Una estrategia que surgió una y otra vez fue la de trabajar dentro de un marco de triunfo, no de fracaso. Desde esta perspectiva, los pensamientos positivos toman el lugar de los negativos.

La reincidencia en las comilonas es una oportunidad para entender mejor la compulsión, y se recompensan los éxitos con estímulos, sentimientos positivos y resultados tangibles.

Una mujer que leyó mi folleto original, *Come sin temor*, me escribió una larga carta a principios de los 80. Ella había sido anoréxica y después bulímica durante 12 de sus 28 años. Al principio, se sintió animada al leer que otra persona, que era bulímica, se había "aliviado", y pasó varios días sin hacer comilonas. Abrió su corazón a su esposo, que la apoyó, y entonces se sometió a terapia profesional. Cuando se puso en contacto conmigo, ya se consideraba "curada" desde hacía varios años. El pasaje siguiente describe sus avances iniciales. Por cierto, nos mantuvimos en contacto a lo largo de los años, y ahora, casi dos décadas después, no ha tenido más problemas con la alimentación.

Al principio, me vi obligada a tomar decisiones muy difíciles respecto a hacer algo más: combatir un impulso que, bien lo sabía, habría de volver a obsesionarme. Hube de aceptar que, cada vez que decidía no vomitar, vivía una experiencia que podía agregar a mi repertorio de mejorías. Esto me permitió aceptar los fracasos, porque ellos no menguaban mis "ocasiones en que había mejorado". Un fracaso no significaba que todo estaba perdido. Podía no vomitar la próxima vez. Aprovechaba las recaídas para examinar las circunstancias que me habían llevado a vomitar, y ello me enseñó a evitar ciertas circunstancias. Conseguí acrecentar mi aceptación de mí misma, lo que me permitió sentirme más contenta con mi persona. Comencé a examinar minuciosamente cómo me sentía después de haber vomitado, y también cuando no lo había hecho. Aprendí a confiar más en mí misma y en mi capacidad para sanar.

Como lo señalé en el capítulo 1 ("¿Cuánto tiempo toma mejorar?"), la recuperación es un proceso permanente.

De las personas que me relataron su historia, en todos los casos la recuperación significó experimentar con diferentes estrategias y soportar presiones, abandonar el cuidado de sí mismas y regresar a él. De hecho, todas hicieron algunas comilonas en las primeras etapas, pero incluso en los muy raros casos en que "pararon en seco", se vieron obligadas a ahondar en el comportamiento bulímico para entender sus emociones, las causas de la bulimia y los estímulos que la ponían en marcha.

Muchas me comentaron que procuraban fijarse metas razonables, y algunas hicieron la prueba estableciendo sencillos contratos, como los siguientes:

Hago planes para el día y me apego al programa, sin permitirme improvisar ni dejarme llevar por el pánico en el primer momento en que me siento sola, hambrienta u ociosa. Si bien no está reglamentado, procuro seguir una guía. Me fijo metas pequeñas y las alcanzo. Utilizo una lista de comprobación.

Procuro no obsesionarme con la idea de una curación de la noche a la mañana. ¡Sé muy bien que toma tiempo! Ahora dejo de comer después de haber consumido menos que en las comilonas de antes: dos panecillos en vez de seis. Mi terapeuta llama a esto "cantidades moderadas". Mis comilonas han disminuido considerablemente. Solían ocupar todo mi día, mi vida entera. El amor a una misma realmente ayuda, lo mismo que el no rendirse. Siempre hay un mañana.

Ponía $5.00 en un frasco por cada día sin comilonas y ahorré para comprar algo que deseaba.

El estímulo: ¿por qué curarse?

Lo más importante que puedo decir acerca de la lucha por terminar con la bulimia es que vale la pena. No obstante que es más un camino que una meta, y que se inicia en lo que se percibe como una oscuridad total, hay una luz que existe en el interior de tu propio ser, que te guiará en tu camino hacia la salud y la integridad.

Es sorprendente que muchas mujeres que se han recuperado de un trastorno de la alimentación piensen que, a la larga, les ha beneficiado haberlo padecido. Consideran que sus problemas con la comida y con el peso han sido sus mejores maestros, sin los cuales quizá nunca habrían cuestionado seriamente sus convicciones y valores, ni hecho frente a sus temores internos.

Haberse recuperado de un trastorno de la alimentación les dio la fortaleza suficiente para oponerse a las presiones culturales para ser esbeltas y para no juzgar a las demás personas con base en su talla o su figura; asimismo, aprendieron a responder a los antiguos modelos de formas novedosas, lo que les permitió atacar otros problemas con confianza y compasión. Muchas de ellas son felices.

Puede ser difícil comprender todos estos cambios cuando una está abrumada por la compulsión y el desprecio a una misma, pero recuerda que los trastornos de la alimentación no tienen que ver sólo con la comida y el acto de comer. Son síntomas de un vacío y un dolor interiores que, cuando sanan, transforman el resto de nuestra vida. Con el tiempo encontrarás otras cosas que te colmen, no sólo física, sino emocional y espiritualmente. Como una persona escribió: "El amor a una misma puede ser delicioso."

En tu interior hay una persona creativa, afectuosa, que vale la pena. En el fondo de tu corazón, sabes que eso es cierto. Cumple tu compromiso, continúa participando en la vida en vez de hacer comilonas. Practica el amor y cree en ti misma. Haz listas, consigue apoyo, sométete a terapia, sigue nuestro programa de tres semanas. Toma tiempo llevar a cabo un cambio tan grande. ¡No te preocupes! Manténte dispuesta a hacer cualquier cosa para curarte. Escucha las palabras de una mujer que me escribió: "Mi vida no ha cambiado con la recuperación, ¡ha comenzado!"

Desde que me liberé totalmente de la bulimia, duermo mejor, tengo más energía, estoy menos nerviosa y me siento más feliz. Río más, y me dicen que soy más extrovertida y que mi compañía es más divertida. También tengo más dinero y tiempo para hacer las cosas que disfruto de verdad.

La mayor parte del tiempo me siento bastante tranquila y más capaz de arreglármelas ahora que la comida ya no es un escape para mí. No obstante, en ciertos aspectos, la vida es más dolorosa, porque debo hacer frente a las emociones en vez de ocultarlas.

Me siento mucho más madura, y eso es maravilloso. Tengo más confianza en mí misma. Abordo cada tarea con mayor fortaleza, disfruto de las cosas pequeñas y ya no soy tan egocéntrica.

Pese a que mi trastorno de la alimentación tenía muchos aspectos negativos, siento que, sin él, no sería la persona que ahora soy. Me brindó una razón para descubrir en efecto mi propia verdad.

Tengo altas y bajas, como todo el mundo, ¡pero la mayor parte del tiempo mi vida es estupenda! Experimento la felicidad todos los días; comparto amor, humor y vulnerabilidad con los demás. Nunca pensé que la vida podía ser así, o que yo podía ser como soy. Con la recuperación, adquirí la confianza en mí misma que antes nunca tuve.

CAPÍTULO 4

¡Consigue ayuda!

La batalla para vencer los trastornos de la alimentación se hace mucho más fácil cuando se cuenta con apoyo externo. Éste puede provenir de muchas fuentes diferentes: grupos de apoyo, profesionales capacitados, familiares y amigos, orientadores de condición similar a la nuestra, clérigos, y libros y cintas de vídeo y de audio.

Cuando una bulímica me dice que soy la primera persona a la que le confiesa su problema, la exhorto a buscar a la "siguiente" persona a quien poder contárselo. Una estudiante universitaria consiguió el apoyo de todas sus compañeras de piso del dormitorio. Declaró en público su problema y les pidió a todas que la ayudaran a dejar de hacer comilonas. ¡Sus amigas respondieron en masa!

Casi todas las bulímicas temen que sus esposos, amantes, padres, compañeras de habitación u otras personas las descubran haciendo una comilona o vomitando. La verdad las avergüenza, y piensan que el acto de estar con el rostro inclinado sobre un escusado es una representación exacta de su valor personal. No sólo la bulimia es repugnante; las bulímicas también piensan que ellas son repugnantes por practicar esa conducta. También temen desagradar a los demás al admitir que tienen un problema tan corrosivo, y que se les juzgue como algo menos que perfectas. A final de cuentas, ellas equiparan la recuperación con una pérdida de dominio y con el consecuente aumento de peso, y ambas cosas las aterran.

Por desgracia, esta falta de confianza, tanto en sí mismas como en los demás, es la razón por la que muchas temen buscar ayuda. Reconocer su conducta ante los demás significa arriesgarse a ser rechazadas, y si han sido lastimadas por alguien cercano en el pasado, este riesgo puede parecer demasiado grande. En vez de dar entrada a otros en su vida, adquieren resentimientos hacia esas personas de quienes se ocultan y se retraen aun más en su obsesión.

Ser sincera y renunciar a la clandestinidad y al fingimiento es estremecedor, pero constituye un enorme alivio. Hacer comilonas y purgarse exige mucha energía, ¡al igual que mantener esa conducta en secreto!

Recuerda que la bulimia no es un reflejo de la persona interior, sino una manera de hacer frente a la vida. Lamentablemente, esta enfermedad refuerza la baja autoestima y también crea una barrera para las relaciones afectuosas sinceras.

El 85 por ciento de las bulímicas que respondieron a la encuesta reconocieron que el sigilo era uno de los obstáculos más difíciles de vencer, pero sus comentarios ponen de manifiesto el valor de ser sinceras y de conseguir un buen apoyo:

Salir de la clandestinidad y hablar con la gente es quizá lo que más me ha ayudado.

Las exhorto enérgicamente a hablar con la familia y con las amistades acerca de la bulimia. Es difícil vencerla una sola.

Contárselo a mi marido después de cuatro años de mantenerlo en secreto es lo que más me ha ayudado. Él me apoya, y ya no me odio tanto a mí misma porque ahora no le miento más.

Apoyo familiar

Es imposible negar que nuestra familia nos afecta de muchas y muy variadas formas. Cuando partimos de casa, llevamos con nosotras estas actitudes y hábitos a nuestro nuevo entorno. Ya sea que vivas en casa o no, y que optes por incluir a tu familia en tu recuperación o no, es importante que reconozcas de qué manera ella ha influido en ti, y también decidir qué es lo que harás al respecto.

Un trastorno de la alimentación no existe sólo en la persona que lo padece; *su entorno lo sustenta de alguna manera.* Por tanto, para que tus padres te apoyen de manera eficaz, deben estar dispuestos a examinar el "sistema" familiar para ver dónde hay problemas. Tal vez existan dificultades de comunicación, de expresión de los sentimientos o de solución de los conflictos. Puede ser necesario que examinen sus propias actitudes en torno a los mismos problemas que tú enfrentas: prejuicios respecto al peso, el papel de la mujer, la intimidad, la espiritualidad, la baja autoestima, la satisfacción de las necesidades. Quizá ellos no hagan comilonas ni se purguen, pero es posible que compartan algunas de las mismas actitudes poco sanas que tienes, lo cual no te ayudará a curarte. Además, los padres sirven como ejemplo en cuanto a habilidades de enfrentamiento de los problemas y hábitos de alimentación, y fijan normas de ambición, perfección y aceptación. Aunque es probable que su intención no sea confundir o no ser sinceros, sus actos pueden transmitir afirmaciones en conflicto. Por ejemplo, quizá al hijo se le ha dicho que no debe comer antes de la cena, pero ve a su madre comer unas cucharadas a escondidas mientras cocina. O bien, al enfrentar el hecho de que su hija alcanza la mayoría de edad, un padre puede retraerse precisamente cuando ella más lo necesita.

Un trastorno de la alimentación es, por lo regular, una forma de manejar los sentimientos en una familia donde su expresión se reprime, niega o pasa por alto, en especial los sentimientos que son negativos o difíciles, como la ira, las críticas o el reto. Tal vez existan reglas tácitas acerca de quién puede enojarse, cuándo y respecto a qué cuestiones. Algunas familias carecen de habilidad para manejar los conflictos o problemas emocionales, y preferirían no oír hablar de ellos. Los hijos que crecen vigilando sus sentimientos encuentran otros medios, menos directos, de expresarlos, por ejemplo, con un trastorno de la alimentación.

Los padres establecen reglas y mitos. Algunos son directos, como la prohibición de comer postre si una no termina toda la comida del plato; las chicas deben tener cuidado con lo que comen; o al padre se le sirve primero. Otros son menos evidentes, como la regla de que las emociones deben expresarse gritando o en silencio; la mejor manera de disciplinar el mal comportamiento es el uso de la autoridad, no el debate racional; o los chicos pueden llegar tarde porque son de fiar, pero las chicas son menos responsables y deben estar temprano en casa. Es posible que estos mitos y reglas hayan tenido un propósito cuando se crearon, pero no necesariamente se aplican al momento presente.

En total, 91 por ciento de las bulímicas que respondieron a la encuesta consideraron que su familia contribuyó a su trastorno de la alimentación de manera directa o indirecta. Algunas pudieron recurrir a sus familiares en busca de apoyo, en tanto que otras afirmaron que no podían identificarse con los problemas relacionados con la comida, porque, o bien comían con "normalidad", o también estaban obsesionados. Las comidas solían ser escenas de enfrentamientos o de dolor y resentimiento ocultos. Muchas usaban la bulimia como una forma de desquitarse de su familia. Como quiera que fuese, *el trastorno de la alimentación era un problema adicional y en nada contribuía a mejorar las relaciones.*

La terapia familiar, combinada con la capacitación para la asertividad, puede ser extremadamente útil, en especial cuando la persona bulímica vive en casa. En ciertos casos, los terapeutas *demandan* que toda la familia se someta a tratamiento. Idealmente, todos sus miembros deberían compartir el compromiso de mejorar sus relaciones. De esta manera, no sólo la persona bulímica se sentiría apoyada, sino que la dinámica familiar en su totalidad mejoraría en profundidad, afectando positivamente a todos los miembros de la familia.

Ya sea que decidas que tu familia participe en tu recuperación o no, de cualquier manera es útil examinar la influencia que ella ejerce. He aquí algunas reflexiones:

Mi madre y toda su familia están obsesionadas con la cocina, la comida y el peso. Las pocas veces que me he abierto a ella, no se ha mostrado dispuesta a comprender; sólo se ríe del asunto y me dice que no debería preocuparme la posibilidad de engordar.

Mudarme lejos de mi familia me ayudó, pues me aparté de sus constantes críticas y juicios.

Mi bulimia ha disminuido casi en un 90 por ciento, y es a mis padres a quienes debo agradecer por ello. Ellos me han apoyado mucho y siempre están a mi lado cuando necesito ayuda.

Lo que más me ayudó a curarme fueron los informes que presentaba a mi madre los domingos por la noche. Después de toda una semana sin hacer comilonas ni purgarme, le contaba de mi triunfo. Podía ver la expresión de alivio en su rostro, y eso bastaba para sobrellevar los momentos difíciles que se presentaban todos los días. A medida que transcurrían las semanas, era cada vez más fácil no vomitar. Pasaban días enteros sin que pensase siquiera en ello.

Cuando llegué a la adolescencia, mi padre parecía evitarme, y yo pensaba que era a causa de mi peso. Cuando hablé con mis padres acerca del vómito, él mostró amor e interés sinceros. Lo que más me ayudó fue que participara de nuevo en mi vida.

Pese a que muchas mujeres afirmaron haber experimentado dificultad para abrirse ante sus esposos o amantes, la respuesta que recibieron fue, en general, de apoyo y ayuda. ¡Casi todos los cónyuges reaccionan muy bien!

El factor más importante para mi recuperación ha sido el apoyo de alguien que me ama incondicionalmente, pese a la fealdad de mi problema. El que ahora es mi esposo, y que fue mi novio durante muchos de los años de mi bulimia, no me rechazó ni me dejó cuando se enteró de mis vómitos. Tampoco me sermoneó nunca para inducirme a renunciar a ella. Sin embargo, no me ocultó la verdad del peligro fisiológico que mis actos representaban. De hecho, me dijo que podría morir de algún efecto directo o indirecto de mi bulimia si no la dejaba. No obstante, la manera como lo planteó dejó en claro que, ya sea que yo decidiese dejar de vomitar o no, lo estaría haciendo principalmente por mi propio beneficio, aunque sin duda también sería bueno para él.

Terapia profesional

Casi todas las bulímicas coinciden en que hablar acerca de sus problemas con la comida es en extremo difícil, cuando han mantenido una apariencia de competencia y bienestar por tanto tiempo. Si bien es probable que les cause vergüenza "contarlo todo" a una amiga o a un familiar, en especial al principio de su recuperación, un terapeuta profesional no tiene interés alguno en verlas como "perfectas". Asimismo, aunque es mucho el trabajo de autoayuda que una puede hacer por su cuenta, las personas con bulimia tienden a confiar en que "pueden hacerlo todo" ellas mismas. Esto rara vez se cumple, y es tal vez consecuencia de un temor a las relaciones en general. Por consiguiente, la terapia es un medio para hacer frente a los problemas difíciles y dolorosos, y también una oportunidad para aprender a confiar en otra persona y a interactuar con ella.

Un sentimiento que algunas expresaron es que sólo una bulímica puede entender de verdad el dolor que se sufre. De hecho, muchas terapeutas se especializan en este campo debido a sus propias experiencias con problemas de la alimentación. Sin embargo, incluso si no han padecido un trastorno de este tipo, dichas profesionales están capacitadas para escuchar, aceptar, desafiar y aportar destrezas de enfrentamiento. Se han preparado para "estar ahí", presentes por entero, para apoyar a sus pacientes, lo que es crucial para superar esos sentimientos de soledad y repugnancia que tienden a preservar la bulimia.

Una relación terapéutica saludable y mutua influye de manera positiva en las relaciones futuras de todo tipo.

Recomiendo ampliamente a todas las bulímicas buscar alguna forma de terapia profesional. Existen muchas clases de terapeutas y de estrategias terapéuticas para tratar los trastornos de la alimentación.

El término "terapeuta" suele usarse con carácter general para referirse a psiquiatras, psicólogos o consejeros matrimoniales y familiares, así como a trabajadoras sociales clínicas tituladas. También podemos obtener apoyo profesional de dietistas y nutriólogas, quienes están preparadas para educarnos en lo que respecta al funcionamiento de nuestro organismo y para elaborar un plan de alimentación que sea razonable y tolerable para nosotras. Asimismo, podemos recibir apoyo de orientadores escolares y clérigos, y de otros profesionales que brindan servicios, como el contacto terapéutico, los masajes o la acupuntura. No obstante, cualquiera que sea el terapeuta a quien elijas para recibir orientación profesional, es importante recordar que su función no es "curarte", sino brindarte los medios necesarios para que te ayudes a ti misma.

Algunos formatos de tratamiento son los siguientes: terapia individual, terapia familiar, terapia en grupo centrada específicamente en la bulimia, grupos con diversos tipos de trastornos o problemas de la alimentación, tratamiento a pacientes residentes o externas, y centros de reinserción social. Por otra parte, para quienes se les dificulta más expresar sus sentimientos con palabras, los formatos no verbales con base en experiencias, como la terapia con danza y movimiento, el arte, la música y el teatro, pueden dar mejor resultado. El entrenamiento por biorretroalimentación es una opción para vigilar y ayudar a modificar la reacción del organismo al estrés.

Aunque la lista de temas que pueden abarcarse en la terapia es interminable, por lo general el tratamiento de un trastorno de la alimentación gira en torno a tres categorías fundamentales: las conductas de los trastornos de la alimentación, los procesos mentales que mantienen esas conductas y las emociones que subyacen en ellas. La terapia conductual cognitiva, que toca las tres, ha demostrado ser muy eficaz en el tratamiento de la bulimia porque se concentra en ayudar a las pacientes a adquirir dominio sobre su conducta de alimentación, al mismo tiempo que reduce su preocupación por el peso y la figura.

El tratamiento con medicamentos, o farmacoterapia, también es una forma de apoyo que puede ser provechosa para ciertas personas. Estos medicamentos deben ser recetados por un profesional —como un médico o un psiquiatra—, y adaptarse a la medida de las necesidades de cada persona. Asegúrate de comentar con tu médico los posibles efectos secundarios, la duración de la prueba inicial, y los posibles cambios de dosis.

De todas las estrategias de recuperación, la terapia profesional fue la más elogiada en las encuestas. Al 80 por ciento de las encuestadas le sirvió y fue calificada como la "más útil" con mucha mayor frecuencia que cualquier otra categoría.

Los comentarios siguientes representan el sentir de muchas otras bulímicas que también escribieron acerca de la terapia:

Mi terapeuta me ayudó a examinar muchos aspectos de mí misma de los que no tenía conciencia, o bien, a los que había hecho a un lado porque me resultaba demasiado doloroso ocuparme de ellos.

Ver a mi psiquiatra yo sola, y a veces con mi mamá, ha sido la mejor ayuda para mí.

Lo que más me ha ayudado es mi terapia en grupo. Me permite encontrarme con otras personas que tienen el mismo problema que yo, y es el único lugar en el que siento que puedo ser sincera.

Una de mis profesoras me recomendó acudir al centro de orientación de la escuela. Fue lo mejor que pude haber hecho.

El tratamiento más eficaz que he experimentado ha sido trabajar con un equipo formado por una psicóloga y una dietista. Comenzamos con un plan impulsado por metas, al cual agregamos una meta cada semana.

Centros de tratamiento de trastornos de la alimentación

Algunos hospitales y clínicas cuentan con programas de tratamiento especializados en trastornos de la alimentación. Es común que estos centros ofrezcan servicios tanto a pacientes residentes como externas, y en ciertos casos disponen de programas residenciales, en los que las pacientes se alojan en casas o en algún tipo de dormitorio mientras se someten al tratamiento. Casi todos los centros de tratamiento emplean una estrategia multidimensional en la que participa un equipo de profesionales capacitados que incluye: un director médico que suele ser un psiquiatra titulado, un psicólogo especializado en trastornos de la alimentación, un director de programa, trabajadoras sociales clínicas tituladas o consejeros matrimoniales y familiares, una dietista registrada, así como personal médico y de enfermería muy completo. El tratamiento puede incluir sesiones de terapia individual y en grupo, orientación sobre nutrición, capacitación en asertividad, programas de relajamiento y de ejercicio, terapias con base en experiencias y, a veces, el uso de medicamentos.

Un día típico incluye sesiones de terapia, reuniones con nutriólogos, citas con médicos, grupos de apoyo, clases y comidas estructuradas. Los grupos y las clases pueden abarcar aspectos como: imagen corporal, manejo del estrés, habilidades de enfrentamiento de los problemas, educación sobre nutrición, prevención de recaídas, capacitación en asertividad, terapia artística o musical, y terapia de escritura expresiva. Este tipo de estrategia intensiva para la recuperación es valiosa, ya sea que asistas a un centro o que idees un programa de autoayuda por tu cuenta.

Otros apoyos

Se puede encontrar apoyo en todo tipo de relaciones. Algunas mujeres de nuestra encuesta describieron el valor que daban al amor incondicional de las mascotas, ¡desde caballos hasta perros y peces! Otras mencionaron que las caminatas al aire libre aliviaban su depresión y angustia. En todos los casos, el apoyo provino de profundos sentimientos de conexión que afirmaban el sentido de valor personal y autoestima. Además de los familiares y los profesionales, las buenas amistades nos brindarán apoyo si lo pedimos. Busca ayuda de maestros, consejeros espirituales y personas que se han recuperado. Hoy día, parece como si todo el mundo conociese a alguien que ha luchado contra un trastorno de la alimentación y ha conseguido mejorar. Una mentora recuperada puede entender por lo que tú estás pasando y ofrecerte algunas perspectivas de su propio proceso.

Haz averiguaciones. Las organizaciones dedicadas a los trastornos de la alimentación, los hospitales locales, las universidades, las escuelas de enseñanza media y los grupos de mujeres son buenos lugares para pedir recomendaciones.

Por lo regular se puede encontrar ayuda gratuita poniéndose en contacto con centros de salud o de orientación de universidades locales que quizá cuenten con grupos de apoyo permanentes. En algunos casos, los hospitales y los terapeutas individuales patrocinan grupos gratuitos o de bajo costo abiertos al público. Los grupos de conversación (*chat*) de la Internet son otro medio para compartir ideas y triunfos.

Otra opción gratuita es *Overeaters Anonymous* (Comedores Compulsivos Anónimos), un grupo de autoayuda que tiene como base los principios de los doce pasos de Alcohólicos Anónimos.

Un comentario: si bien Comedores Compulsivos puede ofrecer apoyo y estímulo en grupo, algunos de los principios que se aplican al alcohol y a las drogas quizá no sean aplicables a las personas que intentan recuperarse de un trastorno de la alimentación. Pensamos que diferentes vías funcionan para las distintas personas. Aprovecha lo que te dé mejores resultados. Insistimos en que existe apoyo para quien esté dispuesta a buscarlo. Esto lo afirmaremos una y otra vez, porque establecer vínculos significativos es muy importante, como lo indican estas citas:

El mejor remedio que he encontrado es expresarme y tender la mano en busca de ayuda. Al hablar con otras bulímicas y pedir a las personas que me escuchen, gano una sensación de identi-

dad, alivio de la angustia y la ira, y un sentimiento de seguridad respecto a que estoy bien. Hoy cumplo más de siete meses de no vomitar, lo que en parte considero un milagro espiritual, y en parte fruto de mi disposición a mostrar a otros quién soy en realidad.

Me sentí mucho menos aislada después de abrirme y desnudar mi alma ante dos amigas en quienes confío. Sus oraciones y su apoyo incesante significaron mucho. Comprendí que no era inaceptable como persona, a pesar de tener un trastorno de la alimentación, el cual detestaba.

Hice que una amiga me llamara todas las noches para contarle cómo me había ido. El hecho de saber que hablaría con ella me ayudaba a tomar durante el día la decisión de no vomitar.

Cualquier grupo de apoyo en el que las personas expongan sus sentimientos sinceros es útil. El aislamiento es el mayor enemigo de la bulímica.

Exámenes médicos y dentales

Si eres bulímica, tu organismo ha debido pasar por una dura prueba. Por tal razón, es conveniente que te sometas a un examen físico completo a manos de un médico familiarizado con la bulimia, quien te alentará a comenzar a cuidar de ti misma. La naturaleza reservada de esta adicción mantuvo a la profesión médica en la ignorancia durante mucho tiempo. Por fortuna, ya hay muchos médicos que conocen bien sus síntomas y sus efectos secundarios. Cerciórate de que el tuyo sea uno de ellos. Si no lo es, pide una recomendación en algún centro local de tratamiento o con algún terapeuta especializado en trastornos de la alimentación.

A veces los médicos nos intimidan por sus limitaciones de tiempo y por su estatura profesional implícita. Sé firme. No busques excusas para evitar un examen físico. Recurre a alguien con quien te sientas cómoda pero que también te inspire confianza. El costo no es mayor que el de unas pocas comilonas, y en muchas zonas hay clínicas disponibles con escala móvil de honorarios. No olvides hablar con el médico de todo tu historial bulímico. Es muy importante que seas sincera. También es esencial hacerse revisar la dentadura, y más en los casos en que hay vómito. El ácido del estómago destruye el esmalte de los dientes, y la exposición constante a la comida, en especial a los carbohidratos simples, causa un grave deterioro de la dentadura y las encías.

Mis dientes han sido un completo desastre durante años y me han costado muchísimo dinero en tratamientos dentales, pero desde que dejé de hacer comilonas no he tenido una sola caries.

Tenía temor de someterme a una revisión médica, pero mi terapeuta insistió. Finalmente, acudí al examen, aterrada ante la posibilidad de que tuviese todos los problemas que las bulímicas padecen, según había leído. Me sentí aliviada al saber que estaba bien, y eso me hizo sentirme mejor respecto a mí misma y a mi recuperación. Era una bulímica sin remedio y estaba hospitalizada por falta de potasio. ¡Los médicos no podían creer que no estuviese en coma!

Mientras yacía en mi cama recibiendo una infusión intravenosa de suero, decidí que definitivamente ya no valía la pena seguir con las comilonas y el vómito.

CAPÍTULO 5

Lo que ha funcionado para muchos

Si bien consideramos muy recomendable buscar ayuda profesional como parte de tu proceso de recuperación, también sentimos que es mucho lo que tú puedes hacer por tu cuenta. Este capítulo ofrece sugerencias en cuanto a temas por explorar, muchas de las cuales provienen de personas que nos han enviado cartas y han respondido a nuestras encuestas, así como de terapeutas especializados en este campo. Piensa en el interés que estos temas tienen para ti, y concéntrate en los que, a tu modo de ver, podrían ayudarte más.

Recuperarse de la bulimia no es tarea sencilla. Si has decidido emprender esta travesía, es muy probable que te encuentres explorando un territorio poco conocido y sobrecogedor. No sólo habrás de investigar los orígenes de tu problema, sino que tendrás que transformar radicalmente tus conductas actuales. Por incómodo que esto pueda parecer al principio, piensa en ello como en el comienzo de una nueva empresa, que se facilita cada vez más con el tiempo y es gratificante en muchos niveles distintos. Si es necesario, hazlo a pasos cortos.

Te exhortamos a hacer de la recuperación de la bulimia la más alta prioridad de tu vida. Aun si piensas que eres egoísta por anteponer tu recuperación a otros compromisos, recuerda que *todos los demás aspectos de tu vida mejorarán si entiendes y curas tu relación con la comida.*

Mira más allá de los síntomas

Hay un dicho que afirma que "aquello a lo que te opones, se impone". Si tienes un trastorno de la alimentación, es probable que te estés resistiendo a algo en tu vida o dentro de ti misma y lo manifiestas a través de tu conducta. Puede tratarse de un trauma que se produjo hace mucho tiempo, una creencia que reduce tu autoestima, emociones no expresadas, o algo relacionado con tus circunstancias actuales que te trastorna. Sea lo que sea, el hecho de resistirse al recuerdo, a la realidad o al sentimiento de ello le da vida en algún aspecto de tu bulimia.

Así pues, este mal no tiene que ver sólo con la comida. Es evidente que los síntomas inmediatos giran en torno al alimento, pero hacer comilonas y purgarse, planear comidas, contar calorías y otras conductas habituales son formas de hacer frente a otros problemas de tu vida. Son estos problemas subyacentes, a los que tú te resistes, los que alimentan tu bulimia. Necesitas explorar estos problemas ocultos para ser totalmente libre.

Si no has conseguido detener las comilonas y purgas, te será provechoso dirigir tu atención hacia los demás aspectos implicados. Tu bulimia intenta decirte algo, en un lenguaje totalmente propio, y el conocimiento de este hecho priva a esta enfermedad de una parte de su poder. Ya no desperdiciarás tu energía en tratar de dominar sus síntomas, y podrás emplearla en explorar posibles soluciones. La bulimia tiene una función en tu vida, y tu tarea consiste en averiguar cuál es esa función.

Estar consciente de que existen razones de fondo que explican tu bulimia no significa condonarla, ni ello debe minar tu motivación para cambiar. Por el contrario, la comprensión de que la usas para lograr un propósito puede aliviar los sentimientos de culpa y de aversión a ti misma asociados con la conducta bulímica, y dejar en claro que dispones ahora de nuevas opciones, cualquiera que haya sido tu pasado. Entender el papel que la bulimia desempeña en tu vida es un medio para conocerte a ti misma y, en último término, para ocuparte de la persona interior que has estado ocultando. ¿De qué manera ha cuidado de ti la bulimia?

Un trastorno de la alimentación es sólo un síntoma de que algo anda muy mal en nuestra vida. De hecho, es una invitación a crecer, tanto emocional como espiritualmente. Toda crisis es una oportunidad.

Le dije a mi novio que no me importaba si subía (cinco kilos). Iba a probarme a mí misma que podía liberarme de la bulimia durante dos semanas. Y, ¿saben qué? ¡Lo hice! En vez de concentrarme en la comida, concentré la atención en mis pensamientos y sentimientos y llevé un diario todos los días. Aprendí mucho, y él me apoyó todo el tiempo.

Escribe tu historia

Escribe la historia de tu vida, destacando especialmente los sucesos relacionados con tu bulimia, por ejemplo, la primera vez que tomaste conciencia de tu cuerpo. ¿Cómo te hicieron sentir esos acontecimientos? ¿Cuándo comenzó tu trastorno de la alimentación? Explora con detalle lo que te venga a la mente, con el fin de conocerte a ti misma y entender cómo la bulimia te ha ayudado a defenderte. Si lo deseas, traza una línea cronológica en la que señales los acontecimientos importantes. También podrías dibujar un árbol genealógico. ¿Hay otras personas en tu familia que tienen problemas con la comida y el peso, o problemas afines, como depresión, alcoholismo o retraimiento social? ¿Puedes aceptar el hecho de que tu bulimia fue una respuesta razonable a tus experiencias? ¿Por qué intentas recuperarte?

Nota: este ejercicio puede requerir días, meses o años, conforme aprendas a conocerte mejor en el curso de tu recuperación.

Escribe en tu diario

A muchas personas que padecen trastornos de la alimentación les resulta difícil comentar sus ideas y sentimientos íntimos; por eso, un diario es un lugar seguro donde explorar esta vida interior.

Estas personas también tienen dificultades para aflojar el paso, porque, cuando lo hacen, los pensamientos y sentimientos resultan abrumadores. Escribir en un diario es un medio excelente, no sólo para encontrar un rato de tranquilidad, sino también para explorar las cuestiones que surgen cuando una se toma el tiempo para ello.

Escribir es una forma de intimidad, porque para ello necesitas tener una relación sincera y afectuosa contigo misma. Dar a tus ideas y sentimientos más íntimos una forma tangible los hace más reales.

Un diario puede poner al descubierto modelos que quizá debas cuestionar, que puedes utilizar para seguir atentamente tu avance a largo plazo, o que te ayudarán a resolver los problemas. Un diario es como tener una buena amiga que siempre está ahí para apoyarte y que valora lo que tienes que decir. Cuando tengas ganas de hacer una comilona, mejor utiliza el diario.

Compra una libreta bonita o crea un sitio especial en tu computadora. Si te sientes más cómoda hablando que escribiendo, utiliza una grabadora.

Trata a tu diario con amor y respeto, porque es una representación de tu experiencia interior. Sé espontánea y deja que las palabras fluyan. Nadie más leerá lo que escribes, no se te calificará el contenido ni la gramática, y no tendrás que dar explicaciones. Puedes ser sincera sin sentir miedo. Programa cierto tiempo cada día para escribir, y recurre a tu diario en los momentos de estrés y también en los de contemplación. Considera la posibilidad de llevar además un diario de sueños.

Recuerda, no hay reglas de ninguna especie: escribe sobre lo que estés pensando. De hecho, al registrar tus pensamientos, ¡literalmente los estarás *ahuyentando* de tu mente!

TEMAS PARA EXPLORAR POR ESCRITO

- ¿Qué ocurrió en tu vida poco antes de que la bulimia comenzara? ¿Hubo algún incidente que desencadenó tu primer episodio de comilona y purga?

- Haz una lista de opciones para llenar tu vida en vez de hacerlo con comida, por ejemplo: relaciones reconfortantes, respeto a ti misma, una nueva destreza.

- Elige un familiar o una amiga y escribe tus impresiones de él o ella, además de describir su relación. ¿Cómo ha influido esta persona en ti? ¿Qué te gustaría decirle que hasta ahora nunca le has dicho?

- Describe un momento particularmente venturoso que te haga sentirte bien con sólo pensar en él. Aférrate a ese sentimiento durante el resto del día.

- Redacta una descripción física objetiva de ti misma. Después, escribe una descripción, también objetiva, de tu carácter. ¿En qué difieren estas descripciones de tus dogmáticos puntos de vista habituales?

- Haz una lista de 10 personas a las que admires (cinco a las que conozcas personalmente y cinco que conozcas de la sociedad contemporánea o de la historia). ¿Cuáles son los atributos que admiras en ellas? Enumera tus propios atributos. ¿Cuáles admiras de ti misma?

- Haz una lista de cinco a 10 mitos y de cinco a 10 reglas que desees cambiar. Un mito puede ser algo como: "Las personas delgadas son más felices"; una regla podría ser, por ejemplo: "Si como postre, tendré que vomitar".

- ¿Qué puedes hacer para sentir más amor por ti misma?

LOS SIGUIENTES SON OTROS TEMAS IMPORTANTES
QUE PUEDES EXPLORAR:

- Lo que mi figura significa para mí

- Cómo utiliza mi familia el escape para manejar los conflictos

- Cómo utilizo yo el escape para manejar los conflictos

- Mi relación con la autoridad

- Mi sentido de identidad social y sexual

- Mis impulsos y cómo los manejo

- Mi carrera profesional presente o futura; por qué la elegí

Cuando inicié mi recuperación, intenté que mi diario fuera mi amigo, en vez de la bulimia. En él decía todo lo que se me antojaba, sabiendo que nadie me juzgaría ni me rechazaría.

El hecho de poner mis ideas y sentimientos en el papel los hizo parecer más reales. Me ayudó a sentirme menos aislada, y supe que, con el tiempo, podría comunicarme mejor con la gente.

Practica la autoestima

Cuando intentas cambiar y buscas amoldarte a los modelos externos, te preguntas constantemente si lo estás haciendo "suficientemente bien". Esforzarte por alcanzar metas poco razonables y compararte con los demás te convierte en tu crítica más despiadada. Te distancias de ti misma y te sientes vacía en tu interior. La bulimia tiene que ver con este vacío. Es una búsqueda implacable y simbólica que pretende "llenar" el lugar vacío una y otra vez, lo cual, evidentemente, no funciona.

La práctica de la autoestima es al mismo tiempo un medio de recuperación y la meta. El mejor autoconocimiento y el aprecio por tu persona te harán sentirte "llena" de amor por lo que eres: un ser humano importante, que vale la pena; una fuente de compasión, creatividad, sabiduría, satisfacción y felicidad. Por alguna razón, que sin duda descubrirás en el proceso de curación, has quedado aislada de este conocimiento y ni siquiera piensas que podría ser verdad. Sin bases firmes de conciencia de ti misma y de amor por tu persona, no obstante, nada de lo que hagas, compres, pienses o comas te llenará lo suficiente.

Por consiguiente, el elemento más importante para recuperarte de la bulimia, o, de hecho, de cualquier clase de "problema" personal, consiste en elevar tu autoestima. Esto significa crear una relación con tu ser interior, con base en la convicción de que mereces tener una vida dichosa. En el pasado, has tenido un concepto muy pobre de ti misma. Y eso, ¿a dónde te ha llevado? ¡A un trastorno de la alimentación! Como escribió una mujer fuerte que participó en nuestra encuesta: "¡Soy una persona, no una talla!"

La autoestima no es algo que sucede por arte de magia. Es algo en lo que hay que trabajar y que es forzoso practicar, al igual que las afirmaciones o la escritura. Conócete. Aprende a escuchar tu voz interior. Sé tu mejor amiga tratándote con las atenciones que son importantes en una amiga íntima: respeto, honestidad, confianza, compasión, consideración, sentido del humor, sensibilidad, comprensión, indulgencia y amor sin condiciones. Si las practicas, estas cualidades fructificarán en tu vida.

La transformación debe darse en un nivel interno muy profundo. Es inútil concentrarse en el cambio externo. Ser más esbelta no te hará sentir mejor ni perfeccionará tu vida. Es posible que te proporcione sentimientos fugaces de autoestima, pero lo más probable es que continúes reprochándote por no ser aun más delgada, extrovertida, o lo que creas que te hace falta. Sin embargo, nada de esto importa, porque lo que es más significativo es cómo te sientes acerca de lo que eres en tu interior. Cuando aprendas a reconocer tu propia grandeza interna, la talla de tu cuerpo te parecerá insignificante.

La verdad es que la gente se da en todas las formas, tallas, colores, aptitudes, intereses, religiones y tantas otras variables. El número de combinaciones es infinito; por ello, cada una de nosotras es única. Sin embargo, nos parecemos en que todas compartimos una similitud divina: la fuente del amor a nosotras mismas habita en nuestro interior.

Todas las personas enfrentan retos y dificultades en su vida. Deja de menospreciarte por padecer una enfermedad tan extraña, porque incluso la bulimia ha cumplido un propósito. Deja de concentrarte en esas cosas de las que pareces carecer, porque tú eres quien les da vida. Aprecia lo que eres en vez de intentar ser "perfecta" de alguna manera. Tú eres siempre una *tú* perfecta.

La repetición de afirmaciones es una forma de practicar la autoestima. He aquí unas cuantas para comenzar a hacerlo. Haz un esfuerzo consciente por articular al menos una aseveración positiva una y otra vez a lo largo del día. Si es posible, dila en voz alta, frente a un espejo y antes de hacer cualquier otra cosa por la mañana, mientras te vistes, al abrir y cerrar puertas, al conducir el auto o mientras estás sentada detrás de tu escritorio. Sé amable contigo misma y sustituye el diálogo interno negativo por afirmaciones positivas.

AFIRMACIONES

- Merezco cosas buenas.

- Mi peso nada tiene que ver con mi valor personal.

- Tengo un buen corazón.

- Todos los días, en todos sentidos, estoy cada vez mejor.

- El universo es benévolo.

- Mi cuerpo es un templo.

- Soy entusiasta y tengo confianza en mí misma.

- Le agrado a la gente.

- Estoy agradecida por las lecciones que la recuperación me ha enseñado.

- Respeto mi individualidad.

Mi valor como ser humano no tiene que ver con mi talla.

Mi bulimia era un síntoma de mi muy escasa autoestima, de mis sentimientos de culpa e impotencia. La terapia me enseñó cómo tratarme a mí misma con respeto, que tengo dominio sobre mis emociones y cómo utilizar las afirmaciones frecuentes, todo lo cual ha hecho dar un giro completo a mi mundo.

¡Nunca pensé que podía agradarme tanto lo que soy!

Exprésate

Casi todos los expertos coinciden en que un trastorno de la alimentación es una forma de expresar por medio del cuerpo algo que no se puede decir con palabras. Por ejemplo, expresar la ira atiborrándose de comida y vomitando violentamente puede ser más fácil que encarar a alguien que nos ha herido. Incluso la expresión de opiniones sencillas, si éstas son diferentes de las de nuestra familia o de nuestras amistades, puede causar suficiente angustia para iniciar una comilona.

Para renunciar a utilizar la bulimia como un amortiguador, debes correr el riesgo de poner al descubierto quién eres en realidad y de exponer tu yo más interno. Debes dejar de intentar complacer a los demás cuando eso significa devaluar tus propias necesidades. "No" es una respuesta aceptable si refleja tus verdaderos sentimientos. Sé sincera y sé tú misma. Eres diferente de otras personas —todo el mundo lo es— ¡y así es como debe ser! He aquí algunas sugerencias para comenzar:

FORMAS DE EXPRESARTE

- Piensa en lo que dices y en cómo lo dices, a ti misma y a los demás. Utiliza más el pronombre "yo" y compleméntalo con verbos activos como siento, pienso, quiero, deseo, ¡soy! ¡Dí "sí" en vez de "no"!

- Deja de pensar en ti misma como en una "bulímica". Tú te estás "recuperando de la bulimia".

- Utiliza el diálogo interno positivo. La mente puede crear problemas o soluciones, según lo que tú practiques. Repite frases como "Me quiero mucho" y "¡Soy estupenda!"

- En vez de tragarte tus emociones, déjalas salir. Intenta averiguar qué es lo que tu bulimia está diciendo y expresa esos sentimientos con palabras. Dale voz.

- Si estás enojada, golpea o da puntapiés a un saco de arena. Grita.

- ¡Dibuja, pinta, baila, canta!

- Si necesitas encarar a alguien y no estás segura de cómo hacerlo, ensaya con una amiga comprensiva o ante un espejo. O escribe lo que te gustaría decir. Considera la posibilidad de representar la conversación.

- Haz a un lado tu miedo de hablar con la gente. Sé sincera. ¡Expresa tu opinión!

- Busca amigas que te levanten el ánimo y apóyense mutuamente. Permite que tu familia y tus amigas conozcan cómo eres en realidad.

De ser una persona que estaba de acuerdo con todo lo que cualquier otro decía o hacía, me he convertido en alguien que tiene opiniones propias y las expresa, y que sabe lo que quiere.

Desde el momento en que por primera vez les dije a mis padres que me estaba "recuperando" de la bulimia, mi concepto de mí misma cambió por completo. Comencé a sentirme más al mando de mis propias decisiones.

Siempre me habían dicho que no tenía imaginación. Sin embargo, durante la recuperación comencé a pintar retratos a partir de fotografías y descubrí algo que me encanta y que sé hacer bien. Mi vida ha tomado un rumbo nuevo, totalmente distinto, porque cada vez más prefiero pintar que hacer comilonas.

Relajación

Las personas que padecen trastornos de la alimentación están sometidas a un estrés muy intenso. Aunque la bulimia puede ser calmante en cierta medida, en virtud de su repetición mecánica y su distancia emocional, sus efectos no duran.

A la larga, la presión y la actividad excesiva originadas por una adicción a la comida intensifican el estrés ya existente. Una consecuencia particularmente negativa de esta actividad excesiva es que te desconecta de tu yo interior y te engaña haciéndote pensar que sólo es buena en la medida de sus logros. Es entonces que te conviertes en un "hacer humano" que debe mantenerse ocupado para valer la pena, en vez de un "ser humano" que es valioso por el solo hecho de estar vivo. La relajación te hará aflojar el paso lo suficiente para sentirte en contacto contigo y con tus razones para vivir. Al mismo tiempo, hará posible que tu cuerpo recupere su estado equilibrado natural.

Ésta es la magia de la relajación. Aunque sientas que nada haces al estar inmóvil, es mucho lo que está ocurriendo en realidad. En vez de encontrarte en la modalidad de "combate o fuga", tu vista, tu oído, tu presión arterial, tu ritmo cardiaco, tu respiración y tu circulación vuelven a la normalidad. En vez de agitarse y dar vueltas sobre sí misma, tu mente se vuelve hacia adentro y reposa. Te sientes más tranquila, más conectada. Después, cuando regresas a tu vida cotidiana, te encuentras más relajada, más capaz de manejar no sólo las tensiones de la vida diaria, sino también los retos de la recuperación.

Sin embargo, para una persona que se está recuperando de un trastorno de la alimentación, la relajación puede llegar a ser muy difícil, incluso aterradora. Esto se debe a que, como ya explicamos, la actividad constante asociada con el ciclo bulímico es una forma de evitar otros problemas, especialmente los sentimientos difíciles.

Ten en cuenta que la relajación puede dar lugar a que algunos de estos problemas afloren a la superficie, y procura dejarlos que existan sin pensar en ellos más que en los momentos en que surgen y desaparecen de tu mente mientras intentas tranquilizarla. Afirma tu derecho al reposo. Después, defiéndete de todas las "ideas viejas" que hayan surgido con rostros nuevos hablando con una amiga o terapeuta, escribiendo en tu diario o aplicando alguna otra estrategia.

Existen libros y cursos que tratan de algunas de las sugerencias siguientes:

- Medita.

- Guarda silencio.

- Escucha música tranquilizadora.

- Toma un baño.

- Da un paseo a pie.

- Contempla una laguna o una fogata.

- Aficiónate a observar a las aves.

- Practica yoga o t'ai chi.

- Hazte dar un masaje.

- Siéntate en un lugar hermoso o sagrado.

- Contempla una pecera, acaricia a tu gato, cepilla a tu perro.

Ejercicio de relajación:

Concédete al menos un espacio de 15 o 20 minutos de tu tiempo. Siéntate o recuéstate cómodamente en un lugar apacible. Cierra suavemente los ojos y recuérdate a ti misma que eres una persona buena, que mereces mucho amor y respeto. En silencio, cuenta hasta seis mientras inhalas, de nuevo hasta seis al tiempo que retienes el aliento, y una vez más al exhalar. Repite esto tres veces para desacelerar y concentrar su mente. Luego, repite "Yo soy" con cada respiración; continúa con esto hasta que haya transcurrido el tiempo. (Puedes usar otras palabras, plegarias, o un mantra, en lugar de "Yo soy", pero es útil mantener la repetición.) Procura no ocuparte en tus pensamientos; permite que pasen por tu mente y concéntrate de nuevo en la repetición. Si tienes un problema o una pregunta en el primer plano de tu mente, toma nota de él y después regresa a la repetición. Esto requiere práctica, y habrá ocasiones en que tu mente se rehúse a aflojar el paso, pero tarde o temprano conseguirás disfrutar de un estado de relajación profunda.

Tener momentos de tranquilidad me facilitó decidir no hacer comilonas. Me sentí más unida a esa parte de mí que ansiaba curarse.

A veces, durante una sesión de relajación, veo un pequeño rayo de luz y experimento un sentimiento de esperanza que me inspira a seguir adelante.

Trabaja en tu imagen corporal

Lamentablemente, en nuestra cultura la mayoría de las mujeres (y más hombres que nunca antes) están descontentas(os) con su apariencia física. Nuestras madres, hermanas y amigas hacían dieta cuando éramos pequeñas, y *todavía* les preocupa su peso. El mercado está saturado de nuevos programas de reducción de peso y técnicas para modelar el cuerpo; los publicistas y los medios de comunicación continúan empleando principalmente modelos delgadas y jóvenes (aunque en tiempos recientes han comenzado a surgir modelos de tallas más grandes), y se mantiene el estereotipo de las mujeres obesas como personas sin control de sí mismas y que son una plaga para la sociedad. Nos han bombardeado a tal grado con el mensaje de que lo más delgado es mejor, ¡que es casi un pensamiento revolucionario la posibilidad de sentirnos a gusto con nuestro cuerpo!

Este descontento es incluso más profundo de lo que parece, porque el concepto que tenemos de nuestro cuerpo mantiene un estrecho paralelismo con la imagen que nos hacemos de nosotras mismas. Ambas ideas van de la mano. Por tal razón, no importa cuán bien te haga sentir el ajustarte a un ideal externo, no te agradará verdaderamente tu yo externo en tanto no te guste tu yo interno. Aun si otras personas te dicen que eres hermosa, si no sientes amor por ti misma, estarás insatifecha con tu cuerpo.

Sé bien que ya lo mencioné, pero vale la pena repetirlo: los cuerpos se dan en todas las formas y tallas, y tú has nacido con un cierto tipo de cuerpo que puedes identificar en algún punto de tu árbol genealógico. Puedes modificar tu talla natural hasta cierto punto en función de los alimentos que ingieres y la cantidad de ejercicio que haces, pero no puedes cambiar de modo radical tu tipo de cuerpo heredado sin hacerte daño con ejercicios obsesivos, cirugía o un trastorno de la alimentación. Sin embargo, como sabes, las recompensas por tales excesos no llegan a materializarse. Hazte la siguiente pregunta: la obsesión por la esbeltez, ¿te ha traído las relaciones afectuosas, los empleos satisfactorios y los triunfos significativos que esperabas?

Aunque podría llegar a parecer que así es, el desagrado por el propio cuerpo no es parte de la condición femenina. Es una respuesta aprendida en una cultura que exalta la delgadez. El prejuicio del peso es la forma de odio que goza de más aceptación social entre todas las que conocemos.

Que te recuperes de la bulimia depende en parte de tu capacidad para aceptar tu cuerpo, así como el cuerpo de todas las personas. El valor personal no es una talla. Tu cuerpo no es bueno ni malo, es sólo el que heredaste. Considera la posibilidad de que no exista el cuerpo ideal, y de que frases como: "Me siento gorda" y: "Me veo fea" son indicios de que hay algo más que te molesta y que va más allá de tu apariencia física.

Hacer comentarios desdeñosos sobre tu cuerpo puede ser tan adictivo como las comilonas y, al igual que ellas, es una señal de problemas soterrados. Debes enfrentarte a las influencias culturales y amar tu cuerpo. ¡Tienes que ser una revolucionaria!

Es mucho lo que puedes hacer para mejorar el concepto que tienes de tu cuerpo. He aquí algunas ideas:

SUGERENCIAS PARA MEJORAR TU IMAGEN CORPORAL

- Sonríe más, muéstrate más contenta.
- Camina y habla con dignidad. Permite que tu lenguaje corporal refleje este orgullo naciente.

- Asiste a una clase de baile o de yoga y deja tus inhibiciones en casa.

- Utiliza afirmaciones para cambiar el diálogo interno negativo.

- Ensaya técnicas de uso de imágenes con orientación y de visualización para apoyar tu autoaceptación y manejar los temores asociados con los cambios corporales.

- Haz amistad con algunos hombres o mujeres obesas.

- Advierte que el cuerpo de cada persona es diferente y deja de compararte. No se debe juzgar por su cuerpo ni a las modelos ultraesbeltas ni a las de peso completo; tampoco tú debes hacerlo.

- Practica ejercicios de movimiento que te pongan de nuevo en contacto con la sensación que tu cuerpo te causa.

- Aprecia tu sexualidad. ¡Experimenta un orgasmo!

- Agradece a tu cuerpo por todas las cosas buenas que hace por ti. Consiéntelo con masajes y baños tibios.

- Tómate un par de días de asueto como vacaciones personales durante tu menstruación.

- Haz diariamente ejercicio en forma moderada.

- Compra ropa que te ajuste a la medida.

- Deja de mirarte al espejo tan a menudo y de juzgar las partes de tu cuerpo. Observa la totalidad.

- Tira a la basura —o destruye — tu báscula.

- Acepta los cumplidos de buena gana, sabiendo que la belleza exterior refleja la belleza interior.

- Lee libros sobre cómo mejorar tu imagen corporal.

Ejercicio de visualización

Ponte en calma y cierra los ojos en un lugar tranquilo y cómodo. Luego de algunas respiraciones para limpiar tu organismo, imagínate como una bebé. Ve cuán redonda eres al rodar por el piso o al ponerte de pie. Escucha a los adultos decir: "¡Qué niña tan encantadora!" Siente felicidad de saber que hablan de ti. La gordura en una niña es buena, porque es natural que todos los niños tengan grasa cuando son bebés. Después, imagínate como una joven adolescente, que apenas comienza a madurar. Tu cuerpo necesita crecer en esta época de tu vida, y también requiere alguna grasa adicional. Ahora, mírate llegar a la edad adulta, adquirir algunas arrugas y dejar que la gravedad haga un poco de las suyas. ¿Puedes aceptar esos cambios? Por último, imagínate a los 90 años de edad. ¡Cuán lejos te ha llevado tu cuerpo! ¿Cuál es tu apariencia? ¿Cómo te sientes ahora respecto a tu cuerpo? Los cuerpos cambian. Tranquilízate. Siéntete cómoda con esta idea y aprecia lo que la naturaleza te ha dado.

¡Me gusta mi cuerpo! Y eso, no obstante que tengo cinco o seis kilos más del peso con el que pensé que podía vivir.

Yo no veía mi cuerpo de igual forma que los demás. Ahora, la diferencia está en que reconozco que mis percepciones están deformadas por mi escasa autoestima, y hasta ahí. Reconozco que no me "sentía delgada" cuando pesaba 38 kilogramos, de modo que perder peso ya no es la respuesta para mí.

Ahora, cada vez con mayor frecuencia, tengo momentos en que estoy en paz con mi imagen corporal porque me siento más en paz internamente. Me alegro de estar sana y no escuálida, como solía estarlo.

Durante la mayor parte de mi vida he utilizado mis dimensiones corporales para evaluar mi valor como persona. No fue sino hasta los cuarenta y tantos años que finalmente comencé a reconocer que los demás me valoraban por lo que yo era, no por mi apariencia.

Ejercicio físico saludable

El ejercicio es un medio estupendo para intensificar tu sensación de bienestar y salud general, pero hay una diferencia entre el ejercicio moderado saludable y las rutinas obsesivas. Para una persona que padece un trastorno de la alimentación, el ejercicio se convierte en un tipo de purga. Si bien puede ser saludable trotar de 16 a 24 kilómetros por semana, correr esa misma distancia todos los días va mucho más allá del simple propósito de mantener una buena condición física.

Algunos investigadores afirman que los cambios químicos que ocurren en el organismo causan una "euforia" adictiva por ejercicio que no necesariamente es nociva. Aunque esto es muy posible, el ejercicio excesivo puede ser una forma de: dar salida a emociones abrumadoras; purgar las calorías indeseables; recuperar (en apariencia) el dominio que se perdió durante una comilona, o escapar de responsabilidades o de problemas difíciles. El entrenamiento en exceso puede tener la apariencia de un régimen de acondicionamiento y engañarnos, haciéndonos creer que somos buenas con nosotras mismas, cuando con toda seguridad no es así.

Por otro lado, el ejercicio saludable es una parte importante de todo programa multidimensional de autonutrición. Las personas sanas disfrutan el ejercicio regular, y más de 80 por ciento de las bulímicas recuperadas que respondieron a nuestra encuesta lo calificaron como satisfactorio en alto grado, mental, emocional y físicamente. Cuando una hace ejercicio, se siente bien, a menos que se comporte de modo obsesivo y compulsivo respecto a él.

No deseamos sugerir una forma de ejercicio en especial. Los deportes en equipo o las actividades en grupo son tan útiles como ejecutar una rutina a solas, y es mucho lo que se gana al estar con otras personas. ¡Camina con una amiga! Veinte o 40 minutos de actividad vigorosa hasta seis días por semana es razonable, y muy bien puedes complementar eso con otros movimientos menos aeróbicos de estiramiento, fortalecimiento, yoga, etcétera.

Para obtener el máximo provecho de tu rutina, conviene hacer hincapié en la importancia de una actitud positiva, del estiramiento y de darte tiempo para relajarte y reflexionar después del ejercicio. ¡Aprovecha todos los buenos sentimientos que afloran al mover tu cuerpo!

ACTIVIDADES RECOMENDABLES

Rutinas aeróbicas

- Trote
- Montar en bicicleta

- Natación
- Patinaje en fila
- Excursionismo
- Caminatas rápidas
- Baloncesto
- Tenis
- Frontenis
- Voleibol
- Saltar la cuerda
- Artes marciales

Actividades complementarias
- Entrenamiento con pesas
- Yoga
- Golf
- Jardinería
- Baile en grupos o con pareja
- Caminatas tranquilas

El ejercicio me ha resultado muy útil. Después de hacerlo, tiendo a comer de forma normal en vez de atiborrarme, como acostumbraba. Practico la carrera al trote, pero supongo que cualquier tipo de ejercicio que la haga a una sudar en serio funciona.

Para ayudar a reducir la angustia y la frustración, nado o monto en bicicleta. Esto me permite dar salida a mucha energía acumulada que habitualmente utilizo para hacer comilonas, que son agotadoras. Después de hacer ejercicio me siento mucho mejor respecto a mi persona. Me enorgullezco porque opto por hacer algo que es bueno para mí en vez de las destructivas comilonas.

El ejercicio diario es indispensable para mi salud mental, emocional, física y espiritual. Procuro hacer ejercicios aeróbicos todos los días, caminar, nadar, montar en bicicleta. Pero si un día no me ejercito, nada tiene de malo.

Experimenta hambres y sentimientos

Los seres humanos tienen diversos tipos de hambres: físicas, emocionales, sociales, espirituales y sexuales, entre otras.

Las personas que padecen trastornos de la alimentación tienen dificultad para reconocer las diferencias, porque están separadas de su experiencia interior por la adicción a las comilonas y purgas. Por consiguiente, un aspecto importante de la recuperación consiste en dejar de lado las conductas, delicadamente, dando el tiempo suficiente para distinguir entre estas hambres —en especial las físicas y emocionales— y alimentarlas como es debido.

El hambre física es el ansia fisiológica de alimento que nuestro cuerpo experimenta. El hambre emocional es una mezcla compleja de necesidades, deseos y sentimientos. Incapaz de enfrentar estos problemas interiores, o renuente a hacerlo, la bulímica responde de forma simbólica, comiendo hasta que literalmente ya no le cabe más alimento; pero ni toda la comida del mundo alcanzaría para satisfacer las necesidades emocionales.

Por lo regular, las bulímicas se ven empujadas a hacer comilonas por lo que ellas mismas describirían como sentimientos abrumadores de angustia, como una "masa" de presión emocional. La comida, y el acto de engullirla lo más rápidamente posible, es una distracción respecto a esta angustia y en muchos casos un medio para evitarla por completo. Pero si tú estás en vías de recuperación, necesitas hacer un alto y preguntarte *antes* de que comience la comilona: "¿De qué tengo hambre en verdad? ¿Qué sentimientos necesito expresar? ¿Hay alguna forma de satisfacer mis hambres directamente, en vez de encaminarlas a través de la bulimia?" Sé amable y compasiva contigo misma en tu intento por detener las comilonas y permite que tus sentimientos afloren a la superficie, sabiendo que puede haber dolor o miedo debajo de ellos. Consigue apoyo para este difícil reto.

Toda comilona es una maestra, porque nos ofrece la oportunidad de aprender un poco más acerca de nosotras mismas y de por qué abusamos de la comida. Cada una de nosotras tiene una vida interior rica y vigorosa; negarla es negar una parte de lo que somos. Las hambres emocionales son legítimas y es necesario satisfacerlas por los medios adecuados. Por ejemplo, si te preocupa cierta relación, en vez de hacer comilonas comenta tus inquietudes con otra persona o escribe acerca de ellas. Si te sientes sola, en vez de pasar el tiempo comiendo, llama a una amiga, asiste a un curso o inscríbete en un grupo de apoyo. Si el dinero es lo que te angustia, habla con un asesor financiero o intenta conseguir un mejor empleo. De lo que se trata es de experimentar tus emociones en vez de sepultarlas con comida. Recuerda que, no importa cuánto comas, con ello no conseguirás satisfacer tu hambre emocional.

Para una persona que ha sido bulímica durante varios años, puede ser sumamente difícil reconocer las señales de hambre física.

Algunas bulímicas en recuperación responden bien a los planes de alimentación, los cuales las liberan de la responsabilidad de elegir cuándo y cuánto comer. Estos planes pueden ser una gran ayuda en las primeras etapas de la recuperación, cuando las hambres emocionales salen a la superficie y te sientes más tentada a sucumbir a tus antiguos hábitos de enfrentamiento de los problemas.

Otras optan por "legalizar" ciertos alimentos y quitar restricciones, en un intento por experimentar sus indicios de hambre cuando se presentan de manera natural. (Consulta el capítulo 6: "Alimentación saludable y peso saludable".)

Solía hacer comilonas cuando estaba disgustada, aburrida o angustiada. Ahora, pienso en mis sentimientos y procuro encontrar otras cosas que hacer.

A través del autoconocimiento y la terapia estoy aprendiendo que a menudo he optado por comer en vez de sentir ansiedad y enojo. Ahora soy capaz de expresar mi enojo y aceptar mi ansiedad. Entiendo que los sentimientos pasan y que puedo elegir no comer.

El hecho de ser terriblemente maltratada por el hombre al que amaba fue el precursor de mi bulimia. Hacía comilonas para rellenar la herida y colmar el vacío. Ahora, estoy llena de amor, pero de uno que viene de mi interior, no de alguien más.

Cultiva relaciones

La clandestinidad y el aislamiento son parte del estilo de vida de la persona bulímica porque su relación primordial es la que mantiene con la comida, no consigo misma ni con otras personas. Por tanto, a nadie debe sorprender que la recuperación signifique derribar las barreras que impiden la intimidad y aprender a cultivar relaciones saludables y afectuosas.

Es crucial encontrar personas a las que una pueda hacer confidencias, en especial si no tenemos nuestras fronteras bien definidas o hemos sido lastimadas en el pasado. Las o los terapeutas son una buena opción, porque saben cómo orientar, enseñar, poner en tela de juicio y estar presentes cuando una las necesita.

Una amiga o pariente bien dispuesta puede ser una caja de resonancia que ofrece seguridad. También se puede encontrar ayuda en los grupos de apoyo, con personas que han enfrentado o enfrentan problemas similares. Lo importante es interactuar con otras personas que reflejen sus serios esfuerzos por amar y ser amadas. Poco a poco, y con delicadeza, permite que más personas sepan quién eres tú en realidad. Te sorprenderá la actitud tan solidaria que algunas pueden tener. Con el tiempo, te sentirás cada vez más a gusto con tu propia persona, y conseguirás mantener esa sensación de identidad al establecer vínculos con los demás.

A medida que adquieras la confianza para expresar tus ideas, tus sentimientos y tus necesidades, podrás abordar las relaciones con algunas de las personas más difíciles de tu vida. Ten presentes los antiguos estereotipos restrictivos y, muy especialmente, no permitas que abusen de ti.

La separación y la independencia son mejores opciones que la incomprensión o el maltrato. Asimismo, si tu autoestima es baja, es probable que tiendas a mantener "amistades" superficiales con otras personas cuya autoestima también es baja.

No necesitas personas que te depriman mientras te esfuerzas con sinceridad por recuperarte. Cultiva relaciones positivas con personas dispuestas a animarte y a aceptarse a sí mismas. ¡Busca buenas compañías! Esto es importante y merece repetirse:

¡Busca buenas compañías!

Por otra parte, es probable que necesites abordar cuestiones relacionadas con tu sexualidad. A veces, se utiliza la bulimia para evitar la intimidad de las relaciones sexuales como una respuesta a la inmolación sexual, que puede ir desde la violación hasta el trato a la mujer como un objeto en una sociedad dominada por el varón.

La bulimia es un medio para gozar a solas de un placer físico predecible. Atiborrarse y purgarse es similar al acto y a las sensaciones de la unión sexual: la lenta acumulación de intensidad, el ansia emocional de amor, las caricias corporales, la explosión de placer o dolor físico y, para algunas, un sentimiento de culpa condicionado. Sin embargo, la recuperación crea la oportunidad de disfrutar de todo tipo de amor en tu vida. A medida que tu autoestima y tu capacidad de intimidad crezcan, también estarás más preparada, y serás más capaz de sostener relaciones sexuales satisfactorias.

Las personas bulímicas tienen miedo de las relaciones. Su sentimiento de culpa y su sigilo las orillan a sentir temor por lo que la gente piense de ellas. Pero todo el mundo siente miedo, en alguna medida, de exponer su verdadero ser al mundo exterior, y tu recuperación será más fácil si consigues ser más abierta y sincera al seleccionar a otras personas. Renunciar a la bulimia como tu "mejor amiga" significa descubrir de nuevo la amistad y la intimidad, lo cual exige valor y práctica. He aquí algunas sugerencias:

IDEAS PARA CULTIVAR RELACIONES SALUDABLES

- Sé sincera en todo momento.
- Comunícate con tus amistades que vivan lejos por medio de cartas, llamadas telefónicas y correo electrónico.
- Busca a una amiga a la que no hayas visto por largo tiempo y que te haya conocido y estimado antes de que tuvieras bulimia.
- Si presientes que una conversación va a ser difícil o polémica, intenta ensayarla antes con una amiga o con tu terapeuta.
- Mira a las personas a los ojos.
- ¡Sonríe, ríe, diviértete!
- Dedica tiempo a estar con niños pequeños o con animales: ellos te aceptan incondicionalmente.
- Hazte valer; dí lo que piensas.
- Sé positiva.
- Plantea preguntas, escucha y apoya.
- Ve a Dios en todas las personas, especialmente en ti misma.

Debido a que a casi todas las bulímicas nos avergüenza nuestra conducta, tendemos a ocultar y a mantener nuestra adicción en secreto. Nos aislamos de quienes se interesan por nosotras y quieren ayudarnos. Fueron muchas las veces que deseé recurrir a alguien en busca de ayuda, pero el temor al rechazo me mantuvo en el aislamiento. No podría expresar el alivio que sentí cuando mi secreto quedó por fin al descubierto: todos los que lo conocen me han apoyado mucho y se han mostrado comprensivos.

Mi salvación han sido tu libro y mi hermana, que es una anoréxica en recuperación. He dudado de contárselo a mi mejor amiga, quien irá conmigo a la universidad el próximo año, pero sé que, a menos que lo haga, la relación no será sincera y acabaremos por distanciarnos.

Pienso que quizás al principio estaba mejorando por mi esposo y tenía la esperanza de que con el tiempo desearía mejorar por mí misma. Esto es precisamente lo que ha ocurrido. Cuando fui sincera, nuestra relación se tornó más profunda y descubrí que soy una persona buena. Eso me proporcionó confianza. Ahora tengo una amiga íntima y, en general, me siento más a gusto cuando estoy con otras personas.

Búsquedas espirituales

Los trastornos de la alimentación tienen que ver con una sensación de vacío interior, no sólo físico o emocional, sino también espiritual. Son herramientas para habérselas con una vida carente de amor, de sentido, de esa necesaria sensación de seguridad, de vínculos con los demás y, más que nada, de autoestima. La exploración de estos aspectos es lo que llamo la "búsqueda espiritual", o el reconocimiento del espíritu que habita en nuestro interior y en el de todos los demás, aparte de nuestra mente y nuestro cuerpo. Este espíritu recibe muchos nombres, por ejemplo: Dios, Poder Supremo, el Ser, el inconsciente colectivo, y muchos otros. Cuidar de la salud de nuestro espíritu nos conecta con el misterio de la vida y nos satiface en un nivel que no comprendemos en su totalidad.

El acto más satisfactorio a lo largo de mi recuperación ha sido la práctica del amor. Éste ha sido mi camino: amarme a mí misma y amar a los demás. Esta simple enseñanza me obligó a examinar las barreras que me impedían disfrutar el amor en todas las facetas de mi vida, aquello de lo que más hambrienta estaba. No me refiero sólo al amor a mi esposo o a mis hijos, sino más bien a un estado constante de amor con el cual pude abordar a toda persona, lugar y situación. El hecho de hallarme en este camino espiritual ha dado a mi vida un significado, y me ha satisfecho de un modo que la comida nunca consiguió. Irónicamente, ¡todo se lo debo a mi bulimia!

En años recientes, es cada vez mayor el número de terapeutas que integran la espiritualidad a su tratamiento de los trastornos de la alimentación, como lo explica la terapeuta Carolyn Costin:

> He llegado al punto de considerar el tratamiento que aplico a mis pacientes de trastornos de la alimentación como el cultivo de almas olvidadas, y a la psicoterapia como una forma de práctica espiritual. En vez de concentrarse en erradicar síntomas o en resolver problemas, la meta de la terapia es hacer nacer el significado, la realización y la satisfacción en la vida de las pacientes.

A este enfoque hacen eco los autores de un artículo de una revista clínica, en el que escriben lo siguiente: "El papel de las influencias religiosas y espirituales en el desarrollo, funcionamiento y curación del ser humano recibe un reconocimiento cada vez más amplio en las profesiones médicas y psicológicas". En dicho artículo, que reseña un gran número de estudios sobre espiritualidad y trastornos de la alimentación, los autores sugieren diversas actividades, algunas de las cuales se incluyen en la siguiente lista ampliada:

ACTIVIDADES RELIGIOSAS Y ESPIRITUALES

- Acoge conceptos espirituales como la gracia, la honestidad y el servicio.

- Lee libros religiosos o espirituales, incluso las escrituras de la religión de tu elección, u obras sobre la "Nueva Era".

- Ora.

- Practica la visualización, la meditación y otras técnicas de relajación que calmen la mente.

- Alienta el perdón a ti misma y a los demás.

- Busca orientación espiritual por parte de dirigentes religiosos que muestren una actitud positiva y optimista (y no una controladora o que te provoque vergüenza).

- Participa en una comunidad religiosa.

- Realiza un trabajo voluntario o un "servicio desinteresado".

- Participa en actividades "con alma", como escribir sobre conceptos que te inspiren, estar en contacto con la Naturaleza, cultivar intereses musicales, labores artísticas, jardinería.

- Busca buenas compañías; comparte tu tiempo con otras personas interesadas en búsquedas espirituales.

Casi 60 por ciento de las personas bulímicas encuestadas mencionaron que la espiritualidad les fue de gran utilidad. Por lo regular, todas se sintieron inspiradas y motivadas, cualquiera que fuese su religión. Se mencionaron muchas religiones y prácticas específicas, pero el mensaje subyacente fue que la fe en Dios, como quiera que la definiese cada una, las ayudó a recuperarse. Algunas de ellas practicaron el amor a sí mismas y el amor a su "prójimo" con el mismo efecto espiritual y consecuencias positivas similares.

Lo que más me ha ayudado es mi fe y mi confianza en Dios. Quienes padecemos trastornos de la alimentación tenemos un problema de falta de seguridad, y saber que Dios se ocupa de mí me brinda consuelo y paz. Todos necesitamos a alguien en quien confiar, de quien sepamos que nos ama incondicionalmente, no por nuestra apariencia ni por lo que hacemos, tan sólo por lo que somos.

Ahora, estoy rescatando mis sentimientos y trabajando mucho para entender que soy digna de afecto y valiosa. Merezco vivir una vida gozosa, plena y serena. En muchas ocasiones he salido a caminar en vez de hacer una comilona, y nunca he regresado a casa sintiendo aún el deseo de atiborrarme. Acostumbro orar mientras

camino, desahogando todas mis cargas, temores, alegrías y espe-
ranzas; sabiendo que Dios me escucha y se deleita conmigo. De
verdad disfruto estos ratos a solas con Él.

Cambia tu modo de pensar

Las personas que padecen trastornos de la alimentación viven atormentadas por modelos de pensamientos negativos que las inducen a mantener su dañina conducta. Estas murmuraciones internas constantes pasan de un tema a otro, reproduciendo las mismas "cintas" destructivas una y otra vez, y les impiden escuchar algo positivo. Hacer comilonas y purgarse es un medio para silenciar esta implacable voz crítica, aunque sólo sea por breves momentos.

Algunos ejemplos de modelos de pensamientos negativos son los siguientes:

- **Ver todo como blanco o negro.**

La comida se convierte en buena o mala; un aumento de peso equivale a obesidad. Siempre te miras en el espejo de cuerpo entero, pero no te agrada lo que ves.

- **Amplificar los aspectos negativos.**

Filtrar y desechar los aspectos positivos y dejar pasar sólo los negativos. Los problemas de poca monta se ven como catástrofe, y los comentarios crecen fuera de toda proporción. Si ves una lectura más alta en la báscula, tu día se ha arruinado. Si alguien disiente de tu opinión, piensas que los demás te odian.

- **Tomar todo de forma personal.**

Pensar que el mundo gira en torno a ti. Si ves una fotografía en una revista, te comparas para decidir si eres más esbelta o no. Tienes sentimientos de culpa por cuestiones que en muchos casos nada tienen que ver contigo, o sientes que la gente te juzga o que el mundo está en tu contra.

- **Los "debe".**

Tener reglas rígidas acerca de cómo debes actuar tú y todos los demás; por ejemplo: "No se debe expresar la ira" o: "No debo comer aderezo de ensalada". Los "debes" te empujan a pensar que tienes dominio sobre cosas que muy bien pueden estar fuera de tu control.

Estos modelos de pensamiento definen tu existencia en ciertos sentidos, porque lo que piensas es también lo que experimentas. Si tu mente se concentra en lo mala que es tu vida, entonces la vida es mala para ti.

Si te concentras en avergonzarte de ser bulímica, entonces la vergüenza es tu realidad. En cambio, si te esfuerzas conscientemente por combatir estos modelos habituales, puedes cambiar la manera de experimentar todo lo que te rodea. Concentrarte en lo que es positivo en tu vida te inducirá a sentirte más positiva. Sentir compasión del dolor que sin duda te empujó a la bulimia borrará la vergüenza. Es así que *lo que piensas tiene el poder de cambiar tu vida.*

ACTIVIDADES PARA CAMBIAR TU MODO DE PENSAR

- Atiende a lo que piensas y a lo que dices. Esto puede parecer una simpleza, pero la claridad es importante en este ejercicio.

- Practica un diálogo interno diferente, más positivo, tanto verbal como escrito. Intenta "reformular" tus ideas, desechando lo negativo y contrarrestándolo con un aspecto positivo.

- Cuando surjan pensamientos negativos, obsérvalos con indiferencia. Si lo deseas, toma nota de las ideas, pero déjalas pasar sin sostener una conversación mental.

- Haz una lista de afirmaciones para decirlas en voz alta, por ejemplo: "Soy una persona estupenda". Aun cuando no creas en estas afirmaciones al 100 por ciento, el acto de verbalizarlas te ayudará, no sólo en términos emocionales, ¡sino también en un nivel celular!

- Practica la visualización, la meditación y otras técnicas de relajación que calman la mente.

- Acepta que estás haciendo las cosas de la mejor manera posible en este momento. Incluso la bulimia es una forma de cuidar de ti misma cuando no conoces otra. Ahora, escríbele una nota de agradecimiento y dile adiós.

La transformación de tus pensamientos negativos en positivos es una poderosa herramienta para cambiar. Sin embargo, esta "limpieza general mental" brinda el beneficio adicional de hacer posible que escuches tu propia voz interior con más claridad. Aunque es probable que hasta el día de hoy haya sido muy tenue, posees una sosegada voz de sabiduría y guía que proviene del centro más hondo de tu ser. Es tranquilizante, cómoda, sabia, divertida, segura de sí y totalmente digna de confianza. La voz interior busca sólo lo mejor para ti desde el fondo de tu corazón, que es donde reside, por cierto. Es la voz de tu yo interior; esa fuerza benéfica pura que yace en el interior de cada una de nosotras.

Con un poco de práctica, podrás escuchar esta voz cada vez con mayor claridad. ¿Cómo practicar? Con tenacidad y fe, sigue las sugerencias de este capítulo, que son, entre otras, las siguientes: escribe en tu diario; mejora tu autoestima; concéntrate en lo positivo; exprésate tú misma; toma tiempo para relajarte; cultiva relaciones, y atiende lo espiritual. Esto requiere trabajo, pero el resultado final te traerá más felicidad, mejores sentimientos acerca de lo que eres, y más satisfacción con el mundo. Cuando una se toma el tiempo para cambiar su modo de pensar y abrirse a la voz interior, ocurren milagros.

Solía sentirme como si estuviese en piloto automático. Dejaba que mis pensamientos gobernaran mi vida. Ahora, ¡yo dicto lo que pienso!

Me gusta imaginar que en mi mente hay una trituradora de papel, en la cual destruyo todos mis pensamientos negativos.

Cuestiona las influencias culturales

Vivimos en una cultura que idolatra la delgadez. Para nadie es noticia esto, menos para quienes padecen trastornos de la alimentación. En los medios de comunicación abundan imágenes de modelos esbeltas que parecen saludables, felices, triunfadoras, inteligentes y sexualmente atractivas, con el mensaje implícito de que la clave para una vida tan estupenda radica en ser delgada. Las industrias de la dieta, la moda y la belleza gastan verdaderas fortunas para convencer a las mujeres, y a un número creciente de hombres, de ser diferentes de como son de manera natural. La implacable andanada de publicidad nos hace pensar que nuestro cabello "debería" ser más claro o tener más cuerpo, nuestros dientes "deberían" ser más blancos, y "deberíamos" ser más delgados.

Nuestra obsesión por la delgadez nos hace odiar la gordura. En los medios nos muestran estereotipos de las personas obesas como seres estúpidos, carentes de voluntad, indeseables y fracasados. Nuestra sociedad se muestra ya más aceptante de las diferencias de raza, religión o género pero los prejuicios respecto al peso prevalecen. Bombardeada por los conceptos y las imágenes que equiparan la delgadez con lo bueno y la gordura con lo malo, no es extraño que te aterrorice subir de peso y desees ser más delgada.

Asimismo, y pese a que mucho hemos avanzado en el campo de los derechos de la mujer, aún vivimos en una cultura orientada hacia el varón. En general, a las mujeres se les paga menos que a los hombres; rara vez alcanzan puestos políticos o empresariales altos; son víctimas de acoso y de violencia, y se las mira inevitablemente como objetos sexuales. La bulimia las ayuda a hacer frente al temor y a la falta de realización como seres humanos, que no son otra cosa que el resultado de ser devaluadas y tratadas como objetos sexuales o como ciudadanos de segunda clase.

Por añadidura, se alientan los rasgos masculinos, como la competitividad, la independencia y la agresión, en tanto que las características femeninas, como ser protectoras, interdependientes y cooperativas se valoran menos. Un trastorno de la alimentación puede ser un recurso para escapar de la confusión de lo que significa ser mujer en un ambiente tan orientado a la masculinidad. Los hombres que adquieren bulimia, ya sean heterosexuales u homosexuales, son típicamente más sensibles que el varón "promedio", y ellos también utilizan su trastorno para retraerse de una sociedad tan hostil.

Pese a décadas de lucha, las activistas del movimiento feminista y en pro de la aceptación de la talla corporal, trabajando hombro con hombro con educadoras y terapeutas de trastornos de la alimentación, han logrado pocos avances en cuanto a cambiar las irracionales normas de belleza y los limitados estereotipos sexuales de nuestra cultura. Sin embargo, cada una de nosotras, como individuos, podemos optar por situarnos por encima de la obsesión y la opresión culturales; tu recuperación te obliga a hacerlo.

DIEZ FORMAS DE CUESTIONAR LAS INFLUENCIAS CULTURALES

- Hacer dieta es una forma de opresión; ¡no hagas dieta!

- Advierte cómo la televisión fija estereotipos de personas de acuerdo con su peso, y no veas ese tipo de programas.

- Recorta de las revistas y tira a la basura las fotografías de mujeres delgadas. ¿Cuántas fotografías de mujeres quedan?

- Escribe cartas de protesta a los publicistas y fabricantes que fomentan el valor de la esbeltez, y aplaude a aquellos que empleen modelos de tallas más grandes.

- Respeta a las personas cualquiera que sea su talla.

- No toleres los comentarios negativos que otras personas expresen acerca del peso.

- Participa en organizaciones que fomenten la aceptación de las tallas grandes o la prevención de trastornos de la alimentación, o apóyalas financieramente.

- No compres revistas "para mujeres" que fomenten la pérdida de peso.

- Replícale a la televisión denunciando verbalmente las imágenes denigrantes.

- Acepta tu individualidad; afirma tu propia y peculiar identidad.

Nadie me dijo que cuando las chicas llegan a la pubertad, suben de peso como preparación para un posible embarazo. ¡Pensaba que yo era la única! Cuando hacer dieta no funcionó, recurrí a la bulimia y quedé atrapada en ella durante 13 años. Ahora lucho por recuperar mi cuerpo "natural" y lo amo, ¡no importa cuál sea su talla o forma!

El año pasado me hice el propósito de decir algo siempre que alguna de mis amigas mencionase que se sentía demasiado gorda o que deseaba perder peso. Ha sido difícil ser tan sincera, pero cuando ellas se enteran de todo aquello por lo que he tenido que pasar, se aceptan un poco más a sí mismas. ¡Incluso yo puedo enseñar!

CAPÍTULO 6

Alimentación saludable y peso saludable

En algún momento de tu recuperación, necesitarás un plan para comer sin temor. Al enfrentar las decisiones cotidianas acerca de qué y cuánto comer, te será de gran ayuda conocer la verdad acerca de la alimentación saludable y el peso saludable. Así pues, antes de analizar la planificación de las comidas y cómo superar los temores relacionados con el alimento, repasemos algunos de los hechos que ya hemos mencionado:

HECHOS ACERCA DE LA ALIMENTACIÓN Y EL PESO SALUDABLES

- La bulimia no tiene que ver sólo con la alimentación.

- Los cuerpos tienen todas las formas y tallas; tu tipo de cuerpo está determinado en su mayor parte por los genes familiares.

- Toda persona tiene un rango de peso genéticamente determinado que es, de manera natural, el óptimo para ella: su punto de equilibrio.

- Las personas obesas, en promedio, no comen más que las delgadas.

- Las bulímicas hacen comilonas para satisfacer hambres emocionales, no físicas.

- Una dieta saludable y bien balanceada incluye carbohidratos complejos, proteínas, grasas, vitaminas y minerales.

- El cuerpo de cada persona es diferente, y a final de cuentas a ti te toca decidir qué y cuánto debes comer.

Las dietas y el punto de equilibrio

Reconozcamos un hecho crucial en relación con las dietas y la reducción de peso: *hacer dieta no funciona*. Haciendo un promedio conservador, millones de mujeres y hombres hacen dieta activamente y el 95 por ciento de ellos recuperarán ese peso, y quizá más. La mayoría de estas personas se culparán a sí mismas por este fracaso, pero en última instancia lo que es falso es la premisa de bajar de peso haciendo dieta.

La razón fundamental por la que las dietas no dan resultado es que el cuerpo humano cuenta con diversos mecanismos de supervivencia cuyo propósito es mantener su peso óptimo. Estos mecanismos perciben una restricción de la ingestión de alimentos como una emergencia, como inanición, y realizan ajustes para que el organismo retenga los valiosos kilos en vez de dejar que se pierdan. Creo oportuno dar una sencilla explicación.

El cuerpo de cada persona tiene un rango específico de peso aproximadamente dos a cuatro kilos) en el cual se encuentra más saludable y trabaja con más eficiencia. En este "punto de equilibrio" o "rango de punto de equilibrio" pueden influir en cierta medida la dieta, la herencia, la edad, la salud y el nivel de actividad; sin embargo, en términos generales, *cada una de nosotras tiene un peso natural que nuestro cuerpo busca alcanzar.* De hecho, lucha por mantener este peso óptimo.

La escasez de alimento se interpreta como inanición; ello provoca que nuestro metabolismo disminuya y que el organismo afloje el paso para conservar calorías. En el otro extremo, una cantidad mayor de alimento constituye una señal para acelerar el metabolismo, y así contrarrestar el exceso de calorías innecesarias. De esta manera, nuestro cuerpo trabaja para mantenernos en un peso saludable y natural, que puede ser mayor o menor que el que tú consideras deseable, pero es el que tu organismo busca mantener.

En tanto no pases hambre ni te atiborres, puedes comer diversos alimentos —más en unos días y menos en otros— y conservar una talla estable. Conviene repetirlo: no te corresponde a ti determinar cuál es esta talla; sólo te toca aceptarla y, en último término, amarla.

Otro sistema estabilizador del organismo se encarga de manejar el agua. La pérdida acelerada de agua explica prácticamente toda la reducción de peso durante las etapas iniciales de una dieta restrictiva. Cuando se priva al organismo de azúcar en la sangre mediante un consumo restringido de carbohidratos, el hígado primero degrada su propia azúcar almacenada (glucógeno) y después convierte los aminoácidos de las proteínas musculares en azúcar. Tanto el glucógeno como las moléculas de aminoácido están rodeadas de agua, la cual sale de las células, se transporta a los riñones y se excreta en forma de orina. Por esta razón, quienes hacen dieta pueden perder inicialmente, con rapidez, varios kilos de agua. Sin embargo, los riñones se adaptan a esta pérdida de agua reteniendo sodio y, por consiguiente, agua. Esta adaptación es lo que muchas personas que hacen dieta experimentan como una "meseta" de peso.

El principio anterior de retención de agua, combinado con una reducción del metabolismo, puede causar un rebote del peso cuando comienzas a comer normalmente y tu organismo percibe que ya no está en peligro. ¡Ten muy presente este hecho! Tu organismo debe pasar por un periodo de ajuste a una nueva forma de vida, y es importantísimo equilibrar el agua y el metabolismo. Es probable que experimentes señales de hambre particularmente intensas o no estés muy segura de qué o cuándo comer. Esto es natural. Sigue el plan de alimentación que hayas elaborado con ayuda de una nutrióloga o dietista, y confía en que tu organismo sabrá cuidar bien de ti.

En realidad, el peso corporal no es indicio de un organismo sano. *Las investigaciones han probado que ser más delgada no es ser más saludable.* De hecho, entre las personas que están en buena condición física general, quienes tienen un peso superior a las normas "ideales" de las tablas de peso presentan una tasa de mortalidad significativamente más baja que quienes pesan menos que lo "ideal". La idea de que un cuerpo grueso pudiese ser saludable resulta una verdad difícil de aceptar, dado el intenso lavado de cerebro al que nos someten las industrias de la dieta y de la moda, las absurdas normas de las compañías de seguros y nuestros errados prejuicios contra la obesidad. Tener un trastorno de la alimentación, hacer ejercicio en demasía o reducir drásticamente nuestro consumo de grasas puede dar por resultado una reducción temporal de peso, pero no te hará sentirte mejor ni estar más sana en el aspecto físico.

El mejor medio para alcanzar y conservar tu punto de equilibrio es el ejercicio regular moderado, combinado con una dieta saludable permanente, como veremos más adelante. Pero las dietas restrictivas, las purgas o cualquier otro método encaminado a alcanzar un peso significativamente por debajo de este rango de punto de equilibrio no funcionarán. En cambio, lo que se crea es hambre física, depresión, sentimientos de privación, debilidad, irritación, pérdida de concentración y preocupación por la comida... así como un probable aumento de peso.

Cómo superar los temores relacionados con la comida

Por lo regular, las personas que padecen bulimia tienen fuertes convicciones y siguen reglas autoimpuestas en relación con la alimentación. Apartarse demasiado de estos modelos les causa temor. Etiquetan los alimentos como "buenos" o "malos" en función del efecto que, en su opinión, comerlos puede tener sobre su peso. Cuando ingieren alimentos "malos", sienten que han roto las reglas y han perdido el control de sí mismas. Ello suele desencadenar comilonas, con la expectativa de que la purga ponga todo "en orden" una vez más. Es obvio que no es así. De hecho, los alimentos no son ni "buenos" ni "malos". Algunos son más nutritivos que otros, pero eso no les confiere un valor intrínseco. Comer postre no te convierte en una mala persona, ni debe orillarte a hacer una comilona.

Primero, conviene que identifiques algunos alimentos "no peligrosos". Prepara una lista para saber qué puedes permitirte comer sin sentimientos de culpa. Con esto, se establece una mentalidad de "puedo comer" en vez de una de "no puedo comer". Poco a poco, cuando estés en condiciones de hacerlo, arriésgate un poco y amplía esa lista. Todo alimento nuevo hará surgir ideas y emociones, pero tú conseguirás manejarlas si avanzas a tu propio ritmo. Las asociaciones negativas que una atribuye a los alimentos *se pueden* reconocer y eliminar, en especial si se las ataca de frente de una manera sistemática y decidida. Utiliza tu diario. Busca personas que te apoyen. ¡No menosprecies este reto! Por más que entiendas los "porqués" de tu bulimia, es una realidad que deseas ser capaz de comer sin temor. La comida no es el enemigo.

En muchos casos, los temores son alimentados por falsas creencias acerca de la alimentación y del peso. Por ejemplo, la idea de que comer cualquier cosa que contenga azúcar te hará aumentar de peso no es cierta. Igualmente falsas son las creencias de que se debe eliminar toda grasa del menú o de que comer sólo frutas y verduras es una dieta vegetariana saludable. Si bien estas deformaciones pueden ayudar a mantener una sensación de seguridad y de identidad, se interponen en el camino hacia la recuperación y es necesario ponerlas en tela de juicio. Aumenta la variedad y la cantidad de alimentos que consumes, con más confianza cada día.

Para algunas personas aficionadas a las comilonas, ciertos alimentos, en especial el chocolate, tienen efectos adictivos. Lo mismo que un alcohólico, sufren una dependencia psicológica y saben que, si consumen la sustancia a la que son adictas, es probable que pierdan el control. Muchas de ellas aplican la estrategia de la "abstinencia" a esos alimentos específicos. Con todo, aún tienen necesidad de descubrir nuevos alimentos porque su menú anterior estaba encaminado a un solo propósito.

Un método para introducir nuevos alimentos consiste en elegir uno "prohibido".

¡Hazlo, aunque sea sólo un bocado! Concéntrate en su textura y sabor. Persiste en hacer a un lado los pensamientos molestos concentrándote en la sensación de masticar o el paso del alimento por tu garganta. Recuérdate continuamente que el alimento está lleno de amor, y que tú lo mereces. Cuando termines de comer, ajusta una alarma para que suene en 10 minutos y permítete tener todos tus pensamientos habituales, como: "No podré conservar en el estómago este alimento; quiero vomitar", ¡pero no lo hagas! Cuando la alarma suene, dí en voz alta y con firmeza: "¡Sólo es comida! ¿Qué importa?" Enseguida, oblígate a hacer algo diferente. Por ejemplo, escribe en tu diario, llama por teléfono a una amiga o ve al parque. Sigue adelante con tu vida.

Ten paciencia contigo misma. Toma tiempo cambiar las conductas y reacciones de tantos años. Pero es posible hacerlo, y tú eres capaz de ello. He aquí algunas ideas que te ayudarán a superar tus temores respecto a la comida:

SUGERENCIAS PARA SUPERAR LOS TEMORES RELACIONADOS CON LA COMIDA

- Come para estar sana, no para hacer dieta.

- Afirma que mereces comer lo mejor, y que lo hay en abundancia.

- Si sufres recaídas en cuanto a hacer comilonas, aprende de ellas.

- Experimenta con diferentes alimentos y estilos de cocinar (aunque sea probándolos). Asumir algunos riesgos pequeños puede brindarte sentimientos de competencia y dominio.

- Intenta "comer con delicadeza" y apreciar lo que comes, en vez de devorar tus comidas mecánicamente, en un estado de trance.

- Para introducir un alimento antes prohibido, ensaya intercambiarlo por uno de tus alimentos "no peligrosos".

- Quizá sea buena idea probar un alimento nuevo cada semana, o prometerte a ti misma un postre delicioso cada día, semana o mes.

- Permite que otra persona cocine para ti y te sirva una comida.

- Ve de compras al supermercado con algunas amigas, para ver qué alimentos les agradan. Habla con ellas acerca de sus inquietudes.

- Recurre a tu grupo de apoyo para calmar tus inquietudes; por ejemplo, asegúrate de tener una "camarada para la hora de la comida" que se siente contigo en esos momentos.

- ¡Cocina con devoción o sirve con elegancia! ¿Te parece un anuncio publicitario? ¡Estoy tratando de convencerte de comer y de disfrutar de ello!

Organización de las comidas

Para muchas pacientes en recuperación es útil abordar el aspecto de la comida siguiendo un plan estructurado. Colabora con una nutrióloga o dietista que conozca bien los trastornos de la alimentación y su tratamiento. Lo que necesitas es un plan alimentario balanceado e individualizado, a la medida de tus necesidades. Una profesional puede proporcionarte información sobre nutrición y apoyo emocional; pero, si no dispones de ayuda profesional o prefieres no recurrir a ella, tú misma puedes elaborar tu propio plan. Describe por escrito cuáles alimentos vas a consumir, en qué proporción y a qué hora. Comienza con aquellos con los que te sientas a salvo; después, introduce poco a poco nuevos alimentos a medida que adquieras confianza. Esfuérzate por apegarte a este plan, y regresa a él aunque en algunas comidas te apartes de lo previsto. Nada tiene de malo comer a intervalos preestablecidos en tanto aprendes a reconocer el hambre física y a responder a ella.

Algunos especialistas recomiendan tomar tres comidas balanceadas y dos o tres bocadillos entre comidas cada día. Tampoco es malo comer simplemente cuando sientas hambre, una vez que aprendas a distinguir entre el hambre física y el hambre emocional. Algunas personas se sienten bien con seis comidas ligeras o comiendo cada dos horas. Si el hecho de apegarte a un horario libera a tu mente de preocupaciones por la comida, ¡excelente! Si deseas más libertad, sé flexible. Haz lo que te dé buen resultado.

Una dieta bien balanceada y saludable incluye carbohidratos complejos, proteínas, grasas, vitaminas y minerales. A menos que una nutrióloga o dietista te haya prescrito un plan de alimentación con una cantidad específica de calorías, no te recomiendo contar las calorías. En vez de ello, atiende tus señales de hambre física y apóyate en las pautas para la dieta diaria que sugerimos a continuación, y que se basan en las recomendaciones del Departamento de Agricultura de Estados Unidos:

DIETA DIARIA BALANCEADA RECOMENDABLE

- De 3 a 5 porciones de verduras. Una porción es aproximadamente media taza de vegetales crudos, una taza de verduras de hoja o tres cuartos de taza de jugo.

- De 2 a 4 porciones de fruta. Una manzana o una naranja es una porción, lo mismo que media toronja o tres cuartos de taza de jugo.

- De 2 a 3 porciones de alimentos ricos en proteínas, como productos lácteos, carne, pescado, aves, tofú o legumbres. Una taza de leche, un par de huevos o 3 o 4 cucharadas de mantequilla de maní equivalen a una porción.

- De 6 a 11 porciones de granos, como pan, cereal, arroz o pasta. Una porción es una rebanada de pan, 30 gramos de cereal, 2 o 3 galletas o media taza de arroz o pasta cocidos.

- Los alimentos ricos en grasa, como la mayonesa, la mantequilla, la margarina, los aderezos para ensaladas y los postres no deben excluirse, pero sí comerse con más parquedad. Procura que de 20 a 30 por ciento de las calorías que consumes sean de grasas, pero no las cuentes de manera estricta.

* Bebe de 8 a 10 vasos de agua.

Situaciones especiales

Comer en restaurantes y acudir a fiestas puede ser causa especial de tensión para las personas con trastornos de la alimentación. A menudo se resisten a comer en público por temor a excederse. En vista de que son muchos los restaurantes que sirven raciones demasiado grandes para cualquier persona, es necesario que seas firme en cuanto a la cantidad que decidas comer. No hay regla alguna que te obligue a comer todo lo que te sirve. Si estas situaciones te angustian, usa una técnica de relajación para llegar al término de la comida, o habla acerca de tus temores con acompañantes que te apoyen. Si te sirven más comida de la que apeteces, aparta la cantidad que te parezca razonable en tu plato y come sólo esa porción. Otra opción es ordenar del menú de aperitivos, o compartir la comida con una amiga. Si algo de lo que te sirven te incomoda, no estás obligada a comerlo. No te asustes; tranquilízate.

No esperes sentirte a gusto de inmediato al salir a comer; sin embargo, es parte de la recuperación sentirte cómoda con el aspecto social de las comidas. Ponte a prueba haciendo y aceptando invitaciones. Con el tiempo, disfrutarás al salir a comer con tus amigas.

Me dije que siempre habrá tarta de queso o chocolate, pan, ¡lo que sea! Si no los como ahora, siempre habrá otra oportunidad.

Me permito todo lo que me apetece, pero con moderación. Tomo pastel y helado, pan y mantequilla; incluso le pongo crema al café. El tamaño de la porción es adecuado para mis necesidades del momento. Ser capaz de permitirme comer cualquier cosa ha disipado el sentimiento de culpa, cuando antes un bocado de un "alimento prohibido" desencadenaba una comilona; como el alimento, lo disfruto, y se queda en mi estómago.

Procuro comer varias veces al día en raciones pequeñas. Los alimentos que ahora consumo me dejan satisfecha, y ya no tengo deseos de hacer comilonas.

Mi prioridad es la salud, no la delgadez.

CAPÍTULO 7

Qué hacer en vez de las comilonas

Pese a que un trastorno de la alimentación causa muchísimo dolor y sufrimiento, es difícil renunciar a él. Cualquiera que haya pasado por esto seguramente coincidirá conmigo. Sin duda alguna, tú enfrentarás retos e incluso contrariedades a lo largo del camino; sin embargo, no importa cuán difícil parezca, las recompensas están a la vista: dinero para divertirte, tiempo para tus amigas, energía para experimentar una gama completa de emociones, claridad para conocer tu verdad interior, ¡más amor!

Dedica un momento a pensar en las razones por las que quieres terminar con tu bulimia. Concretamente, toma una hoja de papel y divídela a la mitad con una línea vertical. Del lado izquierdo de la línea, escribe "Bulimia" y todas las razones que te impulsan a conservarla y del lado derecho, las que te motivan a renunciar a ella. ¿Estás dispuesta a hacer el cambio? ¿Tal vez? En una escala del 1 al 10, ¿en qué medida estás dispuesta a hacerlo? Lo suficiente como para comenzar en este momento. Así lo espero.

Al mismo tiempo, es necesario que entiendas que no puedes renunciar a algo si no tienes otra cosa con qué sustituirlo. ¿Con qué actividad puedes reemplazar a la bulimia? Es importante pensar en esto, porque debes estar preparada. Establece contacto con otras personas que puedan ayudarte. Consigue los libros que deberás leer, las velas para tus baños calientes, unos zapatos nuevos para excursionar si la Naturaleza va a ser su maestra.

Elabora tu plan y reúne las "herramientas" que necesitarás para sustituir tus antiguos rituales y hábitos por otras actividades.

A continuación te ofrezco algunas sugerencias de "cosas qué hacer" que han ayudado a miles de mujeres y que seguramente te ayudarán también. Son tres listas, cada una con un propósito diferente. Cuando sientas la tentación de hacer una comilona, elige una idea de la primera lista, la de acciones "inmediatas", ¡y ponla en práctica! Después, usa la lista de "corto plazo" para prever cómo no hacer comilonas en el futuro y la de "largo plazo" para hacer cambios de estilo de vida, de mayor magnitud. Personaliza estas listas a tu gusto, en cualquier momento, agregándole tus propias ideas. Después de todo, se trata de *tu* recuperación.

Si estás comprometida con la recuperación, es imperativo que suspendas las comilonas y las purgas. Independientemente de cómo abordes a fin de cuentas los problemas subyacentes, es necesario que asumas una postura en este momento. Copia la lista de actividades "inmediatas" y pégala a tu refrigerador. Cuando te sientas tentada a atiborrarte de comida, elige en cambio una sugerencia de la lista.

ACCIONES INMEDIATAS PARA EVITAR LAS COMILONAS

- Pospón la comilona por 15 minutos. Pon la alarma. Esto te dará el tiempo suficiente para elegir otra estrategia.

- Cepíllate los dientes; date una ducha o toma un baño.
- Remoja en agua los alimentos destinados a la comilona.
- Apártate del ambiente que te empuja a hacer una comilona. Ve a un parque, a una biblioteca o a otro lugar "seguro".
- Llama por teléfono a una amiga que te apoye, simplemente para hablar o para tratar tu problema. Cultiva más amigas sensibles, compasivas y capaces de levantarte el ánimo. Alguien que ha superado un trastorno de la alimentación se mostrará especialmente identificada contigo.
- En situaciones de pánico, relájate con respiración profunda. Inspira profundamente hasta contar 10, contén el aire durante el mismo tiempo y exhala. Repite esto varias veces y después reflexiona a fondo en tu angustia. ¿Qué es lo que siento? ¿Puedo manejar lo que está ocurriendo? ¿Estoy a salvo?
- Piensa en otra cosa. Mastica goma. Enciende el aparato de radio o el televisor. Distráete de tus deseos imperiosos el tiempo suficiente para recobrar el juicio.
- Da salida a tus emociones de alguna forma agresiva. Golpea una pera de boxeo o grita contra una almohada. Lucha con una persona que te apoye y que sepa hacerlo sin peligro. Golpea tu cama con un palo. Gritar fuertemente puede proporcionar un gran alivio.

- Participa en una actividad física. Camina, corre, nada o monta en bicicleta.

- Detente un momento e identifica el hambre real. ¿De dónde viene? ¿De la garganta? ¿Del estómago? ¿Del corazón? Escribe tus respuestas más espontáneas. Así podrás identificar la fuente de tus carencias y necesidades legítimas.

- Escribe en tu diario o registra en la grabadora tus ideas. Hazlo de forma íntima y sincera. Revisa las anotaciones anteriores para descubrir modelos y advertir los avances. Plantéate preguntas como: "¿Cuáles son los beneficios de esta comilona?"

- Elabora una lista de los alimentos con los que fantaseas, pon el papel en un sobre y tíralo a la basura.

- Como incentivo, marca con una gran estrella en el calendario cada día que pases sin comilonas ni purgas, o pon dinero en un frasco. Cuando alcances determinadas metas, ya sean de corto o de largo plazo, otórgate recompensas.

- Si puedes hacerlo, detente a la mitad de una comilona. Quizá esto te parezca imposible, pero quienes lo han hecho afirman que es un logro muy poderoso. Intenta inspirar paz dentro de tu incómodo cuerpo atiborrado. Haz lo que tengas que hacer para impedirte comer más o purgarte. Después, digiere tus sentimientos en tu diario o con una persona que te apoye.

PLANES DE CORTO PLAZO PARA NO HACER COMILONAS

- Elabora tu propia lista de actividades "inmediatas" para sustituir las comilonas. A medida que descubras cuáles actividades te dan buen resultado, repítelas y agrega opciones del mismo tipo.

- Incorpora técnicas de relajación a tu rutina diaria. Asiste a una clase de yoga, medita durante 20 minutos todas las mañanas y por la noche, o simplemente tómate un "tiempo de tranquilidad" lejos de los demás y a solas con tus pensamientos.

- Permítete comer lo que se te antoje, pero en compañía de una persona capaz que te apoye y que entienda que lo que buscas es intensificar tu conciencia de ti misma, no hacer una comilona. Dedica tiempo a hablar acerca de tus sentimientos o a ponerlos por escrito. No te purgues.

- Investiga tu infancia. Examina álbumes de fotografías y recuerdos familiares, haz preguntas a tus padres, comparte tus notas con tus amigas y hermanas y dedica tiempo a reflexionar. Identifica tantas causas de tu bulimia como puedas.

- Escribe una carta a un familiar acerca de tu bulimia; sin embargo, *no es forzoso que la envíes*. Ten el valor de decir quién eres y qué necesitas. Escribe una serie de cartas a esa persona a lo largo de un periodo prolongado. Sé sincera, afirmativa y honesta.

- Llama por teléfono o visita a una amiga de la infancia en quien hayas pensado a lo largo de los años, pero que no hayas visto desde hace mucho tiempo. Búscala. Ponte al tanto de la vida de cada una. Ella no te juzgará por tu bulimia; sin duda tendrá su propia y singular historia que contar.

- Come "normalmente" durante un día con base en las pautas señaladas en el capítulo 6, y observa lo que comes y qué sientes al hacerlo. ¿Podrías habituarte a comer de esa manera?

- Haz planes por adelantado y asiste a algún evento cultural, como un concierto, una obra de teatro, una exhibición de pintura o una exposición en un museo. Antes de acudir, estudia acerca del tema. Por ejemplo, si vas a oír una sinfonía, escucha una grabación de ella por adelantado y lee acerca del compositor.

- Elabora listas referentes a tu vida: lo que te gusta y lo que te desagrada, metas, prioridades, logros, cosas por hacer, personas a quienes llamar, etc. Las listas son buenas para organizar nuestras ideas en vez de dejarlas revolotear por ahí.

- Practica decir "no". Sé afirmativa y expresa tus necesidades, ya sean grandes o pequeñas. Esto puede parecerte arriesgado al principio, pero se facilita a medida que tú te fortaleces. Recuerda siempre que gozas de un derecho humano fundamental a tener tus propias opiniones y decisiones.

- Toma unas vacaciones. Aléjate de tu rutina habitual y decide no hacer comilonas ni purgarte mientras estés lejos de casa. Sé una persona "nueva" durante las vacaciones, y piensa en cómo hacer para mantener esa actitud cuando regreses a casa. Quizá descubras que vale la pena realizar cambios en tu entorno normal.

- Prueba con imágenes visuales; éstas te pueden ayudar más adelante a representar una situación en una forma positiva. Imagínate haciendo algo antes de ponerlo en práctica. Por ejemplo, antes de la cena, mentalmente mírate caminando hacia la cocina, preparando una comida saludable, comiéndola en un lugar agradable y limpiando los platos después. Imagina esa escena como algo totalmente placentero. Después, reprodúcela en la realidad.

- Comienza a sonreír a los demás. ¿Por qué no darles un abrazo? Recuerda que la mayoría de las personas son un poco tímidas. Algo tan insignificante como una inclinación de la cabeza o una señal con la punta del sombrero puede establecer conexiones de un modo espléndido.

ACTIVIDADES DE LARGO PLAZO
PARA TERMINAR CON LA BULIMIA

- Participa en obras voluntarias. Ofrece tu ayuda en un asilo de ancianos, en una escuela, en un organismo para la protección del ambiente, en un albergue para animales o en un puesto político. Al dar con generosidad, tu propia bondad irradiará de vuelta hacia ti.

- Practica cuidando mascotas amorosamente. Un perro o un gato ofrecen aceptación incondicional, afecto y compañía. Mirar a los peces te relajará. Las personas tienen mascotas de muchas clases por razones de todo tipo.

- Aprende algo nuevo: un idioma extranjero, primeros auxilios, un instrumento musical, un medio de expresión artística, mecánica o electrónica, o programas de computadora. Ensaya a tomar cursos que pongan énfasis en la independencia, la reafirmación personal o el mejoramiento de la imagen corporal.

- Piensa en cómo ganar dinero en vez de obsesionarte por la comida, y después pon en práctica tus ideas. Esto puede ser un pasatiempo, un plan de inversión o una nueva profesión.

- Utiliza un lenguaje positivo. Prueba a decir en voz alta que eres una buena persona y mereces vivir venturosamente. Habla ante una grabadora. Repite las afirmaciones.

- Procura no ser tan perfecta. Las bulímicas suelen ser muy ordenadas en todo, salvo en lo referente a su paz interior. Concéntrate en las necesidades de tu yo interno.

- Comienza a llevar un registro de tus sueños en el papel. Busca modelos y significados sutiles. Si el tema te interesa, busca un libro sobre análisis de sueños.

CAPÍTULO 8

Consejos para los seres queridos

Un breve comentario de parte de Leigh

Lindsey y yo nos enamoramos a primera vista. Poco después de que admitimos nuestro amor, ella me dijo que tenía un "horrible" secreto. Me sentí aliviado cuando resultó ser "sólo" un trastorno de la alimentación. Pero cuando ella describió en su totalidad el alcance de sus comilonas y vómitos, comprendí que había subestimado su gravedad. En realidad, en esa época la palabra "bulimia" ni siquiera se utilizaba comúnmente, y nadie percibía cuán generalizado estaba este trastorno.

Pronto descubrí que no existía una cura instantánea para la bulimia de Lindsey, y ambos temíamos que —a menos que ella renunciara a su hábito—, nuestra relación estuviese en peligro. Durante nueve años la bulimia había monopolizado su tiempo y su atención, y le había impedido apreciar la bondad que existía en su interior y que yo reconocí de modo tan inmediato. Aunque yo nada sabía acerca de los trastornos de la alimentación, respondí con compasión y con la promesa de ayudarla a recuperarse. Ella me permitió apoyarla.

La batalla de Lindsey con la bulimia fue el centro de nuestra atención durante muchos meses, mientras ella se esforzaba por dejarla atrás. Durante ese tiempo, yo debía recordarme constantemente que ganar la libertad dependía de ella. Podía hacer sugerencias, ser una caja de resonancia, o incluso recibir puñetazos con los guantes de boxeo, pero no era yo quien tenía que hacer el trabajo. Yo no podía "componerla". Desde luego, no era simplemente un espectador indiferente: nuestra unión se fundaba en su recuperación. Por otra parte, sus esfuerzos me obligaron a examinar mis propios valores en aspectos como las relaciones familiares, la obsesión por el peso corporal, los estereotipos en los medios de comunicación, el feminismo y la alimentación saludable. Con todo, nunca perdí de vista el hecho de que era ella quien experimentaba una crisis.

A veces, las personas que han escuchado su historia me dan más crédito del debido. Yo simplemente le brindé apoyo e ideas: sugerencias similares a las que llenan este libro. No tuve problemas con la comida ni con la autoestima, por lo que nunca experimenté de primera mano el dolor que Lindsey enfrentó o su valor. En cambio, coseché los beneficios de su entrega a la recuperación. A consecuencia de todo ello, nuestro amor ha florecido durante más de veinte años, y yo he encontrado la obra de mi vida. Nunca esperé escribir y publicar libros sobre trastornos de la alimentación como una profesión, ni interactuar con miles de personas preocupadas por problemas con la comida. He tenido la fortuna de haber ayudado a muchas de ellas y a sus seres queridos, y confío en que los consejos que ofrecemos en este capítulo serán útiles para usted.

SUGERENCIAS GENERALES

- Recuerda que es ella (o él) quien tiene el problema con la comida, y le corresponde a ella (o él) hacer el trabajo.

- Hagan un pacto de honestidad total.

- Sé paciente, evita juzgar y escúchala. Hazle saber que te importa y que deseas lo mejor para ella.

- Acepta que la recuperación es un proceso y que no ocurre rápidamente. Ayúdala a ser paciente ella también.

- Cuando su conducta te afecte, exprésate sin atribuirle a ella la culpa. Procura no tomar sus actos de modo personal.

- Ten compasión. La persona amada puede sentirse abrumada al establecer contacto con los dolorosos problemas que dan origen a su conducta. En estos momentos, ella necesitará tu amor y tu apoyo más que nunca antes.

- Acuérdate siempre de que tu ser querido utiliza la bulimia como un sustituto para no enfrentar sentimientos o experiencias dolorosas. Aliéntala a encontrar medios saludables para aliviar su dolor.

- No intentes adivinar lo que ella desea. Aliéntala a expresar sus necesidades. Si tienes preguntas que hacer, formúlalas.

- Estimúlala a someterse a una terapia profesional, sin olvidar que no hay una estrategia de recuperación que funcione para todo el mundo. Procura estar disponible para participar en sesiones de orientación conjunta. Sé flexible y abierta(o) a apoyarla en cualquier método que ella elija.

- Reconoce que ella necesita aprender a tomar sus propias decisiones y es la encargada de dirigir su recuperación. No la vigiles constantemente a menos que ella así te lo pida.

EL ALIMENTO Y LA FORMA DE COMER

- Recuerda que el problema no es la comida, y que la bulimia es un síntoma. Mira más allá de la situación inmediata, para entender los problemas más profundos.

- Permítele establecer reglas y metas razonables acerca de la comida y la forma de comer, pero también afirma tus propios derechos. Establece sólo reglas que se puedan hacer valer; trabaja dentro de un marco que sea conducente a triunfos, no a fracasos.

- Deja en claro que ella es responsable de las consecuencias de su conducta bulímica. Por ejemplo, si se atiborra de comida que es de la familia, deberá reponerla con su propio dinero. Si vomita, deberá limpiar el baño. Si roba, deberá restituir lo robado.

- Si ella hace una comilona, deberá hacer frente al hecho más tarde, hablando de por qué ocurrió, escribiendo en un diario o examinando opciones para no hacer una comilona la próxima vez que se encuentre en una situación similar.

- No permitas que las comidas se conviertan en un campo de batalla. Evita que la forma de comer de ella se convierta en una lucha por el poder. Las conversaciones a la hora de comer no deberán girar en torno a su bulimia.

- Alienta a la bulímica a idear un plan de alimentación seguro y saludable, por cuenta propia o con ayuda de una nutrióloga o una dietista. Apoya todos los pasos que dé, por pequeños que sean.

- No hables acerca de su apariencia. Quizá pienses que le estás haciendo un cumplido, pero éste puede interpretarse de diferentes maneras. Por ejemplo, si le dices que se ve "bonita", podría interpretar tu comentario en el sentido de que habitualmente se ve fea. Afirmar que se ve esbelta no hace sino poner un énfasis excesivo y destructivo en el peso.

- Organiza actividades que no giren en torno a la comida. Hagan caminatas juntos, visiten museos, vayan al cine, practiquen deportes. Si comer le resulta incómodo a ella, entonces busquen otras formas de diversión distintas de ir a restaurantes.

- No tomes decisiones relacionadas con la comida por la bulímica. Ésas le corresponden a ella. Apóyala en lo que ella elija. Por ejemplo, si ella no come postres y tú sí, no esperes que ella los prepare o que los compre para ti. Hazlo por tu cuenta.

CENTRA SU ATENCIÓN EN TI

- Considera la posibilidad de buscar ayuda profesional para ti. Tener una hija u otro ser querido con un trastorno de la alimentación es una de las situaciones más estresantes que existen. Cuida de ti mismo(a), y podrás apoyar mejor a quienes te rodean.

- Ábrete a la posibilidad de que, de alguna manera, estés contribuyendo al problema de ella, y que quizá necesites cuestionar algunas de tus propias conductas y convicciones.

- Infórmate acerca de los trastornos de la alimentación y de cuestiones afines, como: presiones que la sociedad ejerce sobre las mujeres, la explotación de la delgadez, el prejuicio del peso, el punto de equilibrio, la dinámica familiar y la autoestima.

En nuestra encuesta aplicada a bulímicas ya recuperadas y en proceso de recuperación, preguntamos: ¿Cómo pueden la familia y los amigos ayudar? Las respuestas nos brindan más pautas excelentes:

Sé sincero y apoya a la persona en su búsqueda de una cura, sin apoyar la conducta.

Examina sus sentimientos acerca de la comida, o si contribuyes de algún modo a la bulimia de tu ser querido.

Estoy firmemente convencida de que los seres queridos necesitan admitir, en primer lugar, que se trata de un problema serio y que se requiere mucho trabajo, a veces desagradable, para que la bulímica mejore.

¡La comunicación es muy importante! La persona bulímica necesita contar con la posibilidad de comentar libremente los sentimientos e inquietudes que pudiese tener, sin sentirse amenazada.

Es necesario que los seres queridos ayuden a las bulímicas a buscar su reafirmación personal. Yo necesitaba sentirme tranquila respecto a que estaba bien decir "no" a los demás.

Procura informarte acerca de este trastorno; en especial, los problemas y causas subyacentes.

Alienta a la bulímica a someterse a terapia.

Sé paciente y no esperes resultados "instantáneos".

¡Ofrece pagar el costo de la terapia!

Acerca de los autores

Lindsey Hall y **Leigh Cohn** forman un matrimonio, y son autores de varios libros sobre trastornos de la alimentación y temas relacionados con la recuperación. Entre sus obras más conocidas están *Cómo entender y superar la anorexia nerviosa* (Lindsey y Monika Ostroff), *Herramientas de autoestima para la recuperación* y *Vidas plenas: mujeres que se han liberado de la obsesión por la comida y el peso*, todas las cuales han sido traducidas a otros idiomas, como francés, italiano, japonés y chino. Su compañía, Gürze Books, publica libros relacionados con los trastornos de la alimentación, escritos por un buen número de autores reconocidos.

Lindsey es licenciada en psicología por la Stanford University (1971) y fue la primera bulímica recuperada en aparecer en televisión de alcance nacional en Estados Unidos para relatar su historia. Lindsey fungió como Directora Ejecutiva de Eating Disorders Awareness and Prevention, Inc., y a finales de los años setenta fue pionera en el arte de la escultura blanda al diseñar y vender más de medio millón de muñecas Gürze en todo el mundo. Leigh, quien tiene una maestría en enseñanza por la Northwestern University (1975), es Director Ejecutivo de *Eating Disorders: The*

Journal of Treatment and Prevention, un boletín de reseñas para profesionales clínicos, y ex presidente de la Publishers Marketing Association. Lindsey y Leigh tienen dos hijos, Neil y Charlie.

Si deseas obtener más información y conocer los recursos para el tratamiento de trastornos de la alimentación, consulta la página: www.bulimia.com.